Jayme,

A little summer reading,

Best regards,

Bill.

RULES
of
ENCOUNTER

RULES
of
ENCOUNTER

WILLIAM P.
KENNEDY

ST. MARTIN'S PRESS NEW YORK

Design by Judith Christensen

Library of Congress Cataloging-in-Publication Data

Kennedy, William P.
   Rules of encounter / William P. Kennedy.
     p. cm.
   ISBN 0-312-06182-X
   1. World War, 1914–1918—Fiction. I. Title.
  PS3561.E429R8 1992
  813'.54—dc20   91-36516
                                                CIP

First Edition: April 1992
10 9 8 7 6 5 4 3 2 1

For Dorothy

"She was a marvelous asset,
dignified as befitted her achievements,
more vivacious than her years
would suggest,
and with a beauty that made
a mockery of youth."

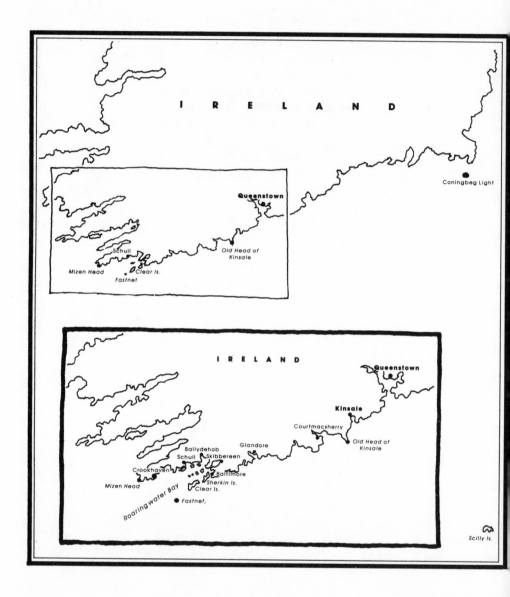

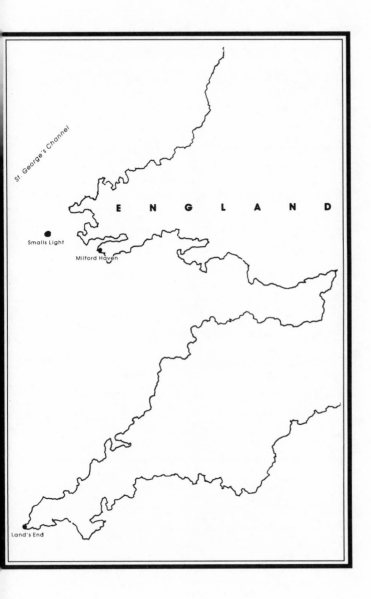

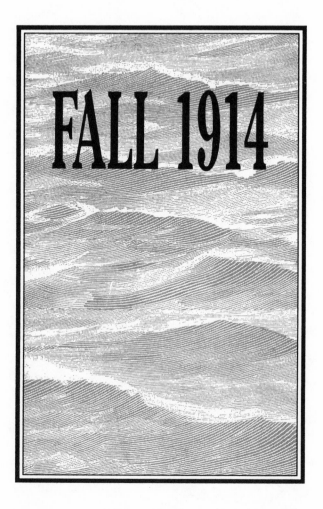

FALL 1914

LONDON

"THE UNITED States is a peace-loving nation, committed to peace throughout the world. President Woodrow Wilson is pledged to keep our country neutral in this terrible world war, a friend to every nation involved on every side. And it is as a friend of England that I present his proposals for an honorable peace."

Colonel Edward House was Woodrow Wilson's personal friend and confidant, his hand-picked emissary to the warring nations of Europe. He had brought with him Wilson's idealistic plan to bring the war out of the trenches and to the more civilized setting of the conference table and was in the process of presenting it to the leaders of His Majesty's government.

No one was really listening. What England needed to end its war with Germany was not a peacemaker but an ally. An ally to tip the terrible balance of terror in its favor.

Germany had struck into France with incredible swiftness, its armies swinging in an arc through Belgium and rushing down from the north toward Paris. England's expeditionary army had crossed the channel to aid its French ally, but the British troops, like the French, had been driven back by the German onslaught. Then, when it seemed defeat was inevitable and the fall of Paris a certainty, help had come from the most unlikely of places: Russia. The ragtag Russian army, still loading its rifles through the muzzle, had attacked Prussia, threatening the castles and estates of the German generals. One of the German armies was pulled away from the attack on Paris and sent to deal with the Russians. The loss of that army had turned the German advantage to a stalemate, and the war had dug into a line of trenches across northern France.

But the standoff wouldn't last forever. Once the Russians were defeated, the Germans would return. The only hope of victory that British generals and admirals had was that their own lines could be strengthened before the Russians collapsed. And their only source of new strength was the United States. They needed America in the war, on their side. Not at the head of a conference table.

". . . and therefore, the president proposes freedom of the seas, guaranteeing to the ships of all nations access to the ports of any nation," Colonel House droned on.

Absurd, the British leaders thought. Their most effective weapon was the naval blockade they had thrown across the North Sea, cutting off all maritime commerce with Germany. They had no intention of letting any ship, from any nation, get within a hundred miles of a German port.

There was polite applause as House finished his presentation. No one was terribly enthused, but, on the other hand, there was little sense in offending a personal friend of President Wilson's. House poured a glass of water from the pitcher that had been set next to his lectern and sipped it as he waited for questions.

"Colonel House." The questioner was a young man, barely forty, with a cherubic face and a soft body. He wore the gray morning attire that was the the the uniform of civilian government officials.

"Yes, Mister . . ." House had been introduced to all the guests, but he remembered only a few names. This man's wasn't one of them.

"Winston Churchill," the young man said. And then, with a mischievous grin to the other British officials, "I believe I'm First Lord of the Admiralty."

"Yes, of course," House pretended.

"While we are most respectful of your president's commitment to neutrality," Churchill said, "I wonder if there is anything that might pursuade him to take a more active role in the war?"

"More active?" House had just presented the president's offer to serve as the architect of a lasting peace. What could be more active than that?

"To declare war on Germany," Churchill said, clarifying any ambiguities.

The colonel stiffened. "Mr. Churchill, there is nothing that will bring the United States into this war."

"Nothing?" Churchill pressed, blinking in astonishment. "Nothing at all?"

"Well," House reconsidered, "nothing short of a German attack on American citizens. If the Germans were to kill American citizens, then certainly we would be forced to fight. But, of course, that would be highly unlikely."

"Highly unlikely," Churchill agreed as he settled back into his chair.

He was buoyant as he walked from the meeting, in clear contrast to the heavy shuffle of the other British officials. General French, commander of the British armies in France, caught up with him. "Not much hope from that quarter," he said.

"Oh, I think we can count on the Americans," Churchill contradicted.

French was stunned. "I thought he made it quite clear that there would be no help from across the Atlantic."

"Unless the Germans attack American citizens," Churchill reminded the general. "What we have to do is assemble some Americans, and then pursuade the Germans to attack them."

"You can't be serious," French said. "How would you ever get Americans in front of a German gun?"

"I was thinking of a ship," the First Lord of the Admiralty answered.

THE NORTH SEA

DAYLIGHT.

A pale knife edge cut through the mist, separating the night from the distant outline of the Dutch coast. The wet wind seemed suddenly to die, and from the east came the first squawking of the gulls. Standing on the wing of *Aboukir*'s bridge, Commander William Day could suddenly make out the bow of his own ship and the white foam that washed out of its way. Overhead, he could see the cloud of soot that rose from the ship's funnels and blotted the deep gray of the awakening sky.

"Sunrise, quartermaster," Day called as the small leaden arc of the sun appeared. The North Sea was colorless in the fall, and in the rain even the tint of the sun was difficult to discern.

"Sunrise at zero six one four hours," the quartermaster chanted as he made the appropriate entry in the log. He leaned out of the wheelhouse and looked up at the signal bridge. "Morning colors," he ordered, and in response the Union Jack slid up the signal mast.

"Inform the captain," Day called, his cadence almost singsong from the boredom of the routine.

"Aye aye, sir!" The quartermaster disappeared into the passageway behind the helmsman.

They were steaming north by northeast, running parallel to the coastline, in a broadly spaced triangle. *Hogue* was closest to the beach, and *Cressy* was in the van. Day was just able to make them out as the feeble sliver of daylight lifted the night a bit higher. Neither ship could see *Aboukir*, which, from their positions, was still hidden against the black backdrop of the night.

"Number One."

Captain Drummond always addressed his officers by their billet titles. He stood beside Commander Day wearing his greatcoat over his pajamas and slippers.

"Good morning, captain."

"Nothing much good about it," Drummond mumbled, sniffing at the heavy air. "Where's the barometer?"

"Holding at twenty-eight and a half," Day answered.

"Damn. Looks like we're in for another day of this muck. The rotten coal dust falls all over you before you can get out from under it." The captain rose up on his toes, pressed his hands into the small of his back, and leaned backward. A chain of cracks sounded from his spine. "The dampness gets into everything. You can catch your death of cold just lying in your bed."

"We're supposed to get a high front through this afternoon," Day offered.

Drummond sneered. "No such thing as a high in the North Sea. This time of year, the nearest high is off Egypt. We should get ourselves transferred to the Mediterranean, Number One. It's the best place to winter."

"I'm all for it, sir," Day agreed.

As the two men stood side by side, they seemed to be from different planets as well as different generations. Day towered over his commanding officer. He was over six feet tall, with broad shoulders and powerful arms inherited from his longshoreman father. Drummond was diminutive, a short, slight man whose physique suggested scholarship more than hard work. Day had a dark complexion with angular features chiseled around deep-set, brooding eyes. Drummond's thin hair had turned to white, blending easily into a soft, pink face. Day, at the age of thirty, still seemed to be growing. Drummond, who was a few weeks past fifty, was becoming even more frail with his advancing age.

"Any orders from the flag?" Drummond had started back toward the wheelhouse when he remembered to ask whether the squadron commander, who had his flag aboard *Cressy*, had sent any signals.

"Turn to two eight five at oh seven hundred," Day answered.

"Jesus," Drummond cursed. "Back to the west and then to the south and then back in here to the coast. Why in hell are we steaming in circles off the Dutch coast? If the German fleet comes out, they won't be heading in our direction. They'll go north."

Day shrugged. The captain looked into the wheelhouse and focused on the chronometer. "I'll take my breakfast before the maneuvering starts, Number One. If I'm not here by oh six fifty, send someone for me."

"Aye, sir."

Day looked back toward the coastline. He could now make out details on the superstructures of *Hogue* and *Cressy*, the masts streaming their wireless antennas and the four stacks that rose above each hull. The hulls themselves were still lost in the darkness of the water, but Day could see the white wakes trailing behind them.

They were ancient ships, laid down before the turn of the century, trying hopelessly to steam into a new era of warfare. God help us, Day thought, if the German High Seas Fleet ever does come out. *Cressy*-class cruisers were only 450 feet long, with 9-inch guns as their main battery.

The new German cruisers were nearly 200 feet longer. With their 15-inch guns they could drop shells on *Cressy*, *Hogue*, and *Aboukir* for half an hour before the English ships could even bring them into range.

The Admiralty called them "The Fishbait Squadron," in cynical reference to their fate if they should ever be forced into combat. But when the kaiser's armies tore through Belgium and into France, they were the only ships available for patroling the northern approaches to the English Channel. They were hurried into service, their crews augmented by volunteers from the merchant marine, freeing the British dreadnaughts for patrols north of the Orkneys, to keep the German fleet from breaking out into the Atlantic.

Day checked the chronometer. Zero six twenty-five. In half an hour, the signal flags on *Cressy* would drop, ordering the squadron to turn to the west. As the ship on the pivot point, *Aboukir* would have to slow to just a few knots, allowing her two sister ships to swing around. Then, when the new heading was established, she would have to put on speed to hold position in the formation. He stepped through the hatchway into the wheelhouse and pulled the cap from one of the voice tubes.

"Engine room, this is the bridge."

"Engine room, aye." The voice came from deep within the bowels of the ship, fifteen feet below the water line.

"We're going to be maneuvering in a few minutes," Day said. "You might want to bring up your steam."

"Aye, aye, sir," the hollow voice responded. And then it added, "Thank you for the warning, Mr. Day."

Among *Aboukir's* watch officers, Day was the only one who understood what happened below decks when the bridge rang down for abrupt changes in speed. He had spent scores of off-duty hours in the stokehold, where soot-stained stokers fired endless shovels of coal into unquenchable boilers. He had stood beside the towering reciprocating engines while machinists struggled to shift them from ahead to reverse. He had talked with the engineers over cups of tarlike coffee that was cooked on the boilertops. On the bridge, it was a simple matter to swing the handles of the telegraph to a different direction or a higher speed. Below decks, there was hell to pay.

When he rang down for "ahead one-third" enginemen had to leap to the huge throttle valves and wind them down, slowly cutting the flow of steam to the engine cylinders. Steam pressure between the boilers and the throttles would climb, lifting safety valves and venting the lines. Then, moments later, when he called for "full ahead," the giant valves would be twisted wide open, sucking steam from the lines.

To respond to his orders, the engineers needed extra steam capacity. And that meant they needed white-hot fires in all the boilers. His warning gave the black gang time to break out extra coal from the bunkers, stoke the fires, and bring up steam volume and pressure. The other watch officers muttered and swore when the engines were slow to answer their commands. On Day's watch, the engines seemed more lively.

He raised his binoculars and scanned the horizon. To the east, there was a faint trace of light, broken by the flat landfall of Holland and the silhouettes of the two sister ships. To the north and west, still nothing but murky darkness. He looked back to *Cressy*, where the flags that ordered the turn to the west were still flying from the yardarm. There was no hurry. The Fishbait Squadron wasn't going anywhere. The squadron commander could wait until there was more daylight before executing his signal.

Suddenly, the ship lurched as if struck by a giant hammer, its steel side crashing like a cymbal. Day staggered as he tried to hold his footing, then toppled and slid across the deck until he smashed against the wheelhouse. He looked up to see a wall of black water rise high above the port wing, followed by a cloud of hissing steam. Instantly, fire alarms began clanging deep within the coffin of the hull.

"Sweet Jesus, a torpedo." The scream came from the helmsman, who had been slammed to the deck by the violent twisting of the ship's steering wheel.

"Hold her on course," Day yelled as he struggled back up onto his feet. He ran into the wheelhouse and uncapped the voice tube.

"Engine room. This is the bridge."

A deafening roar came back up the pipe.

"Engine room. This is the bridge."

A voice shouted back above the hellish howl of escaping steam. "We're taking water into the boiler room, Mr. Day. We've got a hole clean through the portside bunker. And we've got busted steam lines."

Day was going to ask if they had steam pressure to the engine, but he was suddenly aware that the deck was tilting over toward the port side. In an instant he understood the significance of the sea water pouring through the bunker.

"Open the starboard seacocks," he screamed back down the voice tube. "Flood the starboard coal bunkers."

"Flood 'em? Mr. Day, we're already taking on more water than we can handle."

"Flood them. Now!"

There was a pause, and then "Aye aye, sir."

Aboukir was built with longitudinal coal bunkers running down each side of the ship. The explosion, Day realized, had blown a hole through the hull, opening the port bunker to the sea. They had been cruising for two weeks, which meant that the coal supply was half gone, so sea water was filling the port bunker. The imbalance in weight would roll the ship over in a matter of minutes. He had to open the starboard bunker to keep *Aboukir* upright.

He charged out of the wheelhouse and started up the ladder toward the signal bridge. But the ship was already listing fifteen degrees to port, and the angle of the steps made it difficult for him to keep his footing.

"Signal to *Cressy*," he screamed above the deafening alarm bells that seemed to be clanging everywhere. "Struck by mine or torpedo. Losing speed and listing."

"Aye aye, sir," the signalman acknowledged as he tore the weather cover off the carbon arc signal lamp.

"Number One!" Captain Drummond had staggered out onto the wing, a table napkin still tucked into the collar of his jacket. "What happened? Do we have damage reports?"

"I think it was a torpedo," Day snapped. "Our port coal bunkers are open to the sea."

"Can we keep up steam?"

Day shook his head. "I've ordered the starboard bunkers flooded. That will bring water over the stokehold floor. I'm going to tell the black gang to vent steam and get themselves topside." He had his hand on the voice tube when Captain Drummond caught up with him.

"Why are you flooding the stokehold? We need to keep the fires going."

"With the portside bunkers flooded, we'll roll over and turn turtle," Day shot back. "I'm buying a few minutes to get everyone up on deck."

Drummond nodded. He knew Day was right. Once one bunker was open, *Aboukir* was doomed. All they could do was prolong the death agony until the crew could make it safely over the side.

"Signal *Cressy* to come alongside and take off survivors," Captain Drummond decided.

Commander Day hesitated.

"Number One?"

"If it was a torpedo," Day answered, "then there's a submarine waiting out there. This is the last place *Cressy* should stop dead in the water."

"Message from flag!" the signalman screamed.

Captain Drummond started out onto the bridge wing, then grabbed the edge of the hatchway to keep from falling. The list to port was increasing rapidly.

"*Cressy* . . . coming . . . alongside . . . to render . . . assistance," the signalman mouthed as he read the flashing light on *Cressy*'s bridge. "*Hogue* . . . will . . . provide . . . protective . . . screen."

Drummond was satisfied. "If there's a submarine out there, *Hogue* will keep it covered," he told his Number One. They watched as *Cressy* leaned into a tight turn, swinging her bow until it pointed straight at the stricken *Aboukir*.

Forty feet below, the engineers were racing against a rising tide. Inky black water reached to the top of the port bulkhead, rolled across the engine room at a twenty-degree angle, and lapped at the base of the starboard bulkhead. They waded waist deep, choking on the coal dust that filled the air, as they went from valve to valve, venting away the ship's steam. In the boiler rooms, the stokers were raking out the fires. The white coals they pulled out of the fire doors exploded into clouds of steam as they touched the water.

"Bridge. This is the engine room."

Commander Day uncapped the voice pipe. "This is the bridge."

"Mr. Day, we've got all the seacocks open," the chief engineer said. "It's no good. The starboard cocks must be out of the water."

"Get all your men topside," Day said.

"We haven't got all the fires."

"Forget the fires. Get everyone up here now."

They had only a few seconds left. *Aboukir* was tipped so far to port that the starboard bilge was high out of the water. Even with the seacocks open, it was impossible to flood the starboard bunker. The ship was already listing twenty degrees, and the rate of its roll was increasing. Within the ship, everything that was loose was falling. Heavy machines would soon begin to tear free and smash through interior bulkheads as they slid to the port side. With each degree of list the forces causing even greater list would increase. At some point, only moments away, the ship would roll over and die.

Day heard screams from the boat deck and turned to see a seaman dangling from the gunwall of one of the lifeboats. Because of the list, the boat had swung out away from the ship as soon as it was raised from its chocks. The seaman, who tried to hold it back, had been dragged across the lifeline. A second later, he dropped into the sea.

Captain Drummond was looking straight down from the port wing, waiting for the rush of water along the side of the ship to slow. Incredibly, *Aboukir* was still moving, her bow nearly submerged as it drove into the sea. Drummond wanted the ship dead in the water before he ordered the boats lowered and his crew over the rail. But even as she moved forward, the ship was twisting over onto her side. If he waited for her to stop, it might be too late to save his crew. He made his decision.

"Abandon ship!"

The quartermaster pulled the whistle cord to sound the signal. The deep-throated roar faded quickly as the steam blast began to sputter.

"Cut the boats free," Day screamed. "Get the life rafts overboard."

He couldn't fill the boats and lower them. Even if there were time, the boats on the port side were hanging ten feet away from the ship. No one could reach them. Those on the starboard side were hanging in over the deck, where they couldn't be lowered.

Crewmen formed firelines, passing life jackets out from their lockers. As quickly as the men were able to fasten on jackets, they jumped over the port rail into the ugly black stain of coal grime that was trailing behind the ship.

Drummond looked around at the bridge watch. The quartermaster and the helmsman were still at their stations. The signalmen were clinging precariously to the railings of the signal bridge.

"You heard my order. Abandon ship!"

The crewmen broke from their stations and slid down the sloping deck until they were at the end of the bridge wing. Then they stepped over and dropped into the sea.

"You too, Number One."

"We'll go together, captain," Day said.

Drummond shook his head. "I'll stay put until *Cressy* comes alongside."

"You don't have time," Day began to argue, but his words were lost in a screech of tearing metal. The number one stack broke free and fell like a tree, crashing down on top of the seamen struggling in the water. Then the signal mast began to topple as the ship lurched further to port.

Day wrapped his arms around Captain Drummond and wrestled him over the lifeline. As *Aboukir* continued to roll, the rising sea lifted them off the bridge and floated them clear. The ship paused on its side for only an instant as sea water poured into the tops of the remaining stacks. Then its decks and superstructure fell under while the keel and bilges broke out of the sea. She turned completely over, the whalelike curve of colorless steel broken only by the propeller shafts and the two idle propellers that slowly began to rise into the air.

For a half mile behind the sinking ship, its crew was stretched out in a line of bobbing heads. Choking men struggled toward the overturned boats and rafts. Broken men clung to shreds of debris. Some voices called out orders as they tried to rally the men into rescue parties. Other voices screamed out in pain. Some were still and silent, blank faces kept afloat by the collars of the life jackets.

Commander Day held Captain Drummond in his arm as he kicked out toward the floating flag cases from the signal bridge. The older man struggled for a handhold, and then Day vaulted him onto one of the cases. Drummond reached back to help haul Day on top, but the commander was already swimming back toward a signalman who was thrashing in the water.

The signalman pounced on Day as soon as he was near, driving him under the surface, and for a moment they struggled as if they were mortal enemies. Then Day got an arm around the boy's neck, dragged him over onto his back, and started kicking back toward the floating flag cases. It was then that he saw *Cressy* as she appeared around the capsized hull of *Aboukir*.

The flagship had slowed and was drifting toward the line of men who were suddenly screaming and waving frantically toward their rescue. Aboard *Cressy*, crewmen lined the life rail, lowering cargo nets and ropes over the side. The ship's boats were swung out, one of them already lowered halfway down the side. Then, well behind *Cressy*, Day saw *Hogue*. She was moving at full speed, belching clouds of thick smoke from her funnels as she searched for a submarine that might be lurking beneath the water to the west.

Drummond reached down and caught the signalman by his shirt collar. Day got his shoulder under the boy, and together they were able to lift him up next to the captain.

"Get aboard," Drummond called to Day. The commander was reaching up when the sky suddenly flashed with light, and the air vibrated in a thunderclap. In the distance, *Hogue* shuddered beneath a billowing cloud of smoke.

"Good God," the captain prayed.

Hogue seemed to skid sideways, kicking up a wave of white water as she stopped dead. Then there was a second flash, this one near her stern. As Day and Drummond watched incredulously, the old ship began to roll to starboard, her decks and then her gun mounts disappearing into the sea. Her deck crew fell like raindrops into the water.

Aboard *Cressy*, the boatswain's pipe sounded and the crew scampered away from the railing, abandoning the nets and lines they were lowering over the side. The sea churned around her propellers, and the flagship moved away from the drowning men, rushing off toward the sinking hull of *Hogue*.

Cressy had no choice but to attack. If she stopped dead in the water to rescue the crew of *Aboukir* she would be an easy target. The submarine had to be somewhere beyond *Hogue*, probably already moving away from her victim, but perhaps moving in for still another kill. As soon as she had gathered enough speed, *Cressy* began zigzagging, turning from side to side like a blinded boxer stalking an opponent. In the water around *Hogue*, sailors waved deliriously at what they thought was approaching rescue. Their calls turned to screams of horror as *Cressy* charged through their midst, her wake tossing them aside like bobbing corks.

Her deck guns began firing at phantoms. The daylight still had not burned through the mist, and visibility was limited. Lookouts scanned the sea and directed gun crews toward every wave that might be the wake of a moving periscope. The gunners poured round after round into invisible targets, hoping for a flash of light or a puff of oily smoke that would signal a hit.

Still clinging to the sinking flag boxes, Day, Drummond, and the signalman watched *Cressy* turn abruptly to starboard, taking up the second leg of her search pattern. She raced a thousand yards to the north, then turned again and headed eastward, back toward the rising stern of *Aboukir*. Screams came from the water around them. *Aboukir's* crewmen had seen *Cressy* steam over *Hogue's* survivors in her frantic chase toward her invisible tormentor. Now she was coming straight toward them.

And then she exploded. The blast threw a water spout up along her starboard side, and a cloud of coal dust belched from her shattered hull. Immediately, she began to lean to starboard. Like her sister ships, her longitudinal coal bunker was flooding quickly, its weight dragging the ship into a roll from which there was no hope of recovery. *Cressy's* whistle sounded her death groan. One of her stacks broke free and tore across her sloping deck like a scythe, cutting through the crew members who were scampering toward the railing. Then she began to settle into her own black stain, joining *Hogue* and *Aboukir*, which had already vanished.

Now there were a thousand men thrashing in the water, struggling toward the broken pieces of debris that bobbed in their midst. *Aboukir's* men were stretched out in a line. The few survivors of *Hogue* and *Cressy* were bunched in two groups a few hundred yards apart. Cries echoed across the flat surface of the still water.

Day identified one of the voices, slid down from the flag box, and struck out toward the helmsman who was screaming for help. As he pushed the man back up next to Captain Drummond, he heard another voice nearby, this one just the choking gasp of a drowning man. A pale face bobbed up a few yards away, and he was able to reach out, seize the man's life jacket, and drag him alongside. In just a few seconds he gathered six of *Aboukir's* crew: three on top of the floating flag locker, three with him in the water holding on for support.

By now, there was enough light coming through the haze so that he could make out individual forms. He saw two members of the engine room crew clinging to a piece of wooden decking and was thrilled they had made it up out of their tomb before the ship had capsized. But the next instant he recognized a young gunner, his face staring blankly as the sea splashed over it. For every moment of hope, he found another moment of despair.

Then, through the pained wail that blended hundreds of individual voices, he heard a new sound, the dull, rhythmic throbbing of an engine. He looked around, trying to see over the waves that were lapping at his face.

"The murdering bastard." It was Captain Drummond, sitting up on top of the flag locker, who saw it first. Day turned in the direction that Drummond was staring and saw the ghostly shape of a submarine cutting through the mist. But as he blinked in disbelief, the gray form vanished.

When he saw it again, the decks were awash so that the forward edge of the conning tower was breaking the water. She was so low that she kept disappearing behind swells in the sea, only to reappear a few hundred feet closer. The droning noise of her engines grew louder, and the details of her structure began to take solid shape. He could make out the deck gun, which broke through the surface and then sank away as the boat pitched. He could see the top of her bow as it occasionally sent up a misty spray. And then he saw the shape of a man standing atop the conning tower, looking around in disbelief at the destruction he had caused.

The submarine came closer, and as it moved, the air around it became deathly still. Voices stopped in the throats of the men in the water as they came face to face with the image of death moving like a shark through their midst.

"Bastard," Drummond suddenly screamed, his voice cracking the momentary stillness. "Murdering bastard!" The captain of the submarine looked down as his boat drew close. Then he raised his hands in a gesture of helplessness and turned slowly to take in the thousand heads bobbing in the sea around him. As the U-boat drifted past, he stretched out his arms, embracing the tiny size of his craft. How, he seemed to be asking, can this little boat rescue so many men? He wagged his head in bewilderment. Drummond, who had raised himself to his knees, sank helplessly back down onto his haunches. The flag locker rocked precariously in the wake of the submarine. The beat of the engines suddenly quickened, and the ghostly craft kicked up a backwash as she accelerated. It took just a few seconds for her to disappear into the low-lying mist.

Day tightened his grip on the edge of the flag locker. He was exhausted, and the weight of his clothes was dragging him down lower into the water. He could taste the sulfur in the coal that was floating in a slick just an inch under his chin.

LONDON

ALFRED BOOTH raised the glass of port to his lips, letting it pause for a moment so that he could savor the sweet bouquet. His cousin George looked on apprehensively from across the table.

"Very nice," Alfred pronounced. He sipped, then closed his eyes to block out all distractions. His chin raised and his lips puckered. "Very nice, indeed."

"I'm so glad you like it," George said. He signaled the waiter, who immediately approached with a wooden chest of cigars. "Try one of the Cubans. They really are extraordinary."

Alfred reached for a cigar, but his eyes looked over the top of the box and fixed suspiciously on his cousin. Though they each ran half of the family business, they didn't generally socialize together. As chairman of the Cunard line, Alfred was involved with the shipping barons of the great port of Liverpool and with the industrialists of the north. As the family's financial genius, George spent most of his time in London's central city. It had been over a year since George had invited Alfred to have dinner at his club, and his solicitude was alarming to his cousin.

Alfred rolled the cigar close to his ear. The waiter struck a match and held it steady while Alfred drew in the first breath of heavy smoke. He nodded his satisfaction. "Quite nice," he admitted.

George cleared his throat. "I suppose you've guessed that there is something I need to discuss with you."

"I thought there might be," Alfred said.

"Well, in truth, it's not just me. The fact is one of my associates is going to be joining us." George lifted his watch from his vest and glanced down at it. "In fact, he should be here any minute."

"Who?" Alfred demanded, his eyes narrowing.

"Winston," George mumbled.

"Churchill?" Alfred's eyes widened.

George nodded carefully. "I'm afraid so." He watched as Alfred's jaw tightened into a straight line. "It's important, Alfred. He needed a word with you, and I thought . . ."

Alfred Booth crushed the cigar into the ash tray.

"Please," George said. "I wouldn't have done this if it weren't absolutely necessary."

Alfred pulled back from the table. "This is outrageous," he fumed. "You know my opinion of that . . . upstart."

"It's about the war effort," George tried. "A matter of national security."

"It's about *Lusitania*," Alfred fired back.

"Well, yes. As a matter of fact, it is."

"Then the First Lord of the Admiralty can call at my office," Alfred said, jumping to his feet. "He can make an appointment during business hours. The best thing that Winston Churchill can do for our war effort is to step down and let a true seafaring man take over the Admiralty."

"Sit down, Alfred," George Booth ordered.

Alfred's jaw slackened. No one spoke to him in that tone of voice. He looked as if he had been slapped.

"Sit down," George repeated, his expression hardening.

Alfred settled slowly back into his chair. They sat quietly for a moment, staring at each other across the table.

"I'm sorry," George finally said. "But the truth of the matter is that I arranged this meeting for your sake, not for his. Churchill doesn't have to ask for your cooperation. He has the authority to order it."

Alfred Booth nodded slowly. "I know that," he admitted. "If the Admiralty wants *Lusitania*, it has the right to take her." He toyed with the cigar that was still smoldering in the ashtray. "Probably best if it did. Cunard can't afford to keep her in operation. She loses money every time she crosses. Especially now, with the war on and passenger bookings down. Maybe it's time she did her tour as a cruiser."

Lusitania had never turned a profit. The great liner had been built with Admiralty money to Admiralty specifications that called for twice the engine power that a commercial liner needed. Her advanced turbines, the first ever installed in a large ship, gave her more speed than any vessel afloat. But the twenty-five giant boilers that fed them steam consumed more coal in a one-way passage than most of her transatlantic competitors used in the round-trip. It took a generous government mail contract, on top of the low-interest construction loans, to keep the ship close to breaking even.

From the moment her keel had been laid, she was intended to be converted into a naval cruiser in the event of war. The mounting rings for eight long-range naval guns were already built into her decks, giving her potentially the same broadside firepower as a battle cruiser. Valuable cargo space was given over to ammunition magazines and to the elevators that would hoist six-inch shells up to her gun mounts. True, she didn't have the heavy defensive armor of a true man-of-war. But she had incredible speed. There wasn't a battle cruiser in the world that could keep up with her.

George Booth shook his head. "Winston doesn't want her converted into a ship of the line," he answered. "He wants to keep her in commercial operation. Cunard has to keep her running in regular passenger service."

Alfred's blank expression showed that he didn't understand.

"That's the problem," George continued. "You want to tie her up for the duration. The Admiralty can't allow that to happen. If you insist, then they're going to replace you with a new chairman of Cunard."

"They can't," Alfred blurted. "We own Cunard."

"They can," George said. "There's a war on, and right now we're losing it. I assured Winston that there was no need to bring someone into Cunard over your head. I told him he could count on your cooperation."

"Why? What has passenger service to do with the war?" Alfred asked. "I don't think I understand."

George waved at the waiter, who returned with the wooden cigar chest. He waited while Alfred selected a replacement for the Havana he had destroyed. The he leaned over the table confidentially.

"It all has to do with the supply of war materials. Shells, primarily. We're firing more shells in France each day than we can make in England in a week. And there's guncotton. We have all the mines we need to lock the German navy into the North Sea for the duration. But we have no explosive guncotton to put into the mines. Our only chance is to buy what we need in America. Shells. Nitrates. Cannons. Even warm coats and boots."

"How do you know all this?" Alfred asked.

"I've been asked by His Majesty to make provision for a very long and difficult war. All quite confidential, of course. The official opinion is still that we'll win in one glorious cavalry charge. I've set up a purchasing commission in the United States to buy war materials, and we've hired the Morgan Bank to finance our purchases."

"The United States is neutral," Alfred protested.

George shook his head. "The United States only thinks it's neutral. We've made arrangements right up to President Wilson. We can buy just about anything we need. For a price, of course. But with Morgan working with us, the money is available. Our biggest problem is getting the supplies across. And that's where Cunard comes in. That's what Winston wants to talk to you about."

"You know I can't abide that smug little—"

"Hear him out, Alfred. He's a bright young man. This is a new kind of war we're fighting, and Winston is one of the few who seems to understand it. What's happening in France right now has nothing to do with tactics and very little to do with valor and bravery. It's a war of attrition. Whichever side has the last case of cannon shells is going to be the winner. The generals are still talking about battle lines. Churchill is the only one worrying about supply lines."

As if on cue, Winston Churchill strode into the dining room, his short, round physique impeccably turned out in white tie and tails. He handed a top hat and a walking stick to the porter, paused for an instant to order a bottle of champagne from the maitre d' and to select a cigar, then walked up to the table.

"George."

George Booth rose and gestured Churchill into the chair that the waiter was already holding.

"Alfred," Churchill said, as he held the cigar up to the light that the waiter struck. "How good"—he puffed a few times—"to see you"—one more puff and then a brisk exhale of smoke—"again."

"A pleasure," Alfred managed. He studied the soft, angelic face as

Churchill turned away to examine the label on the bottle of champagne being held by the wine steward. Winston really did look like a grade school teacher's pet, dressed in white tie to pass as an adult.

"That will do nicely," Churchill told the steward. "George, I hope you don't mind that I put this on your bill." George Booth nodded. Alfred winced.

"Alfred," the First Lord of the Admiralty began as he watched the bubbles in his champagne, "George assures me that you're most anxious to help us."

"Naturally, in a matter of national concern."

Churchill nodded as he sipped. "That's very good of you. And has your cousin explained our problem?"

"About transporting war materials? Yes, he has. But I was still a bit confused as to Cunard's role. It would seem you would need freighters rather than passenger ships."

"We need anything that floats," Churchill said, reaching for the bottle that rested in the ice bucket beside his chair. "But for special cargoes, we need passenger ships. Fast passenger ships. You're familiar with the maritime rules of encounter?"

The impertinent little toad, Alfred Booth fumed. His family owned one of the great seafaring empires of the world. He doubted that Churchill had ever been in water deeper than his knees.

"Of course," he responded.

The rules of encounter were recognized by all nations as governing confrontations between warships and commercial vessels in time of war. Warships were entitled to sink commercial vessels, but only after providing for the safety of all civilians aboard. They were entitled to stop them, board them, and search for contraband or for military personnel. If they found nothing, the commercial vessel was entitled to pass. But if it found war materials or military personnel, then the warship was entitled to seize the vessel as a war prize. Or, if it didn't have time to escort the captured vessel into port, it could simply sink her after placing civilians into lifeboats.

"We're planning on using passenger ships to carry munitions from America," Winston Churchill explained. "Submarines can't simply fire torpedoes at passenger ships. According to the rules, they have to surface and order them to stop. And, in the case of *Lusitania*, the submarine crews can't very well board her and search her because there's no way they can hope to catch her. And even if they did, they couldn't sink her. How could they provide for the safety of 2,000 passengers?"

"Submarines?" Booth asked. "I thought you were concerned about the German fleet."

"The German fleet isn't the problem," Winston said as he hunched over his cigar. "If it comes out, we'll sink it. And if we don't sink it, at least we'll know where it is. It's the damn U-boats." He turned to George Booth. "Have you mentioned the *Cressy* affair?" George shook his head.

Churchill turned back to Alfred. "Last week we lost an entire squadron of cruisers in half an hour. *Cressy*, *Hogue*, and *Aboukir*, all sunk by a single submarine twelve miles off the Dutch coast. Fifteen hundred men lost to a boat small enough to float in your bathtub."

Alfred was stunned. "I hadn't heard. None of our insurers mentioned—"

"We're not talking about it," Churchill said. "No point in stirring up a panic. But the fact is that all the battleships and cruisers in the king's navy can't keep the sea lanes open. The German submarines can choke England off from the rest of the world."

"But surely the navy . . ." Alfred tried to offer.

"The navy can't stop them. God, the navy can't even find them. Three ships of the line steamed right up to the submarine and didn't even know it was there. In half an hour one German submarine sank more tonnage than their High Seas Fleet has since the beginning of the war."

Alfred looked at George. His cousin nodded gravely.

"But that was in coastal waters," Alfred protested. "The submarines can't challenge us on the Atlantic."

"We're talking about supplies," Churchill continued. "Not naval victories."

The First Lord reached across the table, took Albert's ashtray, and set it in the center. "Here's England." He put his champagne glass beside it. "Here's Ireland." Then he used his cigar as a pointer. "Every pound of war materials that George buys in America has to come right through here to get to England." He moved the tip of the cigar around the bottom of the glass and then into the space between the glass and the ashtray. "Across the southern coast of Ireland, and up through Saint George's Channel. All coastal waters. All perfect for the submarines. Put half a dozen submarines in the area, and you can shut down England."

Alfred Booth looked up from the diagram. Instead of the smug little man who had ingratiated himself in high places, he saw a statesman who was plainly frightened.

"They could do it to us," he mumbled.

Winston nodded. "This war won't be won or lost in France. Nor on the North Atlantic." He pushed the wet end of his cigar down on the tablecloth. "It will be fought right here, off the Irish coast." He turned back to the ice bucket and poured another measure of champagne into the glass he had used as Ireland. There was a long pause while Alfred digested the map. Then George Booth continued with his cousin's education.

"The only way to get supplies through is to bring them in on ships that the submarines can't attack. Particularly on fast passenger ships that U-boats not only can't attack, but can't even search. How can they board a ship that's over the horizon by the time they can get their deck gun loaded?"

"But if *Lusitania* carries munitions, then she gives up her rights under the rules of encounter," Alfred Booth objected.

"The munitions will never appear on her cargo manifest," Churchill answered.

"But if the Germans even suspect—"

"The ship will be carrying civilian passengers. Many of them Americans. Even if the Germans suspect she's carrying munitions, I don't think they'll want to invite the Americans into the war."

"It's foolproof," George Booth added for his cousin's benefit. "They can't fire on her without making provision for the innocent passengers. And they can't make provision for the passengers because *Lusitania* won't stop long enough to have a conversation with them. She's our supply line, Alfred. She's our link with the arsenal we're buying in America."

"But where will she carry the ammunition?" Alfred questioned. "You can't just stack artillery shells in a stateroom."

"You're going to pull her out of service for a brief overhaul," Churchill answered. "The shipyard already has the plans. Basically, we're tearing out everything below the main deck and forward of the number one boiler room. The entire bow of the ship will become a magazine with very substantial capacity."

Alfred Booth looked from his cousin's fine patrician features to Churchill's cherubic jowls. "You're asking me to be a contrabandist," he said.

"We're asking you to be a patriot," Churchill answered.

Alfred looked hopelessly back toward his cousin.

"I assured Winston that His Majesty could count on you," George said.

Alfred sat in stunned silence for a few seconds. A munitions ship disguised as an ocean liner, with innocent passengers unaware that their lives were being offered to protect the deadly cargo. American passengers, so that Germany would be inviting its own destruction should it dare to attack. It was unthinkable. Absolutely immoral.

Then he looked at the ashtray that represented England and the cigar stain on the white linen tablecloth that marked his country's lifeline. "Yes. Yes, of course," he finally managed. "It all makes perfect sense."

NEW YORK

STRINGS.

Definitely strings. There was no doubt about it. He had made the right choice.

Even from the terrace of his estate on the north shore of Long Island, Sir Peter Beecham could feel a tingle of excitement as he listened to the musicians tuning their instruments in the ballroom. The plucking of the strings and the wailing of major chords on slowly drawn violin bows recreated the electricity that always anticipated a great concert or the curtain of an opera. You just couldn't get that feeling from an upright piano.

He had toyed with the idea of something trendy. Maybe a shirt-sleeved trio playing ragtime, or a colored group doing the new blues. After all, the party was for Jennifer's birthday, and he could explain that the music was for her and her friends. But he had reminded himself that, no matter what the occasion, the party was always for the Americans. And, in the company of Europeans, Americans pretended to prefer strings.

He couldn't explain Americans. Here they were, the most independent, decently democratic people in the world. But he had closed dozens of business deals simply by hinting to an American buyer that there might be an opportunity for his wife to curtsy to an authentic English princess. Any princess, no matter how serpentine her connection to the Crown. American industrialists had revolutionized metalworking and developed processes to make chemicals at half the market cost. But they would still travel across the ocean for the privilege of paying a defrocked Bond Street tailor twice the going rate for a genuine English suit. True, the average American had little use for the English. But Sir Peter Beecham didn't spend that much time with the average American. His dealings were with the capitalist elite, and as Americans rose in stature, their fondness for things British seemed to compound right along with their bank accounts.

There was no doubt about it. He had made the right choice. Definitely strings.

Sir Peter looked out onto a hillside that rolled from his manor house down into Long Island Sound. It was fall, and the countryside was ablaze with color, the trees in tones of orange and yellow, exploding across lawns of vivid green. If he looked north, across the shimmering blue of the sound, he could see New England, where the old world had given birth to the new. If he looked west, the could see the fledgling skyline of New

York City, where the new world was pushing the old aside and striking out on its own. He had made his fortune helping to build the industries of America. Now he was calling on those industries to come to the rescue of England.

The invitations to Jennifer's coming out had been written from a list of America's power brokers. There were the chairmen of two steel companies, both considering contracts for 2 million shell casings. There was the president of the nation's largest chemical concern, the globe's second-largest manufacturer of nitrate explosives. Directors of the two largest electrical manufacturers had been added to the guest list when the British army suddenly realized a need for electrical cable and portable generators. There were invitations for the head of America's telephone cartel, who was pricing an order for field telephones and switchboards, and for two shipping magnates who were deliberating the premiums they would charge for carrying dark cargoes into dangerous waters. With the United States claiming neutrality, all these men were free to sell equally to the Germans or the English. Culturally, they preferred the English. But business was business, and they would manufacture victory for the highest bidder.

To stay ahead in the bidding, Sir Peter needed vast supplies of credit. So, invitations had gone out to Wall Street. J. P. Morgan had been invited along with two of his top lieutenants. Morgan had refused. He detested social events where people sometimes enjoyed themselves. His two lieutenants had accepted. The Chase would be represented, as would two of New York's largest brokerage houses that had recently joined in financing a railroad that would never own even a foot of track. Taken together, the bankers who would dine at his table could lay their hands on more money than the Treasury.

And then there was government. U.S. law prohibited delivering war materials in American or neutral bottoms and clearly frowned upon boarding passengers on the same ships with munitions. Authorities had to be persuaded to look the other way as contraband was being loaded, and to scratch their signatures on cargo manifests that they knew were false. The Honorable Dudley Malone, customs collector for the Port of New York, had therefore received an invitation. And Germany could certainly be expected to file formal protests with the Department of State over America's outrageous breach of its obligations as a neutral power. Which explained why Robert Lansing, counsel to the State Department, was not only invited but was also listed as a guest of honor.

The invitations were not entirely cynical. Sir Peter hadn't selected the names with a hatpin. In the ten-year course of his business dealings in North America, he had befriended at least half of these men. And when George Booth had asked him to head the British purchasing agency in the

United States, Beecham had gone out of his way to make the acquaintance of all the others. In some cases, a personal note from the king on palace stationery had been all that was needed to assure cooperation. "Their Majesties look forward to receiving you on your next visit to Their Country" could make even a tycoon's wife giggle like a schoolgirl. For the others, like the great J. P. Morgan, the opportunity for obscene profit was more persuasive.

"Sir Peter."

He turned to find his butler standing at his side, holding a silver tray with a single wine glass. In his other hand he held a still-smoldering bottle wrapped in a white linen towel.

"The wine, sir."

The butler poured a small measure into the glass. Beecham lifted it from the tray, tasted it, and smiled. "The Louis Norde. How delightful. I thought we were out of it."

"A new supply," the butler answered. "In only last week. I hope it's not still agitated from the journey."

"No," Sir Peter answered. "Not that I can tell. Have you tried it?"

The butler nodded. "I took the liberty. It seemed quite satisfactory."

Beecham set the glass on the tray. But his eyes remained fixed on it as it was carried across the terrace and back into the house. How extraordinary, he thought. France is being blown to pieces, its soil salted with cordite. There isn't a healthy man in the country who hasn't been marched into the trenches to await the fall of the next mortar round. And every ship that isn't eaten through with rot or rust has been pressed into hauling supplies. Yet his wine had been bottled, crated, and carried to a safe port, loaded aboard a vessel, and shipped through hostile waters. All for a few dollars a bottle. There were ways around the war for those who could pay a reasonable price.

His guests began arriving, brought to his door in carriages that had met the special train he had arranged from New York. His wife, Anne, made her entrance down the grand staircase and stood beside him as he welcomed each couple. She was a marvelous asset, dignified as befitted her achievements, more vivacious than her fifty years would suggest, and with beauty that made a mockery of youth. She not only put a name with every face but also recalled some humorous anecdote from a prior meeting, making even the most formal relationship seem like a lifelong friendship. Sir Peter was free to smile his greetings and to gesture the men to his well-stocked bar at the entrance to the ballroom.

Jennifer's guests weren't really her friends. Her true friends had been left behind in England when she was ripped away by her father's critical mission to New York. Her young guests were the children of her parent's associates, young women who had included her at their own presentations to society without even knowing who she was, and young men with the connections that got them included into most fashionable parties. But Anne had made a point to learn something about each of them and was able to offer a greeting more genuine than perfunctory.

Robert Lansing arrived, with his wife, the daughter of a former secretary of state, on his arm. He was a tall man with his full head of gray hair nicely styled, his moustache carefully contoured. His eyes twinkled as he smiled an elaborate greeting to Anne, and his words rolled in an Oxford accent that he had spent years rehearsing as evidence of his good breeding.

"Strings," he noticed, as he stepped to the ballroom door. "I love an evening of strings."

"I thought you might," Sir Peter agreed.

The guests broke into small groups according to industry: the manufacturers in the center of the room, the financial men near the orchestra, and the steamship owners by the rows of French doors that looked out over the sound. The young guests, who seemed to laugh more than talk, stayed close to the bar. Waiters circulated with trays of champagne and hors d'oeuvres and filled special requests for gin and whiskey. Sir Peter was content to move from group to group, but Anne resisted the easy plunge into factionalism. She led a couple from the industrialists' caucus across the room to meet with the shipping magnates, then stole a seafaring couple and took them to the bankers. Within just a few minutes she had organized a microcosm of the American economy.

And then came Jennifer's moment. The orchestra paused from the incidental melodies, then stilled the conversation by playing a spirited fanfare. All heads turned in anticipation toward the staircase, where Jennifer suddenly turned into view and paused on the landing. The women sighed at her beauty.

She was tall and thin, the perfect figure for the narrow, floor-length underskirt and blousey tunic that had been the spring revolution in Paris. Her deep complexion was the perfect shade to complement the almond white of the brocade. She wore her dark hair up, showing the long neck and soft shoulders that were now exposed by the more radical couturieres. The subdued makeup of her high cheeks and small mouth made the diamond tiara in her hair that much more glorious.

Sir Peter crossed to the bottom of the stairs, climbed the first two steps, and extended his hand. Jennifer descended with the carefully paced steps that her tight hemline allowed and reached down to him. When he turned, with his daughter on his arm, there were tears of joy in his eyes. He led her into the ballroom, where his guests exploded in applause.

Jennifer was his life, a fact that his wife, Anne, understood better than he did. Peter Beecham thought of himself as a thick-skinned business-man, a tough negotiator, and a demanding employer. Anne knew him to be an apprehensive father who caved into his daughter's every wish and who asked nothing more than to be allowed to look in on her while she slept.

Her daring dress was a case in point. Would her father allow her to be seen in the new bare neckline look, she had asked her mother. Anne had promised to talk to him.

"Did you see the dress your daughter is hoping to wear to her party?" Anne had begun.

"Outrageous," Peter had pronounced.

"I don't think we should let her," Anne said.

"Certainly not," he agreed.

Peter had turned away from the subject confident that his opinion was final.

"Of course, it will break her heart," Anne had allowed.

"Break her heart?"

"Some of the other girls are wearing it."

"They are?"

"Well, the ones with the more attractive figures."

"More attractive than Jennifer's?"

"The ones who can wear that sort of look."

"My daughter can wear any sort of look she chooses."

"Do you think so?"

"Of course. And if that's what the more attractive girls are wearing, then Jennifer should certainly wear it."

"You're quite sure?"

"Certainly."

He led her to each of his guests, introducing her even though they had been introduced before. It was a rite of passage, the moment when Sir Peter Beecham admitted publicly that his little girl had become a woman and henceforth would be allowed to speak for herself. Anne pretended to be busy with the servants, but she relished the moment as she looked on. The two people she loved the most seemed so happy in each other's company. Would their lives ever know a more exhilarating moment?

The conductor waited until Sir Peter had made his last introduction, then turned to his musicians and whispered the name of a waltz. Peter led his daughter to the center of the ballroom and circled the floor to smiles and applause. Then Jennifer asked the others to join them, and the ballroom came to life.

Peter handed his daughter to one of the young men and did another turn around the floor with Anne. "We can serve at any time," she whispered to him.

"Can you give me a few minutes? Lansing needs a word."

She nodded without even for an instant losing her smile.

Peter carried two whiskeys to their rendezvous in the library and handed one to Robert Lansing. The strains of a waltz filled the room.

"You're a very lucky man, Sir Peter." Lansing tipped his glass in a toast. "Your daughter is lovely."

"A wonderful evening," Peter Beecham agreed. "Thank you, Robert for sharing it with us." He gestured toward one of the leather chairs, and Lansing's expression grew grave as he sat.

"Von Bernstorff was in this morning," Lansing began. "He brought Franz von Papen with him."

Beecham nodded. The German ambassador and his military attaché were overdue. The true nature of the cargoes that he was loading aboard neutral vessels and passenger ships would never be officially acknowledged. But in the course of arranging passage, setting rates and premiums for insurance, loading and unloading under the noses of port commissioners, it was impossible to keep his activities secret. Germany had been asking neutral nations to protest England's flagrant breach of international law. Now they were taking their protest directly to the U.S. government.

"It's a difficult issue," Lansing continued. "They're warning us of their right to sink any ship that carries war materials. Von Papen came right out and said that Germany could assume no responsibility for American citizens who travel on passenger ships carrying contraband." He shook his head in despair. "Technically, they're right, of course."

"Outrageous," Sir Peter sympathized. "I know of no government more diligent in checking cargo manifests than your own."

"That's exactly what I told them," Lansing agreed. "No ship clears an American port until we have verified its cargo."

"Robert, I can absolutely assure you that we are abiding by the laws of your country. Oh, I'm sure there are mistakes made. We're buying so much here in America. But contraband on passenger ships . . ." He lifted his hands in a gesture of helplessness. "I suppose there's no way we can disprove the charge."

"I told them much the same thing," the counsel to the State Department agreed. "Shipping through our harbors has nearly doubled. Our port authorities are overwhelmed. Some irregularities are inevitable. But to suggest that the United States would knowingly sanction embarking ammunition on passenger ships . . ."

"Ridiculous," Beecham said, concluding Lansing's thought.

Lansing took his glass with him as he jumped up from the chair and paced toward the fireplace. "The problem is that this is just the kind of thing that Bryan would love to believe." William Jennings Bryan, the secretary of state, had the traditional midwesterner's distrust of the British. He was anxious to assure that the administration's stated policy of neutrality wasn't tipped in favor of Britain.

"How did he react?" Beecham asked.

Lansing shook his head. "I've kept the Germans away from Bryan. There's no sense in arming the man with unfounded charges."

"Robert, I'm well aware how difficult this is for you. All of us know where your true sympathies lie. We respect your loyalty to your government's policy."

"It's just a matter of time," Lansing said. "Americans are clearly behind the Allies. President Wilson has to begin to see the national will."

"Or his successor. There are a number of very powerful people in England who are hoping you might aspire to the job, Robert."

"The presidency?" Lansing tried to look shocked at the suggestion. "That's not even remotely possible," he protested.

"Perhaps not at this moment," Beecham countered. "But my purchasing committee is dealing with the biggest men in this country. You saw them out in the ballroom. And we'll be working with many more like them in the months to come. Those men are not neutral. They want to help the British cause. When they look to Washington, you're the only man they can agree with."

"But, still . . ." Lansing started.

Peter held up a hand to cut him off. "I'm wrong to even raise the issue. I respect your loyalty to President Wilson. Suffice it for me to say that many of us hope to see a change in American policy by the next election. A change much along the lines of your own thinking."

"I appreciate your candor," Lansing said, setting his glass on the mantel.

Beecham rose to escort his guest back to the party. "As I do yours," he answered. "You're a true friend."

There had been no candor at all. Lansing knew perfectly well that the British were loading their cargoes after they had filed their official manifests. American law allowed for supplementary manifests, covering last-minute cargo and provisions, which were handed to the pilot as their ships departed. Port commissioners and customs inspectors had no way of verifying whether the supplementary manifests were true.

And Beecham knew perfectly well that Robert Lansing thought of little else but the presidency. His hint of support from powerful friends was really a promise. Stripped of the niceties, Sir Peter Beecham was saying, "Robert, you help these men get rich by selling war materials to England, and they'll have enough money to buy you the White House."

Peter knew what he was promising. Lansing knew what to expect in return for his services.

The music grew louder as they walked toward the ballroom, then seemed to explode when they stepped through the doorway.

"Ah, Cinderella has found her Prince Charming," Lansing suddenly said. He was much taller than Sir Peter and could easily see the dance floor over the heads of the gathered guests.

"Prince Charming?" Peter asked. He stepped around a cluster of chattering bankers until he could see Jennifer in the center of the room, swaying in the arms of a tall naval officer in full dress uniform.

"My new naval aide," he said. "Arrived just yesterday. I wasn't sure he'd make it here on such short notice."

"Your aide?" Lansing wondered.

"No. Of course not. Not a personal aide," Beecham admitted. "He's officially attached to our commercial delegation in New York. But he'll be working with me."

"He seems captivated by your daughter."

"Nonsense," Sir Peter protested. "He's much older than Jennifer. Let me introduce him to you. A most interesting chap. One of the survivors of *Aboukir*."

He got them together as soon as the music stopped. "Counselor Lansing, may I present Commander William Day, attached to our commercial office. Robert Lansing," he told Day, "is chief counsel to the United States Department of State."

"An honor," Day said as he offered his hand.

"My honor," Lansing insisted. "I heard about your ship. Three of them, if I remember. A terrible tragedy."

Day nodded, hoping to put the subject to rest. But he was the first actual combatant that the counselor had ever seen. Robert Lansing could almost smell the gunpowder.

"One submarine," he said shaking his head gravely, "sinking three ships of the line. It's hard to believe."

"They were very old ships," Day said. "The tragedy is that they were sailed by very young men."

Sir Peter had been careful in planning the seating arrangements for dinner, interspersing the financial people between the manufacturers and the shippers. The scent of the bankers' money, he figured, would bring the others together the way the smell of death causes vultures to circle. Dudley Malone, the collector of customs, was parked between one of the young ladies—the one who never stopped giggling, if Anne remembered correctly—and Commander Day. Since Day would be loading contraband right under Dudley's nose, Sit Peter wanted them to get acquainted. Given the childish noises that would come from the young lady's side, Malone would certainly turn all his attention to the commander. Robert Lansing would be at Anne's right, where he would keep the conversation alive in order to practice sounding British. That put Lansing's wife, who through her father had more contacts in the State Department than her husband did, next to Sir Peter. Perhaps he could fathom the kind of advice she was giving to Robert. Jennifer was to be at the center of the table, flanked by two of the young men. Directly across from her was the one girl with whom she seemed to be striking up a genuine friendship.

Jennifer destroyed his plan. She brought William Day to a place beside her, sending one of the young men across the table to Day's place. That trapped Dudley Malone between the giggling girl and a young man who was determined to amuse her. Throughout the dinner, they both leaned forward and talked under Malone's chin.

To rescue the customs official, Anne tried to engage him in a conversation across a shipper and a banker. Both fell mute in the presence of a tax collector. And the effort distracted her attention from Lansing, who was left to try his breathy H and flat R on the wife of an Ohio steel maker, whose accent was distinctly Scandinavian.

Sir Peter should have been furious with his daughter for her outrageous breach of etiquette. Instead, he was delighted with her spirited disregard of convention. She was wearing the most daring dress, with her hair in the most modern style. She had reached out and claimed for herself the most interesting man of the evening and seemed to be holding her own in an engrossing conversation. Jennifer was certainly the Cinderella of the ball, and Sir Peter was thrilled that he had provided a uniformed prince for her entertainment.

The ladies withdrew at the end of the meal, and the servants reconfigured the table with brandy and cigars. Lansing should have been the center of attention, with everyone wondering whether President Wilson was tipping away from his avowed policy of strict neutrality. But even Lansing was anxious to hear from the young British naval officer. To Americans, the Great War was a championship fight, and now, in its early months, the fighters had only just climbed into the ring. The bell would sound when the German High Seas Fleet weighed anchor and came out into the North Atlantic to challenge the English first line.

To the midwestern steel makers, who had long ago severed their connections with the ocean, the fight would be a slugfest pitting heavy cannons against heavy cannons. To the east coast shippers and bankers, who saw the ocean from their office windows, the fight would be a boxing masterpiece, with tactical feints and quick jabs that generations of naval officers would study along with Trafalgar and Salamis. The question that all of them waited for William Day to answer was which one was going to win.

He laughed at the question and shook his head slowly. "I don't think my opinion is worth very much. My total combat experience was the two or three minutes it took my ship to turn over. I've never been aboard one of our battleships, and I don't think I've even seen a German cruiser."

"But surely you've heard people talking," a banker pressed. "Is the Admiralty confident?"

"Confident? Yes, I think so. If the High Seas Fleet comes out, I think there's a good deal of confidence that our navy will be up to the test."

"If?" one of the shipping barons asked. "Is there any doubt that they'll come out?"

"What good are cruisers lying at anchor in Wilhelmshaven?" the chemical manufacturer asked. "They have to come out."

"I'm not sure," Day responded. "I think this may be a war of supply. And they don't need to win a naval battle to cut off our supplies. They can do it with their submarines."

"Submarines? Against capital ships?" The shipping baron couldn't believe what he was hearing.

"We had three capital ships," Day reminded the men gathered around the dinner table. "Not the most modern ships. But it wouldn't have mattered. The fact is that the submarine can choose its target. It can let the capital ships sail by, and then slaughter the cargo vessels. If the Germans are content to starve us out, they don't need their High Seas Fleet."

"But surely the Royal Navy can deal with a few submarines?" The question came from J. P. Morgan's banker. "If it can't, why would anyone finance cargo vessels sailing into English waters? Who would insure them?"

Day nodded. His point had been made. Sink a few cargo ships, and the entire shipping industry would refuse to load British supplies. A few submarines could, indeed, isolate the island fortress. "We knew there was a submarine close by," he said, referring to his experience with the Fishbait Squadron. "But we couldn't find it. Our ships charged off in all directions, and when they happened close enough to the submarine, they were sunk."

"Surely you're being too pessimistic," Sir Peter said, realizing that his suppliers might begin to think of England as a lost cause. "There has to be something we can do."

"I think there is," Day answered. "I think the answer may be a large number of small ships rather than a small number of large ships. Submarines can stay down for only a few hours. They have to come up to replenish their air supply and charge their batteries. If we could blanket the shipping lanes with small boats, submarines wouldn't be able to operate there."

"Is that Admiralty policy?" an electrical manufacturer wondered.

"No," Day admitted immediately. "It's just my own thought. I've had a lot of time to think about submarines lately."

There was an appreciative chuckle as the butler made the rounds with more brandy.

"Now that's just enough men talk!"

Sir Peter turned in his chair to find Jennifer standing beside him. He was delighted. Who else but Jennifer would violate the sanctity of the men's after-dinner conversation?

She marched straight down the length of the table until she reached William Day. "Commander Day promised me another dance," she announced. "There are six musicians waiting to accommodate him."

"I did, indeed," Day admitted to the guests. "I hope you'll excuse me."

"Of course they will," Jennifer said, taking his hand. "It's my party." She led the commander out of the dining room.

"A lovely couple," Robert Lansing teased, reminding Sir Peter of his earlier remark. "I hope you've checked out his family."

Peter Beecham smiled. "How could I? He's only just arrived. For all I know, he comes from a family of Laborites."

There was hearty laughter all around. But while he enjoyed his own joke, Sir Peter was making a mental note to check out Commander William Day's service folder. Lansing was right. You could never be too careful.

THE NORTH SEA

Was it smoke? Lieutenant Feldkirchner couldn't be sure. The way the boat was rolling, he couldn't steady his binoculars. And with the height of the seas, he was able to get only occasional glimpses of the horizon.

The timing was right. Submarine Flotilla Commander Bauer's sources had confirmed *Glitra*'s sailing from Oslo at noon the previous day. At twelve knots, her run to Kristiansand should take about twenty hours. Feldkirchner rechecked his watch. 0730. It had to be *Glitra*, running right on schedule.

But he needed to see her to get an angle on her bow. With two ranges and a bow angle, he could calculate her course and speed. Then he could submerge and run under water to the intercept point. He would break surface right beside her and put a shot across her bow before the mate on watch could summon the captain to the bridge.

It was simple. A textbook exercise. But textbooks didn't snap-roll twenty degrees to each side. And they didn't sink down into the troughs between the swells. He needed to lock onto the mast of the ship with his rangefinder. He needed to see the angle on the bow. And right now, he could see nothing except a haze that might be the soot from her coal fires. Or might be nothing.

U-17 had left its home port of Emden three days earlier, following the channel past the Frisian Islands and breaking out into the North Sea. She made one dive to check out her bow planes, then ran due north on the surface to the center of her assigned patrol box, a 120-mile square stretching from the southern tip of Norway, across the Skagerrak and down the west coast of Jutland. That was the way Bauer ran his submarines. He scattered them into patrol areas that surrounded the northern and southern approaches to England. Then he waited for information.

Information from port officers who read the destinations and cargo manifests of parting ships from official sailing documents. Bauer had German loyalists or paid informers in nearly every European and North American port.

Information from insurers who underwrote specific cargoes to specific English ports. There were always low-level clerks who had access to high-level information and would sell it for a price.

Information from coast watchers on the western reaches of Ireland. Irish nationalists would help anyone who might give the English their comeuppance.

Even information from Englishmen who spoke too freely about the ships that were due to arrive and the cargoes that would need transportation.

Bauer had contacted U-17 with the name of a ship leaving Oslo, headed around the Orkneys, past the Hebrides and down the North Channel to Liverpool. It had taken Lieutenant Feldkirchner less than a minute to plot his point of intercept, at the northern edge of his patrol box, off the southern tip of Norway. He had motored there during the night, running on the surface at a leisurely ten knots. Now he was waiting, and paying the price of being a submariner. The heavy seas were tossing his boat about like a cork.

He stood on a conning tower that rose only nine feet above the sea and looked down at decks that barely broke the surface. The narrow hull rolled continuously, slamming to a stop each time the bow plunged into a wave, then shooting forward the instant the bow broke free. Feldkirchner was constantly ducking beneath walls of water that shattered against the front of the tower and then struggling for balance to keep from being battered against the iron rails. He waited in frustration whenever the boat sank into a trough between waves. Then, when it rose to the top of a crest, he snapped the salt-stained binoculars to his eyes and tried to see the horizon through the mist—to find the steamship *Glitra* approaching from the east. To be certain that there was no one on any point of the compass who might be looking for him.

Below deck, inside the U-17's pressure hull, the battering was even worse. The hull was only 120 feet long and less than 10 feet across. Packed into that small tube were 2 engines that burned heavy, paraffin-rich oil, each coupled to a motor generator set. There were banks of lead-acid batteries and hundreds of yards of heavy copper cable. There were pumps connected to runs of steel piping that could shift hundreds of gallons of trimming water fore and aft in just seconds. There were electrical panels, spiked with control levers that moved diving planes and opened doors to the sea. There were fuel tanks and fresh-water tanks. There were compasses, depth gauges, pressure gauges, and a steering wheel. And that was just to run the boat.

To turn it into a weapon there were five eighteen-foot torpedoes. There were compressed-air firing tubes. There was a firing computer, an ingenious arrangement of cams and gears that could take the speed and relative course of a ship and, with watchlike precision, calculate the exact moment of fire. There were ammunition magazines and shell hoists.

And then there were the men, squeezed into the small, awkward spaces that were left over, bashed against their surroundings each time the boat rolled or pounded into the sea. To escape their hellish world of damp mildew, choking air, and glaring electric lights, they climbed out onto the decks whenever the boat was running on the surface. But with the heavy weather, the decks were too dangerous.

One hatch, just aft of the conning tower, was open. The men who weren't at a duty station were grouped under it, sucking at the wisps of fresh air and holding up bed covers to catch the sea water that splashed in. They had to be careful. If they let the water flood into the battery rooms, the boat could fill with deadly sulfuric acid fumes. But if they closed the hatch, the stench of fuel oil would sear their eyes and scald their lungs.

The bow plunged, and a swell of sea water rolled down the deck. Feldkirchner ducked behind the barrier and tightened his grip around the lifeline. The ocean roared over his head, spilling torrents down on top of him, and down through the open hatch on top of the crew.

For an instant, the boat seemed to be stuck in the sea, hanging motionless as the wave drove it backward while the propellers pushed it ahead. Feldkirchner waited for what seemed an eternity. Then the bow broke through the top of the flood, and the boat sprang free.

In an instant, he was standing on the peak of a wave, high above the sea. And there ahead of him was the freighter, plowing across his bow under a cloud of heavy smoke. Feldkirchner raised his rangefinder, fixing the marks on the top of the ship's mast and the water line. He scarcely had time to take his reading before the U-17 slid down into another trough, blocking *Glitra* from view.

He counted the seconds on his watch, waiting for his boat to rise up again. Then he took another reading on his distant target, still several miles away. He reached down, opened the hatch at his feet, and dropped down the ladder, pulling the hatch closed over his head.

"Dive," he ordered his executive officer, as he stepped to a plotting board and began to calculate his course to the intercept point.

At the executive officer's command, a series of orders passed through the boat. A soaked seaman charged up a ladder and closed the hatch aft of the conning tower. Engineers threw the clutch levers that uncoupled the motor generators from the engines. Electricians closed the switches that connected the banks of batteries. The engine air vent closed and the chattering engine suddenly stilled, replaced by the whine of the motors, which now used power from the charged batteries to drive the boat's propellers.

Levers were raised to open the doors of the ballast tanks that surrounded the pressure hull. Sea water flooded into the tanks, tipping the delicate balance of the boat to negative buoyancy. It slowly began to sink. Control wheels were spun, turning the bow planes downward. They caught the flow of the sea and drove the bow down, aiming the boat into a dive.

Suddenly, there was silence. The pounding of the sea was no longer heard. The shuddering of the hull stopped. The boat fell from the wild, pitching surface to the dead stillness below.

"Turn to one one zero," Lieutenant Feldkirchner ordered.

"One one zero," the helmsman echoed as he swung the ship's wheel.

"All ahead flank," the commanding officer intoned.

"All ahead flank," The chief of the watch rang the command on the engine telegraph, and the engine room responded.

"Rig for surface attack."

The gun crew began loading three-inch shells into the ammunition hoist. A machine gun, already armed with a cartridge belt that snaked out of a wooden box, was brought to the conning tower.

"How long?" the executive officer asked Feldkirchner.

He finished his calculations. "Eighteen minutes. We'll check it again in ten minutes."

They stood quietly, listening to the electric motors that hummed in the background. On the surface, *Glitra* was pounding through the sea at ten knots. Forty feet below, the U-17 was moving at six knots, closing in on *Glitra's* track as the freighter overtook her. The preparations were completed. The gun crew hunched at the foot of the ladder to the after hatch, and the boarding party, their hands on the frame of a collapsible boat, waited beneath the forward hatch. The gunner was already at the top of the conning tower ladder, his heavy weapon cradled in his arms. In the deathly silence, Feldkirchner could hear each tick of the chronometer he was watching.

"Some tea, captain?" The cook whispered the question as he offered the steaming mug. Feldkirchner nodded his thanks.

"I'll bring you a dry sweater," the cook offered, turning toward the hatch that led down from the conning tower.

"Later," Feldkirchner answered. He looked down and realized that the sea water had washed through the collar of his oilskin. His black knit sweater clung to him like a wet towel.

"Time." It was his executive officer reminding him that the ten minutes had elapsed. He nodded and turned to the periscope as his second in command pulled down on the counterweight cable. The polished steel tube rose up inside its track.

For a moment, all he could see was a moving hill of water. Then he was looking at a heavy spray at what seemed to be the tops of waves. As the spray cleared, he saw the freighter bearing toward him, its bow pitching as it fought through the white-capped crests.

He called out the bow angle and fixed the image within the brackets of the rangefinder. Then he pushed the scope down. "Right on course," he announced. "Looks about one mile."

"About five minutes," the executive officer commented as he looked over the captain's shoulder.

Feldkirchner nodded. "We'll come to a parallel course in three minutes. I want to get right next to her so the boarding party can damn near jump aboard."

They waited again, hearing their own nervous breathing above the hum of the electric motors. And then there was a new sound like the pounding of distant thunder. It was *Glitra's* screw as it cut through the sea.

"Come right to one five zero."

The helmsman threw the wheel as he called, "One five zero."

Feldkirchner pointed at the periscope. "Let's take another look." The executive pulled on the counterweight cable, and once again the commanding officer dropped to his knees to catch the eyepiece at deck level. He eased the scope up until he saw daylight through the spray.

Glitra appeared off his port quarter, no more than one hundred yards astern.

"Right to one six zero," he ordered, pushing the periscope down. He nodded to his executive. "Another minute."

They both listened carefully for any change in the sound. If a lookout on *Glitra* had spotted the periscope, then the freighter would probably make a sudden turn. The pitch of her propeller noise would tell them they had been seen even before they detected the sound moving away from them. But there was no change. The throbbing continued, growing louder until it drowned out the hum of their own electric motors.

"Everything ready?"

The executive officer responded by raising his thumb.

"Surface," Feldkirchner ordered, starting up the ladder at the heels of the gunner.

The bow planes were tilted upward, raising the angle of the bow. The boat's forward motion drove her back toward the surface. At the same instant, compressed air was fired into the tops of the ballast tanks, making the boat slightly buoyant. The bow and the conning tower exploded through the sea at the same instant.

The gunner threw open the hatch and charged upward through the torrent of water that poured down into the tower. Feldkirchner followed an instant behind him. He saw *Glitra*, running on a parallel course, no more than fifty yards off his port quarter.

"Switch to the engines," he shouted through the hatch as he slammed it closed. A deck port that would feed air to the diesels opened. Below, a compressed air charge started the engines, their roar deafening after the silence of the underwater run. Engineers closed a clutch, connecting the engines to the propellers. Electrical switches reversed the polarity of the electric motors, turning them into generators that immediately began recharging the batteries.

The instant the decks cleared the surface, hatches opened fore and aft of the conning tower. The gun crew sprang from the after hatch, each man connecting a safety line from his belt to a track in the deck. The boarding party climbed through the forward hatch, dragging the collapsible boat up behind them.

Feldkirchner watched his gunner set the machine gun into its stanchion and pull the bolt. He looked back in time to see the first round disappear into the breach of the three-inch deck gun. Then he looked over at *Glitra*. These were his most vulnerable moments. His guns weren't aimed. He was in the process of switching his engines. His crew was standing on decks that were awash, out in the open in plain sight. A trained gunner aboard the freighter could rake his boat with machine gun fire, dropping his men in sequence like ducks lined up in a shooting gallery. Or the freighter, which had much more speed than he had been able to carry to the surface, might turn in toward him. It would take her only a few seconds to cross the narrow strip of open sea and cut his boat in half with her bow.

But there was no activity at all aboard *Glitra*. The lookouts weren't at their posts. The officer of the watch was apparently at the other side of the wheelhouse. No one on the ship had yet seen the submarine.

The gunner's mate at the deck gun held up his hand. Feldkirchner raised his own arm and then let it drop. A second later, the deck gun fired with a sharp crack, and instantly the sea in front of *Glitra*'s bow exploded. A column of water climbed into the air and broke across the freighter's foredeck.

Suddenly there was a face on the wing of the bridge, wide-eyed under a seaman's knit cap. The man looked in disbelief at the submarine, then turned and disappeared toward the wheelhouse. An instant later, another man, this one wearing a greatcoat and an officer's cap, appeared on the bridge. With *Glitra* now abeam of the U-17, Feldkirchner was looking upward over the top of the iron wall formed by the steamer's hull.

"Heave to," he screamed through his megaphone. "Heave to and prepare to be boarded." His English had only the slightest trace of a German accent.

The officer peered down incredulously. The submarine was only a third as long as his own ship, and with her decks awash she seemed barely afloat. He hesitated as he weighed his options.

"Take the cargo rigging," Feldkirchner told his gunner. The man swung the machine gun away from the freighter's bridge toward the jungle of spars and rigging that grew from its foredeck. He sighted for a second and then squeezed the trigger. The gun chattered, and a stream of tracers reached out across the sea. Instantly, pieces of wood tore free from the booms. Ropes frayed and wooden blocks shattered. With a screech of tearing lines, one of the cargo booms broke free and crashed down on the deck. A second later the machine gun swung back, pointing its muzzle into the face of the officer.

"Heave to," Feldkirchner screamed again.

The man spun on his heels and disappeared into the wheelhouse. The lieutenant looked down at his gun commander, raised his arm, and let it fall once again. The second shot was even closer to the freighter's bow. The geyser poured down on top of her bridge.

Glitra was still making good speed, but U-17 had begun building momentum as soon as she had switched from the electric motors to the engines. Now the submarine was matching the steamer's speed, the two craft moving side by side on parallel courses. But Feldkirchner knew he couldn't keep the race up for long. The sea swells were running down his decks and smashing into his crewmen. Those forward were clutching a rail on the face of the conning tower, struggling to assemble their boat. Even with safety lines connected to the decks, they were in constant danger of being taken over the side. The gun crewmen on the afterdeck were keeping their footing only by hanging onto the gun stanchion, they had to release their grips each time the gun fired.

A new figure appeared on *Glitra*'s wing, again in officer's cap, but shorter and older-looking than the watch officer. As soon as he saw the submarine, his hands flew into the air.

"Heave to and prepare for boarding," the lieutenant ordered once more. "My next round will be into your water line."

The raised hands began to wave back and forth. Suddenly the steamer's captain dropped one hand into his greatcoat. When he raised it again, he began to wave a white handkerchief. The gunner burst into laughter at the size of the surrender flag. Feldkirchner drew a deep breath of relief.

Immediately, a blast of steam vented from *Glitra*'s funnel. The engineers were shutting down her throttle valves. The captain on her bridge pointed to the steam with one hand while he waved his handkerchief with the other.

Feldkirchner raised his megaphone. "Put a ladder over the side. My executive officer will come aboard."

The captain lowered one hand and cupped it behind his ear. Feldkirchner pointed down to the boat assembled on his foredeck. Then he shouted, "Put a ladder over the side." *Glitra*'s captain nodded vigorously and darted back toward the wheelhouse.

The freighter was already slowing, and the submarine had to slow its engines to stay abreast. Then, when *Glitra* was nearly stopped, it began to broach across the seas. Feldkirchner backed his engines to bring U-17 into the lee formed by the larger vessel. Immediately, the executive officer, who had climbed up onto the foredeck, ordered the collapsible boat into the water. He jumped aboard, and the small craft bobbed toward the ladder that was lowering along the steamer's side. The executive officer waited until the boat was at the top of a swell before jumping onto the ladder and scrambling up and over the ship's rail.

"First Officer Otto Marx," the executive officer saluted when he reached the bridge.

"Captain Morrissey," the old man answered, the white handkerchief still in his hand. He couldn't bring himself to salute the bearded young man in an oilskin slicker whose soaked trousers were plastered against his legs.

"May I see your cargo manifest," Marx asked politely. And then he added, "You might have your crew break open the forward hatch cover in case I have to inspect the cargo." Morrissey led him through the wheelhouse, where Marx saluted the steamer's watch officer and smiled at an obviously terrified helmsman. When they reached the chart room, the captain opened the ship's safe and found the cargo manifest.

Marx shook his head at the first entry on the listing. "Stainless steel bars," he said with genuine sadness in his voice. He mumbled through the rest of the items, which included ball bearings, electrical wire, and optical lenses. Then he handed the manifest back to Captain Morrissey. "I'm afraid half of these items are war materials," he said.

Morrissey stared at him mutely.

"Captain, I must claim my right, as a military officer at war with Great Britain, to destroy this cargo. We will allow you ten minutes to put your crew in the ship's boat and stand clear. We intend to sink your ship."

Morrissey's jaw hung dumbly.

Marx checked his own watch against the ship's chronometer. "We'll commence firing at zero nine hundred. Do you understand?"

"We won't be safe in a small boat in those seas," Morrissey answered.

"Safer than you'll be staying on board, I'm afraid." The German smiled. "This ship is going down."

He saluted and walked back through the wheelhouse. Captain Morrissey followed him down the ladder from the bridge to the main deck and watched him as he climbed over the rail.

"Zero nine hundred," Marx repeated as his head disappeared from sight.

The small boat pushed off from *Glitra*, the two seamen struggling to get some rhythm into their oars. Even in the lee of the larger ship, the sea was tossing in swells, making it difficult to keep the boat on a steady heading. Just as it reached U-17, a wave caught it, lifted it up, and tossed it over the top of the deck. Then the boat slid down the back of the wave and smashed against the conning tower. Marx reached out and caught the ladder rungs just below the conning tower deck where Feldkirchner was standing. He grabbed the bowline from the boat and took one turn around a cleat. But before he could haul the small boat back against U-17's deck, it broached across another swell and capsized, tossing its crewmen into the water.

One of the swamped sailors caught the boat's gunwall and began hauling himself aboard, hand over hand, along the bowline. The other bobbed up ten feet from the hull and began thrashing about in sudden panic. Marx wasted only a second as he secured the boat's bowline to the cleat. Then he dove from the side of the conning tower into the sea.

Feldkirchner had watched the simple act of landing the boat turn into a disaster. He vaulted over the rail of the conning tower and started down the ladder rungs, reaching the deck in time to haul the first sailor aboard.

Then he unfastened the bowline and walked it back along the deck so that the swamped boat drifted toward the sailor in the water. Marx surfaced next to the sailor and caught him by the collar. Then he began dragging him toward the boat that Feldkirchner was playing out toward them. He grabbed the gunwall as the boat drifted past and worked his way up to the bowline.

On board U-17, one of the gun crew broke from his station and, dragging his safety line along its track, worked his way to Feldkirchner. With his final lunge, he wrapped his arms around his captain just as a wave broke against the tower and washed across the deck. He helped Feldkirchner haul in on the bowline until they dragged the small boat alongside. Then others of the gun crew lifted the executive officer and the sailor aboard.

The frantic rescue had taken only a minute. But that minute could have been fatal. With its gun crew distracted, U-17 had ceased to be a weapon. With no one on the conning tower to issue orders to the helm and the engines, the dreaded submarine had become a foundering hulk. *Glitra* could have turned on her and rammed her. Or, with nothing more than small arms fire, she could have slaughtered the submarine's crew. But when Feldkirchner climbed back to the top of the tower, the steamer was still drifting calmly nearby. Her crew had swung out the ship's boat and were beginning to lower it over the side. Her captain jumped aboard as the lifeboat dropped below the deck.

"Stand clear," Feldkirchner called through his megaphone as soon as the boat was in the water. The crew used the boat's oars to push away from the riveted steel hull and began rowing frantically past her stern.

The lieutenant turned to his gun captain. "Below the water line, directly beneath the funnel." He looked up to be sure the lifeboat was clear.

"Commence firing," he ordered.

The crew aimed the three-inch rifle carefully. But the rolling of the deck made it impossible to fix their elevation precisely. The first round tore through the hull plating three feet above the surface of the sea and exploded inside. The second round hit short and exploded in a geyser along the ship's side without penetrating the hull.

In the lifeboat, *Glitra*'s crew stopped rowing. They watched in fascination as the submarine's gunners tried to time the boat's continuous roll. Even when a wave broke over the lifeboat, dousing them with sea water, they couldn't take their eyes off the gun crew.

The third shot blew a hole right at the water line, and sea swirled through. The next shot hit just below the surface, throwing up another enormous water spout. This one split one of the riveted seams, and *Glitra* immediately took on a list. The final shot tore a gaping hole just above the water line, but within seconds the increasing list dipped the opening into the sea.

"That should do it," Feldkirchner called to his gun captain. "Secure the ammunition and get your men below." He was about to offer a word of congratulations when he was interrupted by a metallic blast within the hull of his victim. Cold sea water had reached the red-hot furnace under one of *Glitra's* boilers. The boiler had exploded, belching out its remaining steam pressure. Bulkheads collapsed, allowing the weight of water to rush forward. *Glitra* immediately began to settle by the bow.

Within a few minutes, her stern lifted out of the water, its enormous weight putting an unimagined strain on the ship's keel. With a sickening screech of metal, the ship tore in half, its bow plunging rapidly while the stern half settled into the waves.

Feldkirchner lifted the deck hatch. "All ahead two-thirds," he called into the control room. "Come to course one seven five." He looked up as the last edge of *Glitra's* transom disappeared under a swell. Then he saw the lone lifeboat, its crew attempting to develop their timing with the oars as they thrashed about in heavy seas.

"Steady on course one seven five." It was his executive officer calling up from the control room below.

"Come topside, Otto," Feldkirchner shouted down. Marx climbed up to join him, still in the soaked clothes he had been wearing when he was pulled out of the sea.

"They're not going to make it," the commanding officer said, nodding his chin toward the bouncing lifeboat. "Looks as if none of them has ever rowed a boat in his life."

"It's a very difficult sea," Otto Marx answered.

Feldkirchner nodded. "I think we better give them a tow. Get a boatswain to break out a tow line. And give me a course to a nice sandy beach where we can put them ashore."

The executive officer laughed. "First we put them in the water. Now we're going to get them out. Does this make any sense to you, captain?"

"Why should it?" Feldkirchner said, shaking his head. "These are English rules we're playing by."

He maneuvered U-17 close to the lifeboat. At first, the English crew sat hunched over their oars, fearing a mass coup de grace from the machine gunner, who still held his position on the conning tower. Then, when they saw the German sailor coiling a heaving line on the submarine's afterdeck, they nearly swamped the lifeboat in their excitement. Wildly waving hands scrambled for the line and secured it to the bow cleat. Feldkirchner ordered his engines ahead at cruising speed and made for the Norwegian coast with his enemies in tow.

Insane, he thought as he looked back at the small boat bobbing in his wake. A few moments before he had been playing the role of an armed cruiser, firing a shot across the bow of his prey and ordering the ship to heave to for searching. Playing that part, he had exposed his boat to senseless danger and nearly lost his crew over the side. Now he was playing a tugboat, motoring on the surface where he could be spotted by any passing ship and where he would be an easy target for a British man-of-war.

His submarine didn't fit the traditional cruiser rules. It was a small, underpowered, barely seaworthy boat whose only weapon was its incredible ability to simply disappear. Lurking beneath the waves, he was more than a match for any ship afloat. He could maneuver undetected, in close, where his torpedoes were unerring in finding the hull beneath the water line. But when he surfaced, his odds changed dramatically. Then he became a pathetic weakling, outgunned by even the smallest cannon mounted on any rusting hulk and outmaneuvered by anything powered with a steam engine.

But the international cruiser rules insisted that he act like a surface vessel. Give warning, which meant giving away his best weapon. Search, which meant loitering dangerously in the open. Make provision for the safety of any civilians. A cruiser could simply take civilian passengers aboard and drop them off at the nearest neutral port. But how could he take passengers aboard a tiny boat that barely had space for its own crew?

The English had promulgated the cruiser rules four centuries earlier to save their merchant fleet from endless European wars. They had enforced the rules through the barrels of their cannons. Now they were screaming in every international forum that civility demanded the rules be strictly observed, depriving Germany of its best naval weapon. Civility? What was civil about the trench warfare that was drawn like a scar across northern France? What was civil about the free-floating mines that the British were dumping into the North Sea?

The Norwegian coast loomed up ahead. Feldkirchner could see the waves breaking on a rocky shore. He turned north, running parallel to the coast as he looked for a safe landing for the small boat he had in tow. It was dangerous. Any coast watcher could fix his position. There were probably radio messages already in the air calling British warships to come and destroy him. But he was still five miles from the beach, and the seas were still dangerously heavy for a lifeboat.

He sighted a break in the rocks and turned U-17 to the east. He would get them in as close as he could. Once he had thrown them a tow line, the Englishmen aboard *Glitra* had become his responsibility. Otto Marx, now in dry clothes, came up through the hatch carrying a chart. He unrolled it into the wind, pinning the corners against the conning tower rail so that Feldkirchner could plot his approach to the shore.

"Clear water right up to 1,000 yards," the captain said.

"You're going in that close?"

He hunched his shoulders. They were already taking incalculable risks. What did another mile matter?

When he could make out every detail of the shoreline, he ordered his boatswain out on the afterdeck to haul in the tow line. In a few seconds, he had the lifeboat alongside.

"This is as far as we can take you, captain," Feldkirchner shouted down from the tower.

Captain Morrissey stood up in the boat and braced himself at military attention. He saluted formally, bringing a stiff hand to the peak of his cap. "Thank you, captain," he said to the ragged, sea-soaked figure above him. "I'll make a full report on your proper conduct."

Feldkirchner returned the salute and watched as the men began rowing their boat toward the beach. A full report, he thought to himself. That should have the English admirals holding their sides in laughter.

"Come to two five zero," he called down through the hatch.

"Two five zero," the helmsman affirmed.

He would head away from the coast, then turn to the south and return to the center of his patrol box. Flotilla Commander Bauer would probably have another ship waiting for him to challenge.

NEW YORK

News of *Glitra*'s sinking hit the Manhattan shipping offices like a torpedo. The Germans had apparently pulled their submarines back from direct conflict with the Royal Navy and had instead aimed them, with equally frightening results, at unarmed freighters. The damn little boats were just as effective against merchant ships as they were against warships. Suddenly, it was dangerous to carry war materials to the British Isles.

Sir Peter Beecham heard about *Glitra* everywhere he went. Scandinavian, Dutch, and Greek flag steamship companies that days before had been courting his cargoes suddenly wanted no part of the nitrates, the shell casings, the field radios, and the generators that he was buying from American manufacturers. Even a shipment of warm winter coats sat unattended on a Hudson River pier. "They're field coats for soldiers," a Swedish shipping company representative protested. "Anyone can wear a warm coat," Beecham argued. But the Swede shook his head. "Who's going to explain that to a German submarine captain?"

Insurance companies, which generally tripped over one another in their rush to write coverage for merchant ships and their cargoes, now put their best people to work writing exclusions. Rates for ships bound for England were suddenly doubled. And if the ships were carrying anything that might be used to bludgeon a German, the rates doubled again. Beecham was suddenly spending more money to get his war materials across the ocean than he was spending to buy them and get them to the docks. He was going through money faster than Morgan's bank could raise it.

"One ship!" Beecham protested to Commander William Day as they left the offices of an insurance company in a building that was the architectural rival of a European cathedral. "A few rounds into the side of a rusting steamer, and the Huns are able to bankrupt England right out of the war."

"It may get worse," Day cautioned. "Once the Germans give up the cruiser rules and start fighting by the submarine rules . . ."

It was a conversation they had often. Sir Peter saw war as a kind a duel between gentlemen. There were strict procedures dictated by good breeding. You turned your back, walked ten paces, then turned and fired. It was unthinkable that anyone would take only two paces, turn around, and blow his opponent away while the poor fool was still counting his footsteps. The Huns were certainly barbarians, with Belgian babies on their bayonets and all that. But even barbarians wouldn't fire on civilians without issuing proper warning.

Day saw war as mindless brutality, a jungle game of kill or be killed. And he understood the unique advantage of the submarine. English mines didn't ask to inspect cargo manifests before they blew holes in the sides of ships traveling to Germany. They didn't pause to allow innocent passengers to take to the lifeboats. Why should the submarine commander go through the niceties of the rules of encounter before firing?

"They'll declare the Western Approaches a war zone, just as we've declared the North Sea a war zone," he told Beecham. "They'll sink anything that comes across their bow."

"Innocent passengers? Without warning? Preposterous," Beecham insisted.

"Naming it a war zone is all the warning they need," Day countered.

Beecham spent every hour trying to find neutral ships to supplement the fleet of English steamers he had commandeered, and William Day was his constant companion. He used Day almost as a patriotic poster, shamelessly displaying him in front of shippers and insurers to wring out concessions. Just as a price was about to be named, he would remind his mark of the true significance of the transaction.

"We're not really discussing tonnage, you know. We're discussing the lives of fine young men. Like Commander Day, here, one of the few survivors of the *Aboukir* outrage. Torpedoed without warning and left to drown without any offer of rescue. What we're talking about is giving these brave men a chance to fight back."

The steely eyes would soften as they looked up from the contract. "You were there? I understand the submarine cruised back and forth, ramming the lifeboats and running over the men in the water. It must have been terrible."

"There were no lifeboats," Day would try. But before he could explain what actually had happened, Beecham would turn back to the contract. The shipper or insurance agent, who could have demanded three times the going rate, would settle for twice.

"It's been an honor meeting you, Commander Day," he would conclude, while Beecham was blotting the ink on the contract.

Day's experience and his uniform were particularly important in dealing with the customs inspectors. With American neutrality regulations prohibiting neutrals from loading war materials and passenger ships from taking on munitions of any kind, cargo manifests had to be falsified.

Dudley Malone, the New York customs inspector, was far too shrewd to be fooled. He had seen every creative ruse for repacking and relabeling cargoes in order to escape his tariff. But even though he lived in a world defined by clerical forms and rubber stamps, his imagination traveled out over the dangerous seas, aboard the ships he certified. He dreamt of glorious sea battles, where he would breathe salt air mixed with cordite. He had admired Commander Day when he first met him at Jennifer's party. In their business meetings he had soaked up every drop of insight that Day could offer on warships and their tactics. The strong, brooding officer in the gold-trimmed uniform had become his alter ego. As he plied Day for information to feed his heroic fantasies, he signed and stamped forms that he couldn't bother reading. Why worry about the real content of a 600-pound crate of cheese consigned to a Welsh grocery broker when he could be listening to the latest technologies for aiming a 14-inch main battery? Who cared whether cartons of screws and nails were intended for use by a carpenter or as shrapnel inside a fragmentation shell? Day was telling him about the unimagined delights of shore leave in Marseilles.

It wasn't that Day enjoyed the ruse. Secretly, he wished that Malone would challenge his cargoes. He was slipping nitrates aboard ocean liners, away from the eyes of their passengers. Would these people sail if they understood the shattering explosive force that was resting against their keels? He protested to Sir Peter about orders to load rifle cartridges into the forecastle of *Lusitania*. "The passengers have nothing to do with our war," he argued. "Do you know what would happen to them if a German submarine put a torpedo into that cargo?"

"But they wouldn't dare," Beecham countered. "Don't you see? That's why the passengers are perfectly safe, and the cargo is perfectly safe. The Germans wouldn't dare fire on a passenger ship."

Beecham's view prevailed. They were breaking the law, but they weren't really endangering the passengers. Day mastered the procedures of duplicity. He held back suspicious cargo until the last minute before sailing. Then he filed a fraudulent supplementary cargo manifest that wasn't presented until the ship was steaming past the Ambrose Lightship. Malone had every right to order the ship into port, or to have the Coast Guard board her and verify the cargo. But that wasn't a right he chose to exercise.

"What's this? More late cargo?" he would ask as Day dropped the supplementary manifest onto his desk and eased into a chair.

"Just some foodstuffs held up in transit," Day would respond, shaking his head in exasperation. "Reminds me of the time we had to steam out to a gunnery exercise without a single bag of black powder to fire. The powder was on the wrong train . . ."

Malone's hand would reach for the rubber stamp while he waited to hear how Day had managed to fire the ship's guns without any powder.

If the young naval commander was essential to Sir Peter's workday, he was almost as important to Beecham's evenings. Jennifer had followed her prince from the party at the Long Island estate into his offices in Manhattan. She had moved with two trunkloads of her belongings into the family townhouse on Washington Square, leaving her mother's watchful eye for her father's more casual supervision.

"What in God's name am I supposed to do with her?" Sir Peter had protested to his wife. "We have meetings until all hours trying to arrange purchases and shipments. I can't possibly take her everywhere she wants to go."

"Send her home," Anne had insisted.

"And break her heart?" Beecham could stare down the most radical labor organizer. But he couldn't manage to mumble a half-hearted "no" to his daughter.

The truth was that he thrilled to her every word and gesture. During her first days in New York, he would find her waiting up for him when he came home late at night, ready to serve him a pot of strong tea and his favorite biscuits. He would listen eagerly as she recounted all the things she had done for the first time during the day. Jennifer could take an hour describing the dinner she had shared with Commander Day at Delmonico's.

"Every eye was on him," she rejoiced. "In his uniform, he was quite the most handsome man in the room."

"I'm sure they were looking at you," Beecham teased.

"No, the women, father! It was the women who were staring. You could read the envy in their eyes. The lady at the next table—a terribly dilapidated thing in an awful green dress—almost fell off her chair sniffing at his cologne. Just to drive her mad, I reached across the table and took his hand."

"You didn't," he protested. "Not in public?"

She laughed mischievously, as if she had just succeeded in smuggling cookies into her bedroom. "I most certainly did. And you should have seen her expression. She stiffened like an old school marm, and her nose shot up into the air as if she'd just sniffed a bad wine. She made a great show of not noticing."

Beecham struggled to maintain a disapproving frown. "Naturally. She was shocked by your behavior."

Jennifer shook her head furiously as she dunked a biscuit into her tea. "Her jealousy was as green as her dress. She kept sneaking peeks over at our hands."

"But what a terrible thing to do to Commander Day," Beecham said over the edge of his teacup. "After he went out of his way to show you such a lovely evening. I'm sure he was mortified."

"Oh, he was," Jennifer sighed. "A big strong man who isn't afraid of anything. But he absolutely blushed when I took his hand. It was wonderful!"

"Positively scandalous," Beecham censured, as he stood to end the conversation. But he was smiling as he climbed the stairs to his bedroom. Such spirit. Such daring. She was light years ahead of other young women her age.

Weeks later, it was he who was sitting up by the teapot waiting for Jennifer to come home. Commander Day would see her to the door, stepping in just long enough to pay his respects to Beecham.

"Join us for tea, commander," Sir Peter offered.

"No thank you, sir. I'm afraid there are still a few requisitions that you'll be needing in the morning."

Beecham nodded. "Very well, then. And thank you for being so kind to Jennifer."

Jennifer would stand in modest silence while these formalities were exchanged. Then she would explode the minute the door closed behind Day.

"Oh, father. William was simply wonderful."

"'William,' is it?" as he poured the tea.

"Well, you can't keep calling someone 'commander' while you're dancing."

"You were dancing? Where?"

"At the Winter Garden. We had the nicest supper." She launched into the details of the menu, telling Sir Peter exactly what Day had ordered for her. Beecham listened through to the dessert.

"And the dancing?"

"There was the most wonderful orchestra. A piano. A bass violin. Drums. And two or three horns. Have you heard the new blues? It's like ragtime, but slower. With more feeling."

"Blues? I don't think so," he confessed.

Jennifer laughed. "You must have. It's all the rage. The horns are so . . . emotional."

Beecham shook his head. "I prefer strings, myself. They're perfect for the waltz."

"The waltz? Father, no one does the waltz anymore. You really have to get away from your office. I know! Why don't you take mother dancing at the Winter Garden? She'd absolutely love it. And I could show her the new steps."

Jennifer jumped up, raised her arms to embrace an invisible partner, and began backing through a slow and somewhat suggestive cakewalk. Sir Peter's face split with laughter. "I think your mother uses a little less of her hips," he said. But then he forced a scowl. "Is that the way you were dancing with Commander Day?"

"William is a marvelous dancer," she replied, throwing her arms into the air and spinning around. "You should have seen the people just standing back to watch us."

"Good Lord. I pray that I may be spared the sight."

"It's just wonderful," Jennifer sighed.

Beecham checked his pocket watch. "It's just two hours past your bedtime."

He was happy to see Jennifer so happy. And grateful to Commander Day for being so understanding of his iconoclastic daughter. With William Day watching her, he didn't have to feel guilty for leaving Jennifer so much on her own. It gave him time for his essential services to the Crown.

Anne began hearing about Jennifer's escapades from friends in the city. And she began to worry about the things she was hearing.

"I saw Jennifer just the other evening," one of the English women from her circle of expatriate friends told her. "She looked so lovely in her bare-shouldered dress. She certainly can wear the latest fashions."

"How she's grown," another harpy cooed. "I couldn't believe it was Jennifer, dancing with that wine glass in her hand."

"Anne, you must tell me. Is it serious?" a friend begged.

"Is what serious?"

"Why, Jennifer and that strikingly handsome naval officer. They're seen everywhere together."

Anne went to the telephone, rang up the local Long Island operator, and asked to be connected to New York. Peter Beecham was angry when he heard her voice. She knew how he disapproved of wives bothering their husbands during business hours.

"I want to know about Jennifer. Have you been keeping a close watch over her?"

"Of course. We speak every evening. She's having a fine time here in the city."

"Too fine a time, from what I'm hearing," Anne fired back. "One friend tells me she's appearing in public half-naked. Another says she's drinking. And everyone is warning me to be very careful of Commander Day. She's much too young to be keeping serious company with anyone, much less a sailor who's years older than she."

"My God," Sir Peter sighed. "Will you have sense, woman? Commander Day is looking after her as a personal favor to me. He has no interest in Jennifer. How could he? He's a commoner."

Anne groaned at her husband's density. "He's tall, handsome, and a war hero. Your daughter is an impressionable child. You don't think, by any chance, that she gives a tinker's damn whether he's in the social register?"

"Your friends are just jealous," Peter snapped back. "My daughter is the toast of Manhattan while their daughters are probably at home embroidering coats of arms on doilies. Pathetic things!"

"Your daughter," Anne said coldly, "likes to rush into things ahead of her time. And the next thing she's scheduled to rush into could leave her with a warm bun in the oven."

Sir Peter gasped. The cigar slipped from his fingers and fell into his lap. "That is the most outrageous thought," he screamed into the telephone as he swatted the hot ash from his trousers. "Commander Day is a naval officer and a war hero. He wouldn't think of . . . of . . ."

"A naval officer and a hero? Does that mean that you have just promoted him from 'commoner'?"

He wanted to slam the telephone down.

For the rest of the day he simply went through the motions, eyeing William Day suspiciously whenever they met.

"Have you seen duPont's price for guncotton?" Day asked, barging into his office with a file of papers in his hand. Beecham never heard the question. He stared dumbly at his naval attaché, trying to imagine the unimaginable.

"The price," Day persisted, waving the papers. "You recall the requisition we placed for sixty tons of guncotton? For the mines?"

"Certainly," Sir Peter finally allowed.

"It's nearly double what they charged for the last consignment. And they want it prepaid. It will nearly exhaust our accounts."

Peter Beecham said nothing, leaving Commander Day staring curiously.

"It's very suspicious," Day finally offered.

"Suspicious, indeed," Beecham agreed, although he wasn't really referring to the guncotton.

"I think you should talk with Mr. Morgan's people," Day suggested. "Maybe they can learn something. It looks to me as if someone may be bidding against us."

Beecham finally caught the drift of the conversation. "Who could be bidding against us for guncotton?" he asked.

"Maybe Germany," Day said.

Beecham waved away the suggestion. "Why? What could the Germans do with guncotton? They can't get a single ship in and out of an American port."

Day thought for a moment, then nodded. Sir Peter was right. The German liners that had been in New York when war was declared were still tied up to their piers in New Jersey. They had asked for asylum to avoid confronting the British cruisers that were waiting at the end of the channel, just outside American coastal sovereignty.

"I'll talk with Morgan," Beecham promised. But his mind was elsewhere. He was really rehearsing the talk he was going to have with Jennifer. Anne, he realized, was right, as usual. Not that he thought for a moment that there could be anything serious between Jennifer and William Day. But she was only eighteen. Perhaps there was no reason for her to charge so enthusiastically into adulthood. It was probably a good idea for her to spend more time with her mother.

He made up his mind. He would help her pack her things, and he would see her personally to the train in the morning. He would simply explain that he and Commander Day would be quite busy over the next few weeks. Neither of them would be able to spend any time with her. She would be much better off out on Long Island.

But even as he was determining exactly what he would do, he was already regretting the conversation that was awaiting him. Jennifer was having such a wonderful time with her Prince Charming in New York. Sending her home would probably break her heart.

LONDON

To WINSTON Churchill, it seemed so obvious. He had explained it in broad terms, and Captain Hall had filled in all the details. Why couldn't the First Sea Lord, Admiral John Fisher, grasp the concept?

"It's illegal! A blatant violation of international law." Fisher's voice was tired and gravelly. The old man, who sat hunched in a wing chair wearing a poorly tailored dark business suit, no longer had the vitality that had carried him to the very pinnacle of the Royal Navy. Nor did he particularly care for Churchill and Hall. They knew his views. And he knew that the two younger men would do exactly as they wished whether he agreed with them or not.

Churchill sat behind his desk at the Admiralty offices in Whitehall, idly fingering the rigging on a perfect two-foot model of the *Golden Hind*. He was nicely dressed in a pearl gray cutaway, his pink complexion darkening to red with the mounting anger he was suppressing. Reginald Hall sat at military attention in a straight chair drawn up beside the desk, so that he and Churchill were together as a team, facing Fisher, who was alone on the other side of the net. Hall's strong face, under prematurely white hair, was nearly expressionless. As head of Naval Intelligence, he had mastered the art of camouflaging his thought processes.

Churchill would just as soon have ended the meeting. He didn't need Admiral Fisher's advice. But the admiral was a national hero, admired throughout the government, and Churchill did need Fisher's support. When he went to brief the prime minister on his new strategy for dealing with the submarine menace, he needed to be able to say that Fisher was thoroughly briefed and approved of the idea. So, he drew a deep breath and tried again.

"The submarine is writing its own body of law on naval warfare, admiral. You yourself have said that a submarine commander would have to be insane to adhere to the rules of encounter."

Fisher's puffy eyes widened. "I did, indeed. But I never said that would give us the right to fly foreign flags on our merchant ships."

Churchill glanced in despair at Captain Hall. It was he who had suggested the idea. Perhaps he could get through to his elderly senior officer.

"Sir, we know from our radio intercepts that the German government is taking great pains to avoid involving neutral countries in the war," Hall explained for the second time. "They have set up extensive spy networks so that they can track British ships sailing with military cargoes and avoid ships of neutral nations. By flying our flag on our merchant ships, we simply make their job that much easier for them. In effect, the flag says, 'Here I am. I'm the ship you're looking for.'"

"Then fly no flag at all," the admiral still didn't understand what they were talking about. The gulf that separated the old seafarer from his younger colleagues was wider than the ocean.

Fisher was a lifelong naval officer who had begun his career under sail and blossomed in an age of heavily gunned dreadnaughts. He understood the kind of naval warfare in which ships set out against ships, and the best fleet won. Show him the enemy, and he would weigh anchor and steam out to meet him. But don't talk to him about the political uses of naval power. He had no interest in the grandiose aspirations of governments, and absolutely no respect for the bureaucratic landlubbers, like Churchill and Hall, who tried to tell him how to sail his ships.

As far as Fisher was concerned, Captain Hall shouldn't even be wearing a uniform. He had no command. It had been years since he had even stood on a deck. All he had were a nest of radios and a staff of college professors who copied German wireless messages and deciphered their codes. They never fired guns. All they fired were memos and reports. And who had ever decided that Winston Churchill was fit to serve as First Lord of the Admiralty? The only ship he had ever handled was that infernal model of Drake's flagship that he kept on the corner of his desk. He was nothing but a political opportunist who would have taken a position in the Foreign Office more eagerly than one in the Admiralty if it had brought him closer to the seat of power. The man probably got seasick on the Dover ferry.

To Churchill, talking with Fisher was like talking to a fossil. The Lord Admiral was the perfect image of a world that had been left behind, an expert in fighting wars that would never be fought again. Here he was worrying about flags and their proper use according to the rules of chivalry. He was concerned with what history would say if he hid his ships under foreign colors. Fisher simply couldn't understand that modern warfare was a struggle for survival, and that the survivor would write history any way he chose. He couldn't grasp that the issue wasn't the conduct of a few damn ships, but rather the very existence of the British Empire.

"That simply won't do, admiral," Winston Churchill said, taking up the cause. "The absence of a flag will be just as much a giveaway as the presence of a British flag. What we have to do is to instruct our merchantmen to fly the flags of neutral nations. Even paint their funnels with the colors of steamship lines operating out of neutral countries. We're going to hide our merchant vessels in a sea of foreign ships."

"Then the Germans will have to attack everyone," Fisher argued. "Neutrals and British ships alike."

"Exactly," Churchill nearly shouted, thrilled that Fisher had finally gotten the point. "Or, they will have to *avoid* attacking anyone. If they can't tell a British ship from an American ship or a Swedish ship, then they will have to treat them all alike."

"Then what difference will it make?" Admiral Fisher argued. "They'll simply stop each ship, board it, and demand its papers. That will tell them soon enough which ships are British and which are neutral."

Churchill's eyes closed in despair. His face fell into his soft hands. Captain Hall came to the rescue.

"That's why we need the second part of the plan, sir. British merchantmen will be forbidden to obey a submarine's order. Instead, they will be ordered to ram any submarines that challenge them. What we are hoping is to put the U-boats in a bit of a dilemma. They will have to inspect the ship to be sure that it's British. And if the ship should happen to be British, then the submarine is going to find itself under attack."

Fisher's dark expression began to brighten. It wasn't just a matter of flags. It was a counterattack that would blunt the submarine threat. The little boats were death traps when they were caught on the surface. Fisher had predicted that sooner or later they would have to fire on British ships from their safe haven under the seas. But if they couldn't be sure it was a British ship, then they were forced to give up their only protection. It was genius. Provided, of course that the neutral nations didn't raise a ruckus.

"We're also planning to install guns on the fantails of our merchant ships," Hall continued. "Concealed, of course, under some sort of deck house or cargo crate. If the submarine avoids being rammed, then she'll come under cannon fire as soon as the freighter steams past her. The U-boat really won't have much of a chance at all."

"Of course, the neutral powers won't like it," Fisher thought aloud. "Which flags are you planning to use?"

"Several," Hall responded immediately. "But principally the U.S. flag. Our traffic intercepts tell us that the Germans are particularly determined to keep the Americans neutral."

"And Washington will go along with this?" the admiral asked.

"We're not planning on asking them," Churchill responded through clenched teeth. "We'll change flags at sea and switch back to the British flag when we enter port."

"But surely they'll find out," Fisher protested.

"How?" Winston drummed his fingers while he waited for the admiral to come up with his answer. Fisher looked to Captain Hall for help.

"The only ones who could possibly see the flag would be German submarine captains," Hall said. "Most likely they will take the flag as genuine. But suppose one of them knows the ship. Suppose he is able to positively identify it as one of ours flying a foreign flag. What can he do other than inform his government, and what can the German government do other than raise a protest? In that event, we will simply deny the charge."

Fisher nodded slowly. The mischievous twinkle returned to Winston Churchill's eyes.

"Well," Fisher gasped as he lifted himself out of the chair, "I wouldn't want my name on the order. But I suppose I'm in favor of anything that could make life a bit more difficult for Admiral von Pohl."

"Wonderful," Churchill said, jumping up from his chair and rushing to assist the admiral. "There's no need for your name to appear anywhere. But I do hope you understand how grateful I am for your counsel on this matter."

Fisher brushed the helping hand aside. He was perfectly capable of getting himself back to his quarters. He retrieved his hat and his walking stick from the rack next to the door and let himself out.

"Well, that wasn't too difficult," Captain Hall volunteered as he pushed his chair back to its place near the wall. "Once he got the general drift of the plan, I think he was quite enthusiastic. As enthusiastic as Jack Fisher ever gets." He started for his officer's cap, which was resting on a side table, but the First Lord of the Admiralty motioned him into the soft wing chair that Admiral Fisher had just vacated.

Churchill slid the model of the *Golden Hind* back to the corner of his desk. "Tell me, captain, which of our codes are the Germans reading?"

Hall looked shocked. "Absolutely none that I'm aware of."

"That's comforting news," Churchill allowed. "But I'm afraid I can't buy it. I'm sure they're copying our messages just as diligently as you're copying theirs. And I'd venture that they have just as many mathematicians as we do serving as code breakers. If they haven't gotten through one of our ciphers yet, it's certainly only a matter of time before they do."

"You want them changed more frequently?" the naval officer asked.

Churchill shook his head, a conspiratorial smile spreading slowly across his face. "To the contrary. I want to find one code they are reading, and then I want to make sure that we never change it."

Captain Hall's eyes narrowed. "You want to be able to get information to the Germans. Information that they'll assume is highly classified."

The First Lord of the Admiralty leaned back in his chair and aimed a ring of smoke at the ceiling. He was enjoying watching Hall sort the pieces of the puzzle.

"Information about ships . . . and their cargoes," Hall guessed, thinking back to the conversation they had just shared with Admiral Fisher.

"Not ships," Winston Churchill said. "A particular ship." He looked at Hall from the corner of his eye. He could see that his intelligence officer was baffled.

"I'm afraid I don't understand," Hall admitted.

"When our ships begin turning on the German submarines instead of meekly submitting to search, what do you think the Germans will do?"

"Begin firing without warning," Hall said. "They'll have no choice." Then his eyes glowed in recognition. "And you have a particular ship you'd like them to fire at."

Churchill nodded. Good boy, he seemed to be saying.

"You'll use the compromised radio code to direct them toward the ship you want them to attack."

"If you can find me a compromised radio code, Captain," Churchill added.

Hall jumped up and took his cap. "Then we'll have to find you one, First Lord." He juggled the cap in his hands for a moment. "May I ask which ship you have in mind?"

"Of course," Churchill answered. "A ship that will bring the Americans into the war. On our side."

NEW YORK

THE CITY stopped and turned to face the Hudson River as *Lusitania* appeared around the tip of Manhattan.

In downtown office buildings, bank clerks and stockbrokers slipped away from their desks and pressed against the windows. On the docks, longshoremen left the crates they were loading and wandered to the water's edge. On the dozens of ships fitted between the piers, crewmen deserted their posts and gathered on the sterns. On the streets of the west side, pedestrians ran toward the waterfront to get a better look.

New Yorkers called her "The Greyhound," which seemed a more fitting name for the fastest ship afloat. And they never tired of seeing her, even though she arrived like clockwork every other week. At each appearance, business stopped, and New York turned toward the river for a moment of enthusiastic tribute.

She was not the largest ship in the world. *Olympic*, sister ship of *Titanic*, was both longer and beamier. Two German liners, now sitting idly in Bremerhaven, displaced more tonnage. But The Greyhound seemed to be the tallest. The rapier-shaped black hull climbed five stories from the water line. Three more decks, painted glistening white, were built above that. And then there were the four enormous funnels rising another seven stories. As she slipped around the tip of Manhattan, she was one of the tallest buildings in the city. Blocks away from the river, her stacks could be seen moving steadily northward above the skyline.

William Day heard The Greyhound's mournful whistle signal to the tugboats that came alongside to assist her. Slowly, they began swinging her bow in toward the Cunard piers and pushing her into the narrow space of stagnant water that would briefly be her home. She would spend the next two days loading her cargo and filling her coal bunkers. Then the passengers would come aboard, and she would head back to her true home, the cold, hostile waste of the North Atlantic.

He watched as the black steel wall of her hull, bristling with rivet heads, slid along the dock, suddenly blocking out the sun and casting the Cunard offices into shadow. High above his head, on the protruding wing of the bridge, he could make out the ship's master as he kissed *Lusitania* cautiously against the pilings. Caution was Captain Fairweather Dow's trademark in maritime circles, where it was rumored that he had never so much as scratched the paint from his ship's hull in making a landing. It was Captain Dow's caution that had summoned Commander Day from a chemical plant in New Jersey, where he was inspecting a production run of rifle cartridges, to the Cunard offices in New York.

Charles Sumner, the Cunard Line's American representative, looked up from behind a cluttered desk as Day was shown into his office.

"Ah, commander!" He immediately began digging through stacks of accounts and correspondence until he found the typed copy of the message that had preceded *Lusitania* into port. "And what, in the name of God, am I supposed to do with this?" He pushed the wireless message toward Day.

UPON ARRIVAL, DEMAND IMMEDIATE BRIEFING BY ADMIRALTY OF ALL STRUCTURAL CHANGES MADE TO LUSITANIA. DEMAND FULL ACCESS TO ALL AREAS OF SHIP NOW CLOSED OFF BY ADMIRALTY ORDER. HAVE NO INTENTION OF SAILING UNTIL I AM FULLY SATISFIED AS TO SAFETY OF SHIP AND INTENDED CARGO. CAPTAIN DANIEL DOW, MASTER.

"It's not as if *Lusitania* weren't causing me enough problems," Sumner chattered while Day read. "Alfred Booth is constantly haranguing me about costs. Everything from the cost of coal to the cost of oysters for the first-class dining room." He picked up a handful of bills, weighed them momentarily in his palm, and then tossed them aside. "I can't keep a crew aboard. Stewards and seamen jump ship each time she reaches port. Who can blame them? Why should they risk their lives steaming back and forth through submarine-infested waters? How am I supposed to replace them in three days? And the Admiralty is always late bringing cargo aboard. It costs me twice as much to load cargo at night. We just can't get the longshoremen. I told Booth that he should lay the ship up for the duration. But do they listen to me?"

"What does this mean?" Day asked, dropping the message back into the pile of rubble on Sumner's desk.

"Just what it says," Sumner answered curtly, annoyed that his litany of grievances had been interrupted. "The man is responsible for everything on the ship. He can't accept that responsibility unless he's fully informed."

"Do you have another master available?"

Sumner gasped. "For *Lusitania*? My dear commander, you don't pick a master for a ship like *Lusitania* out of shapeup. A man trains a lifetime for a command like that."

"Then Captain Dow will have to remain the master," William Day conceded. "What kind of man is he?"

Sumner began to snicker. "He's a little old lady, that's what he is. He got the name 'Fairweather' because he'll take a ship a hundred miles off course to avoid a rain squall. Bad weather makes him seasick. Every time he comes into port, he has a long list of things he wants changed. Not just important things. Nonsense things. New tablecloths. A different brand of bath soap. How am I supposed to keep costs down when the ship's master is constantly forcing me to spend money?"

"Can he be trusted?" Day asked.

"Trusted? You mean—"

His secretary interrupted him. "Captain Dow is here," she announced.

Daniel Dow marched into the office, handing his cap to the secretary without sparing her even a glance. He was a slight man, seemingly too small to command a ship. Even before he was seated, his eyes darted apprehensively between Sumner and the naval officer.

"Commander William Day, from the Admiralty," Sumner said. Day offered his hand and took care not to crush the thin, manicured fingers he grasped.

"I've seen your wireless, Captain," Day said to end the introduction. "Is there something wrong with *Lusitania*?"

"Something?" Fairweather Dow asked sarcastically. "Everything is wrong. Since you put her in the yard, she's a different ship. Structurally different. Less seaworthy."

Sumner's eyes widened. "Less seaworthy? Ridiculous," he snapped, dismissing the charge.

"Have you sailed aboard her?" William Day challenged.

Sumner bristled at the affront.

Day turned to the master. "Captain Dow has. I think we should listen to his views."

Dow sneered in the general direction of Charles Sumner. He felt an immediate fraternity with the naval officer who had just put Cunard's pencil pusher back in his place behind a desk. What could a glorified bookkeeper know about the sea-keeping characteristics of a ship? He directed his comments to Day.

"She's lost her snap. *Lusitania* was always a roller. But when the sea put her over, she snapped back into trim. Now she's unsteady. Unsure, I might say. You've changed her balance by adding shell plating to her sides above the water line. Unless she's fully ballasted, she has no footing. I'm steaming with coal bunkers only half full, and I'm forbidden to flood the ballast tanks. That makes her top heavy."

"Who forbids you to take on ballast?" Sumner interrupted.

Day held up his hand. "The Admiralty," he answered Sumner without taking his eyes off Captain Dow.

"That's one problem," the captain continued. "Even worse is the yawing of the bow. Whatever you did to her, you took the stiffness out of the bow. She doesn't track in a straight line. If the Admiralty removed any structural stiffeners, they have to be replaced."

"Are the problems just westbound, when you're traveling empty?" Day asked.

"It's certainly worse when she's light," Dow said. "The cargo we take back to England helps keep her tighter. But that's another problem— these last-minute cargoes that are sealed into the holds before I can inspect them. How can I assure the safety of my ship when I don't even know what I'm carrying? How can I inspect when whole sections of the ship are closed behind locked doors?" He turned to Sumner. "Well, I won't have it. I demand to be shown the holds. I demand to know exactly what cargo is being put aboard. I'm the ship's master, not some hired crewman."

"Captain Dow, may I remind you that we are at war," Sumner began to scold. "Those cargoes—"

"I agree with Captain Dow," Commander Day interrupted. He stood up abruptly. "I have the keys for all of the areas that the Admiralty has secured," he said to the ship's master. "Would you like to inspect them now?"

Fairweather Dow was stunned by the Admiralty's acquiescence.

Charles Sumner was flabbergasted. Even he was forbidden from venturing beyond the new hatchways that the Admiralty had installed.

"Commander Day," Sumner said, rising from his chair, "I don't think you have the authority to countermand the instructions I have received from the chairman of the company."

"And I don't think you have the skill to take *Lusitania* back to England without Captain Dow," William Day answered. He turned back to Dow. "Are you ready, captain?"

They boarded the ship at the shelter deck level and walked forward, around the great rotunda that rose like the dome of a statehouse above the first-class dining room. Whenever he boarded *Lusitania*, it was hard for Day to believe that he was on a ship. The dining room was three decks high. White doric columns on the first deck supported the ceiling, surrounding a well that opened through to the second dining level. The dome, decorated in gold and white and supported by another circle of columns, rose up through the third deck, fifteen feet over their heads. The two dining levels could accommodate all the first-class passengers at a single sitting.

They passed the first-class entrance where two caged elevators waited to carry passengers down two levels to their staterooms, or up two levels to the lounges, libraries, and music rooms. Farther forward, Captain Dow turned into a stairwell and began leading Commander Day down into the lower decks of the ship. They descended two levels, past the third-level saloon on upper deck, until their passage was blocked by a heavy steel door. A chain was fitted around the latch, secured by a padlock. A small metal sign warned in etched letters, "Secured by order of the Admiralty." Fairweather Dow stepped to one side, making no effort to conceal his anger that he should be barred from any quarter of his own ship. Day took out a ring of keys and began comparing the numbers with the number on the lock. At last he selected a key, opened the padlock, and unfastened the chain. He pulled the door open and stood back so that the ship's captain could enter. Dow stepped through the hatch and turned into a passageway that he assumed would lead him to the third-class cabins on the main deck. He stopped so abruptly that Day charged into him.

There were no cabins. Before him stretched nearly a hundred feet of open cargo deck, divided by heavy storage racks. Steel cargo rings were embedded in the deck and on the bulkheads.

The ship's master staggered forward, his head turning from side to side in bewilderment. Sixty cabins, with accommodations for nearly 200 passengers, had vanished.

"The deck below is exactly the same," Day told him. "It's built directly on top of the boiler hatch for the number one boiler room."

The cargo deck narrowed as they walked forward, the bulkheads coming together to form the ship's prow. But they were still a hundred feet from the bow when the deck ended abruptly. Above them was the cargo chute that rose up to the hatch on the promenade deck. Below them, the chute continued downward all the way to the ship's keel.

"From this point forward," Day said, "there are four levels of cargo space, running from the forward boiler room all the way to the bow."

"What about the athwartship coal bunker?" Dow asked.

"Removed," Day answered. "It was valuable cargo space."

Fairweather looked around mentally measuring depths and dimensions.

"All the bulkheads," he calculated, "and portions of six decks have been removed. There's nothing left but a hollow shell."

Day nodded. "That's the yawing motion you're noticing when she's empty."

"Without cargo, this could be dangerous," the captain cautioned.

"Not according to the builders," Day said. "We use these holds to carry war materials, captain. Things that we're not supposed to put aboard a passenger ship. Do you want to leave it at that, or do you want me to be more specific?"

"What kind of war materials?" the master persisted.

Day tried to remember the last cargo that Fairweather Dow had carried to England. "Artillery shells. Rifle cartridges. Flares. Range finders . . ."

"Artillery shells?" Dow's thin face was turning ashen.

"They're not particularly dangerous," Commander Day assured. "The detonators and fuses are shipped separately. They're nearly impossible to explode."

"But if we took a torpedo?"

"I don't want to sound smug, captain. Certainly there are safer cargoes. But we store the explosive materials well above the water line. It would be difficult for a torpedo to score a direct hit. And nothing short of a direct hit would pose any significant danger."

Dow did not look reassured.

"You mentioned that you were forbidden to take on sea water as ballast," Day continued. "That's because on your return trip we fill the ballast tanks with light oil. We can't risk contaminating the oil with sea water. The oil may sound dangerous, but it is completely nonexplosive when carried in bulk."

Dow shook his head in disbelief. "If it's all so safe, then why all this damned secrecy?" he demanded.

"Because it's completely illegal. American law doesn't allow us to ship any war materials on passenger ships."

"Then put it on freighters," Dow said.

"Submarines can stop freighters and inspect the cargo. They can't even catch up with *Lusitania*. And they would hardly begin firing at a passenger ship that refused their order to heave to. Particularly one known to carry neutral passengers. I think when you weigh all the alternatives, Captain Dow, you'll agree that *Lusitania* is the safest way we have of getting essential materials across the Atlantic."

The captain turned away from Commander Day and walked in a small circle as he took in the cavernous cargo space that had been created inside his ship. He tried to comprehend how many artillery rounds could be packed into the giant hold, containing how many tons of powder. And oil in the ballast tanks. A torpedo could open the tanks and spill a film of oil out onto the sea. Which would mean that he could end up lowering his lifeboats into a blazing inferno.

"I'm sorry, commander," he finally concluded. "I simply don't feel that it's safe."

Day nodded his understanding. "Nor do I. But I wonder, captain, how many Englishmen don't feel safe. I think I can speak for the crews of our warships who are not trying to avoid submarines but are actually trying to find them. I'm sure the same is true of our soldiers. I doubt if they feel safe in the trenches. I wonder how many of them would be willing to change places with you right now."

"Dammit, man," Captain Dow snapped, "it's not my own safety I'm thinking about. I'm thinking about my passengers."

"I know, captain. I think about them, too. But I try to give equal thought to our soldiers and sailors," Day responded. "Without these materials, they don't stand much of a chance."

Dow took one last glance around the cargo hold. "I've seen enough," he said as he turned and started back toward the exquisite beauty of the ship's dining room.

They were at the companionway leading from the ship to the pier when Fairweather Dow announced his conclusion.

"I'll take her out." He took one step onto the wooden catwalk, then stopped and turned back to the naval officer. "I appreciate the truth, commander. I've heard nothing but lies from the Admiralty in England. And from the owners of my company."

"They were simply trying to protect you, captain," Day answered.

Fairweather seemed offended.

"What I've told you is a top Admiralty secret," the commander explained. "Secrets are dangerous. If you should ever breathe a word of what you now know to anyone, I think you can count on spending the rest of the war in a naval prison."

*   *   *

IT WAS mid-afternoon when Beecham's motor car retrieved Day from the railroad station and brought him to the estate of Long Island's north shore. By the time they reached the house, the winter sky had already darkened. Through the bare trees, Long Island Sound took on the color of tarnished silver.

The two men took their supper in the library, eating off serving trays while they worked before an open fire. Beecham had delivery schedules for hundreds of orders that he had placed with American manufacturers, and Day had the list of ships on which cargo space had been requisitioned. They had to match the delivery dates with scheduled sailings.

They came to a cargo that was being loaded aboard *Lusitania* that night, and Day recounted his conversation with Fairweather Dow.

"I think you handled it perfectly," Beecham concluded.

"But he's right, you know," Day added. "When we put ammunition aboard *Lusitania*, she becomes a legitimate target. The Germans have every right to sink her."

"Only after they stop and search her," Sir Peter reminded. "And they can't stop what they can't catch." He reached for the next shipping order, but Day persisted.

"The day will come when they won't challenge our ships. They'll simply fire. A torpedo hit probably wouldn't even slow *Lusitania* down. But if one of our cargoes exploded . . ."

"Fire without warning? Abandon the international rules of encounter?"

"Isn't that what we're doing?" Day asked.

"My dear boy, there are Americans traveling on *Lusitania*. They'd never give the Americans cause to enter the war. Now, enough of this talk. We have work to do." Sir Peter began studying the next shipping document.

Jennifer paced the hallway outside the closed library door as she rehearsed the list of grievances she had been saving for William Day. She was a prisoner, locked away in a secluded castle by uncaring parents who had stolen her from the city she loved. There were no romantic dinners, no nights of dancing, no carriage rides home with her naval officer by her side. There was nothing. Not even the hope that her friends from the city might stop by for a visit. People who lived in Manhattan didn't even know where Long Island was. She knew that Day would listen and understand. She hoped that, somehow, he would find a way to rescue her from her exile.

Each time she passed the door, she stopped and listened for a

boisterous exchange which might indicate that the meeting was adjourning. All she heard was the dull mumble of dull business.

"Jennifer!" Anne had come down the stairs and caught her daughter
with her ear pressed against the library door.

Jennifer rolled her eyes in exasperation. "I haven't seen William in
two weeks. He's come all this way to see me, and father has him locked
up in the library for the whole evening." She followed her mother into
the living room.

"Commander Day didn't come all this way to see you," Anne said
without looking back. "He came to see your father. They have important
business to discuss."

Jennifer pleaded her case as she followed at Anne's heels. "What's so
important about a lot of papers that it can't wait until tomorrow?"

"That's not your affair," Anne scolded as she continued through the
dining room toward the kitchens and the servants' quarters.

"William *is* my affair," Jennifer yelled, stopping her mother in her
tracks. Anne turned, and they stared at each other, she stunned by her
daughter's rude outburst and Jennifer choking back a hint of tears. Then
Jennifer turned abruptly and rushed off to the music room. Seconds later,
there was the sound of a lullaby being banged out on the piano keys with
furious hands.

Anne brought a silver tray with a teapot and cups into the library and
tried to be unobtrusive as she set it on the desk. When her husband took
his tea, she always served it herself. It was a gesture of caring that she
couldn't leave to the servants.

"We've just about finished," Sir Peter said, gathering his papers into
his briefcase. "Please join us." His attention suddenly turned to the door
that Anne had left open behind her. "What is that infernal banging?"

"That's your daughter enjoying a cultural moment," Anne said. "I
believe the piece was intended to be soothing."

"Sounds like a confounded marching band," Beecham growled. And
then he asked, "Is she all right?"

"She was anxious to see you, commander," she said to Day. "Perhaps
she thinks the ruckus will drive you out of your meeting."

Day looked from Anne to Beecham. "Will you excuse me, Sir Peter?"
Beecham nodded as he closed his briefcase.

Anne brought Peter his tea. "I don't suppose the commander will
want any," she noticed.

Beecham looked up at the unused cup, still resting on the tray.
"Probably not. Pour for yourself and join me."

They sat on opposite sides of the fire, Anne attentive to her husband,
who seemed lost in thought.

"You're working too hard," she said, trying to retrieve his attention.

Peter turned to his tea cup. "Apparently not hard enough. We're falling behind." He raised the cup to his lips, but then set it down again without drinking. "Our guns are rationed to firing just six rounds a night. The Germans never let up, but our gunners fire one star shell and then just six rounds for each field piece. I'm told one of our reserve divisions had to borrow grenades from the French before they could go to the front."

"One man can't provision an army, Peter."

"Oh, it's hardly one man," he told her. "We have enough people over here working on it. But we just can't seem to hurry the Yanks. They take their time with each order, making sure they get the highest bid. If they'd just name a price and manufacture the stuff, we'd be all right. But they seem to put every round up for bidding."

"Auction?" she asked. "Who else is buying war materials?"

"The Germans," he answered. "And they make wonderful customers. They don't want to take delivery because they have no way of shipping anything to Germany. No ships, and even if they had ships, no way of getting through our blockade. In fact, they don't even care if the Americans actually manufacture their order. They're just soaking up factory capacity to keep the materials out of our hands. So the Americans can take their order, and their money, and they don't have to deliver anything. Makes it damned difficult for us to compete."

"That's absolutely scandalous," she said in genuine shock.

Sir Peter smiled at her. "Perhaps you should be doing the purchasing. I don't think the Yanks could resist you."

They sat quietly with their tea while Anne tried to think of the best way to introduce the subject that was bothering her. Finally she decided to plunge right into it.

"I suppose you've noticed that Jennifer is very much taken by your naval officer."

Peter chuckled. "I think *infatuated* is a better word. After all, she's just a girl."

"She's eighteen," Anne answered. "I was nineteen when I became infatuated with you. I think *taken* proved to be the right word."

"A totally different situation," Peter reminded her. "We were from the same stock. Good Lord, it was our parents who introduced us."

"And you think your daughter is concerned over Commander Day's stock?"

"I think a serious relationship is the farthest thing from his mind. I think he's realistic enough to know that he can't be in love with Jennifer. It's the war that has brought him into our household. And while he's in our household, he's simply paying the appropriate courtesies to our daughter. Would you have him simply ignore her?"

Anne picked up the empty cups and set them on the tray. "I hope you're not underestimating what may be happening between them. It could be very difficult for Commander Day, and shattering for Jennifer."

"Believe me," Sir Peter said lightheartedly. "I work very closely with Commander Day. If he were in love with my daughter, I would certainly know it."

DAY FOLLOWED the furious tempo of the lullaby to the music room and walked to the piano, where he stood beside Jennifer. For a few moments she chose to ignore him, playing on even though he was in plain sight.

"Try for a bit more feeling," he finally teased.

"It's exactly how I feel," she shot back, continuing for another few bars. Then she jumped up from the keyboard and threw her arms around Day, burying her face in his shoulder.

"Oh, William. I've missed you."

"I've missed you, too," he admitted. Then he held her at arm's length and tried to wring a smile from her tear-stained face. "In fact, the whole city has missed you. The spirit is gone from the dancing at the Winter Garden, and Delmonico's is thinking of shutting for the season."

"I don't care about the whole city. I care about you. I thought for sure you would come out to see me."

"I couldn't. I have work to do," he reminded her. "They're fighting a war back home."

"I know that. I know you don't have much time. That's why I should be in the city, so that I'm there when you're free."

Jennifer looked over his shoulder to make sure they were alone. Then she decided that even the empty room wasn't safe enough. She took his hand and led him toward the French doors that opened out onto the terrace.

"Come outside," she said, not waiting for his answer.

He felt the cold draft as soon as she opened the door.

"Jennifer. You'll catch pneumonia out there."

But she never broke stride until she reached the stone wall that marked the edge of the lawn, which sloped down to the sound. Day unbuttoned his jacket and slipped it over her shoulders.

"I have a friend who lives in Manhattan," she began in a whisper. "I know she'd take me in. She's already invited me to stay with her."

"Jennifer . . ." he tried to interrupt.

"If I were living there, then we could be together whenever you weren't busy. Even if it were only a few hours during the week. And on the weekends, when you might have a whole day free . . ."

"You can't spend weeks on end waiting for me to have a few hours off. There are so many wonderful things you should be doing."

"There are no wonderful things," she argued, her voice rising well above her conspiratorial whisper. "Nothing is wonderful without you. Isn't that how you feel?"

He tried for a change of subject. "Does your father know this friend?"

"Yes, of course. He knows her family."

Day looked at her suspiciously. "And he approves of your going back to Manhattan and staying with her?"

"He doesn't know yet," she admitted. "But once I'm there he certainly wouldn't come and drag me away."

She looked up at him anxiously, waiting for his approval. But he turned away, walking a few steps across the terrace before he turned back to face her.

"Do you always get exactly what you want?" he asked.

Her eyes widened in surprise. Then they dropped slowly in embarrassment. "I thought that was what you wanted, too," she said softly.

He turned away from her, leaning his hands on the top of the wall and looking absently out over the water. "I want so many things," he said, as much to himself as to her. "I want a ship. I want to get back into the war. I'm a naval officer, not a stocking clerk. And, I want very much to be with you." He looked back at her. "For the time being, all those things are beyond my reach. I don't suppose I'll ever have them all."

"You think I'm selfish," Jennifer concluded. "Just an empty-headed brat like my spoiled, rich friends. But I'm not. I know what's important. And I can give my whole life to something that's important."

Day walked back toward her. "No, I don't think you're selfish. I think you're impatient. I think you want your whole lifetime, right now."

"Is that wrong?" she asked honestly.

"It's just not possible." he said.

He reached down and pulled his oversized jacket more closely around her. "I should get you back inside," he said, taking her arm to lead her back to the open door. But she stood her ground.

"I don't need everything right now," she decided. "I can wait for you. Tell me that I should wait, and I will, no matter how long it takes. I don't give up easily."

"Jennifer . . ."

She was looking up at him, her arms pinned to her sides by his jacket, waiting for his answer. He took her in his arms and kissed her gently.

Peter Beecham raked the coals with the poker until he was sure that the fire would die. When he looked up, he saw Jennifer and William Day through the window. They were at the edge of the terrace, outlined in the light that came through the French doors from the music room. His daughter was in the officer's arms.

He should have been furious. But instead, something about the way that Day was holding Jennifer filled him with a great sadness. She looked pathetically small, childishly costumed in the oversized jacket with gold braids and buttons. And Day, despite the brutal strength of his arms, was holding her as carefully as if she were a precious crystal that might shatter at his touch. Their kiss was soft, a shared breath of life rather than an urge of passion. Beecham suddenly understood what his wife had seen so clearly. It was not that Jennifer was in love with her prince. It was that Commander Day was hopelessly in love with his daughter. He felt ridiculously foolish for not having noticed it. He felt heavy with grief, because it was all so futile.

Beecham and Jennifer walked Day out into the driveway where the car was waiting to bring him back to the station. He had to catch the last train back to the city because there was a ship waiting to be loaded at daybreak. Jennifer leaned up against her father as the car pulled away. When it disappeared at the end of the road, he suddenly took her hand and held it as if they both were sharing some great loss.

He climbed out of his bed in the middle of the night, slipped on his bathrobe, and walked silently to the library. There, he sat at his desk and, in the dim light of a shaded lamp, penned a letter to the First Lord of the Admiralty.

> *My dear Winston,*
>
> *May I ask, as a personal favor, that you recall Commander William Day, Naval Aide to our commercial delegation here in New York.*
>
> *Commander Day has been an invaluable asset to our activities and is to be highly commended for his intelligence, energy, and professionalism. My request is made entirely for reasons of harmony within my household and should in no way affect his career adversely. I therefore hope that you will keep this letter in strictest confidence and assure that it is not attached to his service record.*
>
> *I am deeply grateful to you for accommodating me in this matter.*

He was about to scribble his signature when a final thought occurred to him.

> *I hope that Commander Day can be assigned to an important, yet safe, duty station. I would regard his loss as the loss of my own son.*

Sir Peter read his letter and underlined the word *safe*. Then he folded it into an envelope, sealed it, and addressed it to Churchill.

The next day, it would be included in the diplomatic pouch headed for London and put aboard the *Lusitania* just before sailing.

He turned off the lamp and glanced out through the window to the place on the terrace where Day and his daughter had stood. Once again, he felt the depressing sadness.

WASHINGTON

"AMBASSADOR von Bernstorff," Robert Lansing's secretary whispered through the half-open office door.

"Is he alone?" Lansing asked in a stage whisper as he stood and reached for his suit jacket.

The secretary shook her head slightly and then rolled her eyes.

"Von Papen?" Lansing mouthed.

She tipped her head to signal that Captain Franz von Papen had, indeed, accompanied the German ambassador.

Lansing responded by rolling his own eyes as if pleading for mercy, then held up one finger to signal that she should stall the guests for a minute. As soon as she closed the door, Lansing began scurrying around his office, tidying up like a housemaid.

He could abide von Bernstorff. The man was a bore, but he was basically well meaning, polite, and therefore tolerable. He might drone on for hours about some insignificant point, but that was a habit born of his passion for orderliness. Not only did he insist on dotting every *i*, but he needed to be certain that everyone else in the room was in full agreement that he had dotted it properly.

It was von Papen who was unbearable. He was a youthful, miniature clone of Kaiser Wilhelm, firmly convinced that the German officer was the final evolution of the human species, and that he himself was its most perfect specimen. Von Papen was never seen without his full military uniform, a dark blue jacket with a three-inch-high collar of gold brocade, fringed shoulder boards, and an array of medals across the chest representing a dozen of the insignificant orders that German officers liked to confer on one another. A scabbarded sword inevitably hung from his side. And square on his head he wore a spiked brass-encrusted helmet, its point adding a full four inches to his height.

Captain von Papen was always on duty. He inspected every room he entered, reacting in horror to even a book misaligned in a bookcase. Reflexively, he ran a white-gloved hand over every surface and then examined his palm for microscopic traces of dust. Rarely did he engage in genuine conversation. Instead, he spoke orders and listened to responses. On any issue, there was only one correct position—which was, of course, his own. Officially, he was only an aide to the German ambassador, Count von Bernstorff. But in his own mind, their relative importance was precisely reversed. The ambassador was nothing more than a velvet glove, useful only to soften his own iron fist.

Lansing was running his handkerchief over the arms of the chair that he would offer to von Papen when his secretary announced, "Ambassador von Bernstorff and Captain von Papen." He jammed the handkerchief into his pocket and tried to look as if he were stepping casually around his broad mahogany desk.

"Count von Bernstorff, how good to see you," he oozed.

The count responded with a trace of a smile in poor imitation of Lansing's toothy grin and accepted the hand that was offered.

"And Captain von Papen. A pleasure." Lansing began to extend his hand but let it falter when he saw von Papen's gloved hands permanently pinned against his sides. A small leather briefcase was inserted under his left arm.

The Captain responded with a window-rattling click of his heels. His body snapped downward from the waist in a formal bow that aimed his spike directly toward Lansing's heart. Then he racheted back up to his perfectly vertical position.

Lansing pirouetted back around his desk, gesturing to the two armchairs that were set across from him. "Please be seated, gentlemen."

The ambassador spread the split in his coattail like a concert pianist and settled into a chair, his weight coming to rest on one elbow, which he propped against the chair arm. It was more difficult for von Papen, who first had to fit his sword under the arm of his chair before he could lower himself to its edge in perfect attention.

"To what do I owe this honor?" Lansing began, trying to follow von Papen's eyes as they panned around the room in search of clutter.

"Most distressing information concerning the maritime policy of the British government," von Bernstorff began. "Information that, I believe, requires an immediate and most vigorous protest on the part of the government of the United States."

Lansing frowned his expression of concern. He looked earnestly at the ambassador, and then toward von Papen when the ambassador turned to his military aide. Von Papen opened the flap of the leather briefcase that he carried under his left arm, withdrew a gray folder, and snapped it down on Lansing's desk.

"These are Admiralty orders found among the papers of a British steamer, stopped by a German military vessel two weeks ago," von Papen said. "They reached us in our diplomatic pouch just this morning."

Lansing looked at the folder, lifted one corner carefully, and asked, "May I?"

"Of course," von Papen ordered. The American opened the folder and began to read. Simultaneously, von Bernstorff delivered an analysis.

"The first order instructs British merchant captains to fly the flags of neutral nations, which, as you know, is a flagrant violation of international law. You will note, in particular, the third paragraph, which stresses that the flag of the United States is the preferred neutral flag."

He waited until Lansing had finished reading and had turned to the next page.

"The second document forbids British merchant captains from obeying the lawful search orders of German submarines. When confronted with a submarine and ordered to receive a boarding party, they are to steer into the submarine with the intent of sinking her. Further, they are to use all firearms at their disposal to attack the submarine." He let Lansing read on for a few seconds and then added, "As you can see, the British merchantmen are warned that they will be prosecuted by the Admiralty should they submit to a submarine search."

Lansing nodded. "Most disturbing," he agreed. He turned to the third paper, which was an operations schedule that merchant ships were required to file with the Admiralty. Each ship reaching certain listed ports was to be held over for several days so that a naval gun could be installed on its fantail.

"You're convinced that these documents are genuine?" the counsel to the State Department asked, already organizing his defense.

"We are," von Bernstorff answered immediately. "They were found aboard a British ship, stopped and searched by U-19, thirty miles west of Cape Clear. The ship had sailed from Liverpool on the date that the orders were issued."

"Yes," Lansing said. "And, of course, it is precisely that point which I find puzzling. Here's a ship carrying orders forbidding it to submit to search, and yet it stops and allows the search in which these documents were obtained. I wonder if your correspondence specified which flag the ship was flying?"

Von Bernstorff blinked at the question. He glanced to von Papen for help, but the captain was still sitting at ramrod attention, his eyes fixed straight ahead. "I don't think it specified a flag," the ambassador admitted.

"Then, I'm sure it wasn't a foreign flag," Lansing noted, using his lawyerly skills to pick apart the Germans' testimony. "If it were, that fact certainly would have been noted. So again, the British ship appears not to have been following the orders that you say it was carrying."

"The orders that it was carrying," von Papen corrected.

Lansing closed the folder and then tapped it thoughtfully with his fingertips. "Well, I will certainly bring this matter to the attention of His Majesty's ambassador. If such an order had actually been issued, then I'm certain my government would protest the use of the U.S. flag."

"The order was issued," von Papen corrected again. "Whether the ship's captain had not yet read it, or whether, when faced with a submarine, he simply chose to ignore it, is completely beside the point. What is obvious is that the British government is abandoning the rules of encounter."

Lansing pursed his lips. "I'm not quite sure I would come to that conclusion."

"There is no other conclusion," the captain pressed. "If British passenger ships and merchantmen intend to ignore a submarine's warning shot, then the submarine is left with no alternative but to attack. England cannot claim the protection of the rules of encounter if her captains are ordered to ignore their obligations under those rules. It is that simple."

Lansing's eyes flashed the anger he felt at being lectured by the ridiculous character. "Captain von Papen, these few papers, even if genuine, in no way constitute an excuse for German submarines to attack ships without making provision for civilian passengers."

Count von Bernstorff immediately tried to calm the exchange. "My dear counselor, I'm sure Captain von Papen didn't mean to suggest—"

"What I am suggesting," von Papen said, completely ignoring his own ambassador, "is that England is attempting to embroil our submarines with neutral nations. If we follow the cruiser rules, they will ram us. If we don't, then we run the risk of sinking neutral ships. Or of sinking English ships that carry neutral passengers. It is English policy, not the German submarine, that threatens your citizens. We must insist that you warn the English that you will hold them strictly accountable for any loss of American lives or property."

It took all of Robert Lansing's considerable decorum to keep him in his chair. "Insist" went well beyond the conventions of diplomatic language. Who did the little bastard think he was, issuing orders to the government of the United States?

"Captain von Papen," Lansing said slowly, "we cannot hold England 'strictly accountable' for events that have not occurred."

For the first time, the German military attaché broke from his statue-like pose. He leaned across Lansing's desk and pressed a gloved fingertip against the gray folder. "These orders have already occurred, Herr Lansing. Their consequences are inescapable. If you and the other neutral nations cannot convince the British to retract these orders, then

Germany must follow England's lead and abandon the rules of encounter. The consequences will be disastrous."

Lansing looked at von Bernstorff. "Your aide, sir, is threatening U.S. civilians with submarine attack." The count looked in confusion from one man to the other.

Von Papen snapped to his feet. "The threat, Herr Lansing, comes from England, not from Germany. Will you be so kind as to convey our views to your secretary of state."

He placed the leather briefcase back under his arm and snapped into his bow. The ambassador, realizing that his aide was adjourning the meeting, pushed himself up from his chair. Lansing rose as well, his eyes burning at the miniature Prussian warlord who had just addressed him as if he were a messenger boy. Von Papen's heels clicked like a rifle shot. He turned abruptly and marched out of the office with the German ambassador stumbling at his heels.

"Damn," Lansing cursed as soon as the door closed behind his visitors. He picked up the gray folder and then slammed it down on his desk. Of course the documents were genuine. It was exactly the kind of move that the British ambassador had been suggesting in their recent conversations. "The cruiser rules," the ambassador had said when they stood together at a State Department reception, "were intended to give merchantmen the opportunity to avoid combat. But if a freighter chose to ignore the warning to stop for search, it could certainly do so at its own peril." The English meaning was clear. American policy should insist the cargo ships be protected from submarines. But the submarine should be afforded no similar protection from the cargo ship.

Lansing had, of course, recognized that the British were quibbling over their own rules but expressed his sympathy for their problem. He fully expected them to tell their merchant captains to turn on their U-boat attackers. But he had never expected the Admiralty to issue a formal order.

And the foreign flags? Had they lost their minds? What could have ever prompted the British to put such a blatantly illegal decision into writing? He could already hear the secretary of state's righteous outrage at the misuse of Old Glory.

William Jennings Bryan was the price that Woodrow Wilson had to pay for the support of the populist wing of his party. The old silver species warrior had nothing in common with the president, and Wilson had hoped to satisfy him with a less important position—postmaster general, or perhaps ambassador to some Central American puppet. But the man had twice come within a few votes of the White House, championing the agrarian middle American Democrats against Wilson's intellectual eastern wing of the party. The president had no hope of getting any of his programs through Congress unless William Jennings Bryan seemed to be a contented member of his team.

Lansing's job was to keep Bryan from embarrassing the administration. And with these documents in hand, the old cornball could cause serious trouble. Imagine if his prairie constituency learned that England was hiding its mighty merchant marine under the American flag. They'd be burning the king in effigy at all their tent meetings.

If Bryan took these documents to the president, then Woodrow Wilson would have no choice. He would have to prohibit Americans from traveling on British passenger ships and deny use of American ports to England's armed merchantmen. He would have to demand, under threat of severing diplomatic relations, that England give up the use of American flags. It would mean the end of all the material support that a supposedly neutral America was providing to the side it unofficially favored. It would also mean the end of Robert Lansing's usefulness to the industrialists and the bankers who were profiting so handsomely from filling the British arsenals, and whose support was certainly important to his heady political ambitions.

Lansing lifted the captured documents from his desktop and slipped them beneath a stack of personal records he kept in his bottom drawer. At his next meeting with Secretary Bryan, he would casually mention the "forged British orders" that had gotten the ridiculous von Papen into an uproar. William Jennings Bryan always enjoyed stories about von Papen's Wagnerian behavior.

But there would be nothing casual about his next meeting with the British ambassador. He would warn the man most vehemently to find every copy of those damned orders and personally supervise their destruction. How could he orchestrate the United States' outrage over Germany's departure from the cruiser rules if England's own abandonment of the rules was a matter of written record?

LONDON

CAPTAIN Reginald Hall entered Churchill's office from a side corridor, tapping a rhythmic code and then opening the door as soon as he heard Winston's grunt of approval. It was not that the head of Naval Intelligence didn't have every right to meet with the First Lord of the Admiralty. But Hall was a uniformed officer, reporting in the chain of command to Admiral Fisher. Both men thought it prudent not to call the admiral's attention to their frequent meetings of which no minutes were ever published. Sooner or later, Fisher would begin to ask questions, and they knew it was unlikely that he would approve of most of the answers they would be forced to offer.

Churchill was at his desk, poring over lengthy estimates of the navy's reserves of critical war materials. The information had sunk his generally optimistic outlook into a sea of despair. All mining in the English Channel and along the North Sea coast would have to be suspended in three months because the supplies of guncotton used in the mines had been exhausted. Submarine patrols had been curtailed to conserve dwindling reserves of light oil. The North Seas fleet had restricted gunnery practice because of a shortage of black powder. Everywhere he looked, scarcities of supplies were proving to be a more lethal enemy than the Germans.

"I hope you have some good news for me," he mumbled without looking up to greet his guest. He slapped the back of his hand across the reports he was reading to indicate that the news was anything but cheering.

"I think so," Captain Hall said as he settled into a side chair. "I think we've found that mailbox in Germany that you were looking for."

The First Lord dropped the papers on his desk as he tried to shift his mental gears. Supplies reports involved the details of tactical operations. His conversations with Reginald Hall centered on the broader strategic issues that he found more stimulating.

"A communications channel?" he asked.

Hall nodded.

"Where?"

"Ireland," the intelligence officer said. "The Germans seem to be reading our traffic through the radio station at Crookhaven."

Churchill's face showed its mischievous smile. "Ireland. I might have known. The damned Fenians actually hope that the Germans will finance their next rising."

"With good reason," Hall corrected. "There have been quite a few German rifles smuggled into Ireland. If we're not careful, the Fenian brotherhood will be better armed than we are."

"How did you find which channels were compromised?" Churchill wondered.

Hall smiled broadly. He took great delight in the schemes he devised to outflank the enemy. In his office, war had nothing to do with the wholesale slaughter that was occurring in the trenches of France or with the agony of sunken crews clinging to life rafts. It was an intellectual game, and his delight in it complemented his passion for chess.

"We invented a ship, and then broadcast messages to it using different radio channels and different ciphers. Quite a number of combinations, actually. And, of course, we continued listening in on the German submarine frequencies. The first time we used the Crookhaven transmitter, we picked up a German broadcast referencing our fictional ship. Now, they couldn't have learned about the ship from any other source because, as I said, the ship doesn't exist. They have to have gotten it through our broadcast traffic."

The First Lord of the Admiralty growled with pleasure.

"Then we invented other ships and radioed to them through Crookhaven using several different ciphers. Ciphers that the Germans were unable to read when we used them over different transmitters. No matter which code we used, if we sent the message from southern Ireland, the Germans learned about it."

It didn't take Churchill a second to solve the riddle. "Then it's not our codes that have been broken. The Germans seem to have found a spy in Ireland."

"Precisely. If they could read our codes, then they would be acting on them no matter what transmitter we used. You're absolutely correct. We've got a German agent somewhere along the lines of Crookhaven."

"Any ideas?" Churchill asked.

"That's a bit sticky," Captain Hall confessed. "We deliver our Irish traffic to Admiral Coke, in Queenstown. We use telephone lines between Queenstown and our communications center at Crookhaven. So there are two possibilities. It could be that the Irishers have a tap on our phone lines."

He hesitated long enough for Churchill to ask, "And the other possibility?"

Hall grimaced. "The other is that it's one of our own people. Someone at Queenstown or Crookhaven. Or one of our operators along the line."

"How would they get the information out?"

"They could be broadcasting it directly to Germany using one of the codes we haven't broken. Or, they could be signaling it to a submarine lying off shore. That's a very bleak coastline. There's no way we can cover it closely enough to prevent communications from the shore to submarines."

Churchill lifted himself from behind his desk, selected a cigar from his desktop humidor, clipped the end, and then carried it with him to the window. He sealed it carefully in the flame of a wooden match, then puffed it like a steam engine.

"For the time being," he concluded, "let's leave things alone. I'd like to find out who the spy is, but I want to leave him in place."

Hall nodded. "And feed him bogus information."

"No. I think the information should be valid," the First Lord answered. "I'd rather not give the Germans any reason to suspect that we're on to the Crookhaven leak."

"Valid shipping information?" Hall's eyes narrowed. The First Lord of the Admiralty was telling him to put incoming ships in jeopardy in order to preserve the communications link with Germany.

"We don't have to send everything through Crookhaven," Churchill answered. "But what we do send should be authentic."

"Then I won't look too hard for the spy," Hall decided. "If we want the channel to stay open, we don't want to spook anyone. But still, the Admiralty should do something, if only for appearance's sake. We should put someone in charge out there."

Churchill brightened. "Perhaps an area commander. An officer with impeccable credentials. Admiral Coke has been asking for help in Ireland."

He opened his desk drawer, fumbled about briefly, then withdrew a handwritten letter and slipped it across the desk to Hall. "I was asked to find a position for this man. Something that wouldn't get him killed. I don't think there's much danger along the southern coast of Ireland."

"William Day," Hall said as he read Sir Peter Beecham's letter. "Isn't he the chap who rescued half a dozen of his shipmates from *Aboukir?*"

Churchill nodded. "A fine officer. We could assign him to Admiral Coke in Queenstown, and then have Coke put him in charge of the southern coast."

Hall dropped the letter back on Churchill's desk. "I'll put through the transfer," he said.

He stood and walked to the side door. His hand was on the knob when he paused and turned back to the First Lord.

"You appreciate, of course, that if we use Crookhaven, we run the risk of handing the Germans one of our own ships. It could be disastrous."

Churchill lifted his cigar from the corner of his mouth and examined the perfectly shaped ash. "If we pick the right ship, it will be disastrous. For Germany."

NEW YORK

"YOU'LL BE joining us for Christmas?" Sir Peter Beecham asked as he pushed an enormous stack of papers into his briefcase.

Commander Day was standing by the window of the British Purchasing Mission's fourth-floor office, looking out at the snow that was beginning to accumulate in the street below. "I'd like that very much," he answered. Then he turned to Sir Peter. "If you're sure it won't be an intrusion."

"Nonsense. You're one of the family." He suddenly looked up from his papers, embarrassed at his choice of words. They both knew it was not true. William Day was most certainly not one of the family.

Day's recall orders from the Admiralty had come through the day before, and Beecham had launched into a tirade, complaining that the navy had no right to rob him of such a valuable assistant. But William knew it was just posturing. He was well aware that Sir Peter had considerable influence with Winston Churchill and that the orders never would have been issued without Beecham's approval. It was obvious that his transfer had been requested, and he had little trouble guessing that he was being sent back to England precisely to assure that he would never become one of the family.

"That's very kind of you," he said as he turned back to the window.

"Not kind at all," Beecham said, trying to recover from his gaffe. "Well, deserved, if you ask me. We both could do with a holiday. It's been a difficult month."

They had been working long hours and long weeks and had had only modest success as their reward. They had beaten the Germans to 15,000 barrels of diesel oil and gotten a respectable buy on 20,000 time-delay shell fuses. They had won a bidding war for 4,000 cases of rifle cartridges, at a price that had brought groans from their bankers. But the order for 8,000 bags of black powder had slipped through their fingers when German purchasing agents topped their final price. And they had lost three months' production from North America's largest barbed-wire factory when the Germans had laid an enormous bribe on one of the company's directors. And then there was the guncotton. Twice they thought that they had a contract for a chemical company's entire production of the highly explosive material, only to have the company quote a new and higher price.

"We've done our best," Day consoled the older man. "And you should have better luck in the new year. The Germans will run out of bank credit long before we do."

Beecham had slipped into his topcoat and picked up his briefcase from his desk. "I'm sure you're right. Things have to get better. But I feel personally responsible whenever I can't fill a requisition. Our boys need these things."

He stopped when he reached the door. "I really wish we could have gotten the guncotton. The Admiralty is absolutely desperate for it." He lifted his hat from the rack and squared it on his head. "It would have made a great Christmas present for Winston."

Day stayed by the window until he saw Sir Peter cross the street below. He went to Beecham's desk and thumbed quickly through the stack of open contracts until he found the unsigned agreements for the guncotton. Then he took his cap and greatcoat, locked the office door behind him, and pushed the button for the ornate iron elevator that traveled in a wire-caged shaft in the center of the stairwell.

The snow, which had begun falling at midday, was turning into a blizzard. The electric trolleys had stopped running, and the taxis and carriages had disappeared from the streets. Day set his head into the wind and walked up Broadway, dodging the hunched-over businessmen and the hobble-skirted secretaries who were making an early exit from the city's financial center before they were trapped by the storm. He could only hope that Harry Sinclair was still in his office.

He reached the Nassau Building, asked the elevator operator for the duPont offices, and stamped the snow from his shoes as he rode to the fifth floor. Then he opened a glass-paneled door and entered the railed-in reception area, where a matronly secretary greeted him and led him back to the executive offices.

"Commander Day. Did we have an appointment? I was just about to get an early start for home." Harry Sinclair was a bullet-headed man with a mournful expression that seldom knew joy. He lifted a watch from his vest pocket as he spoke and made a great show of checking the time, indicating that he expected Day's visit to be brief.

"No, we didn't," Day answered, crossing to the uncomfortable leather chair that faced Sinclair's oak desk. "I just dropped in on the chance that you might spare me a minute."

"That's about all I have," Sinclair said. He glanced toward the door that his secretary was closing. "Sir Peter isn't with you?"

"As a matter of fact, he's not. But I thought you and I might be able to wrap this up without him."

"The pyroxylin?" Sinclair said, using the technical name for guncotton. Then he leaned forward with sudden interest. "Are you entering a new bid?"

Day lifted the unsigned contract from his jacket pocket. "No. I was simply hoping that we might come to an agreement on the outstanding bid. I've been called back to sea duty, and I'd feel a good deal better about it if I knew we had the pyroxylin instead of the Germans. It's nasty stuff when it bangs against the side of your ship."

Sinclair looked confused. "But I thought I made it clear that we have limited production. We can't fill all the orders, and we're expecting a higher offer from . . . other parties."

"You did," Day conceded. "Very clear. But after you get the German price, you'll be expecting a higher offer from us, and with all the bidding, our deliveries will be delayed for weeks. The fact is, we can't afford to waste all that time. The war, you know."

Sinclair sat silently while his confusion gave way to anger. "Commander Day, I can sympathize with your patriotism. But we are a neutral country, and this is simply a business transaction. I don't care who gets the pyroxylin. I do care about getting the best price."

Day opened the contract. "I thought our offer was very generous. It's 60 percent higher than your list price."

Sinclair rose from his chair, signaling the end of the meeting. "I can see you don't know a great deal about business, Commander Day. Perhaps you can ask Sir Peter to stop in and see me."

William Day remained comfortably in his chair. "I'm sure you're right, Mr. Sinclair. On the other hand, I don't think you know a great deal about war. You're talking about your associates getting rich. I'm talking about my associates getting killed. I think that gives me the greater claim." He set the contract on the desk and smoothed down the corners. "Sir Peter has already signed. All we need is your signature. Then we can make the first payment, and you can order the production started."

Sinclair looked down at the document, then looked back up in disbelief at Day.

"Do you need a pen?" Day asked, reaching into his jacket pocket.

"I have no intention of signing anything," Sinclair sputtered.

The humor disappeared from Day's eyes. He nodded slowly at his adversary. "That's very brave of you, Mr. Sinclair." He rose slowly from the chair, walked back to the office door, and turned the key in the lock. Then, as he walked back across the room, past the desk, he said, "I'm sure the shareholders will remember you kindly when they divvy up all the profits you've earned for them." Sinclair's head spun slowly as he followed Day's progress across the room. His eyes widened as the British naval officer went to his window.

Day released the catch and threw open the lower pane. Sinclair recoiled from the blast of icy air that rushed into the room. "Are you crazy? What the hell are you doing?" he demanded.

Day responded with two strong hands that grabbed the astonished businessman under the arms, snapped him off his feet, and lifted him steadily toward the open window. "Diplomatic immunity," the commander explained patiently as he tilted Sinclair's head into the opening. "All they can do is send me back to England, which is exactly where I'm going in any event. And without that guncotton, I'll be safer in jail."

"You can't do this," Sinclair screamed.

Day dropped Sinclair's back down on the window sill, grabbed his knees, and began pushing him out over the edge. Sinclair let out a blood-curdling scream, but it was hardly a whisper into the wind that was rushing along the side of the building.

"You could have been a hero," Day yelled into the terrified face. "Sixty percent extra profit. You probably could have had a raise!"

Sinclair's arms were flailing in space. Day's grip had slipped down to his ankles.

"I'll sign. For the love of God, I'll sign!"

Day leaned out the window and gave Sinclair a suspicious look.

"I swear. I'll sign. Pull me back."

Day hesitated for a moment of exaggerated indecision. Then he dragged Sinclair back through the window and set him carefully into his chair. The man sat wide-eyed, the buttons on his vest split apart, his tie turned halfway around to the back of his shirt. Melting snow dripped from his bald head down over his face.

"For God's sake, close the window," Sinclair panted.

Day nodded toward the contracts, which were scattered across the desk. Sinclair spun in his chair, opened his desk drawer, and found a pen. He scribbled a shaky signature across the bottom of the agreement.

"Both copies," Day reminded. He waited until Sinclair had signed again before he lowered the window and shut out the storm.

"I think you've made a wise decision," the commander commented as he gathered up one of the copies. "You can tell your people that the Germans never met the price. And I'll tell mine that you wanted us to have it. You'll be a hero to both sides."

"You're crazy," Sinclair blurted, his eyes still wide with terror.

"Desperate," Day answered after a thoughtful pause. "I think *desperate* is a better word."

He turned back after he had unlocked the door. Sinclair was still at his desk, disheveled, frightened, and beginning to tremble from the cold. "We'll have our check to you right after the holiday. And if there's anything you can do to speed up the production, we would certainly appreciate it."

Sinclair reached over his shoulder and retrieved his necktie. But his eyes never left Day. "You would have done it. You would have dropped me out the window."

"Dropped you out the window?" Day asked. "What kind of a way is that to conduct business?"

PETER BEECHAM was the Christmas elf, determined to bring magic to the holiday. For weeks he had refused all of Anne's efforts to take care of his shopping, insisting on selecting each of his gifts personally. He weighed each purchase, visualizing the exact measure of joy it would bring to its recipient and chuckling at the moment of delight that opening the present would bring.

Anne had suggested that just this once she call in a professional to decorate their home for the holidays. "You're so busy with the war, Peter. Everyone will understand that you simply don't have the time to see to all the details." But Peter relished the details. "An outsider?" he had protested. "How will they know what we like? They'll turn our home into a department store window."

He had supervised everything. The evergreen ropes that draped from the bannister of the staircase and fell gently across the mantel. The sprigs of holly that were affixed to every door. The candles, one carefully placed in each of the house's windows. The bright red bows and mistletoe that hung over every entrance and passageway. The soft lighting on the crèche, with its real straw and lifelike plaster figures. The stockings that hung above the fireplace. And, of course, the Christmas tree.

"Not another like it in all England," he had said each year as he stepped back from the carefully decorated evergreen. Now, with his horizons broadened, he had confidently proclaimed that there was not another tree like his in all the world. It was a perfectly tapered blue spruce, thick with branches and reaching to within a few inches of the fifteen-foot ceiling in the music room. It was decorated with the traditional ribboned fruit, and candy canes hung from its branches. Then, as a tribute to his fondness for the colonies, he had wrapped the entire tree in a garland of strung popcorn. Delicate candles were set at the tips of the branches, filling the room with a warming glow.

He rubbed his hands in anticipation as Anne found her gift under the tree, a small package that he had wrapped personally in silver paper with a bright red bow. He chuckled at her delight in finding a jewelry box and followed her eyes to the antique silver ring that she slipped on her finger and modeled with great joy. Then it was his turn to slowly unwrap the small box Anne had given him. "Ahh . . ." he sighed, and then he held up a gold tie pin that he pronounced the most beautiful he had ever seen.

"Well now, what have we here?" He lifted a box that showed Anne's touch for tasteful decoration. "Saint Nick seems to have left a gift for you, William."

Day carefully removed the paper despite Jennifer's urging that he tear through to his gift. He found a small ebony chest, fastened with a gold clasp. He opened it and from its soft felt interior lifted a snowy white meerschaum pipe with a curved stem and an oversized bowl.

"Peter says that sea captains need a good pipe to smoke on the bridge," Anne explained. "And we all know that you'll soon have your own command."

Day held the pipe as though it were a relic. "It will take a fine ship to deserve such a pipe on its bridge," he told Anne.

"It will take a fine ship to deserve such a commanding officer," Sir Peter said sincerely.

Day reached under the tree and found a small, flat box, decorated in store paper, that he gave to Anne. She thanked him profusely, insisting that he should never have thought of bringing her a Christmas gift. She opened it carefully, lifted out a beautifully embroidered handkerchief, and carried on as though it were the one thing she had wanted since childhood. Then he took a plain envelope from his jacket pocket.

"Merry Christmas, Sir Peter."

Beecham's eyes widened. "Well, really now. This is an unexpected pleasure." He weighed the envelope on his fingertips, then looked suspiciously toward Day. It was a letter of some kind, and he thought quickly of all the things that the commander might want to say to him. The things he most deserved to be told weren't thoughts that he would want to share with his family. "Should I open it? Now?" But even as he asked the question, he knew he could trust William Day. He ran his finger under the flap and drew out an official-looking document.

"You said it would be a fine Christmas present for Mr. Churchill," Day reminded him. "I thought you deserved it more."

Beecham glanced at the familiar contract for the guncotton, then flipped to the last page, where he found Sinclair's signature next to his own.

"We have it all," Day said. "Delivery guaranteed by the first of May."

"But how . . . ? He was so firmly decided that it should go to auction."

"I appealed to his best instincts," Day said.

Beecham looked to his wife and daughter. Both, he could see, were bewildered.

"A very important contract that I thought I had lost," he told them. "William has saved it for me."

Anne turned to the naval officer. "I won't pretend to understand, Commander Day. But I think you have given my husband the finest present of his entire life. I'm very grateful to you."

"William . . ." Sir Peter tried to begin. But the best he could do was shake his head. "I think there are many men who would want to thank you," he finally managed.

Day saved his gift for Jennifer until they were alone, walking on the packed snow path that led across the hilltop to the carriage house. Even as he reached into his pocket, he still had doubts as to whether he had made the proper choice. He knew she expected something personal, and he had stripped his bank account to find a gift that would tell her how much she meant to him. And yet, that was exactly the wrong message he should be delivering to someone whom he would probably never see again. His choice was between what he wanted to say and what he had to say. He had decided to let the present come from his heart and had determined that the words would come from his head.

She opened the package eagerly, gasped when she saw the soft jewelry box, and lifted the string of pearls slowly into the light. Then she stared at them, reading their meaning.

"I thought you could wear them for your triumphant return to Delmonico's," Day said, trying to make light of his message.

"I want to wear them now." Jennifer suddenly sprang to life, handing him the pearls and turning her back to him. "Put them on me!"

"Now? I don't think they go with your jacket . . ."

"I don't care. I just want to wear them. I don't think I'll ever take them off."

He laughed when she turned back to him, the pearls hanging outside her coat. "You'll have to take them off if you ever want to get out of that coat."

Now Jennifer reached into her pocket and carefully produced a small, square package that she had trimmed with lace. "And this is for you. Merry Christmas, William."

He examined it curiously. "Can't be another pipe," he said.

"Open it!"

He held it to his ear. "It isn't ticking, so it can't be a grandfather clock."

"Will you open it!"

He took out a heavy gold signet ring, his initials cut in the plain block letters that were the current fashion. "Now this is something *I'll* never want to take off. It's beautiful." He began slipping it onto his ring finger.

"Read it. It's inscribed."

He searched the ring, rolling it in his hand.

"Inside." Jennifer turned it in his palm and pointed. "Right there!"

I'll always love you. Jennifer.

Slowly, he closed his fist around the ring. His muscles tightened as if he were fighting against an intense physical pain. She took his strong hand in hers.

"Take me with you. We can go back to England together."

She saw his knuckles whiten as if he were crushing the ring in his palm. Then, slowly, his grip relaxed.

"You mustn't say such things," he told her.

"But it's true. I'll always love you."

Day pulled away from her, took a step back toward the house, then stopped and turned back to her. "You're so young. Just a—" He wanted to say that she was still a child, but that certainly wasn't true.

"You do love me?" Jennifer asked.

Day looked down at the ring in his hand. "If I were half the man your father wants for you, I'd be able to tell you, 'No, I don't love you.' That would be the right thing for me to say."

"Then you do love me," she answered joyfully. "So how old I am doesn't matter. We're in love, and love changes everything, doesn't it?"

He looked at her, and then shook his head slowly. "No. Not everything."

She launched into a speech that she had been rehearsing for days, ever since the moment when she told the jeweler what to inscribe on the ring. "I know there's a war on. I can't help that. And I know you'll be away and that I won't see you for months on end. But thousands of women are waiting alone. I even know that something could happen to you. That you might go off and . . . never come back. I've thought of all the things you're going to tell me. But if something were to happen to you, then we would never be together. That's why we should be together now. While we can."

He found himself smiling at her enthusiasm. Carefully, he took the ring and slipped it onto his finger. He held out his hand and took hers. He began walking toward the carriage house.

"I never told you how I became an officer. I think I should, because it's not the usual way. A year or so ago, all the officers in the navy were from important families. They were selected for the academy, given their commissions, and told they were seafarers. They were put in charge because their families have always been in charge. I became an officer because, with the war, they needed people to command their ships. I was a merchant officer, so they made me a naval officer.

"In these uniforms, you can't tell the difference. I look just like the men from the important families. But when the war ends, we'll all go home. And then you'll be able to tell the difference. They'll all go back to their great estates. I'll go back to the merchant ships."

"Do you think I care about great estates?" Jennifer interrupted angrily. "I told you once that I knew what was important. I don't give a damn how I live."

"No. Not now. But I think you will. I think you should. Jennifer, my father is a longshoreman. He carries heavy cases up the sides of ships on his back. The house I live in—that I'll go back to after the war—is smaller than that carriage house."

"I'd be happy with you in a carriage house," she insisted.

"And when would you wear your pearls?" he asked.

She pulled her hand away angrily. "You're making fun of me!"

He reached for her, but Jennifer backed away, tears showing on her cheeks, which were already red from the cold.

"I'm not making fun of you," Day insisted. "I could never do that."

"Then trust me. I'm stronger than you think. Trust that I can make everything work."

He answered the only way he could. "No. I can't do that."

Her eyes filled with rage. For a moment, he thought she was going to strike him. But she turned away, lifted the hem of her coat, and began running back toward the house.

"Jennifer!" He tried to call her, but the sound died on his lips. He had ended it. And whether now or later, he knew it had to end.

When he finally returned, the music room was empty, the light from the Christmas tree pretending to a joy that seemed to have fled the house. He walked through the quiet, empty rooms. The library door was open a crack, and he could see Sir Peter sitting hunched in front of the fire. He entered quietly, crossed the room, and rubbed his hands together in the warmth of the crackling logs.

"I'm sorry, Sir Peter," he said, speaking toward the hearth. "I'm afraid I've ruined your Christmas."

"Not your fault," Beecham mumbled. "She's quite headstrong. Perhaps I let her grow up too quickly."

Day forced a smile. "I don't think there's much you could have done about it." When he turned away from the fire, he found Beecham with his hands folded in his lap, staring idly at the patterns in the carpet that stretched in front of the fire.

"You must think me a terrible snob," Beecham said without raising his gaze.

Day lowered himself carefully into the chair next to Beecham's. "No, I don't think that. I think you love your daughter very much."

"I've been realizing," Sir Peter continued, still unable to raise his eyes, "that you might get your head blown off protecting my family. I know how damned unfair I've been. I want the very best for you, William. And yet . . ."

"The war will end," Day said softly. "And then we'll all go back to where we belong. You're a good man, Sir Peter. You've made me feel very welcome. But there are rules among people. Rules that none of us can change."

WINTER
1915

SCHULL

EMMETT HAYES narrowed his eyes behind his wire-framed glasses and bounced a ruler in the palm of his hand. He stared down at the red-haired boy whose face was rapidly draining of color.

"Are you telling me, Terrance, that this is the best you can do?"

"Yes," the alto voice answered in a whisper.

"Yes what?" Emmett Hayes snapped.

"Yes, sir."

Hayes looked down at the page of penciled printing that rested on his desk. He studied it for a moment, then pushed it aside in disgust.

"Well, your best isn't good enough. Not good enough, at all. And you know what that means."

"Yes, sir," Terrance managed.

"What? What does it mean?"

The boy shuffled his heavy shoes, one without laces and the other open at the toe. "That I have to try harder."

"Try? Try?" Hayes pretended to be aghast at the answer.

"That I have to do better," Terrance offered in desperation.

"Ah! That's more like it, lad. You have to *do* better. Trying is nice, but it's results that pay the piper."

He picked up the paper and studied it again. "You tried, but you didn't succeed. I've taught a thousand English lads your age, and they all wrote better compositions than this." He jammed the paper into the boy's chest and waited until the small hand took it. "So do it again. Tonight. I want a composition without a single mistake. I want a composition that I can hang on the wall of the best schoolhouse in England. Is that clear?"

"Yes," Terrance whispered, rolling the paper in his nervous fingers.

"Yes what?"

"Yes, sir."

The boy turned and tiptoed a few steps before he broke into a run. He nearly collided with Father Brendan Connors as he flashed through the doorway.

The priest sauntered into the room, his biretta square on top of his close-cut white hair, the buttons of his cassock turning in a detour around his ample paunch.

"I thought it was a murder I was hearing, Emmett."

"Just a dose of encouragement, Father," the schoolteacher answered as he took his topcoat and umbrella from the clothes tree. "The boy is lazy."

"He's just a farm lad," Father Connors tried.

Hayes slipped his arms into his coat, holding the cuffs of his threadbare suit jacket. "He can be more, that one. He has talent."

"You're too hard on them," the priest advised. "They're just tenants. In Ireland, it's enough if we can teach them their prayers."

Emmett hooked his umbrella over his arm and gathered up his books. "We've been using prayers for 500 years, Father, without much to show for it. I think it's time we started using our heads."

Connors laughed. "Hayes, you may not know it, but you're on your way to sainthood. You've got no faith, and God knows there's not a drop of charity in you. But I've never met a man so blessed with hope." He waited as Hayes locked the schoolhouse door and dropped the heavy key into his pocket. "Will you be stopping by the rectory for a game of chess?"

"Not tonight," the teacher answered, "much as I'd like to. I have a translation that I have to finish. Tomorrow?"

The priest nodded. "Tomorrow then." He patted Hayes on the back and started down the narrow street.

"Father Connors," Hayes called after him. "I don't really have hope." And then, with a mischievous smile, "What I have are plans."

Father Connors cackled with laughter.

Emmett was an oddity in Schull, always dressed in a jacket and tie in a population of rough shirts and shapeless sweaters. Carefully manicured fingers among callused, dirt-hardened hands. Shined brogues walking beside work shoes and boots. He was small and slim to the point of being delicate, while most of the men he passed on the street were brawny. He was always armed with books, which were a curiosity to neighbors who could neither read nor write. Only forty years old, he carried himself along the single main street like the village patriarch.

And yet they loved him. His hat tipped politely to each of the women he passed, and his umbrella waved in response to the hoarse greetings from the men. Even the children, driven mercilessly in his schoolhouse, were pleased to be recognized by their teacher. In Schull, Emmett Hayes was a symbol of an impossible value, like the statue of the Virgin on the steps of the church. The Virgin represented paradise to people living in the hell of poverty. Hayes represented intelligence to people buried in ignorance.

"Nasty weather, Mr. Hayes," James Corcoran said from behind the counter as Emmett entered his store.

"Nasty indeed, Mr. Corcoran," Hayes echoed. "The dampness cuts to the bone."

Corcoran made a great show of stretching his back. "Terrible for the rheumatism," he said.

"Just a bit of cheese, today." Emmett hung his umbrella on the counter while he opened his coat and dug for his wallet. "And a pint of milk."

Corcoran lifted a cheese wheel onto the counter and positioned his knife to outline a wedge.

"A bit more," Hayes said, and Corcoran moved the knife to widen the wedge before he cut down. Emmett counted out the coins while Corcoran wrapped the cheese in paper. Then he stuffed the package and the bottle of milk into a brown paper bag. Hayes pushed his books into the bag on top of the food and lifted the package in one arm while he retrieved the umbrella with the other.

"I hope your rheumatism is better, Mr. Corcoran." He caught the door with his toe and swung it closed behind him.

He walked to the end of the main street, then turned down a row of small stone houses that led up the hill away from the water. His house was on the end of the row. There were two steps up to the door that opened into a parlor, with the kitchen behind. A narrow staircase along one wall led to the two bedrooms on the second floor.

Hayes went straight to the kitchen, set the paper bag on the porcelain-topped table, unwrapped the cheese, and carried it with the milk to the icebox. He hung his hat, topcoat, and umbrella on a hook attached to the back of the kitchen door, then took the cheese wrapper with him as he climbed the stairs to the front bedroom.

Emmett dropped the wrapper on the bedspread, lifted the small brass key that hung from his watch chain, and unlocked the armoire that was centered on the back wall. He took a starched white shirt from a stack on one of the shelves, unfolded it carefully, and removed the shirt cardboard. With the cardboard in one hand and the cheese wrapper in the other, he sat down at the desk beneath the front window.

Carefully, he copied the words that were written on the wrapper.

Steamer Edmund Hampton. Dep. Philadelphia 8 January, Arr. Liverpool 19 January. Escort rendezvous 180 Fastnet 10 miles, 2300 GMT 18 January. HMS Juno assigned.

He opened the fold in the shirt cardboard and spread out a code table that substituted random letters for each letter of the alphabet. Over the next two hours, he calculated the proper random substitution for each letter in the message until he had translated it into gibberish.

When he finished, he slipped off his spectacles and spent a moment pressing his fingers into his burning eyes. Then he folded the shirt back around the cardboard, placed it carefully into the stack of other fresh shirts, and locked the armoire. He crumpled up the cheese wrapper, dropped it into an ashtray, and took a match to it, nudging the paper into its own flame. Then he carried the coded message down to the parlor, turned around the back of the staircase, and followed a flight of creaking steps down to the cellar.

The radio was built into a sewing machine cabinet. Hayes lifted the top, swung the radio up into position, and sat with his feet resting on the ornate metal treadle. As he rocked his feet, the belt, which had been designed to spin the sewing machine, turned the armature of a generator. He watched as the needle climbed into the required power range. Then he tapped out a call sign on the telegrapher's key. Immediately, the signal was repeated by a distant radio station, telling Hayes that a German operator was ready to receive.

He keyed his coded message, and then he signed it with his identification name, sending the single word, *Leprechaun*.

The signal traveled up a wire he had strung through the chimney and connected to an antenna that was stretched inside the peak of the roof. From there, it radiated out over Europe.

CROOKHAVEN

"ATTENTION on deck!"

Chief Radioman Richard Gore rolled off the dilapidated sofa and sprang to his feet, buttoning his uniform jacket in the process. Radio Seaman Tommy Halliday, who had shouted the order, stood at ramrod attention, still holding the tea pot he had been pouring from when Commander Day pushed open the door.

"Stand down," Day responded. He opened his greatcoat and shook the mist from his cap.

"Welcome to Crookhaven radio station," Gore said. "We wasn't expectin' you 'till tonight. Otherwise . . ." he looked around in embarrassment at the stacks of unfiled messages, the checkerboard on the table, and dirty tea cups piled in the sink, ". . . we would've tidied up a bit."

"I got an early start," Day explained, offering his hand. "Commander William Day. It's good to be here."

"Radio Chief Richard Gore," the petty officer responded, shaking Day's hand. "This is Radioman Halliday."

Halliday gestured with the tea pot. "Pleased to have you aboard, commander."

"Get the commander a cup," Gore ordered the radioman.

"Not yet," Day said. "I'd like to have a look around first."

Crookhaven station stood atop a rocky mountain that rose 200 feet out of the sea, the last of a row of giant rocks that seemed to have been scattered like a handful of pebbles from the southwestern tip of Ireland. On its western end was Mizen Head Light, the first point of warning for ships coming in from the Atlantic. Sheltered under its eastern bluff was the small protected harbor of Crookhaven, with a few small houses and a dozen fishing sheds along its edge. The gate to the station was just outside the tiny village, where the road from Skibbereen ended. From there, a narrow path climbed up to the top of the mountain.

There were two small buildings set between the two iron towers that hung the low-frequency radio antenna like a clothesline. The two buildings were identical to any of the stone cottages that dotted the coastline, and the rolling matted grass that grew right up to the edge of the cliffs would have been perfect for grazing sheep. It might have been a farm, except for the towers, steel lattice structures stained with red lead that stabbed 100 feet into the sky above the land line.

One of the cottages, the one Chief Gore stepped out of with Commander Day at his heels, served as the communications office. It housed the transmitter and receiver, giant boxes filled with glowing vacuum tubes, two operator's desks with their telegraph keys and telephones, and the filing cabinets for messages. A sink and stove served as a mess for the people on duty, and old household furniture made each watch comfortable. One of the rooms, the bedroom in the original floor plan, served as the coding room. It had the only substantial door in the building.

The other cottage served as the crew's quarters, with one bedroom that had been commandeered by the chief, and a loft fitted out with a row of narrow beds and footlockers. The sink, stove, and long kitchen table functioned as the station's mess hall.

"We've got six men out here," the chief explained as they walked through the deep, wet grass. "Myself, two radio ratings, and three able bodies who stand guard watches."

"Only three guards? Is that enough?"

"I think so, commander. For show, mostly. The locals aren't fond of us, but they mind their business for the most part. Shiela keeps 'em in line."

"Shiela?"

"Miss McDevitt. Our coding clerk. Irish, originally, and raised right around here. We've had a few spats with the neighbors, but she's been able to smooth them over."

"Isn't she on duty?" Day asked.

"Oh, she's always on duty, commander. Only coding clerk we have. But she can't live out here, you know. A woman with six men? That would really give us trouble with the parish priests. She keeps a place near Schull and comes out every morning with the army patrol car. She has a bicycle at the gate."

Day looked up at the sun, a blotch of light in the heavy sky. It was already at its mid-morning height.

"Every morning?"

"She was doing some shopping today, sir. We wanted a nice table in the mess. In honor of your arrival."

They walked to the edge of the station, where the grass ended abruptly and a sheer wall of stone dropped down into the crashing sea. They were standing at the western tip of Europe, leaning into cold winds that had blown over 3,000 miles of ocean, looking at the sea lane that carried the blood England needed to stay alive. The radio tower was essential to keep that blood flowing. Yet all Day had to keep it in operation were a few seamen and a coding clerk who seemed to double as a housekeeper.

Day pointed out to the flat water, just beyond the rollers that pushed inland and crashed against the cliff. "A single U-boat could surface right there," he told his chief radioman, "and blow this place away in less than three minutes."

Gore looked where he was pointing and nodded. "I suppose it could," he agreed. "But why would they waste a shell on this godforsaken place? They probably don't even know we're here."

Day started back toward the communications office, the chief scurrying to keep up with him. He was halfway there when he stopped abruptly.

"Chief, can I ask you a personal question?"

"Certainly, commander."

"What in hell did you do to get yourself stationed out here? Put a ship up on the beach?"

Gore laughed. "Just let myself get old, I suppose. The spit-and-polish types in Queenstown don't have much use for an old salt six months from puttin' in his papers. But I was thinkin', here you are, a strapping young officer and a full commander, at that. I was trying to get up the courage to ask you the same question. What was it that you done to get put out to pasture?"

Day nodded. "A fair question, chief. I guess I broke one of the rules."

They turned the corner of the cottage, and Day saw a woman on a bicycle riding up the path from the guard gate. "Looks like our coding clerk is back from her shopping," he said to Gore.

"I wouldn't go jumpin' to conclusions, Commander Day," the chief responded. "She gets her job done. We couldn't make do without her."

Shiela McDevitt pedaled closer, working hard to move the bicycle, with its baskets full of packages, into the face of the wind. She wore a wool hat and a heavy knitted sweater over a long skirt that she had hitched up over her knees. She was breathing hard when she rolled up to Day and his chief and stepped down off the seat.

"A devil of a wind," she said. She pulled off the knit hat and let long red hair fall down around a fair, Celtic face with striking green eyes. "You must be Commander Day."

"Our new area commanding officer," Chief Gore added unnecessarily.

"Well, I hope you like fish, commander," she said, gesturing to the packages in the handlebar basket, "because there isn't a piece of beef in any store in Schull. And the turnips aren't what they should be."

"You shouldn't have troubled yourself," Day smiled. "Fish will be perfect."

"We'll get it started right away," the chief offered, reaching for the package.

"In the meantime," Day asked Shiela, "I wonder if we could take a look at your coding operation.

Shiela took off the heavy sweater, revealing a long-sleeved white blouse tied at the collar with a green bow. She was an athletic-looking woman in her late twenties, slim and yet strong, with square shoulders and strong hands that somehow seemed comfortable beneath the frilled cuffs. Day guessed that she was much more at home in a working environment than she would be in a drawing room. She had a businesslike appearance, which she confirmed by asking Day to produce his security authorization before she unlocked the door and admitted him to the coding room.

Inside, the room was bare except for a rolltop desk against one wall and a heavy iron safe against another. There were iron bars fixed across the only window, which looked out onto the ocean.

Messages, Shiela explained, were delivered in plain language from Queenstown over an Admiralty-operated telephone line. The duty radioman copied them and slipped them under the door. Shiela used the code books, kept in the locked safe, to translate the messages into the day's cipher, and then gave the coded copies to the radioman for transmission. She collected the coded copies and destroyed them, then gave the chief the plain language copies for filing. The coded version and the English version were never together in order to safeguard the integrity of the code.

Incoming messages were handled in the same way. The radioman copied a coded transmission slipped it into the code room. Shiela translated it into plain language and destroyed the coded copy. Then the message was telephoned to Queenstown.

But despite Shiela's best efforts, Day saw immediately, the system was anything but secure. Anyone tapping the phone line would have access to the plain language text, which defeated the entire reason for coding the message. Worse, anyone with a radio could copy the coded version from the air. Put the plain text together with the coded text and it would be relatively easy to compromise the cipher.

"Why use a telephone line," he asked. "Couldn't the traffic be handled by a messenger?"

"I saw your car by the gate," Shiela answered, "so I suppose you've driven the roads. You could spend a whole day getting here from Queenstown. Longer, when it's raining."

"Or, code the message in Queenstown," he speculated, "and telegraph it here in its coded version."

She shook her head. "If the transmission were garbled, we'd have no way of checking its accuracy."

Day nodded grimly. "Then we have to be damn sure of that telephone line."

"Do you think we're being compromised?" she asked.

"No. Just worrying, I suppose. If German submarines were reading our traffic, then we'd be leading them right to their targets. We have to be sure there are no possibilities of leaks."

Shiela locked the coding room behind them. Day helped her on with her sweater, took his own coat, and they started across the field to the quarters cottage, where the new commanding officer's welcoming dinner was waiting."

"Chief Gore tells me you know this country," Day said as they struggled with the wind.

"I lived here as a child. Until I was twelve. Then the family picked up and moved to Liverpool, looking for work. When I was sixteen, I got a job in a Liverpool naval office. After a few years, the Admiralty trusted me enough to teach me how to work with their codes. I suppose it's because I'm Irish that they assigned me here. I've been away for seventeen years, but nothing has changed. Nothing ever seems to change in Ireland."

"Maybe I can borrow you for a few hours each day," he asked. "I'd like to get to know the area. Particularly the coastline."

"You're the commanding officer," Shiela said.

"I also need to find quarters. A small house, or even a few rooms. Maybe you can plead my case with some of your neighbors."

"A house would probably be better," she thought aloud. "I think we might have problems putting you up as a boarder, unless we can get you into one of the landlord's homes. The locals will be happy to take your money. But I don't think that an Irishman would feel right about sharing his table with an English officer. We're the enemy, you know. The Germans are their liberators."

He was wearing a civilian suit and a peaked cap when he met Shiela early the next morning at the radio station. They began along the time-worn road that followed every curve of the coastline and headed into the sun that was just breaking on the eastern horizon.

"What do you want to see first?" she asked, as soon as Crookhaven had disappeared behind them.

"The fishing harbors," he said. "I'm hoping to put a fleet together that can give us some help with the German submarines." She glanced across at him suspiciously, then smiled, wondering if he had any idea what he would find.

It was a motley group of battered boats, tied to a sinking pier. Wooden dories with pegs for oarlocks, piled with fishing nets. Rusted bum boats with single-cylinder steam engines and wood-burning boilers. Ancient gaff riggers, with patches on their canvas and rot in their keels.

The crews were as suspect as their vessels. Toothless old men wearing rubber boots over colorless suits. Wide-eyed boys with windburned faces under knitted woollen caps. Even women, with men's shirts buttoned over their long dresses and shawls pulled up over their heads.

They stood on the main street of the village, looking down a grassy slope, over the harbor at Schull. The pier reached out from the end of a street that wandered down from the town. Beyond it was Roaringwater Bay, dotted with barren, rocky islands and Cape Clear set into the distant mist.

"They could do it," he told Shiela, who was standing beside him, holding her sweater closed against the wind.

"Battle submarines?" she asked incredulously. "They can barely survive the sea."

"The don't have to fight the submarines," he answered. "All they have to do is keep them from surfacing."

Day and Shiela had spent most of the day touring the coastal towns, a string of weatherbeaten villages that stretched along the southern cliffs from Glandore all the way to the western tip of Mizen Head. It was a broken shoreline, with hundreds of inlets cut by the sea into its rocky walls, each a safe haven for the tiny boats that hopscotched along shore, trafficking in poverty. "There's some fishing," Shiela had explained. "And some of them carry small cargoes down from Cork. Then, of course, there's a bit of smuggling. But it's all coastal traffic. None of these boats would ever venture out into the ocean."

But Day hadn't been thinking of long voyages. He had been thinking of the coastal waters that ships inbound from America passed through on their way to Coningbeg Light and Saint George's Channel. Waters that the German submarines could turn into a killing ground if they were able to operate freely.

"The submarines can stay under for only a few hours at a time," he said, sharing the plan that he had been formulating. "They have to come up for air and to recharge their batteries. If we could keep a fleet of small boats stationed out there, the submarines couldn't operate in the area."

Shiela pointed down to a twenty-foot sloop that was struggling into the harbor, its rails nearly in the water. "A submarine would be afraid to surface next to that?"

Day nodded. "Yes, if it had a machine gun aboard." She looked at him skeptically.

"A submarine is helpless when it first breaks the surface. It's completely unarmed until its crew can get out on deck and man the guns. Any one of these boats, with a single machine gun, could get the crewmen before they ever cleared the hatches."

Shiela shuddered at the image of the human shooting gallery that Day was describing.

"And if the boat had a radio, or even a signal flare, then the submarine would be giving its position away. In a couple of minutes, there would be other little boats, all firing away. No U-boat commander would ever come up in the middle of a fishing fleet. And if he can't surface out there, then he can't operate out there."

"But they don't have guns," she said, dismissing the idea.

"I can get the guns," Day said. "And I can get some sailors to man the guns. What I need are the boats, and the people to sail them."

"These people?" she said, looking down at the worn figures who were working on the pier. "Irishmen? You need Irishmen to help the British navy?"

"There are Irishmen fighting in the British army," he reminded her.

"Not from out here," Shiela answered.

"What have you shown me today?" he asked. "Two, maybe three hundred small boats? We need only fifty or sixty of them out there. Just during the daylight hours. Three or four of these towns could supply all the boats we'd need."

"You expect them to give up their livelihoods and just sit out in the sea lanes waiting for submarines?"

"We'd pay them. How much can they earn with one of these boats, even with a bit of smuggling? There are people making a fortune out of this war. Why shouldn't the Irish get a bit of it?"

Shiela smiled and shook her head. "I don't think you'll have much luck. A man who agreed to take money from the English would have a hard time finding a friend in Schull. Or Glandore, or Baltimore. And that's all they have. Friends and families."

They climbed back into the canvas-topped touring car, which had attracted a circle of gawking children. The children followed Day around to the front of the car, watched him turn the crank, and screamed with delight as the engine coughed and finally caught. Shiela pulled her scarf up over her head as Day climbed up behind the wheel, turned the car carefully through the throng of cheering children, and started down the town's single main street.

"Who are the leaders in these towns?" he asked, breaking a silence that had lasted several minutes. She seemed not to understand his question. "The people we need to win over if we're going to recruit the boat owners. Are there mayors? Constables?"

"There are," she said. "But they're only figureheads. The English run Ireland. You'd probably have to talk to the parish priests. Very little happens that the priests don't approve of. Depending on the town, there might be a small land owner with a bit of influence. Or the school-teacher. It might even be the pub owner. But I can't see any of them getting excited over an opportunity to help the Royal Navy."

"Still," he thought aloud, "if we could just recruit one town, and the people were making some money. The other towns might want their fair share, too."

Shiela turned to him sympathetically. "I don't think you know what you're up against. The Fenians would come down hard on anyone who helped you. They think of themselves as a secret army, and they're hoping that the Germans will give them the guns they need to drive the English out of Ireland."

He nodded. "I don't expect to win over the radicals. But what about the rest of the people? I can't believe they'd rather be working for the kaiser."

"I was born here," she answered. "But I became English, and now I come back working for the English. I have cousins in Schull who won't even speak to me."

"Insanity," he said.

They were on the main east–west road that ran along the coast, from Skibbereen to Crookhaven. It was just gravel and dirt, but it was graded with only occasional ruts and potholes. "Could we go right, here?" Shiela asked as they reached a small intersection. "There's something I want you to see."

Day hesitated. "Do you have time? I've kept you from your work all day."

"It's important," she answered. "It won't take long."

He turned inland, away from the coast, and bounced over the ruts at the intersection. They were driving through treeless country, large mounds of stone, with occasional green pastures growing between the rocks. There was a desolation to the landscape—starkly beautiful and yet sadly barren.

Day tried the question he had been weighing. "Whose side do you think they should be on?"

Shiela answered immediately. "Ours. But it's easy for me. I was Irish for half of my life and English for the other. To me they're both the same. The hatreds seem stupid. But in Ireland, hatred is a disease. The men give it to their women and then the women pass it on to the babies. You said it was 'insanity.' And you're right, commander. But you have to understand what drove them insane."

She leaned forward toward the windscreen as they came to a bend in the road. "You can stop anywhere along here."

"Here?" He looked around as he braked the car at the edge of the grade. "There's nothing here."

Shiela got out and came around the car. "It's just a short walk," she said, and she started up a slope into a grassy field. Day caught up with her, his eyes scanning the rough open country ahead. "Where are we going?" he asked.

"A cemetery. It's right ahead of us."

He was bewildered. There was no trace of a wall or a gate. Not a single monument, or even a headstone that he could see. And then, half buried in the grass just ahead, he spotted a small, stone marker leaning awkwardly to one side.

As she walked, Shiela pointed at the marker, which bore no inscription. Day hesitated at the stone, then ran a few steps to catch up. There was another headstone, this one broken. And then another behind that. Shiela stopped and turned to her right, sweeping her hand at the field they had been walking in. Now Day could make out uneven rows of stones, stretching out into the distance, their tops hardly visible over the swaying grass.

"The children's cemetery," she told him.

"Children? Only children?"

"Three hundred of them," she answered. "Most of them never had headstones. And some of the stones that were here have fallen. They were buried 65 years ago. During the famine."

He was angered by the sight. "Why in God's name doesn't someone take care of this place?"

"Who?" she challenged.

"Their families."

"They have no families. When they died, no one even knew their names. See. The stones have no names. Just a year. Eighteen fifty-one."

"They all died in the same year?"

"At the worst of the famine. There was no food, so the families gave whatever they could scratch from the ground to their children. The parents ate grass. And when they died, there were hundreds of orphaned children roaming the countryside. The English governor, who visited here once or twice a year, built a workhouse so that the children could earn their keep. But, of course, there was no work, so the place turned into a soup kitchen. The governor left one of his relatives in charge. A cousin from London, if I remember."

He looked at the tiny stones, thinking of frail children who had nothing to eat. "We didn't feed them?" he asked, looking at the evidence of the answer he knew he would hear.

"Parliament tried," Shiela said, her eyes looking straight ahead to the edges of the cemetery. "They allocated money and gave it to the cousin. But he put it in his pocket and never left London. The children died in the fields around the workhouse, trying to graze like cattle."

"Sweet Jesus." He walked to one of the markers, dropped to one knee, and brushed the dirt from the stone. He could see the faded outline of "1851." "Who buried them?" he asked.

"The governor. He found the bodies on his visit and brought in workers from Cork to bury them. Then he had the workhouse razed. You can't find a trace of it. It was as if he wanted to forget that the place had ever existed. But he couldn't hide the facts. After all, there were witnesses." She gestured to the headstones. "Three hundred of them."

Day climbed slowly back to his feet. "What happened to the cousin?"

"I understand he made quite a success in finance. They tell me he was knighted."

He pushed his hands into his pocket, then walked slowly down a row of stones. He found one fallen and bent to straighten it. When he reached the end of the row, he turned and walked across to the next row. The wind suddenly gusted and blew the cap off his head, sending his dark hair flying. He bent, picked it up, and twisted it in his hands as he walked. Finally, he stopped and looked across the small cemetery at Shiela.

"I should be getting back," she told him.

Day nodded. He went to her, took her hand, and led her back to the car.

They drove in silence, facing into the clouds that were forming in the east. When they reached the main road, Day asked whether he should take her home. "It's late. You'll go all the way out to Crookhaven, and then have to come all the way back."

"There may be messages waiting," she said. "They have to be coded before the radiomen can send them. I should at least check."

"Then I'll wait until you finish."

They left the car at the gate, where the seaman on watch exchanged salutes with the commander. Then they walked up to the radio cottage.

"It has to be difficult for you," he said, telling her what had been on his mind for the entire journey from the cemetery, "working for the English in a place where Irish children are buried."

"I have a job to do," Shiela answered.

"So do I," Day said. "And I have to have those boats. I don't know of anyone else I can turn to for help."

Shiela nodded. "We're fighting a war, commander. I'll do everything I can. I just wanted you to know what you're up against."

THE IRISH COAST

LIEUTENANT Walter Schwieger raised his binoculars and scanned the crystal night air, tracing a horizon illuminated into a silver line by the thousands of glowing stars. He swept the glasses from fifteen degrees north of his bow to fifteen degrees south, then turned his face back slowly to the west. Still no sign of the British steamer *Hampton*, due from Philadelphia with a cargo of smokeless powder and electrical apparatus. But he had to be patient. There was no way the ship could escape him with so much light in the sky.

He stamped his boots against the icy steel deck plate, and pounded his gloved hands together. The temperature was below zero, tolerable only because the wind had dropped and there was little spray off the flat sea. Schwieger turned in the conning tower and aimed the binoculars back over his own thin wake to the east. There was still no sign of the cruiser *Juno*, which he had plotted to be circling thirty miles behind him, awaiting its rendezvous with *Hampton*, near Fastnet Light. If his information was correct, it was a rendezvous that would never be kept.

He had been vectored to his position southwest of Mizen Head, by Flotilla Commander Bauer. An Irish agent named Leprechaun had relayed orders intended for *Juno*, assigning the cruiser to meet *Hampton* ten miles south of Fastnet Light. Bauer had ordered U-20 to take up station thirty miles farther west, along a course line from Cape May, New Jersey, to Fastnet. To meet up with her escort, *Hampton* would have to steam across U-20.

Thirty miles out into the open sea was a long way off the coastline for Bauer's boats to operate, pushing the limits for any of the older, smaller submarines with their critically limited range. But U-20 was the second of a new class, over 200 feet in length, with the newer, more powerful diesel engines and an extra thousand miles of cruising radius. And Schwieger would need every bit of 30-mile margin. When he challenged *Hampton*, it would take her captain possibly 10 minutes to bring her to a complete stop—more than enough time for her to get off a radio message to *Juno*. He would lose another 15 minutes allowing her crew to take to the lifeboats. Then, how long to sink her? Only 3 or 4 minutes to pound the necessary rounds into her water line. But perhaps 15 more minutes to assure that she was finished. In that time, *Juno* could close to within 15 miles, only minutes away from the range of her main battery. Schwieger didn't want to be waiting on the surface when 9-inch shells began crashing down around him.

He ran his hand over his face, scattering the ice crystals that his breath had formed in his beard. Then he turned back to the west and once again began the slow scan with his binoculars across his bow.

He saw her, so clearly that he wondered how he could have missed her on his last search. *Hampton* seemed to have just jumped up from the horizon, a black hull with the silhouettes of her funnel and masts etched clearly in the light sky. He bent down toward the open hatch, a few inches behind his heels. "Haupert," he called to his executive officer in the control room below. "She's here."

He turned the glasses back to *Hampton* as Lieutenant Willi Haupert climbed up to the top of the tower. "Angle on the bow, ten degrees," Schwieger said. Haupert was cranking the hand-held rangefinder. "Still too far," he said, which meant that *Hampton* was still outside the range of the instrument.

"Let's take her down," Schwieger decided. "With the seas this flat, we can line her up through the periscope." He dropped through the hatch, sliding down the ladder rails inside the tower. Haupert came behind him, pausing to spin the locking wheel that secured the hatch.

"Dive the boat," Haupert ordered. The clatter of the diesel engines stopped, replaced almost immediately by the hum of the electric motors. There was a gurgling sound as sea water was let into the ballast tanks. Water closed over U-20's deck, smashing against the tower. And then, in an instant, everything was silent.

Schwieger remembered the bow angle. "Come to two eight zero," he told the helmsman, turning his boat ten degrees to the north. He guessed that his target was more than five miles away and calculated that he should wait at least fifteen minutes before raising the scope. "Weiser," he said to his gunnery officer, "break out ammunition for the deck gun."

"You want the boarding party ready?" Haupert asked.

Schwieger shook his head. "She's British. We just tell the crew to get off and then sink the son of a bitch. I don't want to get any closer to her than a hundred yards."

They waited in silence, listening even though the steamship was still too far away to hear. Schwieger used the time to wrap his bare hands around a steaming mug of tea and coax circulation back into his fingers.

"I hope they have warm coats," Haupert commented idly.

"They'll probably be aboard *Juno* in an hour, telling tales of yet another German atrocity," the commanding officer said.

He checked his watch, then pointed to the periscope. He bent over to catch it as it came up from its tube. As soon as it broke the surface, he saw *Hampton* framed against the sky, no more than two miles away. "Dead on the bow," he announced. Then he juggled the rangefinder to bracket the ship from the water line to the top of its mast. "Three thousand yards."

He stepped back from the scope as it lowered. "Come left to one eight zero." The helmsman acknowledged the order as he spun the wheel. He would run 5 minutes to the south of *Hampton*'s course line and then come about. That would bring the freighter about 500 yards across his bow. Schwieger watched the time tick past on the chronometer. "Full left rudder. Come about to north." He waited patiently as the compass rose spun in its fluid. When it settled at north, he dropped down on his knees and signaled Haupert to raise the scope.

Hampton was still running in a straight line, carving a smooth white wake. He could picture the lookout on the bow aiming a pair of binoculars in his direction. He pushed the scope down and climbed back to his feet.

"Right on schedule," he said to Haupert. "We'll hear her any moment."

"This is almost too easy," Haupert said, allowing himself a broad smile.

"We've earned an easy one," Schwieger answered.

They heard the propeller, a faint throbbing, almost like water pouring through the narrow neck of a bottle.

"Standby for surface attack," Haupert shouted down into the hull. Two seamen charged up the ladder and into the conning tower, one carrying a machine gun, the other a battery-powered carbon lamp. They took positions directly under the hatch. Then they listened to the propeller noise, which seemed to be rising in pitch.

"One last check for the cruiser," Schwieger said. Haupert reached for the periscope cable. "Bring it up slowly. I don't want to stick it into the face of the freighter."

He raised the periscope gently, stopping it as soon as it broke the surface. Then he spun it quickly to the east, and scanned the horizon in the direction where *Juno* was waiting. There was no sign of the warship.

He spun it around to the north, and then panned westward until he picked up *Hampton*. She was about 700 yards away, approaching off his port bow.

He pushed the scope down and exchanged a glance with Haupert to be sure that everything was ready.

"Surface!"

There was a whistle as valves were opened to release compressed air into the ballast tanks. The lightened boat began to rise immediately, and then there was a crashing sound as the conning tower broke through the surface. He waited until the gunner had thrown open the hatch cover.

"Surface running! All ahead one-third!"

The diesels chugged for an instant, then roared to life. Schwieger scampered up the ladder with Haupert at his heels. The boat was already moving forward when he reached the bridge.

Hampton was still to port, steaming directly across his bow, close enough so that he could see shapes moving in the dimly lighted wheelhouse. He waited a few moments until the freighter's bow reached a point dead ahead. "Right standard rudder," he ordered, bringing U-20 to a parallel course.

He looked aft. His gun crew was already on deck, releasing the locking stops and swinging the gun out toward the target. The first round of ammunition was being passed up toward the breech. Next to him, the gunner had set the machine gun into the portside pedestal. Schwieger heard the bolt close, stripping the first round from the belt into the chamber.

A searchlight switched on aboard *Hampton*. Its beam swung abruptly, first into black water, and then down the gray hull of the U-boat. Schwieger ordered his own light turned on and aimed directly at *Hampton*'s bridge. He lifted his megaphone.

"Heave to! This is the German submarine U-20. I order you to heave to immediately."

The beam of *Hampton*'s light found the submarine's conning tower and lifted until it hit Schwieger in the eyes.

"Turn off that light," he ordered.

The beam painted the tower, then dropped down to illuminate the gunners, who raised their hands to shield their eyes.

"Turn off that light," Schwieger screamed.

The glowing circle danced on the gunners, then swung back up to the conning tower.

"Get the light," Schwieger ordered the machine gunner.

The chatter of the gun exploded through the still night. Glowing tracers shot across to *Hampton*, hitting high on the wheelhouse. Then they dropped down to the hot white carbon lamp. There was a puff of flame, and then the light went black.

Now it was the U-20's light that searched the bridge of the *Hampton.* "Heave to!" Schwieger ordered again. He could see that the freighter was pulling ahead of him. "All ahead full!" he shouted down through the open hatch.

"She has a deck gun!" The frightened scream came from Weiser, who was stationed with the gun crew. "On the fantail. She has a deck gun."

The U-20's light snapped to the freighter's transom. Seamen had knocked down the two oval life rafts that were stored on edge. Behind them, other seamen were cranking a five-inch deck gun, swinging its muzzle toward the German boat. At the same instant, Weiser's crew was bringing the U-20's gun to bear.

"Fire!" Schwieger ordered. Then, into the hatch, "Hard right rudder!" He was turning his boat to present the smallest possible target to the freighter.

The U-20's gun flashed, its crack setting the small hull ringing with vibration. There was no explosion aboard *Hampton.* The shell had sailed over the steamer's stern.

The breech snapped down, tossing the spent casing out onto the deck. Frantic hands pushed another shell into place, and the breech snapped closed. An endless second passed. Then the gun cracked again, followed instantly by a flash against *Hampton*'s hull. The shot had been well below its mark. *Hampton*'s deck gun was now aimed over Schwieger's head, its barrel slowly depressing toward his face.

The machine gunner swung the muzzle of the gun aft. His first blast sent tracers ricocheting off the steamer's after superstructure. Slowly, he depressed his fire toward *Hampton*'s gun crew.

"Hard left rudder!" Schwieger ordered. At this range, even the narrow width of the submarine's hull was an easy target. He had to maneuver out of *Hampton*'s sights.

The steamer's gun roared, a sound twice as deafening as the crack of the U-20's deck weapon. There was a rush of air like the sound of a passing freight train. The sea just beyond the submarine's hull leaped up into a frothy geyser. The round had passed just inches over U-20's deck.

"Christ," Haupert cursed, just as the submarine's gun fired again. *Hampton*'s afterdeck house flashed into flame, tossing shards of steel into the air.

"She's turning on us," the machine gunner screamed.

Schwieger's head snapped to the bow of the freighter. The rising bow wake meant she was adding speed. And the prow was quickly swinging toward him.

"She's going to ram us," Haupert gasped.

Schwieger screamed down at his gun crew. "Clear the deck." He pulled the machine gunner away from his weapon and pushed him and the searchlight operator toward the hatch. "Hard right rudder," he yelled into the opening. Then, "Dive! Emergency dive!"

The two seamen had disappeared and Haupert was jumping into the hole when *Hampton*'s deck gun roared again. The sea next to the conning tower exploded, and the boat lurched with a metallic ringing.

"Dive!" Schwieger screamed again. He saw the water around his boat break into bubbles as the ballast tanks flooded. Then he dropped through the hatch and pulled it down on top of him.

"We're hit!" The scream came from the control room below.

Schwieger looked down and saw jets of sea water flying across his control room. He pushed Haupert toward the hatch. "Get me a damage report." Haupert disappeared down the ladder rails without ever touching a step.

Schwieger was suddenly aware of the throbbing echoing through his boat. It was *Hampton*'s propeller, no more than fifty yards away and closing rapidly.

The deck beneath his feet was pitching. In an emergency dive, the bowplanes had been turned all the way down, driving the bow down a steep incline. That meant his stern was rising. If the propellers broke water, the boat would lose the little speed it had gathered. The freighter would be on him before he could get under its hull.

He heard a new sound. *Hampton*'s bow was cutting through the sea almost directly over his head. The surge was loud enough to drown out the churning of the propellers. He braced himself against the steep dive and cringed from the roar of the charging steamer.

There was a terrifying howl of metal as *Hampton*'s hull grazed across the conning tower. U-20 lurched suddenly, snapping over onto its right side. The impact fired Schwieger across the tower and smashed him against the steel wall. He dropped like a dead man. Screams echoed through the hull. The entire crew had been tossed from their stations and had fallen against the bulkheads. And still there was the deafening pound of the propeller, cutting through the water inches above the overturned hull. Schwieger listened for the slice of the guillotine and the death rattle of water rushing into his boat. The sound peaked, and then its pitch suddenly lowered like the howl of a passing train whistle.

Schwieger opened his eyes to find his world totally disoriented. He was lying on one of the walls of the tower, looking up, not at the overhead, but at the other wall. The top of the tower was to one side. The access ladder to the overhead hatch ran from side to side instead of vertically. He felt himself rolling along the wall toward the forward bulkhead, which was dropping away from him. U-20 was still diving, even though it was lying on its side. The bowplanes, still in their full down position, were now acting as a rudder, turning the boat to port. And the rudder, locked in a hard right turn, was acting as a diving plane, pushing the stern up and increasing the angle of dive.

"Amidships," he screamed, crawling up the inclined deck until he could see down through the hatch. "Rudder amidships." But the wheel, which now seemed to be mounted on the side bulkhead, was unmanned. Streams of water were still firing into the control room. And U-20, driven by the now audible hum of its electric motors, was spiraling into a deadly dive.

Schwieger pushed his legs through the hatch opening and scrambled along the ladder. He reached down, grabbed the helm, and began cranking the wheel to the left. A seaman was fighting his way up the nearly vertical deck toward the bowplane control. "Neutral," Schwieger yelled to him. "Neutralize the bow." He clung to the ladder until the man had reached the control wheel and was able to turn it.

Haupert had dragged himself forward to the ballast control levers. "Lighten the starboard tank," the commanding officer ordered. "Carefully. Just a bit." Haupert, his hand already on the lever, tapped it to a slightly open position. Compressed air began seeping into the starboard ballast tank, forcing sea water out. Instantly, the boat began rolling to the left, bringing itself to an upright attitude.

"Bowplanes up ten degrees," Schwieger ordered the seaman. Then he watched Haupert as his executive juggled the ballast levers to stabilize the role. U-20 leveled, bringing the deck below and swinging the ladder back to vertical. The bow was slowly lifting out of its dive. But as the control room returned to normal, Schwieger could see that the water washing across its floor was almost knee deep. Streams of water were still pouring in through a ruptured seam high on the port bulkhead. He had to get the boat back up to the surface to relieve the pressure on the hull. And then, there was a new danger. As U-20 righted itself, water began to pour down through the conning tower hatch. There was another leak above, somewhere in the tower.

The control room crewmen were back at their posts. A seaman had relieved Haupert at the ballast controls, and the helmsman, his face bloodied from a gash across his brow, was back at the wheel. Schwieger checked the depth gauge. The boat had dived 160 feet, nearly to its safety limits. It was rising slowly, but its climb was limited by the weight of the water it had already taken aboard. With each passing second, its ability to get back to the surface was diminished.

"Take us up to thirty feet," he told Haupert. "Try to hold us there." He couldn't break the surface until he was sure of his distance from *Hampton*. If he came up under the muzzle of its deck gun, he wouldn't be up for long. Schwieger scrambled up the ladder to get to the periscope.

There was an inch of water on the conning tower deck, fed by a jet of water firing down from the periscope packing. He closed the hatch behind him to keep the water from falling into the hull below. He pulled down on the counterweight cable. The periscope started to slide upward, then suddenly stopped. Schwieger saw the reason immediately. The scope had been bent at the point where it passed through the packing and out through the top of the tower. It was useless.

He cursed and turned toward the hatch to go back down into the control room. It was then that he heard the distant throbbing of a propeller. He listened for a second and realized that it was growing louder. *Hampton* had turned back to the west. She was running back over her track in hopes of finishing off the submarine she knew she had crippled.

Schwieger ripped open the hatch. "Level," he ordered as he jumped on the ladder, pausing only to close the hatch above his head.

The pounding of *Hampton's* propeller was echoing through the control room. "She's coming back for us," Haupert said. Schwieger nodded. "We're going to get that son of a bitch," he told his crew. Then he ordered his helmsman, "Come left to zero nine zero." Haupert's eyes widened. Schwieger was turning U-20 toward *Hampton*, and then toward the cruiser *Juno*, which was probably charging in their direction at flank speed.

Haupert had opened the watertight hatch to the forward torpedo room and ordered the torpedo crew into the control room to help shore up the leaking bulkhead. They had positioned mattresses over the bent hull plate and were using the jacks from the torpedo trolleys to pressure them against the leak.

"We need the engineers," one of the torpedo men told Schwieger.

The commanding officer shook his head. He couldn't open the after watertight door without spilling sea water into the engine areas. If the water reached the storage batteries, the boat might fill with acid gas.

The propellers pounded directly overhead, but Schwieger ignored them. He was still too far below *Hampton's* keel to be in any danger, and he had more pressing matters to deal with.

"Steady on zero nine zero," the helmsmen called.

"All ahead full," Schwieger ordered. "Take her up to twenty feet."

He watched the depth gauge as the bow of the boat struggled upward. Water that had spilled into the forward torpedo room poured back through the hatch into the control room. As the bow lightened, it began to swing into a climb. The depth gauge began to move.

"Lighten her a bit," he said. More compressed air squeezed into the ballast tanks. The rate of climb increased.

"We're going to make it," Haupert said, a smile of relief playing across his lips. "We should get out of here, surface, and pump her out."

"Not while that son of a bitch is still afloat," Schwieger whispered. Haupert's eyes narrowed. U-20 was crippled and, without its periscope, blinded. It had lost its fighting capability. Even the most daring commanders, like Rosenberg and Weddigen, would have accepted the situation and turned tail. Schwieger was noted for his caution. It was frightening that he was even considering a reckless attack.

"She'll make one more pass looking for us," Schwieger said, his voice soft as if he were talking only to himself. "Then she'll get back on course and head for Fastnet. And that's when we'll take her."

"How will you aim?" Haupert asked cautiously. He would never take issue with his commanding officer. Even more than surface ship commanders, U-boat officers were unquestioned gods in their tiny kingdoms. But he was hoping to point out the foolishness of attacking and perhaps lead Schwieger back to sanity.

"From the surface," Schwieger answered factually.

"You're going to *surface?*" Haupert asked. Despite his best effort, his tone of disbelief was obvious to everyone in the control room. Schwieger's eyes instantly focused and darted in his direction. Haupert turned away. He had gone too far.

"Thirty feet," a seaman intoned. "Leveling at twenty feet."

Schwieger nodded. He listened carefully. There was no sound from *Hampton's* propellers. He began to trace his plan with his fingertip on the surface of the maneuvering board.

He was running eastward at about five knots, the best he could do under water with the electric motors. It was about five minutes since *Hampton* had passed over him, running westward at its best speed, probably about twelve knots. *Hampton's* captain, Schwieger figured, would have stayed on his westward course for another minute or so, then turned in a wide circle, either to the north or south, and recrossed the point where he had seen the submarine dive. He'd run another minute or so, then give up the hunt and turn back to his original easterly course. With his finger, Schwieger traced the large S of the maneuver that the freighter would most likely take.

In the intervening time, he would have moved perhaps fifteen hundred yards down *Hampton's* course. If he turned back toward her, he could surface dead ahead of her as she ran to the east. *Hampton's* captain would see him as soon as the conning tower broke the surface. And then what would he do?

He had two choices. He could keep coming, hoping that his bow presented too difficult a target and that he would be able to ram the submarine. Or he could turn away, opening up the distance and bringing his deck gun to bear.

"He'll turn," Schwieger said aloud. "The bastard will turn."

He checked the chronometer. Eight minutes since *Hampton* had thundered past above his head. If he was right, she would have completed her wide arc and would be charging back toward her search area. Still plenty of time.

He looked out to the edge of the maneuvering board. *Juno* would be coming from the east at her best speed. When had he first challenged *Hampton*? Perhaps twenty minutes ago. Twenty minutes would have brought *Juno* no more than seven or eight miles closer. She wouldn't have yet reached the edge of his maneuvering plot. He still had all the room he needed.

"Steady at twenty feet," the seaman said.

"Very well," Schwieger answered. And then to the helmsman, "Steady as she goes."

Haupert stepped away from a voice tube. "The gun crew is ready," he reported.

"Very well," Schwieger acknowledged. But he wouldn't need his deck gun. When he came up, only the tower would break the surface. He would leave his decks awash. And only he would go topside. This was a personal matter between him and *Hampton's* captain. The bastard had broken the rules, and now Schwieger was going to invent a few rules of his own.

He's running through the search area, Schwieger thought. He could envision the steamer's crew leaning out over the lifelines, searching for an oil stain or floating debris to confirm their kill. Perhaps they were hoping to see some of U-20's crew struggling in the water. Would they take them aboard? Would they lower the lifeboat that he had been prepared to afford to *Hampton's* crew? He doubted it. They were the ones who had turned the gentleman's game into cold-blooded murder. And he would make them pay the price for their crime.

"Come right to two seven zero," he ordered. "Prepare to surface." Silently, the control room crewmen eyed one another.

"Haupert! Level her out as soon as the tower is up. I want the decks awash. Open the outer doors and get on the firing board. I want to be ready to fire torpedoes."

"Aye, aye," Haupert answered softly. Schwieger climbed the ladder and opened the hatch into the tower. He ignored the sea water that poured in on top of him and closed the hatch behind him. Then he moved up the next ladder and took his position beneath the hatch to the outside deck.

He felt the tower break the surface and heard the sea suddenly crashing against the outside of the forward bulkhead. He popped the hatch and rushed up into the cold night air.

The tower had buckled under the impact of the collision. The periscope fixtures had been cut away, and the life rails were cut and twisted into a knot. Schwieger had to squeeze himself through a tangle of steel to find a foothold. He looked out and saw *Hampton*, no more 500 yards away, headed just a few points to the south of his own position, giving him a very small angle on the port bow.

"Surprise, you bastard," he whispered. "Now make up your mind. What are you going to do?"

Hampton did nothing. The steamer continued in a straight line, aimed across U-20's port bow. Her crewmen had already survived their terrifying encounter with a submarine. Now they were unconcerned, steaming toward the armed escort ship, which was only an hour away.

"All ahead full," Schwieger called down through the voice tube. He heard the immediate response from the growling diesel engines. Salt spray kicked up from the conning tower. The boat accelerated towards its target.

He was only six feet above the sea, standing atop a small structure that was nearly awash, leaning into the breeze created by his own speed. "Look at me, you son of a bitch," he shouted. "I'm coming for you. Look at me!"

He heard *Hampton*'s emergency whistle sound across the water. Then he saw a white spray kick up from the steamer's bow. *Hampton* began turning to starboard, trying to bring its deck gun around to where it would have a clear line of fire.

"Left ten degrees rudder," he screamed into the voice tube. "Stand by to fire one and two." His bow began to swing, moving down the side of the freighter until it pointed to the open sea ahead of his target.

"Fire one." He heard the hiss of air and saw the explosion of bubbles at his own bow as the torpedo was blown out of the tube.

"Right ten degrees rudder." The swing of the boat was immediately checked. Its bow began moving back toward the freighter. At the same time, *Hampton* was turning, presenting its port beam. Behind the rubble of its damaged afterdeck house, Schwieger could see the five-inch gun coming into view.

"Fire two," he ordered. Again, air bubbles broke the sea above his submerged bow. He leaned forward, studying the calm water between him and the target. He could see the fine trace bubbles that trailed his first torpedo pointing ahead of the British ship. The second trace was aiming directly at her hull. By swinging his bow he had bracketed his prey. If she broke off her turn and headed on a straight course, she would run into the first torpedo. If she kept her rudder over in a tight turn, then his second shot should find her.

"Dive," he screamed. He was starting down the hatch when he heard the roar of *Hampton's* big deck gun. He jumped into the hole, then hesitated just long enough to watch the sea explode twenty yards off his starboard beam. As he pulled the hatch cover shut, the ocean washed over the top of the tower.

He lifted the next hatch and dropped into the control room. Anxious faces looked up at him.

"Hard right rudder. Take her to fifty feet." He was aiming the boat into a diving turn to get well below the impact of the next five-inch shell that would explode on the surface. Immediately, water began leaking in around the mattresses that had been used to patch the leaks.

They listened in silence. The torpedoes should take only seconds to reach their target. The seconds ticked by like hammer blows on an anvil.

U-20 shuddered. A sharp, cracking noise hit the hull of the boat, followed by a metallic echo. Schwieger winced. The second five-inch round had hit the water directly overhead. *Hampton* was still alive, still attacking its tormentor.

And then there was the muffled sound of a distant explosion. Haupert's face broke into a broad grin. Schwieger responded with the thumbs-up signal. A roar of shouting echoed through the boat. One of the torpedoes had found its mark.

"Come to zero nine zero," Schwieger ordered. "Surface."

One seaman swung the wheel that raised the bowplanes. Another pulled the levers to blow the ballast tanks with the joy of an organist listening to the chords of his instrument. Schwieger nodded to Haupert. "Come topside with me. You'll want to see this."

They rushed up to the deck as soon as the conning tower broke the surface. The horizon to the south was glowing brightly. At its center, *Hampton* was ablaze, spewing jets of white fire like the nozzle of an acetylene torch. Schwieger raised his binoculars and scanned the afterdeck. The five-inch gun was lost in an inferno.

He bent over the open hatch. "Crew up." Hatches burst open forward and aft, the torpedo crew scampering out ahead of the conning tower and the gun crew coming up next to the deck gun. They were delirious at the sight of the stricken enemy.

The torpedo had hit just behind *Hampton's* funnel, either in the boiler room or the engine room. Secondary explosions were wracking the ship.

"Should we get closer?" Haupert asked. They wouldn't leave her burning on the surface. If a target didn't sink immediately, they would finish it off with their deck gun.

"Not this one," Schwieger answered. "She's carrying black powder. We don't want to get too close."

As if on cue, *Hampton* exploded in a blinding flash of light, causing U-20's seamen to cover their eyes. The thunderclap was nearly deafening. When the crew looked back, the steamer had vanished, leaving a scattering of burning debris across the surface.

"Bring her to course zero one zero," Schwieger said softly to Haupert. All ahead standard." Haupert nodded, his eyes still fixed on the spot where *Hampton* had been burning.

"Keep lookouts on deck," the commanding officer ordered as he started down into the hatch. "The English will be looking for us."

WASHINGTON

"Barbaric," President Woodrow Wilson said sadly. "Simply barbaric." He shook his head slowly in despair. "I suppose, in the madness of war, these things are inevitable. But still . . . for civilized people . . ." His glance wandered, from the report that State Department Counselor Robert Lansing had placed on his desk, toward the window that overlooked the White House lawn. "I can only hope that we never become involved."

"Let's be sure that we don't," Secretary of State William Jennings Bryan advised. "It's an English ship sunk by a German ship. The United States has nothing to do with it. I don't see any reason why we should file a formal protest."

Wilson lifted the document that had been delivered by His Majesty's embassy only a few hours earlier. He bent over it closely to focus his glasses.

THE STEAMER HAMPTON WAS TORPEDOED WITHOUT WARNING. NO CHALLENGE WAS GIVEN, NOR WAS THERE ANY ATTEMPT TO INSPECT HER CARGO. CONSTANT CANNON FIRE FROM THE ATTACKING GERMAN SUBMARINE PREVENTED HAMPTON FROM LAUNCHING HER BOATS. NO ASSISTANCE WAS OFFERED TO HER CREWMEN, WHO WERE LEFT HELPLESS IN THE WATER.

"The point, here," said Robert Lansing, who was sitting beside Bryan, "is one of international law. As the secretary advises, there would generally be no reason for our government to become involved in actions between foreign belligerents, no matter how repugnant."

Bryan's heavy eyebrows raised. He was delighted to hear his counselor agree with anything that he said, even though he was sure that he was about to be contradicted.

"But," Lansing continued, "we are involved in the maintenance of international law. And when confronted with such a flagrant violation, we have a duty to protest in the strongest terms. We must remember that the rules of encounter protect American ships, carrying innocent cargoes, from being accidentally attacked by belligerents. We can't simply ignore the fact that Germany has violated those rules. We must assure that the rules are honored."

The president pressed his fingertips together and rested them against his lips. His eyes narrowed in concentration. "Robert does have a point," he said to his secretary of state.

Bryan was in the process of pinching an enormous handkerchief against his nose. He blew furiously, then bunched the handkerchief and began stuffing it into his trouser pocket. "Mr. President, I might agree if this were a unique violation of international law. But the English are holding a dozen of our ships in their ports, claiming that they don't have time to inspect their cargoes. We've had a hundred protests from American shippers whose cargoes have been turned away from German ports without inspection. We haven't filed formal protests against these violations. How can we maintain an appearance of neutrality if we protest only German violations?"

Wilson tipped his head in contemplation.

"But surely," Lansing hurried to add, "there's a significant difference between a few procedural blunders in clearing cargoes, and the wanton murder of an unarmed commercial vessel's crew. Can we really treat them as if they were one and the same?"

Wilson's head tipped to the other side.

"Are you sure it was unarmed, Robert?" the secretary challenged. Wilson's thoughtful eyes widened in shock. "There were two English ships in New York last week that had gun mountings on their fantails," Bryan continued, "and von Papen is telling anyone who will listen that the Admiralty is arming merchant ships. He mentioned some documents that he had left with you."

"Crude forgeries," Lansing fired back. "Who told you that there were gun mountings on English freighters?"

The president knocked gently on his desk. "Gentlemen, please. We'll get nowhere squabbling among ourselves. The issue, I think, is how best to keep our country from becoming involved in this madness."

"Simple," Bryan answered. "Insist on equal access to all ports. We won't allow American ships to call in England, if the English won't allow them to call in Germany. If either country harasses our ships, then we cut that country off. That would put some real muscle behind our words."

Lansing shuddered. The British would never lift their blockade of German ports. Bryan's proposal simply meant a sharp reduction in cargoes delivered to England. He waited while Wilson nodded toward the secretary, then rushed his words as soon as the president turned toward him.

"I think, Mr. President, that it is imperative that whatever we do be solidly grounded in international law. You have spoken eloquently on the rule of law as our only hope for peace . . ."

Wilson remembered that he had, with congratulatory notes from several countries, including England and Germany.

"Perhaps I should prepare a brief on the legal precedents involved," Lansing offered.

Bryan's eyes rolled. The legal precedents, he felt sure, would be as crooked as the people who had written them. Why couldn't this damn fool of a university president understand the true roots of the country he ruled? We were a simple, God-fearing people, who took our strength from the soil. We had no business trying to play the world's peacemaker, or—what was that idiotic phrase of Wilson's?—making the world "safe for democracy." Safe for the bankers and the industrial pirates was more like it! Why not just let the Europeans do what they had been trying to do for the past 2,000 years? Let them blow one another to hell.

"I suppose we should be certain of the legal precedents," Woodrow Wilson decided. "Robert, how long will it take you to pull something together?"

"A few days," the counselor thought. "Certainly no more than a week."

"Good," Wilson said, jumping up from behind his desk. "Then we're all agreed. We'll review Robert's brief. And then we'll decide on the proper and honorable course of action."

Lansing flashed his most enthusiastic smile. William Jennings Bryan reached for his handkerchief.

They sat side by side in stony silence as they were driven back to the State Department.

"You'll let me have a look at that brief before we take it to the president," Bryan said as they climbed out of the car.

"Certainly, Mr. Secretary," Lansing promised.

Then, as he closed his office door behind him, he added in a mumble, "Not that you'll have the damnedest notion of what you're reading."

He dropped into his chair with his hands still thrust into his pockets.

"Neutrality," he hissed to himself. Couldn't the simple fools understand where their true interests lay? We were English, not German. It was the English who looked out from Europe toward America. The Germans couldn't see past their senile continent. We shared the Atlantic with the English. We shared nothing with the Germans.

He swiveled his chair until he was facing a wall of heavily bound law books and let his eyes roam over the jurisdictions and dates on their bindings. He'd write a legal brief for them. In his impeccable prose he would trace the righteousness of the rules of encounter all the way back to Henry VIII. He would prove to Woodrow Wilson that there was no more honorable principle among men than respect for the right of an unarmed merchant ship passing through hostile waters. When he was finished, the president would have no choice but to call the Germans to task.

But first, he had to get up to New York. Someone in Dudley Malone's office was obviously blabbing about the defensive guns that the British had been forced to install on their merchant ships. He'd have to find the man and tell Malone to come down on him hard. It was dangerous to give William Jennings Bryan more information than he could handle.

WILHELMSHAVEN

FRIEDERICH der Grosse, flagship of the Imperial Fleet, rose like a castle in the great northern German naval harbor, her iron sides disdainful of the waves that lapped against them. Topped with colorful flags and banners, she was a floating military pageant, bristling with twelve-inch guns that aimed at every point of the compass. But the heavy links of iron that fell from her bullnose and chained her to the bottom of the harbor belied the impression of a fearsome naval warrior. Like the rest of the great German High Seas Fleet, *Friederich der Grosse* was going nowhere.

Flotilla Commander Bauer hated his visits to the flagship. As he stepped from the launch onto the companion ladder, he heard the ceremonial boatswain's pipe announce his arrival. Why, in the name of God, did his every coming and going require that hundreds of sailors stop work and render a ceremonial salute? He had forbidden the ridiculous piping aboard his beloved submarines. When he reached the quarter-deck, a marching band greeted him with the chords of the national anthem. He counted the musicians as he stood in his full dress uniform, saluting the flag that fluttered from the fantail. There were enough horn players to crew a U-19–class boat.

If it had been up to him, Bauer would never have left the submarine docks at Emden, where his little gray boats came and went without a single note of martial music. The only flag flying was the German national colors on a wooden flagpole at the foot of the pier, and the only uniforms were dull blue work overalls, generally worn under oilskin slickers. Commanding officers didn't need to be piped aboard their boats. Their crews knew them as well as their own fathers. And ranks weren't claimed with fringed shoulderboards and gold brocade sewn to sleeves. They were recognized in piercing eyes and windburned faces, and in brass buttons that had been salt-tarnished to a pitted green.

Wilhelmshaven was the safe anchorage for the kaiser's Imperial Navy, the magnificent row of capital ships Wilhelm had ordered, specifying only that they be bigger than the English ships belonging to his cousin, the king of England. He loved to board them, inspect them, and watch them steam past the imperial yacht, dipping their colors in tribute as they plowed before his iron gaze. He had no intention of losing even one of them in armed combat. Emden was the shabby home of the half-sunk, oil-reeking submarines that the kaiser regarded as an intrusion into his glorious line of battle. He wasn't sure how many he owned, or how many had already been lost at sea.

But this visit to Wilhelmshaven was different. Captain Bauer was on a mission much more important that the routine reports he generally carried to the staff meetings. He practically ran up the ladders that led from the quarterdeck up the side of *Friederich der Grosse*'s superstructure to flag headquarters.

When he entered the conference room, Admiral von Pohl was already holding court, surrounded by his staff of admirals and captains in their full dress uniforms. He took his place at the end of one of the flannel-covered tables, nodding an apology to von Pohl for his tardiness. Not that he was afraid he had missed anything important. The staff would report on progress in training, the state of repairs to the ships, the quantities of supplies stored in the arsenals and warehouses. The intelligence officers would review the activities of the British fleet, still lying in wait northeast of the Orkneys. The line officers would update the dusty plans for the High Seas Fleet breakout into the North Atlantic. Nothing mentioned would sound anything like an act of war. He fidgeted as he listened to the bland recital of facts and figures, impatiently opening and closing the report he had brought with him.

"Captain Bauer," he heard von Pohl's adjutant say. He was on his feet instantly.

"I regret that I must ask the general staff's permission for my command to depart from the international rules of encounter." Nodding heads suddenly snapped to attention all around him. "British merchant-men are now complying with the Admiralty instructions that I reported at our last meeting. They are attacking our submarines instead of obeying their challenges."

There was a gasp, followed by a rumble of murmuring. Admiral von Pohl slapped his hand on the table to restore order. "You know this for a fact?" he demanded.

Bauer held up the report from Lieutenant Schwieger, commanding officer of the U-20. "The British steamer *Hampton* was challenged by one of our boats at twenty-three forty hours, three nights ago. She responded with cannon fire from a five-inch gun mounted on her fantail. Then she turned toward the submarine and rammed her."

Another explosion of conversation was quickly silenced by a blow of von Pohl's hand. He turned to Bauer. "Our boat was lost?"

"Fortunately no, sir. U-20 sustained heavy damage. And I'm pleased to add that she carried out her mission. *Hampton*, and her cargo of war materials, was sunk."

"It may be just a single incident," a supply officer challenged Bauer. Then, turning to von Pohl, "I can't believe that the English would depart from their cruiser rules."

"Perhaps that's all it is," Bauer responded courteously. "Perhaps you, captain, are confident enough to sail aboard one of my boats and risk being present for the second incident."

A howl of protest went up from the officers. Was the submarine flotilla commander implying that they weren't all biting at the bit in their desire for combat?

"U-20's captain reports that he can't submerge without taking on water," Bauer continued. "He's going to have to run the British blockade north of the Shetlands without diving. His main battery is a three-inch deck gun."

"We can't fire without warning," a staff admiral shouted in response. "It would bring the whole civilized world down on us."

"And I can't ask my crews to expose themselves to five-inch cannons and to ramming," Bauer fired back. "It would be dead men that I would be talking to."

Shouts rang from every corner of the room. If Bauer's boats could fire from beneath the surface, then there was little need for the Imperial Fleet's magnificent dreadnaughts. And even less need for its staff of impeccably turned-out officers. Without the rules of encounter, subma-rines were the most lethal weapons afloat. *Friederich der Grosse* was a museum rather than a ship of the line.

Von Pohl's hand exploded on the table once more, followed by a deadly silence. "I think the business of this meeting is concluded," he whispered as he rose from his chair. The entire room snapped to attention. And then, almost as an afterthought, he told Bauer, "May I see you in my quarters, captain."

The fleet commander was undoing the top button of his tunic when Bauer was saluted into his stateroom. "How dare you raise such an issue in front of the entire staff?" he demanded. "How dare you embarrass line officers of the Imperial Navy?"

"My apologies, admiral," Bauer responded immediately, his tone indicating that no apology was intended. "But I have a crew out there pumping sea water to keep their boat afloat, and sometime tonight they will be passing under the twelve-inch guns of English battleships. I think their survival is more important than the feelings of our officers."

Von Pohl settled into a chair and gestured Bauer toward a place on the sofa. "One ramming could mean nothing," he said in a suddenly thoughtful voice. "It could be nothing more than a merchant captain panicking at the site of a submarine. But the deck gun. That's a different story. Only the Admiralty could install deck guns. If they are arming their merchant ships, then they are abandoning the rules of encounter."

"Exactly," Bauer agreed. "Which is why we should no longer be bound by them. It's suicide for a submarine to surface and challenge an armed vessel."

The fleet commander wagged his head from side to side. "I have no problem when it comes to English freighters. The English will scream 'atrocity' whether their ships are armed or not. But what about passenger ships that are carrying American civilians? Or American ships. If the English begin flying American flags, you won't be able to tell their ships from American ships. How do you propose to deal with that?"

"The Americans are no better than the English," Bauer answered. He flipped through the report he had prepared and opened one of the pages for von Pohl. "This is an intercept from our Irish agent. It orders an escort for an American ship inbound from New York. Why would they be escorting it if it weren't carrying contraband?"

Von Pohl looked at the compromised message. "You believe this is genuine?" he asked.

"The agent is generally reliable," Bauer said. "He has direct access to British radio traffic forwarded from Queenstown."

He watched as Admiral von Pohl lifted himself from his chair and walked to a porthole. He waited as the fleet commander looked out, down the line of fully dressed heavy ships.

"My dear Bauer," von Pohl said, "I agree with everything you've said. But these aren't just naval matters we are discussing. You are getting into issues of national policy. The emperor has personally forbidden me to risk attack on an American ship. You want permission to fire without warning. And you may not always be able to determine whether the target is an English ship flying the American flag, which I would love to sink, or an American ship, which I am forbidden to sink. You can see the position that you are putting me in."

Bauer nodded. "I believe it is exactly the position that the Admiralty wants to put you in."

"Do you have any suggestions that I can bring to the emperor?" von Pohl asked. It was the question that Bauer was waiting for.

"I would declare the waters around Ireland and England a war zone," he said. "I would warn all neutrals that, because of English duplicity in flying foreign flags and placing war materials aboard neutral freighters and passenger ships, all ships entering the war zone do so at their own risk."

"Illegal," von Pohl answered immediately.

"Exactly the same warning that the Admiralty has issued to all ships entering the North Sea. They call it a blockade because it is enforced by surface ships that take no risk in challenging freighters. We would have to call it something else, because our submarines are at too great a risk when they issue challenges."

"A war zone," von Pohl considered. "I wonder how President Wilson would respond to a war zone."

"It's fair warning. It might encourage him to keep a better watch on the cargoes that the English are shipping out of his ports. It should certainly encourage him to make damn certain that the English aren't flying the American flag on their own ships."

Von Pohl paced his stateroom, his chin raised in thought, his hands locked behind his back. "For the time being," he concluded, "I will allow underwater attack on merchant ships you can positively identify as being English." He turned abruptly to Bauer. "Can you make positive identifications?"

Bauer thought for a moment. "In some cases, yes. Where we have a message intercept that identifies the ship, there will be no problem. And, of course, if the ship is flying the English flag . . ."

"Good," von Pohl agreed. "Then under those two circumstances, no warning will be given."

Bauer tapped the open page of his report. "And here, where we have an intercept that tells us a neutral ship is carrying contraband?"

"Not yet, my dear Bauer," Admiral von Pohl said. "Not until I have the permission of the emperor."

"War materials will get through," Bauer warned. "Most of the messages we are getting through Ireland concern passenger ships and neutral ships. That's where the English are loading their supplies."

Von Pohl was nodding even as Bauer was speaking. "I know that. And I will make exactly that point to the emperor. Perhaps, together with the idea of a war zone . . . who knows what His Imperial Majesty will decide."

Bauer looked back at the iron wall of *Friederich der Grosse* as his launch pulled away. Who knows what His Imperial Majesty will decide? Certainly not to risk his battleships in combat. And probably not to risk angering the Americans over something as trivial as the lives of a submarine crew. He didn't have much reason to hope. But at least he had won a partial victory. As far as the British merchant fleet was concerned, the rules of encounter had been repealed.

THE IRISH COAST

"MIZEN HEAD Light. Wake the captain."

John Moore, first mate of the British steamship *Ikeria*, turned back to the distant light and timed its alternating flashes once again. The exercise was hardly necessary. It was his fifth crossing from New York, and Mizen Head had become an old friend, visible from far out at sea, long before the dark shape of the Irish shore came into view. "Sharp lookout," he reminded the seaman stationed on the wing of the bridge. "We're on our own this time." He walked back into the wheelhouse to escape the cold wind.

Captain Henry Timmons came up beside him, buttoning a heavy overcoat over a thick sweater. "Right on time," he announced as he watched the light's distinctive cycle of flashes. "Keep bearings on it. We'll have to use a running fix until we pick up Fastnet."

Timmons stepped into the charthouse and looked down at the thin pencil line of his intended course. It was drawn close to the coast, no more than eight miles off the shore. With no warships scheduled to escort him, he wanted to be as close to the beach as possible. Submarines, the Admiralty advisory had announced, were less likely to be operating in full view of land.

He noted the exact time, 0315. It would take him thirteen hours to reach Saint George's Channel, putting him at Coningbeg Light at dusk. Perfect. He needed a little daylight left when he navigated the entrance. And then, his nine-hour run up the channel to the Liverpool bar would be made in darkness, exactly as he wanted it. The channel was a bottleneck for all transatlantic shipping, and a perfect hunting ground for submarines. And, as he had calculated, he would reach the bar at high tide, when there was no problem in crossing. He didn't want to be loitering in open water waiting for a tide.

The difficult part of his plan was the hour immediately ahead. He had to fix his position with pinpoint accuracy. The first twenty-five miles past Mizen Head would be run before daylight, and he wouldn't dare venture so close to the coastline in darkness unless he were certain of his starting point. He could get a reasonable one-point fix from the light. But he would be much more comfortable if he could shoot simultaneous bearings on Mizen Head and Fastnet, thirty miles ahead, and still hidden in the darkness.

The mate called in a bearing on the light, and Timmons drew it across his course line. Wait ten minutes, shoot another bearing, and he would know approximately where he was. Then he should slow and creep cautiously toward Fastnet until he could get an exact position.

But slowing was the last thing he wanted to do. Speed, the Admiralty had written in its advisories to merchantmen, was the surest defense against the dreaded U-boats. Run at top speed, and they couldn't catch you without surfacing. If they surfaced, they would come up under the barrel of the five-inch deck gun on his fantail. And if they surfaced ahead of him, his speed would make them easy targets for ramming.

On the three prior crossings, a naval escort had been waiting a few miles off Fastnet, one of the ancient destroyers stationed at Queenstown. Certainly not a modern ship of the line, but still enough to take the worry out of passing up the Irish coast. But with the buildup in traffic from America, there were more ships coming in than there were escorts to meet them. This time, it was his turn to complete the run alone.

He stepped back into the wheelhouse and glanced out through the salt-smeared windows. There was no landfill to be seen. His only mark was the light blinking repeatedly off his port bow.

"Mizen Head, bearing zero one zero." Timmons drew in the new bearing line, then advanced the first line by the distance *Ikeria* had traveled since he'd plotted it. The intersection was his best position.

"Come to course zero seven zero," he ordered the helmsman. Then he stepped out to the wing of the bridge to join his first mate.

"We should raise Fastnet Light off the port bow in a few minutes," Timmons told John Moore. "If we don't, I'll want to slow to half."

"Beautiful night," Moore replied. "We shouldn't have any trouble finding it."

He watched Captain Timmons return to the wheelhouse. Then he told his lookout, "Sharp eye on the port bow. We should be raising Fastnet." The lookout, who had been sweeping the port side of the ship, turned his attention ahead.

Moore became restless as the minutes ticked away. This close to the shoreline, there was little room for error. It was a clear night. They should be able to see Fastnet Light, particularly against the dark landfall behind it. He crossed in front of the wheelhouse to the starboard wing of the bridge. "Anything on the bow?" he asked the starboard lookout. The man swung his glasses forward.

"Nothing yet, Mr. Moore," he said.

Another two minutes ticked by. Moore stepped into the wheelhouse, then wandered into the chartroom and glanced down at Captain Timmons's fix. It seemed accurate, and zero seven zero should keep them safely south of the rock even if he couldn't see it.

"Submarine! Submarine to port!" The lookout's screamed warning rang like a shot through the quiet wheelhouse. Moore dashed around the helm toward the wing of the bridge. He had just reached the doorway when the deck pitched under his feet. As he fell, he heard the explosion, sharp and metallic like a cymbal being struck next to his ear. A wall of water jumped into the air just off the port wing.

He struggled to his feet as a deafening roar echoed through the hull. Down below the water line, boilers were exploding, sending walls of high-pressure steam through the guts of the ship. He ran to the wing, where the lookout was lying in a heap on the deck. As soon as he reached the rail, he saw the U-boat.

It was no more than a hundred yards off his beam, a flat deck that barely broke the surface of the sea, topped by a small tower. The officer on the tower was leaning forward, resting on his elbow, as casually as if he were only taking in the night air.

Suddenly Moore realized why he could see the submarine so clearly. A column of flame was twisting out of the number three hatch, just aft of the superstructure, lighting the sky like a fireworks display.

"Swing out the boats! Abandon ship!" It was Captain Timmons, screaming from the wheelhouse. But Moore couldn't tear his gaze away from the submarine, which was turning to a course parallel to his own. His eyes widened as he saw the deck gun swinging into view behind the conning tower. The gun crew was already in position, crouched over the sights that were panning toward him.

Moore ran aft, down the ladder from the bridge to the boat deck. Two seamen were already at work, tugging at the falls as they tried to lift the port boat out of its chocks. Moore leaned against the boat, pushing it free as soon as it was raised far enough. The seamen began tugging at the bow, trying to cant the boat between the davits and push it out over the side.

There was a sharp crack from across the water, followed by an explosion at the water line, directly below the lifeboat. The two seamen dove away from their stations and began crawling across the deck to the starboard side. Moore watched as the submarine gun crew loaded another shell into their weapon. The U-boat commander's plan was obvious. He was going to riddle the port side with cannon fire, hastening the sinking that was already inevitable.

"Starboard boat! Starboard boat!" Timmons was screaming from the starboardside wing. There was no way they could lower the portside boat under the muzzle of the German cannon. The entire crew would have to go over the starboard rail.

Timmons scurried down from the bridge as other seamen pushed the boat over the lifeline. "Load it and lower away," he ordered Moore. "Get clear as fast as you can. You know what we're carrying." Moore's eyes widened. He had seen the cases of artillery shells being loaded in the middle of the night, just minutes before they sailed. There was enough powder in *Ikeria*'s holds to knock down houses on the distant shore he could now barely make out.

"Do we have everyone?" Moore demanded from the ranking deck seaman.

"All the deck crew, and everyone from the watch. But the black gang isn't topside yet."

Moore called up to Captain Timmons. "The enginemen are still below."

"Lower away," Timmons ordered. "They'll have to swim to you."

Moore hesitated, envisioning the engineers climbing up through smoke-filled passageways. If he could just buy them a few more seconds.

"Lower away, damn you!" Timmons roared. At that instant, the deck began to tip to port. The submarine's gunners had opened the port side to the sea, and *Ikeria* was taking on a list. If he hesitated, the starboard boat wouldn't be able to clear the rising side of the ship's hull.

"Lower away," Moore ordered. Then he ran aft to the engine room door. As he opened it, a ball of flame fired out and exploded into the air. Moore was tossed backward and sent sprawling across the deck. The engine rooms, he knew, were an inferno. None of the men on watch would be coming up to the lifeboat.

The lifeboat was already below the rail, dropping slowly as the crew played out the rope falls. Moore jumped out, grabbing one of the descending lines, and rode it slowly down to the boat.

The first explosion had echoed like a thunderclap, bouncing people out of their beds all along the Irish shore. From Crookhaven to Baltimore, people with coats pulled over their nightshirts hurried to the beach, drawn by the eerie light that danced across the water. They could make out the shape of a ship at the base of the towering column of flame, and they watched in fascination as it fired explosive flashes into the air. Then there was a white flash, so brilliant that for an instant the flames were invisible. The impact hit them with the roar of a whirlwind. A moment later, the flames were gone.

The lifeboat staggered into Roaringwater Bay just after daybreak, carrying a cargo of battered, frightened men with white eyes staring from coal-blackened faces. Their hands shook on the cups of hot tea that the people of Schull rushed down to the landing, and they babbled a report of their hours of unspeakable terror. "Poor lads," the women allowed, even though the survivors were English. Even the men, raised on a venom of hatred for their English oppressors, nodded in sympathy. "Bastards," they agreed when they heard of the Germans who had fired without warning and then disappeared without any concern for the survivors.

The bodies began washing ashore the next afternoon. Two came in at Schull, and there were reports of others to the east on Clear Island and Sherkin Island. Only tatters of clothing confirmed that they were men. They were scorched black and bloated with seawater. Some had lost limbs, and one was headless.

"Hun bastards," the Irish agreed, as they gently put the English corpses into deep graves and carefully covered them with stones.

SCHULL

"Barbaric," Father Connors said, shaking his head in disgust. He reached out for the tea that his housekeeper was serving, then turned back to William Day and Shiela McDevitt, who were sitting in soft chairs across from him. Shiela was going through the motions of stirring her tea. Day was resting the cup and saucer on the knee of his naval uniform.

"I'll do everything I can to encourage the people to cooperate with you, commander. Now, mind you, I can't promise anything. There's no great sympathy here for the English. But we're all outraged by what the Germans did, attacking a peaceful ship without even a word of warning. And then to just leave those poor souls floating in the sea."

"There are dangers," Day repeated. "I wouldn't want your people to underestimate them. But there's safety in numbers. The more boats we're able to put out there, the less chance there is of their even seeing a submarine."

Father Connors nodded. "I understand, and it certainly makes sense." He sipped his tea carefully. "And I wouldn't underestimate the attractive-ness of the wage you'll be paying. These are poor people. That kind of money can do a great deal for their families. I think most of them will want to help you."

There was a tap on the door, and then the housekeeper pushed it open without waiting for an answer. She stepped back, and a small, bespectacled man in an ill-fitting suit peeked into the parlor.

"Ah, Emmett," Father Connors announced. And then, turning to Day, "This is our schoolteacher, Emmett Hayes. And this is Commander Day of the Royal Navy, our new area commanding officer."

Day juggled the tea cup as he rose and shook hands with Hayes.

"I think you already know Shiela McDevitt," Father Connors continued.

Hayes bowed toward Shiela. "Indeed I do. She was kind enough to bring me some maps for the school. Very helpful, indeed."

"Emmett enjoys great respect in our community," Father Connors told Day. "I think he could be a great help in your efforts."

Hayes fixed his eyes on Day as the commander explained his plan for using the small boats of the town in his submarine patrols, and he seemed enthusiastic over the plan. "But, I wonder," the teacher asked, "how you propose to fix the positions of the boats. It seems it would take a very great deal of organization. Military training, I suppose you would call it. These are simple people. Not highly educated."

"A grid, based on lines of bearing from the shore," Day said. "Something that any seagoing man with a compass would know. All we have to do is change the bearings to vary the pattern so as to keep the submarines confused."

"A sort of daily code," Hayes ventured.

"Exactly," Day said.

Emmett Hayes smiled. "Well, I could certainly help you there. I'd be happy to rehearse each group on the bearings you assigned."

Day nodded his appreciation.

"Then you'll help persuade the community to take part in the commander's efforts," Father Connors concluded.

"Certainly," Emmett Hayes volunteered. "Although after what they've seen of the submarine's work, I don't think it will take much persuading."

The priest adjourned the meeting with a reassuring smile.

Day was buoyant as he and Shiela walked back to his parked car.

"Easier than I expected," he told her.

"Much easier," she agreed. "I think the Germans did our work for us when they sank that ship."

His flagship was *Hugh O'Neill*, a thirty-two-foot yacht with a white lapstrake hull and gleaming brightwork, and a wood-burning steam engine that had broken down twice on the voyage from Queenstown. His fleet was an assortment of peeling work barges and gut-stained fishing boats, some with engines, some with sails. His crew, a gathering of withered old men and cherub-faced boys, was huddled in groups along the rotting pier, stamping their feet and blowing on their hands as they waited for his order to get under way.

"I won't need my meerschaum pipe," Day said to Shiela. She shook her head and smiled. He had told her about the pipe given as a gift by a close friend in anticipation of his first command. As his ragtag fleet was being assembled, it had become a joke between them.

"Keep it handy," Shiela said. "You'll be wanting it when you see your first submarine."

"The U-boat commander will be laughing too hard to notice."

Shiela and Emmett Hayes had done his recruiting, with Father Connors standing in the background to nod his approval. "It's the French and the Belgians we're helping, not just the English," Shiela had told the townspeople to lessen the sting of working with the occupying army. "The man is paying hard cash," Hayes had added, getting down to business. Eyes had searched both their faces suspiciously, and then turned to God's spokesman for guidance. "A terrible race, the Germans," Father Connors had confirmed. "Lutherans mostly, from what I hear."

They organized their fleets, one based at Schull to cover from Mizen Head to Fastnet Rock. A fleet at Baltimore on the other side of Roaringwater Bay, took from Fastnet to Glandore, and another covered the stretch from Glandore to Courtmacsherry Bay. All in all, they were denying the U-boats fifty miles of hunting grounds, from Fastnet Rock nearly to the Old Head of Kinsale.

In Schull, they used Hayes's schoolhouse for meetings, where Day spread charts on the coastline before the men while the children stood on tiptoes to see in through the windows. He had drawn a grid on the chart, with one of the boats positioned at each intersection. From each point, lines of bearing were marked to obvious details on the shore. All the captains had to do was hold a position at the intersection of the two bearings. That would keep each boat in sight of four others.

"I've positioned the power boats offshore," Day had told his students, "with the sailing vessels closer to the beach." His logic was that the powerboats would be faster to the more distant stations.

"Better put the powerboats in close," old Mike O'Sullivan had mumbled around the stem of his pipe. "That way we'll be able to tow them back on our way home."

"It'll be a cold day in hell when I take a tow line from a sailboat," Tim Sheehy had protested.

The sailboat captain had removed his pipe. "The only thing your engine is good for, Tim, is scaring the fish. It makes worse noises than you do."

Tim had stood in indignation. "I'll not be sailing in any fleet that hangs laundry from its masts," he'd said, then started for the door with Pat O'Donnell, Peter Farley, and his son, and the rest of the powerboat captains at his heels.

"Maybe we should finish this meeting at the pub," Day had offered, bringing order to his squabbling crews. They piled into the wheezing truck that giant Tom Duffy used to haul moorings to the beach and kept up their argument during the short ride to the main street, and then to the saloon.

While he laid out the battle plan, British sailors from Queenstown armed the boats. Machine guns were installed on the bows of boats that had enough good wood on their decks to hold screws and bolts. Rifles were put aboard the others. One of the sailors was assigned to each boat to train one of its crew as the gunner. Day had been able to get enough sailors assigned to his fleet to man only a few of the boats that would be needed. On the others, Irishmen would man the guns.

They had taken their target practice in the fields behind the town, shooting at stacks of hay that were set well below the hill line. His allotment of ammunition gave each of his people only one clip of rifle cartridges for training. The machine gunners had learned their trade by firing just twenty rounds. Day could only hope that submarines made better targets than haystacks.

And now, they were putting to sea for the first time. Thomas McCabe, owner of the long-idled yacht, cast off his lines and stood behind the polished teak wheel, proud in his white cap and blue topcoat. His nephew opened the throttle from the wood-burning boiler to the miniature engine, and *Hugh O'Neill* moved away from the pier. There was the choking of oil engines that sent clouds of smoke into the air, and the screeching of wooden blocks as drab sails were hoisted up dozens of masts. The Schull fleet fell into line in the wake of Day's flagship.

They charged out into Roaringwater Bay, breaking their line as soon as they cleared the harbor and heading toward their assigned stations. Captains leaned out over the prows, breathing in the adventure that had suddenly turned the dull routine of daily voyages into the excitement of the hunt. Faces turned into the salt spray, searching for the dark shapes and probing periscopes of submarines, which they all assumed were as numerous as the fish.

Day watched from the bow of *Hugh O'Neill*, amazed at what he saw. The sailboats angled off a stiff southwest breeze, moving at a clip that left most of the powerboats behind. The tattered sails that hung like dead skin in the harbor flexed with muscle when they reached the open sea. The withered men who seemed as rotted as the dock they had been standing on found new life as they hauled the sheets to trim their sails.

The motorboats were finding their rhythm. Engines that had coughed and sputtered in the safe harbor of Schull began pounding with new energy. Hulls that had seemed to be sinking at their moorings were more than a match for the waves, slicing through the crests and leaving spreading white wakes behind.

Voices called from boat to boat with a camaraderie that had never appeared during the training sessions.

"She's singing like a bird, Tim," O'Sullivan called to Sheehy. "You're in fine trim," came the unexpected response.

"Call me, if you find one," Pat O'Donnell cackled. "I'd like to take a shot at one of them damn submarines."

There were mistakes, just as Day had anticipated. Three of the boats rushed up to the same station, nearly colliding as none of them would give ground.

"Do you have any idea where you are, Peter?" an angry voice called to Farley.

"I'd be right on my mark, dammit, if you'd get that washtub out of my way."

They stood in their boats, waving their charts in the air and pointing to landmarks, their voices echoing over the water.

Hugh O'Neill steamed from station to station, arbitrating the disputes and checking on the bearings.

"You're right on," Day congratulated Jamie Green. The pink-cheeked young man, who was bent over a gurgling heavy oil engine, waved in acknowledgment. Then, as he pulled clear, Day heard, "As if I need an Englishman to tell me where I am." He laughed, then reached into his pocket for his meerschaum pipe. It wasn't such a bad fleet after all.

But boredom came with the sun. Once they reached their stations, the crews had nothing to do, and as the sun moved across the southern sky, tense muscles began to relax, and sharp eyes began to wander.

"Where are your submarines?" Martin Doyle called from his gaff rigger as Day steamed close by.

"Staying clear of us, if we're lucky," the commander answered.

"Then I'll be usin' this for an oar," Doyle said, raising his rifle in disgust.

Just before noon, a trace of smoke appeared on the western horizon, followed by the masts of a freighter. They watched as the ship drew near and sent up a cheer as it slipped safely through their formation. And then the endless waiting began all over again.

One of the sailboats dropped a fishing net over the side, and a powerboat took to the idea and began dragging its own nets back and forth across its station. Then a boat on the perimeter of the formation wandered off its bearings to set its nets in a more promising quarter. Day went after her, urging her back to her station. Then he set *Hugh O'Neill* off after other boats that were wandering away from their marks.

"Can we get any more speed out of her?" Day asked Thomas McCabe, who was leaning up against the gleaming teak wheel.

The captain glanced back at his nephew, who was sitting next to the firebox, whittling the piece of wood that rested in his lap. "Not unless we can get more speed out of him."

Day began heaving logs into the firebox as the nephew watched curiously.

By mid-afternoon, there was no trace of the precise pattern he had drawn on the chart. The outboard boats were farther out to sea, most of them fishing toward the west. The inboard boats, their sails luffing, were drifting back into Roaringwater Bay. The logs in his woodbox were nearly spent. Day looked out toward the silver sky in the southwest and at the calm seas that reached all the way to America. Perhaps his fleet had kept a submarine out of the area. There was no way of knowing. But if one had ventured in, he had to be thankful that it hadn't shown itself. It would take weeks before his squadron would be ready for the encounter.

A flare suddenly exploded in the sky to the west, followed by twisting trails of smoke. Day snapped his binoculars to his face. One of the distant sailboats was coming about smartly, its crew waving wildly at a nearby powerboat. Then another flare shot up from the powerboat as it suddenly kicked up a wake and began rushing toward the sailboat.

"Submarine!" Day heard from a workboat that was drifting off his starboard quarter. The boat's engine coughed and then roared to life as it set off to the rescue.

McCabe's nephew jumped to his feet and began tossing armloads of wood at the base of the boiler. The captain blinked his eyes around the western points of the compass until he found the flare, and then swung the wheel to give chase. "We've got one," he screamed at Day. "Open her up," he ordered his nephew.

In an instant, every boat in the formation was charging toward the flares. Throttles were pushed to the stops, and sails hauled until rails were in the water. "It's a submarine," Martin Doyle called. "A whole damned fleet of 'em," Jamie Green screamed back. The crews leaned into the wind, urging more speed out of their boats.

Through his glasses, Day could see the two boats that had fired flares turning back and forth over a small patch of water. The scattered fleet was beginning to crowd together as it drew like a net around the same spot. It was all wrong. Only the boats nearest at hand were supposed to close. The others were supposed to hold their positions.

A U-boat would have no trouble slipping out from under the boat that had spotted her. She could move a mile away in just the few minutes that it would take the fleet to gather. And then, if she surfaced, she would have all the boats in one place, a perfect target for her deck gun.

Their safety, he had explained to his crews, depended on keeping their stations, giving the submarine no safe place to surface. All had nodded their understanding. But what was logical in Emmett Hayes's schoolhouse was senseless after a day of drifting and waiting. There was action at hand, and no one wanted to be left as a bystander.

Day tried to head off the boats nearest to his yacht, cutting in front of them and ordering them back to their stations. But while he was turning one of his crews around, three others motored past. He could do nothing with the hounds once they had the scent of the fox except follow them.

He heard a rifle shot. In the bow of the closest motorboat, a crewman was aiming a rifle at the center of the area he was circling. Another shot echoed across the water.

A charging powerboat turned abruptly away from the target area, swinging across the bow of a sailboat on a beam reach. The sailboat turned too late and was still carrying speed when she cut into the transom of the powerboat, rolling it onto its side and tossing its crew into the sea.

Then there was a blast of machine gun fire. On one of the workboats, a crewman was bent over a deck-mounted machine gun, aiming into the gap between the two boats that had launched the warning flares. His second burst of fire churned the water that the boats were circling and sent the oncoming boats suddenly scattering in fear of their lives.

Within a fifty-yard radius, Day suddenly had ten boats, turning abruptly in all directions, cutting dangerously across one another. One boat was sinking, its crew struggling for the hands that were reaching over the gunwalls of the boat that had thrown them overboard. A rifleman was squeezing off round after round into the churning water at the center of the chaos. And now the Farley boy, crouched at his machine gun, was beginning to strafe every inch of open water.

He grabbed the cord that hung above McCabe's head and began pulling off short blasts on the steam whistle as *Hugh O'Neill* rushed into the middle of the circle. But the shrill screeches only added to the growing madness. Boats turned blindly away from the yacht. One, a sailboat, jibed across the target area.

Farley turned his powerboat abruptly, throwing his son off balance. The spray of the machine gun bullets walked across the water until it found the pitching hull of Martin Doyle's sailboat, and then chunks of wood exploded out of the sailboat's hull. "Jesus Christ," Doyle screamed as his boat settled to its rails and began taking water over its deck.

"Cease fire!" Day ordered through his megaphone. The response was a new burst of rifle fire off his port beam. Another crew had spotted the U-boat a hundred yards south of the original target. Its captain was shooting into the sea only a few feet ahead of his own bow, and other boats were turning toward him to get in on the action.

"Cease fire!" Day screamed again, punctuating his order with another burst of blasts on his whistle. The screech of the whistle turned into a sad groan as the steam pressure drained.

And then, as suddenly as it had begun, the attack on the German submarine ended. The ridiculous sound of the dying whistle caught the attention of the boat crews, and every head turned toward *Hugh O'Neill* as its engine slowed and its speed died. Then the crewmen turned back to the center of their circle and watched quietly as two of their patrol craft sank into the sea.

"It *was* a submarine," the captain who had fired the first flare announced sheepishly to his neighbors.

"Two of 'em," the captain who had fired the second flare answered.

"Ran for their lives," another voice offered.

"Let's go home," Day said.

McCabe's nephew tossed the last of the logs into the firebox and worked up enough steam to get the ancient engine turning. *Hugh O'Neill* led its sullen squadron back into Roaringwater Bay and toward the tilting pier of Schull.

In Emmett Hayes's schoolhouse, Day handed out the assignments for the next day's grid and spent a moment with each of his captains to argue the importance of holding his station. "Don't fire until the submarine surfaces," he repeated over and over again. Then he joined them in the pub, where the day's adventure was expanded into the great naval battle of Roaringwater Bay. The sunken powerboat, it turned out, had been rammed by the escaping submarine. Doyle's sailboat had come close to winning an artillery duel with the U-boat's deck guns.

As he listened to their stories, Day glanced in disbelief at Emmett Hayes, who was sitting quietly beside him. "Who are they fooling?" he asked.

"Themselves," Hayes said. "This is the biggest day of their lives." Then he advised, "Let them talk. It's the stories that will bring them back in the morning."

Day drove in the darkness to the church in Ballydehob, where he met with the young officers from Queenstown who commanded the other two fleets in his fishing boat navy. Their reports were similar to his own. A morning burst of enthusiasm, followed by a deterioration in station keeping as boredom set in. Fortunately, neither of the other groups had had occasion to fire on suspected submarines.

"It's falling apart after one day," one of the officers said. "What's it going to be like after a week?"

Day shrugged his shoulders. "Keep after them," he said. "As long as they're out there, the U-boats have a problem."

The officers thought of their comfortable quarters in Queenstown. "It's not going to work, sir," the lieutenant, who headed up the squadron at Baltimore, offered.

"It has to work," Day answered. "Either that, or we'll need them to bury the bodies that will be washing up on the beaches every day." He dismissed his officers so that they could get ready for the next morning's patrol.

He motored back to Crookhaven and spent an hour with Shiela McDevitt and Chief Gore reviewing the day's radio traffic. Messages had gone out to six incoming ships, two British and four with neutral registry. Only three were assigned escorts as they approached Fastnet Light. The others were advised to slow so that they would reach the Irish coast at first light when a fleet of fishing boats would be on station to discourage submarine operations. Day allowed himself a smile of satisfaction. Queenstown was already counting on his Irish navy to keep the sea lane open.

He drove Shiela back down the dark road to Schull, telling her about the day's adventure.

"Was it really a submarine?" she asked in disbelief.

"Probably not," he laughed. "Maybe the shadow of a cloud, or a school of fish. Probably just an overactive imagination." Then he added, "I've got to get more sailors to man the guns. We lost two boats shooting at phantoms. We could sink our whole fleet in a couple of weeks."

"But it might have been a submarine," she said, defending her Irish neighbors.

He shook his head. "If we find one, it will be by accident. They're not going to sail under a whole fleet of small boats if they can help it."

He pulled up to her house, a small stone cottage on a long-abandoned farm.

"Let me make you a cup of tea," Shiela offered.

Day followed her into a small parlor, brightly painted and crisply curtained, with a pleasant arrangement of a freshly covered sofa and soft chairs. He dropped wearily onto the sofa while Shiela raked the bed of coals in the cast-iron stove and set a kettle of water over the gasping embers. She spooned the tea into a white porcelain pot and put the cream into a small china pitcher. Then she set a tray with two cups and a plate of biscuits and carried it back into the parlor.

Day was slumped down in the sofa, fast asleep, his head resting awkwardly on his shoulder. Shiela set the tray down and whispered his name, then smiled when there was no response. She brought a blanket from the bedroom and spread it over him, then unlaced his shoes and carefully lifted his feet onto the cushions. His eyes blinked open for an instant, but then his head turned and he drifted back to sleep.

She brought the tray back into the kitchen, banked the fire in the stove, and carried her cup of tea toward her bedroom. As she passed through the parlor, she paused for a moment and looked at the figure sprawled on the sofa, one long arm hanging down nearly to the floor. Shiela remembered what she had been told about her new area commander and pictured him struggling through the debris of a sunken ship, pulling his crewmen from the sea to the safety of a wobbly raft. Then she closed her bedroom door quietly behind her.

At the edge of the town, Emmett Hayes turned down the lamp in his bedroom. He took the coded details of Day's patrol plan for the next morning down the stairs to his parlor, lighted a new lamp, and walked carefully down the steps to his basement. There, he raised the radio from the sewing machine cabinet and began rocking the treadle until the needle on his generator peaked. With a practiced hand, he began tapping out the call letters of the German radio station. He signed off, "Leprechaun."

BALTIMORE

"Stop here for a moment."

Day was startled by the suggestion. "Stop?" he asked.

"Please," Shiela said.

A smile playing across her lips hinted she was about to reveal a delicious secret. He eyed her suspiciously as he pulled the chugging car to the siding.

Shiela jumped out the instant the car stopped, pulled open the back door, and lifted out the blanket she had placed in the back seat when Day picked her up in the morning.

"What are you up to?" he asked.

"Lunchtime," she answered. "We're going to have a picnic."

He was already around the car, standing next to her. "Lunch?" he asked, as if it were an unknown word. "We haven't time."

"You never have time," Shiela answered. "But today you're going to have lunch. In the most beautiful dining room in all of Europe. You can watch your fleet while you eat, so it won't be as if you were wasting a minute."

She started up the rocky hill that led from the edge of the town to a bluff beyond the harbor. Day hung back for a moment, glancing at the automobile and thinking of all the places he had to be. Then he shrugged in resignation and started after her.

They walked out onto a point of land that held Roaringwater Bay to the west and the open sea to the south and east. The warm spring sun, now high over the horizon, sparkled off the crests of the waves. There was even a hint of warmth in the light breeze that played through the grass.

"Where did you get such a crazy idea?" he asked.

"Yesterday, when we drove by here. It was so beautiful, and you weren't even looking at it. I thought that your boats would be able to do without you for an hour."

When they reached the edge of the bluff, where the land broke sharply and a rocky cliff fell down to the sea, Shiela opened her basket and handed Day a tablecloth that he spread as a blanket. Then she sat on one corner and began unpacking the basket while Day looked out at the scattering of small boats that stretched out to Fastnet and then disappeared over the horizon toward Mizen Head.

They had been together for the past two weeks, traveling the broken road from Mizen Head to Glandore during the days and working at the Crookhaven radio station well into the nights. Their days began in the darkness, when William turned his car up the overgrown path that led to Shiela's cottage and found her leaning drowsily against her door. They drove first to one of the harbors, arriving before the boats set out so that Day could talk to the officer, deliver new instructions, and review the day's sailing plan. Sometimes he left her on the docks and rode out with one of the boats to see them set their formations, coming back in when he was satisfied with the coverage. Then they toured the coastline, stopping at vantage points where he could see to boats at sea. Shiela stood beside him as he looked through his binoculars and wrote down his continuous stream of comments that would form the topics for the next day's instructions.

They stopped at the towns and paid calls on the local leaders. Sometimes they met in the drawing room of an English landowner who acted as Day's paymaster, shaping up the crews each morning and then handing over their wages when the boats docked at night. In other towns, the leader was the parish priest, using his church as the labor hall. Shiela and Commander Day would call at the rectory and exchange small talk with the housekeeper while waiting for the priest to return from his morning mass. In one town, it was the pub owner who served as their representative to the locals. He would come out to the benches and sit down with Shiela and the commander, away from the sanctity of the pub. It wasn't that his regulars wouldn't allow an Englishman to stand in their midst. But a woman? That would be a scandal that they wouldn't be able to explain to their sons. Wherever they went, Shiela took care of the social necessities, her Irish conversation winning friends and making Day seem more the ally than the area commander for an occupying force.

They rushed back to Crookhaven to look at the morning's radio traffic. Day covered the routine matters with Chief Gore while Shiela locked herself in the coding room with any classified traffic. If her workload was heavy, Day left her behind, gathering up the notes she had taken for him during the morning and rushing to one of the harbors to meet the incoming boats. Often he was detained for an evening training session or needed to arbitrate a sudden dispute. Sometimes he stayed to join the crews in the local pub, listening to their imagined tales of heroism and heaping praise on their seafaring skills.

"Not a bad sort," he overheard a razor-faced captain say of him after he had praised a squadron for their station keeping.

"About all you can hope for in an Englishman," was the nodded reply.

He didn't delude himself that he was making friends. But he sensed that he was winning respect. The Irish had learned from centuries of painful experience that the English knew how to fight a battle. And here was an Englishman who was happy to have them fighting by his side.

"Not as dumb as you might expect" was about the best he had earned as an expression of admiration.

He had taken Shiela with him on one of his visits to Queenstown, where he made his reports to one of Admiral Coke's staff officers. Admiral Inglefield was a bit of a maverick himself, a man who had tried to train seagulls to circle over the submerged hulls of submarines and perch on their periscopes. Inglefield groaned at Day's requests for provisions and shook his head at each mention of funding.

"I need ammunition to train my gunners," Day had begged. "Without training, they're more a danger to one another than they are to the Germans."

"Out of the question," Inglefield answered. "There's not enough cartridges for the soldiers in France."

"And fuel oil. I had to leave three of the motorboats at the dock this morning. We're burning more oil in a week than these men are used to burning in a winter."

Again Inglefield frowned. "We don't have enough for the admiral's barge."

"Do you have any idea what your Irish fleet is costing us?" Inglefield had complained.

"How many ships have made it through along the coast without seeing a submarine?" Day had countered.

Because the success of his boats was apparent, Day wasn't surprised when a barge carrying barrels of heavy oil pulled into Schull. Admiral Inglefield swore he had personally stolen the cargo the night before. And then a small boat from Queenstown dropped off a case of machine gun rounds. "Compliments of Admiral Inglefield," the sailors explained.

At night, they always returned to the radio station, where he checked the afternoon traffic while Shiela translated any coded messages. Then he would drive her to her cottage and continue on to his own quarters at a boarding house to catch a few hours' sleep before the next day began.

They took their meals wherever they happened to be. Sometimes it was as the car bounced along the roads, a sandwich that Shiela had wrapped in brown paper, or some pieces of fruit. It might be on the benches of the pub, as they were talking to the proprietor, or a meal in a rectory when the priest insisted that they stay. Often it was at the mess in the radio station, where they sat down with the chief and the sailors and talked about their operations as they lifted spoons of scalding stew.

Now, Shiela had spread the picnic fare on the tablecloth. She had sandwiches made with thick cuts of cheese and thin slices of lamb, a salad of pickled vegetables, and a dessert of raisin cakes. Adding to her surprise were two bottles of dark beer, with corks locked in place by wire levers that were hooked into the glass. Day wandered back from the bluff where he had been watching the operations of his boats. His eyes widened when he saw the food.

"You must have been working all night," he said.

She smiled at the compliment. "It's the first quiet meal we've had in a month. I wanted it to be special."

"Special it is." He lifted one of the bottles. "Very special indeed." He started to open it, but then he stopped and set it down carefully. "I've worked you very hard," he told her, as if it had taken a moment of quiet to remind him of the pace they had been maintaining.

"Slavery more than work," Shiela answered.

"And I've never said 'thank you.'"

"Commanders don't have to say 'thank you.'"

"I haven't thanked anyone. You. Father Connors. Emmett Hayes."

"I've thanked them for you," she told him. "They understand."

She was struggling with the wire catch on the bottle. Day took it from her, opened it, and handed it back.

"Do you?" he asked her.

"Do I what?"

"Understand that I'm very grateful for all the help you've given me. I wouldn't be anywhere without you."

She broke a sandwich and shared it with him. "I understand that you've thrown yourself into this with your whole heart. I'm terribly afraid that you're letting yourself in for a disappointment."

"There are still ships being sunk," he said.

"And you can't stop it. The ocean is too big for you to make it all safe." Day nodded, but he didn't seem at all consoled. "You're doing a wonderful job," Shiela continued. "Better than anyone could have expected. The Admiralty is satisfied."

He tasted the beer. "It's not the Admiralty I'm worrying about. It's the ships, and the men sailing them. Fourteen freighters down last month. And as many more in the first few weeks of this month. And every one of them carrying cargoes that we need in the North Sea. And in France."

Day shook his head in despair, then began devouring one of the sandwiches. When he looked up at Shiela, he noticed that she wasn't eating.

"You need a ship," she told him, finally saying what had apparently been on her mind all along. "You could ask them at Queenstown to find you an assignment. They owe it to you."

He smiled broadly. "Sounds as if you'd be happy to be rid of me."

"No," she said, looking away from him. "But I'd be happy to see you out of Ireland. This country is a bog that swallows up good men. The jealousy and the hatred are in the soil. In the air. We take it in with our food. With every breath. Sooner or later it destroys everything that's good."

"They're helping me," he argued.

"They're watching you," she said. "You're paying their wages, so they'll have you to their tables and drink with you in the pub. But God help you if that tin lizzie you're driving goes off the road some night. Or if one of those rotting boats should go down under you. There'll not be a brave hand reaching out to help you. Or if a few of them should get killed by one of the U-boats. Then they'd turn on you in a minute. You're English. And they hate the English because it was the English who taught them to hate themselves."

"You're English," he reminded her.

"Oh, yes," Shiela said bitterly. "And the worst kind. I was one of them, and I left them behind. So I'm not just their enemy. I'm one of their traitors."

"Then you should be getting out," Day said.

"I'm also Irish," Shiela answered. "I have no place to go."

He finished his sandwich, watching her while she tried to eat. Then he reached out and raised her chin with the edge of his hand.

"I'll be careful," he promised.

"Careful isn't enough," she answered, pushing his hand away. "There are things happening all around you that you can't understand. Things that can destroy you."

"What things? Tell me."

She looked at him for a moment, then jumped up and ran to the edge of the bluff. He went after her, but when he reached her, Shiela turned her back to him. He realized that she was crying.

"Please, tell me what's wrong," Day begged her.

He could hardly hear her answer. "I'm afraid."

"Afraid of what?"

"Afraid for you," Shiela said. Then she turned quickly to face him, her eyes red and her cheeks wet. "Make them give you a ship. Get away from here while you still can."

He took her in his arms and held her tightly. He could feel her trembling.

"I'm sorry," Shiela finally managed. "I wanted this to be a happy afternoon for you. And now I've spoiled it." She ran back to the blanket and began gathering up the remains of their picnic.

They drove back to Crookhaven, where Shiela disappeared into the coding room. There were eight ships approaching the Irish coast, all due off Fastnet within the next twenty-four hours. Coded messages had to be prepared for each of them, assigning a rendezvous with one of the Queenstown escorts or indicating a safe course close to the shoreline. While she worked, Day reviewed the day's radio traffic with Chief Gore and drafted his third request for a field piece that could be installed at the edge of the cliff to provide some defense against a surfaced U-boat. The first two requisitions had been turned down by the Admiralty. It was already dark when Shiela handed her last message to the radioman for transmission.

He navigated carefully back down the dark road to Schull with Shiela sitting silently by his side. Until now, they had always filled their journeys with constant chatter about their work. There were hundreds of details involved in the operations of the radio station and in the daily voyages of the Irish boats that he had shared with her.

But now their relationship was changed. She had made it clear that she was more concerned with him than she was with the work that they shared. "Afraid for you," she had said. Not for the success of their naval mission, or for the safety of the ships they were trying to protect. "Afraid for you." And he understood that, because of him, she was frightened for herself. Something had grown, unnoticed, between them. Something that he had taken for granted until it had exploded in her outpouring of emotion during the simple picnic she had planned.

She had warned him that he was falling into danger. And yet, it wasn't his own danger that he was thinking about. "I have no place to go," she had said of herself. He had suddenly understood how alone and helpless she was, caught in the no man's land of hatred that separated England and Ireland. If he were in danger with one enemy, how much greater was her danger? It was Shiela's safety that was troubling him. And in that realization, he understood how important she had become to him. Not simply as an associate in their common causes. But more as the one person in this entire land he was bonded to. In her tears, she had shown him how deeply she cared for him. Now he knew how deeply he cared for her.

He turned up the path to her cottage and swung the gasping automobile to a stop in front of her doorway. On other nights, they had reached her house in the middle of a conversation and continued talking for a few moments before she jumped down from the car. But tonight, Shiela said a simple "Thank you" as she leaned over the seat for her basket. She was stepping out onto the running board when he reached out and caught her hand.

"Thank you for the picnic," Day said.

She forced a smile. "I'm sorry it wasn't a happier afternoon. I wanted it to be lovely for you."

She started to pull away, but he held on to her hand.

"Don't worry about me," he told her.

Shiela studied him for a moment. There was something she wanted to tell him, but she couldn't find the words. "I can't help it," she finally admitted. "Please ask them for a ship. Something that will take you away from here."

Day shook his head slowly. "I can't do that. I can't leave you here alone."

He was still holding her hand, leaning across the empty seat as she stood outside the car. She set the picnic basket on the running board, reached back toward him and covered his hand with hers.

"We shouldn't be holding on to each other," Shiela warned him.

"We have no one else to hold on to," Day said.

Shiela leaned across him and carefully raised the magneto lever that protruded from behind the steering wheel. The engine stuttered and then was suddenly silent.

They lay together in her small bed, her head resting on his shoulder, her long hair flowing across his chest. In the faint light of the dimmed lamp, he could see the white curve of her shoulder until it disappeared beneath the thick quilt. And the sparkle of the signet ring that rested softly against her breast.

Day tried not to think of the inscription that it bore.

NEW YORK

IN JENNIFER'S mind, she already belonged to William Day. He had told her that some things couldn't be changed, but surely he meant that their marriage was impossible only because of his military duty. He was simply trying to protect her from the dangers of the war.

She read the newspapers every day, searching out the most optimistic reports of the war and then nearly committing them to memory. If a foreign correspondent, studying the battle lines from the elevated vantage point of a stool in a Mayfair pub, wrote that a great Allied breakthrough was imminent, she clipped the piece for her scrapbook. If she came upon a more pessimistic report concerning the arrival of German reinforcements, she tried to dismiss it. There was only one kind of news that fitted comfortably with her view of the future.

But even she couldn't ignore the grim reports from the channel and from the windswept waters off the Irish coast. The cowardly submarines were proving effective in their illegal and immoral slaughter. Reports of British ship losses were appearing every day. She assumed that William had his own command. Certainly not a battleship or a cruiser. She accepted that he was still too junior for a capital ship. But probably one of the destroyers that were frequently reported to be hunting the submarines or to be escorting major ships through the sea lanes that the submarines were infesting. She had cut out a photo of a three-funneled "R" class destroyer, reported to be speeding at twenty knots in pursuit of a U-boat. Just like William's ship, she told herself, and she saved the picture for when her father returned from the city on the weekend.

"I shouldn't be surprised if he were commanding one of those," he told her, although he insisted that he had no way of knowing where Commander Day had actually been stationed. "They just don't give out that kind of information in wartime," he'd said.

Jennifer badgered her father for information, assuming that because of his important position he knew much more than the reporters. Sir Peter responded, but he was firmly mindful of his obligation to protect the women of his household from anything that might distress them.

"Are they really sinking so many of our ships?" Jennifer asked.

"The worst kind of sensationalism," he responded. "Irresponsible, if you ask me. Oh, occasionally one of our ships comes across a submarine. But hundreds get through every week. The Royal Navy has things well in hand."

Or, at another time, "Why aren't our soldiers attacking? Are the Germans really so strong that we can't push them out of France?"

"Nonsense! We've blunted their attack. I suppose we'll have them out soon enough once the weather turns for the better. Why do you bother yourself over such things?"

Sir Peter didn't think he was lying, even though the evidence of urgent requisitions and unfilled orders that covered his desk in the library argued quite clearly that the war was going badly. He was simply giving Jennifer the kind of answers that he would have given to Anne or to any other woman who tried to understand the incomprehensible slaughter taking place in Europe. Women had no need to upset themselves with men's concerns.

During the week, when her father was away in the city, Jennifer played the only role available to her. She waited, and she prayed. She wore a widow's walk on the slates of the terrace as she looked out over the water watching for a ship. Certainly not William's ship. At least not his destroyer steaming into Long Island Sound. But the image of a ship, crashing through distant seas, with William in command. He was out there, somewhere, fighting for their future. And then he would be coming home so that they would never be separated again. Often, she walked down the hill to the water's edge, feeling that being closer to the sea somehow brought her closer to him. When the sound was calm, she felt reassured. But when the wind was churning it into whitecaps, and when pieces of rotted driftwood rolled in at her feet, she was suddenly frightened. The sea was dangerous, and William was confronting those dangers alone. It was then that she prayed.

She wrote letters constantly, beginning them early in the week and then hurrying to finish them by the weekend so that her father could take them back to the city and include them in the diplomatic pouches that sailed for London. She addressed them just as Sir Peter had advised, to Commander William Day, in care of the Admiralty. "The navy will see that he gets it," he assured her each time she handed him a letter. "They know where his ship is operating."

But there were no return letters. Not that Jennifer expected William to match her output of trivial news coupled with expressions of concern. She knew that personal correspondence was the least of his priorities. "I'm sure every minute of his day is accounted for," her father advised, and she certainly agreed. But still, just an acknowledgment that he was getting her letters and that they were important to him. And perhaps an expression of his own longing for the war to be over so that they could take up their lives.

As Anne watched her daughter's inexhaustible devotion, her hopes that Jennifer would outgrow her attachment to Commander Day faded.

She tried to offer new interests, involving Jennifer in her charitable work. She encouraged her daughter to join in the activities of the other young people in their social circle and even arranged suitable escorts for their parties. Jennifer complied, but always with half a heart. Sooner or later, all of her conversations turned back to her naval officer, and to the dangers she imagined that he faced every day.

"We're going to have to tell her," Anne finally confronted her husband in the late night quiet of their bedroom.

"Tell her what?" he answered in despair. "That I've been lying to her all along? How will that make things any better?"

"They can only get worse," she warned. "This isn't an infatuation that's going to disappear with the next social season. She's in love with him."

"Perhaps I could ask him to write her. Tell her that circumstances . . . the distance. Things do change."

"Can he say that truthfully?" Anne persisted. "Or would it be just the beginning of more lies?"

"Surely, you're not suggesting that we condone this relationship?" Peter demanded.

"No," Anne said softly. "I suppose I'm suggesting that we tell her what we feel. That this would never be a suitable marriage. And that we admit what we've done. It was in her best interests, and we'll have to help her understand that."

He tossed restlessly in the bed. "You're right, of course. We will have to tell her."

But they didn't. There was never the perfect moment. Anne couldn't raise the issue when Jennifer was telling her friends about her hopes for the life that would begin after the war. And Sir Peter couldn't bring the truth crashing down on her fantasies about William Day's heroic struggles with the dreaded U-boats. He began to think more often about a frank letter to his former aide, with a simple request that Day write Jennifer and put an end to her misunderstandings. He knew where Day was stationed. He thought of him each time he drafted a wireless message about one of his cargoes, assuming that the information might be relayed through the Crookhaven radio station. But each time he was about to take up his pen, he remembered the night when he had seen them together on the terrace, when Day's protective embrace had made him realize that the man was in love with his daughter. How could he ask him to lie about his feelings, just to cover up his own lies?

"Do you think that it might work out between them?" he suggested one evening while he was having tea with Anne. "I mean, the world is changing. The old rules. I wonder if they're still so important?"

Anne admitted, "I've been asking myself the same question. He could have ignored our feelings. He could have asked her to come with him. Or at least written to her. I wonder if Jennifer will ever meet a more honorable man."

Sir Peter nodded. "I've never met a young man with more character." He pounded his fist against the arm of his stuffed chair. "Damn, but we carry these class distinctions too far. There are young men dying for England who wouldn't be welcome at my table. What in God's name is the matter with me?"

Anne reached across and placed her hand over his. "I think we should forward her letters. It's their future. They'll have to make their own rules."

Beecham's heavy eyes brightened. "I'll take them with me on Monday."

He was away from the house when Jennifer recalled an article on British naval operations that she had cut from *The Herald*. She knocked on the library door, then entered cautiously when there was no response. Beecham's huge rolltop desk was open, scattered with folders of papers that he had been working on. She pushed the folders carefully to one side and glanced across the mail slots, looking for the collection of clippings that she knew he kept. When she didn't see them, she slid open the top door reflexively, never pausing to think that she was violating her father's privacy. She tossed a few papers aside with no interest in their content, saw the clippings, and lifted them carefully out of the drawer. It was completely by accident that she noticed the corners of the pale yellow envelopes that were her private stationery.

She glanced at them curiously, her attention divided for a moment between the clippings and the envelopes. Then she set the clippings aside and slid the envelopes out into view. William Day's name was written on the top envelope in her own hand.

She stared at it without at first comprehending the meaning of her find. With the tip of her finger, she pushed the top envelope aside. Beneath it was another, again addressed with William's name. She grabbed the entire stack and tossed through them quickly, remembering the sequence in which they were written. When she reached the last of the stack, she rushed through them again, still bewildered by their presence. When she finally understood she felt a flash of rage. And then, as she squeezed the letters tightly in her hands, she began to feel sick. She pushed the drawer closed and rushed out of the room.

Jennifer didn't come down for dinner that evening and pretended to be asleep when Anne tiptoed into her room to see if she was feeling ill. Early the next morning, she walked into the library where Sir Peter was already hard at work.

She walked up beside him and carefully placed the letters on top of a document that he was reading.

"Ah," he began cheerfully, "more letters for Commander Day." But when he turned his attention from his work, he recognized the stack of envelopes that he had lifted time and time again from its place in his drawer. He picked the letters up slowly, then looked up helplessly at his daughter.

"You sent him away," Jennifer said, a simple statement of fact.

Sir Peter couldn't bring himself to admit his crime. He could only nod, and then he noticed to his horror that her eyes were worn from crying.

"Please," he begged. "Let me try to make you understand . . ."

"I'll be going to join him," Jennifer answered.

He knew that she would, and he could scarcely breathe as he watched her turn away from him and walk out of the room. Like all fathers who have ever lied to a child, he realized that he had forfeited his special place in her life, and that he would never be welcomed back. In an instant, he could see all the empty days ahead without her.

CONINGBEG LIGHT

"LIGHTSHIP, two points off the port bow."

Captain Daniel Dow smiled and raised his binoculars as soon as he heard the message from the crow's nest.

"Thank God," he said to his first mate. He could feel the coiled muscles in his back begin to unwind.

Lusitania was steaming at its best speed. But that wasn't fast enough for Dow. To save coal, the Cunard line had shut down one of *Lusitania*'s four boiler rooms, taking six of her double-ended boilers off the line. That reduced her best speed from twenty-six knots to a hair over twenty knots, still fast enough to outrun any submarine but not nearly fast enough for Fairweather Dow's stomach. He had been frozen in terror during the final hours of his passage along the coast of Ireland.

Dow had proposed shutting down the boiler room in American waters and during the Atlantic crossing, but lighting up the ship's full steam-generating capacity while passing through the war zone. "That's when we need the speed, when we're steaming where the U-boats are," he had said logically.

"We can't pay a team of stokers for six days of steaming when they'll be working for only one day," Alfred Booth had countered with equal logic. Dow was the captain, but Booth was the owner, so the boilers were kept cold for the entire journey.

He had begun searching for submarines as soon as daylight broke behind Fastnet Rock. He had welcomed the sight of the cruiser *Juno* when she had appeared as his escort, but he had begun to worry again when he was forced to shave two knots off his speed so that *Juno* could keep up. The sight of Day's fishing fleet had eased his anxiety, its presence indicating that no submarine could be operating in the area. But then, as he slipped past Queenstown, *Juno* had blinked her parting message and turned off to her anchorage. For the past three hours he had been running alone.

His passengers were completely unconcerned. To their minds, the journey had ended safely at the first sight of land. They had rushed to the weatherdeck rails to catch a glimpse of the warship as it had fallen in beside them, and then across the deck to the landward side, where they'd waved cheerful greetings to the fishing boats. Now the women were in their staterooms, compressing their wardrobes into steamer trunks, while the men were in the lounges, ordering their last drinks before the bars shut down permanently. Fairweather felt himself easing peacefully into their joyful mood.

The lightship was now clearly visible, no more than fifteen minutes ahead. He would swing around her and send The Greyhound charging into Saint George's Channel, past the patrol ships from the naval station at Milford Haven. It would be dark before he had to slow to cross the Liverpool bar. All in all, the dangerous part of his crossing was fading away behind him, he thought. Once he turned the Coningbeg Lightship, he would be home free.

He left the wheelhouse and walked confidently out to the port wing of the bridge, where he stood beside the lookout and looked straight down into the bubbling wash five stories below. Every bit of space forward of where he stood, and from three stories above the water line down nearly to the keel, was given over to the Admiralty's secret cargo. During the entire crossing, Dow had worried about what it might be, battling images of howitzer shells resting on their ends and bags of black powder stacked carelessly like sacks of flour. Now, he didn't particularly care what he was carrying. In a few hours, it would all be hauled up through the deck hatch and swung away from his ship. He stretched his arms out and arched his back until he heard it crack. Then he turned back toward the wheelhouse.

"Submarine! Submarine!"

Fairweather froze in his tracks.

"Periscope to port." The scream came from behind him, from the lookout he had just left.

"Hard right rudder," Captain Dow screamed into the wheelhouse.

Then he turned on his heels and rushed back out to the wing. The periscope, only 500 yards on his port beam, was kicking up a wake as it moved on a course parallel to his own.

At the stern of the ship, a steam engine drove the tiller quadrant through its full arc, pushing one connecting rod while it pulled on the other. The rods twisted *Lusitania's* sixty-ton rudder thirty-five degrees from the centerline, swinging it like a steel door into the enormous force of the onrushing sea. Immediately she began turning to starboard, away from the U-boat, her slender hull leaning into a sharp list. In the cabins below, steamer trunks began to slide, gathering speed until they crashed into bulkheads. In the lounges, tall wine glasses toppled over. Shorter whiskey glasses slid across the polished tables and tossed their contents out onto the Oriental carpets.

Instinctively, Dow rushed to the engine telegraphs to ring down for more speed. His hands were on the high-pressure handles when he remembered that there was no speed left to add. The full output of his working boilers was already racing through the ship's huge turbines. He glanced over his shoulder and saw the periscope swinging toward his stern as *Lusitania* turned away. Just as important as the distance he was opening up was the ever-narrowing target that he was offering to the U-boat's torpedoes. He watched until the periscope disappeared under his fantail. Then he ordered, "Rudder amidships." A few seconds later, the giant ship began to right itself as it straightened into a southerly course, headed away from Coningbeg Light. He squeezed his eyes shut and began to count the seconds it would take a torpedo to overtake his Greyhound.

There was no explosion, only the sound of rushing air as he headed directly into the wind. And then, suddenly, there was a cacophony of voices as the enraged passengers rushed out onto the weatherdeck. They had picked themselves up from the force of the sharp turn, realized that something was wrong, and rushed out to see for themselves.

"Submarine," voices shouted. Hands pointed toward the stern, where the periscope had matched *Lusitania's* turn and was moving into her wake. "Submarine! U-boat!" The shouts grew into a panicky chorus.

Dow rushed back to the wing, where he could look over his stern. The periscope was still there, tossing up a small roostertail of spray. But as *Lusitania* picked up the speed it had lost in the turn, the periscope was falling behind. Just another minute or so, and he would be out of her range. He counted the seconds, his thoughts locked on the bow of his ship and the tons of nitrates it probably contained. One torpedo would hardly make a dent in *Lusitania*. But if it ignited the cargo, then a secondary explosion could lift the bow right out of the water and break the ship in half.

"She's gone!" The submarine's disappeared!" The lookout was search-

ing beyond the wake with his binoculars. "No sight of her now, captain."
But Dow was anything but relieved. He could run away from the
periscope. But now that the U-boat had disappeared beneath the surface,
he had no idea where it was. How could he come about and head into the
channel if the submarine might be lying there, waiting for him?

He dashed back to the wheelhouse and into the chartroom. He had
nearly fifty miles of clear water to the east, all the way up to Milford
Haven on the western tip of Wales. If he ran to the east for an hour, he
could open up fifteen miles between *Lusitania* and the submarine,
assuming the U-boat stayed submerged. Then, if he turned to the north,
he could approach the channel from the east and probably beat the
U-boat back to Coningbeg.

"Left fifteen degrees rudder," he ordered. "Come to course zero nine
zero."

"Zero nine zero, aye," the helmsman confirmed. *Lusitania* turned to
the east.

But no sooner had she settled on her new course than Dow began to
doubt his decision. The submarine commander was no fool. He knew
that *Lusitania* was headed for Liverpool, and one glimpse through his
periscope would tell him that the giant steamer had turned to the east. All
he had to do was surface and make for the eastern approaches to Saint
George's Channel. He could be in position waiting when Dow made his
second approach toward Coningbeg Light.

Dow called his wireless operator to the bridge and quickly dictated a
report of the submarine sighting. "Operational immediate to Milford
Haven," he ordered. The naval station, he reasoned, would forward the
report to the patrol ships at the channel entrance. They would come out
and search the area, preventing the submarine from running on the
surface. All he had to do was wait until the patrol ships were at the
lightship and then turn to the north.

But within seconds, he was again beginning to question himself. He
couldn't simply linger around for a few hours. The high tide at the
Liverpool bar wouldn't wait for even a second. If he missed the tide,
he would be forced to circle outside the great port until the next day,
exposing himself to daylight attack. He had to move north soon enough
to catch the tide.

His first mate was suddenly standing beside him, shifting uneasily
from foot to foot. "Captain, there's a delegation of passengers . . ."

"Jesus Christ," Fairweather answered.

"I tried to reassure them, but they insist on speaking with you."

He didn't have time. But a panic among the passengers was the last
thing he needed. He ordered the mate to plot the point at which he had
to turn north in order to reach the Liverpool bar at high tide. He checked
with his wireless operator to learn that there had not yet been a response

from the Milford Haven radio station. Then he stepped back to the officers' smoking room, where the passengers were assembled, squaring his shoulders and smoothing his jacket before he pushed open the door. Five men, two of them already dressed formally for the final evening's dinner, were waiting. Dow knew the faces. All had dined at his table during the crossing.

"Thomas Astin," their apparent spokesman said, and then mentioned the names of the others. Astin, Dow remembered, was in finance, a London bond trader or some such thing. He was one of the two in white tie and tails. "Apparently, we're in some danger."

"No danger at all," Fairweather Dow reassured, trying to exude a confidence that he certainly didn't feel. "We're taking precautions, of course, but everything is quite in order."

"That submarine was close enough to touch us," one of the committee insisted.

"We're well away from it," Dow answered. And then, with a forced smile, "There isn't a submarine in the world that can catch *Lusitania.*"

The men looked to one another, wondering if their fears had been answered. Dow took advantage of the pause to attempt his escape.

"Now, if you gentlemen will excuse me, I have to be back on the bridge."

He started for the door, but Thomas Astin stopped him with the question that was frightening Dow.

"But he doesn't have to catch us. Don't we have to go back toward him in order to get to the channel?"

"We're taking a different approach to the channel," Fairweather said. "And there are Royal Navy ships coming to escort us. So, there's really nothing to worry about."

But there was, as the first mate informed him as soon as he stepped back into the chartroom. They had to turn north within the hour to catch the tide. That meant they would be racing back past Coningbeg in full daylight. And there was still no response from Milford Haven to indicate that the patrol ships even knew that there was a submarine in the area.

"Have wireless resend our message," he ordered the mate. "Tell Milford Haven that we need an escort ten miles east of Coningbeg by 1630. Demand a confirmation!"

He rechecked his chart, confirming the point twenty miles off the Welsh coast when he would have to make his decision. Turn north, back toward the submarine. Or turn to the southwest and out into the open sea, delaying his arrival at least until the next tide. He paced the bridge as he waited, his fears mounting with each step that he took.

Half his allotted time had elapsed before the wireless operator rushed out onto the bridge. "From Milford Haven," he shouted, waving his typed copy of the message. Dow snatched the paper from his hand and exhaled deeply as he read.

CONFIRM RENDEZVOUS, 090 CONINGBEG, 10 MILES, 1630.

He stepped back into the wheelhouse and ordered a turn to the north.

Again, he checked the chart. Twenty minutes to the north, then a course change to the northwest, and then, half an hour later, a turn to the west. That would bring him to his rendezvous at the eastern edge of the channel right on time. He was carving a large circle, keeping as much water as possible between *Lusitania* and the point where the U-boat had been sighted, up until the final moments when he approached the light. And by then, a navy destroyer should be waiting to take him through.

He doubled his lookouts, sending two men aloft to the crows' nest and additional seamen to the bow and to each wing of the bridge. Then he ordered all his off-duty deck officers to lookout stations. Fifteen pairs of binoculars searched the sea, already beginning to redden from the western sun.

He reached his first turn, plotting his dead reckoning fix, and returned a dozen times to the chronometer as *Lusitania* raced to the northwest. When he reached the second turning point, he ordered her due west, headed directly toward the lightship, and probably the submarine which was stalking him.

"I'll tell the lookouts to keep a sharp eye for the escorts," the first mate suggested.

"To hell with the escorts," Captain Dow snapped. "We'll see the escorts. Look for the damned periscope!"

But they didn't see the escorts. The telltale traces of smoke that he expected on the western horizon didn't appear. The first thing he was able to make out was the distant blinking of the Coningbeg Light.

"Where in God's name are they?" he finally shouted. Milford Haven had confirmed the rendezvous. But had there been any confirmation from the destroyers? Did they even know he was on his way in?

"We could circle a bit," the first mate said. "They may be running a bit off schedule."

Dow nodded grimly. That was one of his alternatives. But it was not without danger. *Lusitania* was now entering the eastern approaches to the channel, exactly where a calculating U-boat commander would expect him. With no destroyers to harass him, the U-boat commander could have surfaced and made his best speed with his diesel engines. He could have beaten *Lusitania* to the intercept point.

Circling as he waited for the escorts would simply prolong the time that *Lusitania* loitered in the danger area. It would also delay his arrival at the Liverpool bar. He had two choices: Turn back out to sea and add another day to his voyage, or rush through the gap between the lightship and the submarine he imagined to be lurking ahead.

Dow thought of the passengers, now gathering at the entrances to the dining rooms, the women totally absorbed in the style of their dresses and the appearance of their hair, the men concerned that their beef not be overcooked. He thought of the unknown cargo in the bow, and of the tons of diesel oil that filled his ballast tanks. The passengers might not survive even a single torpedo hit.

But there was another concern. There was no submarine in sight. The periscope he had seen two hours earlier was probably still where he had seen it, some twenty miles to the west. The maneuvers it had taken to intercept him were, as far as he could tell, the panicky maneuvers of his imagination. How could he explain running away from a submarine that probably wasn't even there? To the Admiralty, which counted on the ship's arrival to get supplies to the front? To Alfred Booth, who could calculate to the penny the enormous cost of keeping *Lusitania* at sea for another day.

"We're going through," he finally concluded. "Break out the zigzag instructions."

The zigzag was a series of turns designed by the Admiralty to confound submarines, preventing them from calculating the ship's relative heading. Varying turns, both to port and starboard, were made constantly, but at irregular intervals. Overall, the ship remained on its intended course. But at any given moment it was turning, preventing the submarine from plotting its heading. Without knowing a target's exact heading, the submarine couldn't aim its torpedoes. *Lusitania* headed for the channel. And then its bow began carving quick turns to both sides of its course line.

In the first-class dining room, Thomas Astin noticed his lobster bisque rolling to one side of his soup bowl. The ice in his water glass began to rattle. He glanced up into the alarmed eyes of his wife, who was struggling to balance her soup spoon over her Paris original dress. "Course change," he told her reassuringly. "We must be in Saint George's Channel." Water splashed out over the rim of glass, and suddenly the bisque was rushing to the other side of the bowl. He glanced around the dining hall and found one of the other gentlemen from his passengers' committee. The man's expression was as white as his tie.

"Submarine!" This time the scream came from the crow's nest. Fairweather Dow looked up and saw the lookout's arm pointing toward the port quarter. He swung his binoculars but could find nothing.

"Submarine," the lookout on the port wing sang out. Dow ran to his side and focused the glasses in the same direction. Immediately, he found the white wake cutting through the sea that was sparkling with crimson. The periscope was high out of the water, one thousand yards off.

He was past her, but still well within the U-boat's firing range. Now, speed was his best hope of escape, and the constant turns of his zigzag maneuver were costing him speed. He made his decision instantly.

"Steady on course zero two zero," he shouted to the helmsman. He was heading straight up the channel, abandoning his evasive maneuver in favor of speed. At the same time, he was narrowing the target he presented to the submarine's sights. Now his fate was entirely in the hands of the U-boat captain. If the German officer realized that *Lusitania* had settled on a straight course, calculated it quickly, and fired immediately, the torpedo could easily overtake the liner. But if he hesitated, then The Greyhound's speed would soon carry her safely out of range.

The seconds fell like hammer blows. Dow kept his binoculars trained beyond his fantail, looking for signs of attack. But a torpedo wake would be invisible in the frothy white turbulence that trailed behind *Lusitania*. His first warning would be the sound of an explosion at the stern.

"Captain Dow."

Fairweather followed the voice down to the boat deck, where Thomas Astin was standing with one of his associates. Both men were in white tie, Astin still clutching the table napkin he had carried with him from the dining room.

"Where are our escorts?" Astin shouted up to the bridge. "What's happening?"

Dow ignored the questions, refocusing his glasses on the periscope, which was fading rapidly astern. How many more seconds, he tried to calculate, as he forced down the bile that was rising up in his stomach.

"Captain Dow!" Astin's voice was now loud and angry. "What the hell is going on?"

Dow waited. One way or another, the question would soon be irrelevant.

"Escorts ahead," the first mate called from the bridge. Dow wheeled around. There was a smudge of smoke on the northern horizon. He could make out the masts of two ships steaming toward him. When he turned back, the periscope had disappeared.

He stepped to the rail and leaned down toward the two first-class passengers. "Dead ahead, Mr. Astin. Just as we planned. Nothing to be concerned about."

The next morning, Fairweather Dow walked into the offices of Alfred Booth and resigned his command. Booth was furious.

"I'll make damned sure that you never get another command," he screamed at his captain. "Nothing. Not even a rowboat."

But even as he was blustering, the Cunard chairman knew it was an empty threat. Fairweather Dow didn't want another command. He wanted out of the war. For one horrifying hour, it had all come together: the innocent passengers, the deadly Admiralty cargo, and the submarine. Dow had no intention of presiding over the slaughter that such a deadly mixture was sooner or later bound to cause. He wanted to go home.

Booth regained his composure after a few moments and gestured his senior commanding officer into a chair.

"Who can replace you?" he asked frankly.

"Bill Turner," Dow answered without a second's pause.

"Bowler Bill," Alfred Booth gasped in horror, thinking of Turner's habit of wearing a bowler hat on top of his uniform jacket in full view of the passengers. "The man's a savage. He puts ketchup in his consommé!"

"Find someone else to dine with the passengers," Dow advised. "Put Bill Turner on the bridge. He's the best seaman you've got. Best chance that *Lusitania*'s got."

It was later in the afternoon when Alfred admitted to himself that Fairweather Dow, for all the stories of his caution, had more courage than he himself. Dow would have no part in an atrocity. He would give up his career rather than hold another passenger hostage to the Admiralty's thirst for war materials. Booth knew that if he had half of Dow's courage, he would resign from Cunard and have nothing to do with its dark cargoes. Let the Admiralty run the line, he thought. Let the passengers' blood be on their hands. He was steeling himself to write a letter to Winston Churchill, rehearsing the words he would use to express his disgust, when his secretary tapped on his door.

"Captain Turner is here," she announced.

The best chance that *Lusitania*'s got, Booth thought.

Schull

DAY's makeshift fleet was doing its job, much to the surprise of Admiral Coke, who commanded the Irish coast from his flagship at Queenstown.

"Astounding," he had admitted to Admiral Inglefield, who had scavenged for the meager provisions that Day needed. The scattering of ludicrous workboats and fishing vessels, armed with nothing more than rifles and light machine guns, was accomplishing off Ireland what His Majesty's mighty armada was failing to achieve in the other waters surrounding the British Isles. Since Germany's proclamation of a war zone, twenty-five British merchantmen had been sent to the bottom in the North Sea, the North Channel, Saint George's channel, and the Western Approaches, along with nearly half a million tons of critical war materials. Only one had been sunk in the stretch of coast that Commander Day patrolled, and that at night, when the Irish boats weren't operating.

Coke had sent a complete report to the Admiralty, coupled with his suggestion that additional civilian fleets be assembled to patrol eastward from Queenstown all the way to the Coningbeg Light. "We seem to be entering a new era of naval warfare," he advised, "when submarines are the main challenge to merchant shipping, and small patrol craft are the only workable defense. It is hard to see what contribution our main, deep-draft battle fleet can possibly make."

But William Day didn't need to see the figures on ship losses or debate the merits of capital ships. He could see the results in the faces of his crews. They had perfected their simple formations and took to sea eagerly each morning with a clear sense of purpose. They were in the war, doing honorable work, and that seemed much more important to them than the fact that they were shoulder to shoulder with their centuries-old enemy.

Most mornings, he sailed out with one of his fleets, using the fastest boat available as his flagship. He raced back and forth through the formations, urging wayward boats back to their stations, shouting encouragement and signaling a "thumbs up" to his captains. Mostly, he was just showing a military presence, reminding the crews during the long hours of idle waiting of the importance of their mission.

If he wasn't at sea, then he was standing on the docks to meet the fleets as they came in at night. He joined the seamen in their pubs, offered his congratulations, and listened attentively to the dozens of tales of imagined sightings.

"We had one right under us," a weather-worn fisherman might say as the barkeeper was sweeping the froth from his ale. "I could see the damn gun on her decks. Just made a couple of turns and headed right back out to sea."

"No place for her to come for a breath of air," another would agree, echoing Day's words as to why the U-boats couldn't operate in their presence. It didn't matter to Day that the stories probably weren't true. What was important was that the crews believed them. The fairy tales reinforced their sense of importance and brought them back to the docks with the next morning's sunrise.

At the end of the day, he was generally at the radio station, reviewing the messages that had been exchanged with incoming ships. Most of the incoming traffic concerned submarine sightings and reports of sinkings, which the Admiralty used to plot the areas in which the U-boats were operating. The outgoing traffic rerouted ships around the danger points, changed ports of call, and set up rendezvous with escorts.

And then there was the time he spent working with Shiela McDevitt. With the increase in coded traffic, she was locked in the security of the coding room, translating messages for hours on end. But at every opportunity, she was with him during his visits to the seacoast towns, serving as his liaison to the priests and town officials whose support for the English was always hanging in the balance. Slowly, patiently, she was winning them over. From "the woman who works for the English" she had become "the Irish girl who keeps the English in line." Father Connors now called her "one of us" instead of "one of them," and the elders of the fishing fleets admitted that "she's as bright as a tack, considering she's just a little girl." Shiela's only detractors were the women, whose eyes narrowed at the mention of her name. "Living like that, with the men," they said to one another, wagging their heads in disapproval. Instead of glimpsing their own potential in her work, they saw her as a threat to their limited roles. "Just a farm girl," was the accepted wisdom among them. "And putting on such airs."

It was the women who first sensed the personal interest that Shiela and Day had in each other. "He's living in her cottage," one of them told a parish priest after Day's car had been seen early one morning, parked beside Shiela's house. "He stayed the whole night." With any hint of encouragement, she would have organized the Rosary Society and marched on the house with a pot of tar and a bag of goose feathers. The ladies knew how to deal with girls who strayed from the straight path of maidenly virtue. But the priest had only turned up his palms in despair. What could the ladies expect? Day was a member of a Protestant church founded by a fornicating king? Prayer was probably a more Christian response than hot tar.

Shiela and Day were careful, well aware that there were few secrets in an Irish village. When they were with the town fathers, or talking to the boat crews, their relationship was official. "Commander Day," she called him in conversation, and she answered his directives, "Yes, sir." He referred to her as "Miss McDevitt," and even when he lapsed into "Shiela" it sounded like nothing more than a casual use of her first name. When he lingered at her cottage, he was usually up and dressing in the middle of the night, taking a few hours' sleep in his own room, and arriving at his housekeeper's table before the eggs were boiled.

"Good morning, Mrs. Martin," as he rubbed his hands together and slipped into his chair. "The coffee smells delicious."

Mrs. Martin looked back wide-eyed, certain that he had not been home while she was looking from behind the curtains of the parlor window.

"You were very late last night, Commander Day. I didn't hear you come in."

"Very late, indeed, Mrs. Martin," he would answer, without offering any reason, "and out very early this morning, I'm afraid."

But Day's relationship with Shiela wasn't easily managed. They were both aliens, without true friends, living under watchful eyes that were only too eager to see their failures. Shiela had warned Day that he was in danger, but the truth was that her own danger was just as great. Her isolation was, if anything, worse than his, because while the men would at least offer the trappings of friendship, the women of the villages were outspoken in their scorn for her. She had left them behind when she went to a better life in England, and now she returned in a position of responsibility that was beyond the fantasies of women who seldom left the chores of their kitchens. Day and Shiela had rushed into the loneliness of each other's lives and found answers to their needs. They couldn't schedule the moments of their intimacy, nor could they time their scattered liaisons by any mechanical clock. Secrecy was important to them, but not as important as their need for each other.

On one day, when Shiela had been vulgarly insulted by a woman on the docks, they had gone from the harbor at Baltimore straight to her cottage without checking back at the Crookhaven station. Day had held her throughout the night and then faced Chief Gore's suspicious glances with her in the morning.

"I was ill," Shiela had lied for both of them before disappearing into the code room. Day hadn't added to the lie with any explanation of his own but had simply dug into the waiting traffic.

On several occasions, the first sound of the morning birds had found them still in one another's arms. Mrs. Martin had dug mercilessly for information when Day returned to her house on those evenings and had been openly contemptuous of the explanations he had suggested. Joseph Martin, her husband, had finally intercepted Day on the docks one morning and steered him aside for a private word.

"She's a fine woman, the missus," he began, leaving no doubt as to his final loyalty. "But a bit under the good father's thumb, if you follow my meaning. Not at all understandin' of the things between young men and women. I mean, she was never alone with a man, even in the light of day, until we was married."

"A fine woman indeed," Day agreed.

"What I was thinkin' was that . . . for your own sake, mind you . . . it might be best if you found another room. Not that we can't use the rent money. It's been a godsend. But thinkin' of your privacy. Mrs. Martin can't help noticin' the comins' and goins' in her own house.

And there's no power on Earth that can keep her from speakin' her mind."

Day nodded gratefully. "I'll find other quarters, Mr. Martin."

"Without makin' a big thing of it," Joseph Martin advised. "I wouldn't want her to think that it was somethin' she done. Maybe if there was somethin' closer to the radio station."

"I understand. And thank you very much, Mr. Martin. It's nice to find a good friend." But while Day was looking for new quarters, he spent more and more nights at Shiela's cottage, until the scandal they had tried to avoid became the truth. He was living with her.

It was while driving to her house at the end of an exhausting day that he first raised a problem that had been troubling him. He had been sullen all day, too distracted for small talk, and in the quiet, she was falling asleep.

"Do you think the Germans are reading our traffic?"

Shiela broke through her weary drowsiness with an expression of fright. "The coded traffic?"

He nodded.

"How?" she asked. "It's a daily cipher. It changes every day."

"Lots of ways. A tap on the telephone line from Queenstown. Or a leak somewhere in the operation. At Queenstown. Or even our own people at Crookhaven."

Shiela went white at the suggestion. "I can't believe it," she said. "Do *you* think we're being compromised?"

He squeezed his lips into a tight line as he thought of his answer. "I'm not sure," he finally concluded. "But there are too many coincidences."

"Coincidences?"

"We send out messages assigning escorts and notify the ships that aren't going to have an escort," he explained. "Every U-boat attack over the past weeks has been on an unescorted ship. Or else, the attack has taken place before the ship reached its rendezvous with the escorts. I just can't believe that the Germans are that lucky."

"But maybe they simply don't attack when they see an escort ship," Shiela contradicted. "They could stay under the water and not attack unless the ship is alone. No one would know that they were there. That would account for their 'luck.'"

It was an explanation that Day had considered. But other "coincidences" weren't so easily explained.

"They've also hit the most important cargoes," he said. "There are scores of steamers running up and down the coast that the U-boats seem to ignore. It's as if they know exactly what they're looking for."

"Didn't you tell me that the Germans watched the cargoes you were loading in New York?" Shiela challenged.

He nodded. "No doubt about it. They know which ships are carrying war supplies when they leave American ports. But how do they manage to intercept those ships on this side? Unless they're damned lucky. Or, unless they have the kind of arrival information that we're broadcasting."

"But most of the important cargoes are getting through," Shiela reminded him.

"They don't have enough submarines to get to all the ships," he answered. "But it seems that the ones they do get to are always carrying important cargoes."

They went silent for a moment, Shiela seeming to weigh the logic that had led him to his conclusions. "There could be other explanations," she finally told him. But Day didn't seem to be considering other explanations.

"The Germans also seem to know where are boats are operating," he continued. "When we move the western end of our area, they attack to the east. And when we move out toward Mizen Head, they suddenly shift their attacks east."

"They can see our boats," Shiela reminded him. Day knew that she was right, but that didn't seem to change his thinking.

"On Monday and Tuesday, we were operating out past Mizen Head, and there wasn't one submarine incident. Wednesday we shifted to the west, and first thing on Wednesday morning they hit *Samuel Tucker*, right in the center of the area we had just abandoned." *Samuel Tucker* was an English steamer, inbound from Halifax. A U-boat had sunk her with a single torpedo just south of Crookhaven, in full view of the radio station. The crewmen, who came ashore in the ship's boat, said that the submarine had never even bothered to surface.

"Coincidence?" he asked.

Shiela was already shaking her head in disagreement. "But we never broadcast our fleet instructions. We hand the assignments right to the crews. It has nothing to do with the radio station."

Day smiled grimly. She was correct, and he knew it wouldn't take her very long to realize the implications. Someone in one of the boat crews, or one of the townspeople who were helping to organize the crews, was talking to the Germans. There was a spy in their midst. And it was probably the same spy who was tapping into their radio traffic. He watched her expression darken as she sorted through the evidence.

"Any ideas?" he asked her.

She stared straight ahead without answering.

"What about Fenians?" he pressed. "This wouldn't be one of our fishermen. Tapping phone lines, and running a radio. Probably even putting the information into a German code." It would take a bit of sophistication, and probably require the kind of organization that the secret society of Irish Nationalists would be able to provide. "Do you think any of the brothers might be close to us?"

Shiela shrugged. "They're everywhere. I don't know of anyone, though, who does more than talk. But I suppose any of the town officials could be part of the movement."

"How about the priests? They seem to be into everything."

"Not the priests," she answered. "Oh, they agree with the politics, and they're always talking about Ireland standing by itself. But there's a dark side to the Fenians. Their opponents get beaten up and burned out. Sometimes they're even killed. The good fathers wouldn't let themselves get involved in that sort of thing. And besides, the Fenians have no love for the clergy."

When they reached the cottage, Day raked the embers in the stove and raised a fire for their tea. Shiela moved around him silently, setting a tray with cups and saucers and a small pitcher of cream. "What are you going to do?" she finally asked.

"Inform the Admiralty," he said. "I'll give them the evidence and tell them what I suspect." He set the kettle on the open fire. "I suppose I'll recommend that they stop sending traffic through Crookhaven. Maybe just close the place down."

"And our local problem?" she said. "You can't just abandon the fleets."

"We won't give out the day's patrol areas until just before the boats leave the dock. That will give the submarines less time to act on the information."

Shiela fixed the tea and carried the tray into the parlor. She poured for both of them. "You can't be everywhere at once," she reminded Day as she handed him his cup. "You'll still be counting on local people to distribute the sailing orders."

"But just a few local people," he said. "If the information still seems to get through to the U-boats, we'll have a smaller number of suspects to watch."

She sent him to bed while she rinsed the cups and banked the fire in the stove for the night. When she reached the bedroom, he was already fast asleep. As she slipped in beside him, she was very careful not to disturb him, even though she knew that her good-night kiss wouldn't wake him. His days were exhausting, and on several nights she had had to pry the teacup from his fingers after he'd collapsed in one of the soft parlor chairs.

Day tossed in the early morning hours and found Shiela sitting up against the pillows, still wide awake. "What's wrong?" he asked as he sat up beside her and pulled her against his shoulder.

"I was thinking. If they close down Crookhaven, then they'll have no need for me here."

"I thought of that, too," he admitted.

"I won't leave you here alone," she said with determination. "I'll resign before I'll let them move me."

He smiled, trying to make light of her worries. "Do battle with the whole Royal Navy, will you?"

"I won't leave you."

He held her closer. "Shiela, they can send me somewhere else anytime they want. We just have to do the best we can."

"No," she said, pulling away from his embrace. "It's dangerous for you here. You should be asking for a transfer."

He reached out to take her back into his arms. "You're the only danger," he teased. But she pushed his hands away.

"Don't be making fun of me," she said, a sudden hurt showing in her eyes. "You shouldn't be staying here."

Carefully, he brushed her hair with his hand. "I'm sorry," he told her. She moved cautiously back against his shoulder.

"Why is it dangerous?" he asked her.

"Because you're asking questions," Shiela said. "They won't want you to have the answers.

LONDON

CAPTAIN Reginald Hall rose from behind his desk as Lieutenant Peter Grace was shown into his office. By rank, he should have remained seated until the junior officer came to attention and presented his salute. Then he could have offered the lieutenant a chair or, if he chose, left him standing throughout the entire interview. But Peter Grace was no ordinary officer. He wore civilian clothes, a bit more casually cut then was generally seen around Whitehall, and his boyish face showed no signs of weathering. He had never been aboard a ship and had no intention of ever accepting a naval command. Peter Grace's services to the Crown were in other capacities.

"Everything tidy on the India docks?" Hall asked as soon as he was finished with the handshake and had guided his guest to a chair. He pulled another side chair up close.

"I think so," Grace answered. "Loughton's friends have all been arrested for pilfering. And Mr. Loughton himself is no longer operative."

No longer operative. Hall had to smile at Grace's nice turn of a phrase. Loughton, a stevedore who had been selling cargo information to a German, had been crushed under a six-ton pallet that unexplainably broke free from a cargo hoist. Positive identification of the body, according to the coroner's board, had been extremely difficult. Even his dental work had been destroyed.

Accidents seemed to follow close behind Lieutenant Grace wherever his work in counterintelligence took him. A cache of German weapons, smuggled ashore to Irish revolutionaries in Londonderry, had exploded in a safe house, killing the leading plotters who were meeting at the time. A junior naval officer, whose code books had fallen into German hands, was washed overboard while his ship was lying at anchor. A merchant captain who had threatened to publish the secret orders for attacking submarines that the Admiralty had issued to all cargo vessels had been the only fatality in an otherwise routine dockside brawl.

The fact was that, in wartime, some transgressions were so potentially damaging to national defense that the normal procedures of arrest and trial had to be bypassed. Hall simply brought them to the attention of Lieutenant Grace, whose efficiency and discretion had earned him the respect of the Admiralty. Once he became involved, problems seemed to just go away.

"What do you know about southwestern Ireland?" Hall asked as a way of getting into Grace's next assignment.

"Admiral Coke's area," Grace responded. "Coastal watch. Escorts." He shrugged his shoulders, indicating that those few highlights taxed the limits of his knowledge.

"Crookhaven?" Hall pressed.

Grace searched his memory. "We have a radio station out there, don't we? Traffic in and out of Queenstown?"

Hall nodded. "Important traffic. Arrival messages for all ships coming across the south coast." He jumped up from the chair and retrieved a folder from the top of his desk. "It's being run by Commander William Day. One of our best young officers. You may have heard his name in connection with the *Aboukir* affair."

"The chap who saved half his crew?"

"Half?" Reginald Hall asked with a smile. "A bit of an exaggeration, but still quite a show." He handed Grace the folder. "He sent this to us. Quite an analysis, and all the information is accurate."

Hall sat quietly while Lieutenant Grace flipped through the pages. He waited anxiously while Grace reread the final page.

"Looks as if he's onto something. As he says, there are too many coincidences."

"He is onto something," Hall answered. "We've known for quite some time that we have a leak at Crookhaven. My guess was that there was one agent, probably tapping the telephone line. But after reading this, I'm inclined to agree with Commander Day. It looks as if we have a fair-sized operation down there that's talking to the Germans every day."

"Any ideas?" Grace questioned.

Hall sighed and held up his hands. "We haven't really looked. But I think it's time we did."

"So you want me to check into it," the lieutenant concluded.

"As soon as possible," Hall answered.

"Any thoughts on what I should use as a cover?"

"You won't need one. Commander Day has called the situation to our attention. It's natural that we respond by adding an intelligence officer to his staff. You'll simply go out to Crookhaven and report to Commander Day. While he's watching the coast, you'll be watching for spies."

Grace nodded. "Seems simple enough." But then his brow tightened. "Too simple, as a matter of fact. Any of your people could handle it. It doesn't seem to fit my specialty."

"Let's hope it doesn't," Captain Hall said. "But there is one complication. We'd like to know who's causing the leaks. But when you find him, we don't want him to become . . . I think *inoperative* is the word you used."

Grace was clearly confused.

"For a number of reasons, we need an open channel to Germany. We want them to read certain traffic that they assume we are trying to keep secure. To be more precise, there are certain ships that we would like to call to their attention."

Grace's lips began spreading into a smile of understanding. "Commander Day's discoveries aren't in the national interest," he suggested.

"They could prove inopportune," Hall corrected. "With you there to follow up on his suspicions, he'll probably focus his attention on his other duties."

"And you're in no hurry for me to find the spies," Grace said.

Hall nodded. "Certainly not for the next few months, at any rate."

Grace handed the folder back to his commanding officer. But his puzzled look indicated that he was still digesting the details of his assignment. "I'm still not entirely certain why you're sending me. I'm not usually your choice when you want nothing to happen."

"Just on the chance that Commander Day finds our German agents, we certainly wouldn't want him closing them down. And I wouldn't want another report like this one. Something that proves Crookhaven is compromised and forces us to shut it down. It's really imperative that the Germans continue to read our traffic."

Peter Grace's eyes turned cold. There was a hint of disgust in the stare he fixed on his country's ranking intelligence officer. "Day is one of ours. One of our best," he reminded Reginald Hall. "This isn't just a traitor, or some loose-lipped ship captain."

"The message we hope to get to the Germans could shave two years off the war," Hall said simply. "It could save thousands of our best from being slaughtered in the trenches."

They sat facing each other for a moment, neither able to think of anything else to add.

Finally Grace stood. "You'll cover my assignment with Admiral Coke."

"Of course," Hall promised. He held out his hand.

But Lieutenant Grace didn't reach for the hand. He turned away and let himself out of the office.

SCHULL

THOMAS McCabe's nephew tossed more logs into the firebox and watched the steam-pressure gauge inch up another two pounds. He opened the throttle valve and listened appreciatively as steam hissed into the cylinder heads.

"Ready to go, commander," he said to William Day, who was standing on the dock, handing the patrol assignments to the boat captains. Day climbed over the gunwall, bringing the bowline aboard with him. His flagship, *Hugh O'Neill*, fell in line with the flotilla of small boats that was heading out into Roaringwater Bay.

Since he had begun holding the patrol assignments until minutes before sailing, Day had gone to sea with his boats each morning. The danger, he reasoned, had become greater with his simple change in operating procedure. He wanted to be there when the danger struck.

The submarines, as he had informed the Admiralty, seemed to know the disposition of his boats along the coast. They had been avoiding his patrol areas, hitting targets in other sea lanes. Now he was denying them that information, making the entire coast a high-risk area for their operations. He knew they wouldn't simply abandon their hunting grounds. Sooner or later, they would have to come to grips with his civilian navy.

The breeze in his face was warmer than it had been in February, when he'd first launched his patrols. The days were growing longer as the sun moved up from the south. Now, instead of tracing its path along the southern horizon, it took a higher arc in the sky overhead. His boats left the docks earlier in the morning and stayed at sea later in the evening.

Hugh O'Neill's owner, Thomas McCabe, had learned the commander's daily routine. At first they steamed among the small boats, checking their bearings to be sure that they were on station. Then they moved to the western end of the formation, where steamers inbound from America would first appear. They loitered there until the first of the scheduled arrivals broke over the horizon, a sign that none of the U-boats had taken up station on the Western Approaches. Then they began to steam in a long easterly arc, tracing the seaward edge of the boat formations all the way back to Glandore. They returned on a westerly course over the same route, always keeping themselves between the Irish boats and the open sea.

McCabe had questioned the procedure. "We should take our station in the middle of the formation, where we've got the shortest distance to the most boats," he argued logically. "Save us all this steaming around, not to mention all the wood we're burning. If this war lasts much longer, you'll put every tree in Ireland under that damn boiler."

But Day knew that the middle of the formation was the last place that a submarine would appear. "If they want to attack us, they'll come in from the sea," he told the yacht's master. "They'll be running on the surface, and their deck guns will already be manned."

He had done all that he could to prepare for the eventuality. A heavy machine gun, begged from Admiral Inglefield, was mounted to the top of *Hugh O'Neill's* wheelhouse and manned by an experienced gunner. It was probably an even match for the machine gun that a submarine would carry on its conning tower. He had considered mounting a cannon on the yacht's forecastle, but Inglefield had laughed at the idea. "First time you fire it, the recoil will tear it right off the deck. You're more likely to sink yourself than you are to do damage to a U-boat." Instead, he had scrounged a simple foot soldier's mortar and placed it on the bow. It was no adversary for the three-inch deck gun that a submarine would be firing. But the sight of mortar rounds exploding in the water around a U-boat commander would probably give him second thoughts.

The boats shaped up quickly, taking stations on the western edge of the patrol area, and the flagship began making its rounds.

"What have we got today?" the captain of a workboat with a small paraffin engine called as *Hugh O'Neill* came alongside.

"First one through is a Yank," Day shouted back. "Should be off Mizen Head in about an hour. Then a British steamer with a destroyer escort."

"Not a lot of air out here, commander," Mike O'Sullivan said, pointing up to the ripples in his sail. "Hope you won't be expecting me to go anywhere in a hurry!"

"Let's hope not, Mr. O'Sullivan," he answered. "It's a nice day for just taking the sun."

He worked his way westward, out to a point three miles southwest of Mizen Head Light, and suddenly saw a trace of soot on the horizon.

"This should be our Yank," he said to Captain McCabe, pointing out over the mortar that rested on his bow. It was McCabe's signal to throw his wheel to port and begin the wide swing out beyond the seaward edge of the formation.

They cruised along leisurely, running at a speed that matched their engineer's efforts to load logs onto the fire. Day kept an eye trained back over his shoulder until the American freighter was clearly in view and had moved into the safe protection of his fleet. As he leaned against the wheelhouse bulkhead, he lifted his pipe out of his pocket and struck a wooden match over the bowl. Then he raised his binoculars and searched ahead, hoping to pick up the Baltimore fleet that would be operating from Cape Clear, back toward Glandore.

They had been moving eastward for over an hour when McCabe called out to him, "Looks like one of your chicks has gotten lost." He pointed to the south, where a dark shape seemed to be drifting on the horizon. Day blinked into the light reflected off the water and raised his glasses. The shape was indistinct, but the white wake it was kicking up indicated that it was moving at a good speed. Faster, he realized, than any of the boats in his fleet.

"Come about," he yelled to McCabe. "That's not one of ours."

As the yacht was turning, Day could make out the crashing spray of a bow just ahead of his target. "Jesus," he whispered to the yacht's captain. "It's a submarine."

He rushed back to the engine and began firing wood into the firebox. "Get me all the pressure that this thing will hold," he yelled at McCabe's nephew. "Pull the goddamn throttle all the way!"

He screamed up to the machine gunner, pointing dead ahead. "Load, and stand by to fire." The gunner, who had been stretched out with his shirt off, jumped up in disbelief.

The mortar crew on the bow had heard the commotion and were already prying the cover off the container of mortar shells.

"Stand by to fire!" Day ordered. One of the crewmen raised a round over the muzzle, prepared to drop it into the pipe. But the gun captain shouted back, "Way out of range. We'll never hit it."

"Aim, dammit," Day snapped.

The gunner turned the crank, tipping the mortar to a thirty-five-degree angle. He raised his hand.

"Fire!"

The crewman dropped the round into the barrel. With a muffled "pop," the first shot Day had fired in the war rose in a high arc and exploded into the water ahead. It was only a fraction of the distance between *Hugh O'Neill* and its target.

"Fire!" Day ordered again.

The gun captain looked back in confusion. The commander had just seen the full range of the tiny infantry weapon. They would just be wasting ammunition.

Day charged toward the forecastle. The gun captain immediately gave the hand signal, and his crewman dropped another round into the mortar. A second explosion shattered the sea halfway to the submarine.

The mortar rounds served one of their purposes. The blasts echoed along the coast, shaking the drowsy captains to action. Sagging sails were suddenly drawn taut, and idle engines crackled to life. But Day's real reason for firing was to turn the submarine, its low shape now clearly visible. The U-boat commander couldn't ignore cannon fire moving closer to his boat. A single hit, or even a near miss, could take away his ability to submerge, leaving him as easy prey for the Queenstown fleet. He would have to dive or turn his attention toward the onrushing *Hugh O'Neill*. Either way, he would be distracted from the murderous attack he was aiming toward the helpless boats in Day's flotilla. But the U-boat wasn't responding. Instead it continued at top speed toward the boats at the outer edge of the formation.

A puff of smoke appeared above the submarine, followed in seconds by the unmistakable crack of its deck gun. At the same instant, a tall geyser of water exploded next to a small, engine-powered fishing boat. The boat, which had turned toward the oncoming submarine, immediately turned away.

"Keep firing," Day screamed to the mortar crew. He saw the submarine's deck gun flash again. This time the geyser lifted the fishing boat out of the water and dropped it on its side. The Irish crewmen spilled out into the sea.

He looked back to the engine, where the young engineer had the firebox nearly glowing. The steam-pressure gauge was already into its redline, and the hissing engine was spinning in a blur. The graceful lapstrake yacht with its richly polished brightwork was moving as fast as it could. But that wasn't nearly fast enough.

The submarine had moved almost to the edge of the formation, bringing the first row of boats into point-blank range. Its machine gun was now chattering, kicking up spray just short of its targets. The next crack of its deck gun splintered a wooden sailing boat and tossed it like pieces of kindling into the air.

The boat captains had seen the submarine as soon as Day's first mortar round exploded and had immediately turned to close in on her. "Get to her before her crew can get on deck," they remembered, not realizing that she had approached on the surface with her gun crews already on station. At the sound of the first cannon shot, they had turned in panic, the closest boats nearly colliding with one another in their rush to escape. But they didn't have a chance. Running on the surface with its powerful diesel engines, the U-boat was quickly overtaking them. Their rifles and light machine guns were useless against its armament. They looked over their sterns at the sleek gray shape slicing the water behind them, and down the muzzle of its deck gun, caught up in a deadly lottery as the German gun crew randomly selected its victims.

The U-boat swung its deck gun toward an ancient coastal tramp with a rusted hull and coal soot belching from a stovepipe stack. It fired, and the round tore through the bow, not exploding until it hit the water on the other side. Immediately, the little boat began to settle, its slowly twisting propeller lifting out of the sea.

The machine gun on the conning tower found its range and shot the rigging off a gaff-rigged sloop. Its crewmen leaped over the side and into the sea. Within a minute, four of the Irish boats were gone, leaving frantic figures struggling in the water. Day could only watch helplessly, the action still beyond the range of his pathetic guns.

The submarine turned, heading inward toward the second line of the patrol, where O'Sullivan's sailboat had its boom swung out trying to run before the light breeze. On the tower, the German machine gunner was switching his weapon to the other side, ready to take aim at the new row of victims. O'Sullivan suddenly appeared on his transom, fumbling with the bolt of his English rifle. Defiantly, he raised it toward the oncoming U-boat.

"Nooo!" Day screamed uselessly. O'Sullivan, in his mad heroics, was designating himself a target. The old man raised the rifle and tried to steady it against the sway of his own boat while the German gunner locked his weapon into the pedestal and pulled the bolt. O'Sullivan fired, the recoil lifting the rifle muzzle into the air. The U-boat's gun crew dropped to the deck for cover. Heads on the conning tower turned toward the sound of the shot, and suddenly the commander was jabbing his finger toward the sailboat, where O'Sullivan was trying to strip a new round into the rifle's chamber.

"Get down!" Day yelled frantically, the sound of his voice dying before it reached the scene of the confrontation. He watched in horror as the U-boat's machine gun swung toward the old man. The gun exploded in a hail of bullets that rippled the water under the sailboat's transom. Pieces of dry wood tore off the hull under his feet as O'Sullivan took aim.

Suddenly, he flew backward, his arms flailing and the gun tossing into the air as he disappeared over the side. The machine gun kept firing, chopping the boat into pieces that dropped quickly into the sea.

On top of *Hugh O'Neill's* wheelhouse, the English gunner took aim and fired a short burst. The bullets skipped into the water, short of the gray hull of the submarine. They were still out of range, and the U-boat was turning toward its next victim. Her deck gun cracked again, exploding the water next to a chugging fishing boat. The sea poured down on the boat's deck. Its engine coughed and died. Then machine gun bullets raked its hull, and it quickly filled with water.

The mortar popped again, launching another shell into a high trajectory. This time the explosion was less than fifty yards from the target. Immediately, the U-boat broke off its attack and turned toward the yacht, its deck gun swinging into William Day's face. At the same time, Day's gun crew began adjusting the range settings on the mortar tripod. They were getting close enough to zero in on their target.

"We're overheating," McCabe's nephew yelled. The crossheads and bearings of the primitive steam engine were moving too fast for him to keep them oiled. "We've got to slow down."

"Full speed," Day screamed back, ignoring the new danger. It didn't matter whether the engine could destroy itself in another minute. The yacht's fate would be decided in the next twenty seconds.

The submarine's deck gun fired, and the air filled with the whistle of the incoming shell. The sea exploded just off the starboard bow, smashing violently against *Hugh O'Neill's* weathered hull. The yacht pitched off its course, sending Thomas McCabe spinning across the wheelhouse and sliding the mortar and its crew across the forecastle. Day grabbed the wheel and twisted the bow back toward the U-boat. He should be maneuvering rapidly to present the German gunners with a more difficult target. But he had to lock onto a steady course so that his own men could aim the mortar. As the two boats charged toward each other, the speed of the gun crews became the life-and-death issue. Whoever got off the next shot would probably be the survivor.

On the submarine, the machine gunner was shifting his weapon to the other side of the conning tower, where he could get a clear shot at *Hugh O'Neill.* Above his head, Day heard his own machine gun begin to chatter. Bullets churned up the sea next to the U-boat's deck gun and then began ringing off the side of her hull as they climbed toward the German gun crew. He saw his crewman drop another round down the barrel of the mortar. The instant the round exploded out toward its target, Day spun the wheel to the right. And at the same instant, the U-boat's deck gun fired.

The three-inch shell traveled in a straight line, instantly ripping into the water where the yacht would have been had she continued on a straight course. A water spout blasted into the air, pitching *Hugh O'Neill* over on its starboard side. As she struggled to right herself, rounds from the submarine's machine gun began tearing into her hull. Day heard the bullets pounding into the wooden strakes, and then he was buried in a shower of glass as the machine gun rounds ripped into the wheelhouse. There was a scream from overhead as the bullets raked his own machine gun position, blowing his gunner over the side.

The mortar round had reached the top of its climb and was beginning to fall toward its unsuspecting target. Aboard the U-boat, all eyes were turned toward the gun mount, where the last rounds from Day's machine gun had knocked down two of the crewmen. The German gunners were trying to drag their wounded comrades down through the forward hatch.

The U-boat commander suddenly looked up, warned by the whistle of the falling mortar round. Then he ducked down behind the conning tower shield just as the mortar shell exploded in the sea only a few feet from his hull.

Day turned the yacht back toward the submarine. His mortar crew had reset their weapon and were cranking in a new range setting. He was rushing right back under the muzzle of the German machine gun, hoping to get off one more mortar round before the U-boat gunner cut him to pieces. But there was no machine gun fire. The submarine commander understood that the tiny field piece, mounted on the yacht, put his boat in mortal danger. He was clearing his decks, preparing to dive.

McCabe, who had been knocked down and dazed by the first shot of the submarine's deck gun, staggered to his feet next to Commander Day. "Hold this course," Day told him, pushing the groggy yacht captain against the wheel. He jumped out through the shattered wheelhouse window and climbed onto the overhead where the unmanned machine gun was still in position.

Through the machine gun sight, he saw crewman scampering down the submarine's deck and conning tower hatches. He threw the bolt and squeezed the trigger. Instantly, bullets began clanging across the diving hull. One of the German crewman dropped before he could reach the deck hatch. Another, halfway into the hatch, threw up his arms and fell into the opening.

In a sudden cascade of bubbling water, the U-boat's decks disappeared. Day aimed his sights toward the conning tower and began firing at the periscope tubes. Machine gun bullets ricocheted off the steel weather shield. But with them came pieces of tubing that protected the delicate lenses of the periscopes. He kept firing, now at point-blank range, as the conning tower sank under his bow. He was still pouring rounds into the U-boat's eyes when they disappeared under the sea.

It was then he realized *Hugh O'Neill* was doomed. The heat from the engine had set the afterdeck on fire. Sea water was pouring in through the bullet holes that had raked the hull and was slowly filling the bilges. With the engine seizing, she was dead in the water, slowly settling on even keel.

Many of the fleeing Irish boats turned back toward him, and toward the crews of the sunken boats who were struggling in the water, clinging to the shot-away masts and deck planking that were still afloat. *Hugh O'Neill* was down to her rails, her engine space still belching black smoke, when a small workboat came alongside and lifted the crew to safety. There was no hint of satisfaction in the faces of the Irish seamen, even though the first submarine to challenge them had been driven off. Some of their neighbors, who had gone into the water, were not to be found among the survivors. One of the young boys who had been clinging to a sailboat's rigging was dead when a rescue boat hauled him aboard.

Day waited on the Schull pier with his crews as the day's toll became a reality. Five of the men from Schull were unaccounted for, their wives and families wandering in a daze among the survivors, crying out when their worst fears were confirmed. Two of the men who had come home were anointed in mumbled Latin prayers by Father Connors, then rolled carefully in sailcloth and carried by their friends toward the church.

William stood aside, suddenly the outsider to the town's grief, feeling compassion that he was unable to express in their language of sighs and embraces. He saw O'Sullivan's wife, suddenly old and frail, standing on the slip where the sailboat had tied up each night for all the years she could remember. He went to her, thinking of words about heroism and valor. But he discarded these and simply touched her hand and said her name. At first she didn't respond. But when she looked up and recognized him, she suddenly screamed, her bony hands flailing out and striking at his face. He backed away, making no effort to block her blows. "Damn you," she cursed in a shrill voice. "What good will your devil's money do him now!"

The people watched while she sagged under the effort of striking at him. She fell to her hands and knees, shaking in muffled sobs. Day knelt in front of her, once again extending his hand and whispering her name.

Emmett Hayes stepped out of the crowd, put his arm around Mrs. O'Sullivan, and carefully helped her to her feet. "She'll be all right," he told Day, as he led her back to her people. They turned with her and walked slowly up the road toward the village, leaving Day kneeling alone on the dock by the empty space between the tied-up boats.

When he started his car, there were no children waiting to hear the engine catch and roar to life. The main street seemed empty, without even a light falling from the window of the pub. As he drove along the street, he thought of himself as an angel of death, with people locked behind their doors in fear of his passing. He turned onto a side road and steered through its ruts until he reached the path to Shiela's cottage.

She was waiting in the doorway. She had been at the radio station when she had heard of the U-boat's attack and had begged a ride on a truck that was leaving Crookhaven. One of the Crookhaven sailors, coming back from the town, had told her that boats had been sunk and that there were rumors of deaths. She knew that, if there ever were a battle, Day would charge into it. And then, as she reached her cottage, a passing farmer had rushed to tell her the first reports, which included the loss of *Hugh O'Neill.*

For reasons she couldn't explain to herself, she never doubted that he was alive. But she knew that once the submarine slipped back beneath the surface, the people would need something else to blame for their miseries. A tall English military officer would never escape their notice.

"A bad one?" Shiela asked as he stepped out of the car.

He answered with a slow nod of his head. "Jeremy Duke," he began, referring to the English sailor they both knew, "shot by the gunner on the submarine. Pat O'Donnell and the Farley kid lost over the side. And old Mike O'Sullivan . . ."

Shiela's hands shot to her face. "Oh, no," she groaned, overwhelmed by the grim litany.

"He just stood there on the fantail, out in the open, loading his rifle as if it were target practice. Mike O'Sullivan, facing off against a three-inch deck gun and a machine gun."

"Sweet Jesus." She turned away from him to hide her crying.

"The son of a bitch came right at us," Day continued as he began to pace the small parlor. "He wasn't after a ship. He was after the boats. He was warning them: 'Keep patrolling out here and we'll make you pay.' We beat him. We drove him off. Maybe even put him out of action. But, damn it, he delivered his message. Point blank into a bunch of small boats. It was a slaughter."

Shiela wasn't listening. She had collapsed onto the sofa and was shaking as she tried to hold back her sobs. Day went to her and tried to take her in his arms. But she pushed him away and rushed into her bedroom. He started after her, then stopped at the door. He had lost good men to the cruelty of war. But she had lost neighbors who had been part of her childhood. She needed her moment of mourning.

He went into the kitchen, found the bottle of whiskey that she kept in a cabinet over the sink, and brought it to the kitchen table, where he poured a heavy measure into a plain glass. Then he ran the dead men through his mind, forcing himself to see their faces. They were his command. Had he wasted them to no purpose? They had trusted him. Had he betrayed their trust? He tried to blame himself, hoping that confession would soften the image of the U-boat as it charged in from the sea, turning Roaringwater Bay into a killing ground. His plan and his leadership had cost them their lives. They hadn't died fighting their war. They had died fighting his.

But there was another image that even the narcotic of the alcohol couldn't dim. That was the thought of faceless seamen falling into the ocean around the hulk of their burning ship. No matter whose war it was, his fleet of small boats had stopped the submarines. His Irish volunteers had saved lives. He hadn't wasted them. He hadn't betrayed them. Old Mike O'Sullivan, standing on the transom of his overmatched sailboat, wasn't a fool. He was a brave man doing, at that particular instant, what he had to do.

"It's not your fault." It was Shiela, her dress wrinkled and her eyes red, standing in the doorway. "It's the damned, senseless war."

"I know," Day answered without looking up from the glass. "But I'm sorry for them." He turned toward her. "I'm sorry for you."

Shiela walked to the table and lifted the glass from his fingers. She emptied the whiskey into the sink and put the bottle back up into the cupboard. Then she stood beside him and pressed his face against her breast.

"We shouldn't be alone," she said. "Not tonight."

She took his hand and led him into the bedroom.

They made love gently, more an act of caring than a surrender to passion, and then lay together quietly as if hypnotized by their own breathing. The first sounds of morning found them still in an embrace, Shiela's hair splayed out on the pillow and over his arms. Day tried to ease out of the bed quietly, but she was awake as soon as he moved. She dressed, went into the kitchen, and began making a breakfast while he shaved and dressed.

"You're going to take the fleet out?" she asked as she poured his coffee.

He nodded. "I have to. If we don't go out today, then we won't go back tomorrow. The submarine will have beaten us."

"Do you think they'll go with you?"

He shook his head slowly. "I can ask them. But I can't blame them if they don't. It's not an adventure anymore. It's grim business, and they know it."

"You've done all you can," Shiela consoled. "There's nothing left for you here."

"But I have to try," he said. "I can't just walk away as if it weren't important. If it's not important, then what did they die for? I have to make them understand that they're saving ships. Lives."

"English ships," she reminded him.

"Human lives," he answered.

She made a lunch for him as he packed his sea bag, then walked with him out to the car.

"If they won't sail with you, what will you do?" Shiela persisted.

He shrugged. "I've told the Admiralty to close down the radio station. If there are no patrols . . . then there's nothing for me here."

"Nor me," she concluded. She looked around at the greening countryside that fell away from the cottage. "It's a beautiful land. But I'll be glad to be rid of it."

When he pulled to a stop at the foot of the pier, only a few men were waiting by the boats. Day took a deep breath and tried to look confident as he walked toward them. Then he saw Emmett Hayes break from the group and start down the pier to meet him.

"I don't think you'll be patrolling today," Hayes said.

Day looked over Emmett's shoulder as the men grouped around no more than half a dozen boats. "Is that what they've decided?"

"It was decided for them," Hayes explained. "Mike O'Sullivan's body came in with the tide. We're waiting on the others."

Day nodded that he understood. "I'll wait with them. I'd like to help bring them to the church."

"We'd appreciate that," the schoolteacher agreed. "But then I think you should give us a day by ourselves. We'll find our own way to decide what we do next."

CROOKHAVEN

"NEW OFFICER'S aboard," the sentry told Day as he was being saluted through the security gate at the radio station.

Day continued a few steps before he stopped short. His mind had been locked on the grim vigil his boat crews were keeping as they waited for the new tide to bring the rest of their friends home to Schull. He had hardly noticed the sentry, and it had taken a few moments before his words registered.

"New officer?"

The young sailor was pleased to be the first with the news. "Yes, sir.

A Lieutenant Grace. Replacement for Miss McDevitt in the coding office."

Day's confusion was obvious. He turned and started up the hill.

"Didn't know we were losing Miss McDevitt," the sentry called after him. "We're going to miss her."

Day didn't respond. He saw Chief Gore standing in front of the cottage and knew that the chief was waiting to intercept him with the news.

"I heard," the commander said as Gore was about to pounce on him.

"Did you know Shiela was leaving?" Gore phrased it as a simple question, but it was really a challenge. He was demanding to know whether Day had arranged Shiela's transfer.

"I had no idea, chief," he answered. "I don't think Shiela knew about it either."

Chief Gore threw up his hands in disgust. "Then why? Why would they move her? Don't they know how important she is to us?"

"Maybe the new lieutenant can tell us," Day said. "Where in hell is he?"

The chief pointed to the quarters cottage. "Having his lunch. He told me to fetch him as soon as you arrived." Day started across the field to the other cottage, and Gore fell in beside him.

"Looks like he's fresh out of school," the chief chatted as they walked. "Brand-new uniform right out of the tailor shop. Probably never stood on the deck of a ship." He paused, but Day didn't take up the invitation to ridicule the new arrival. "Last thing we need is to train a new recruit," Gore continued.

"Let's give him a chance, chief," Day snapped. "He may not be thrilled with his assignment either."

The boyish-looking officer sprang to his feet as soon as Day stepped through the doorway. "Lieutenant Peter Grace, reporting for duty," he chanted. He snapped to attention.

"At ease, lieutenant," Day said casually.

"Jesus Christ," he heard the chief whisper behind him.

"Thank you, chief," Day said. "The lieutenant and I will be over to join you in a few minutes." he closed the door, leaving Gore outside.

Grace had a plate of kidney stew and a pot of tea set in front of him. He looked uneasily at the food and then back at the commander.

"Finish your lunch," Day offered as he dropped his cap on the table and sat opposite Grace. "There's no hurry."

Grace talked between bites. "Heard you had a bad day yesterday. This probably isn't a good time for me to be starting."

The commander nodded. "A very bad day. But a good time to have you aboard. We need help here at the station." He waited while Grace washed down a mouthful of stew with a swallow of tea. "But a bad time to be losing Miss McDevitt. Do you know when she's scheduled to leave?"

"No rush," Grace said. He glanced around, confirming that there was no one else in the cottage. "Fact is, commander, that my assignment is just a cover. I'm with Naval Intelligence." He pushed another kidney onto his fork, ignoring the shock that registered on Day's face. "Nice coincidence, actually. You tell the Admiralty that you suspect your radio traffic is being compromised. The Admiralty tells Intelligence. So, Intelligence has to find a way of getting me in here without kicking up a fuss. And then Miss McDevitt asks for a transfer back to England." He nibbled the kidney off the end of his fork. "What's more logical than for me to arrive as her replacement?"

"She requested a transfer?" Day's surprise was obvious.

Grace shrugged. "That's what they told me. Didn't you know?"

"Miss McDevitt is a civilian," Day answered. "She doesn't need my permission to transfer."

The lieutenant used a crust of bread to mop up the gravy. "Best if you can keep her a while. Changes tend to make spies suspicious. Wouldn't help our investigation."

"Who are you investigating?"

"Everyone," Grace said, carrying his dishes to the sink. "In this business, the last person you'd suspect generally turns out to be the one you're after. Although, if you want my opinion, there are possibilities for leaks all over the operation, with the telephone lines carrying plain language traffic. No reason to think that it would be one of our own."

Day didn't enjoy being lectured by a junior officer. "You're an old hand in intelligence, I suppose."

"I've had a few assignments," Grace said. As he turned back from the sink, he noticed that the commander was staring at his uniform. "Oh, these?" He straightened the jacket and pulled down on the sleeves. "New getup for me. I usually don't like to advertise that I'm military. But in this case, a uniform fits nicely with the cover story, don't you think. Just another wartime officer working at a backwater post."

Day's eyes darkened, but he fought back his anger. "This backwater post just lost some good men to a German U-boat, lieutenant. I wouldn't be so quick to dismiss us."

Grace walked slowly back to the table and leaned down on two strong hands. The smug smile disappeared from his face. "Commander, you're the only one who knows why I'm here. And as long as I'm just a snotty brat out of officer training, we'll be able to keep it that way. Believe me,

I'm very good at what I do. Every bit as good as you are in your work. I won't get in your way. Don't you get in mine."

Day looked long and hard into eyes that were suddenly cold. Then he nodded in respect. "I've misjudged you, lieutenant."

The smile reappeared on the young man's face. "Let's hope everyone else does," he said.

"You'll keep me informed?"

"You'll know everything I know," Grace answered.

Day stood up quickly and picked up his cap. "Let's get you introduced," he said, as he started for the door.

"Aye aye, sir," Grace chimed as he stepped in behind his new commanding officer.

He had no intention of keeping Day informed. If he had, he could have begun by telling the area commander that he had already established, with standard telephone line tests, that no one was tapping the lines. He could have told Day that the teacher who distributed his sailing orders, Emmett Hayes, had spent two years writing inflammatory editorials for a secret Fenian newspaper. Or that a local priest, Father Brendan Connors, had twice been reprimanded by his bishop for harboring Fenian fugitives. Names of three of the local merchants, including the keeper of the Schull pub where Day's crewmen gathered, had been screamed out by an organization courier whose hands were being pressed against a coal stove by British interrogators.

If he had any thought of keeping Day fully informed, he would certainly have mentioned that Chief Gore had been married to an Irish girl in Liverpool who had been sent to an English prison for petty theft, and that it was Gore's outburst against the Crown's justice that had curtailed his navy career. Or that one of his radiomen was into the pants of a local lass whose father was known to be running guns. He might even have warned his commanding officer that the invaluable coding clerk who shared his bed was the daughter of a Free Irish labor agitator.

Lieutenant Grace had done his homework. He was already convinced that the Crookhaven station was surrounded by Irish conspirators. And he knew he could get the names any time he wanted them. All he had to do was find one of the nest who had a young son or daughter, and then make him watch while he pushed the barrel of a pistol into the child's mouth. The Irish certainly loved their country. But they loved their children even more. It was a technique that generally produced more names than Naval Intelligence could possibly investigate.

But he was in no hurry. His assignment was to keep the Crookhaven station operating until it delivered its critical message to the Germans. Then he would shut it down.

"Lovely weather you're having here," he said to William Day as they crossed the field to the radio cottage.

"It's been a bitch of a winter," Day answered.

"Well then," Grace laughed. "I've arrived just in the nick of time."

NEW YORK

SIR PETER Beecham had come to dread his weekends.

From Monday to Friday, he was caught up in the excitement of commerce, using the bottomless pockets of his Morgan bank connections to clobber his German adversaries in the market for war materials. He now owned most of duPont's output of black powder and a whole production line of General Electric's capacity for motor generator sets. Two steel companies in Pittsburgh were now fabricating shell casings to the specifications of English cannons, and three mills outside of Boston had turned their entire production over to British army uniform coats. He was a bigger customer for heavy-duty shoes than the Sears, Roebuck catalogue, and he owned a contract for enough barbed wire to build a fence around the entire perimeter of Europe.

One in every three ships departing an east coast port carried his cargoes. Half of them were British ships, but he had recruited into his fleet freighters that flew the flags of every seafaring nation in the world. True, not all his supplies were getting through. German submarines had sunk over 25,000 tons of precious supplies in the past month alone. But he had so many ships, approaching the British Isles by so many routes, that the few dozen U-boats the Germans could keep at sea were simply overwhelmed. He had passed the crisis in keeping his country outfitted for what was becoming an endless war. And he had earned a personal letter from King George, on palace stationery, that said his services to the Crown could be ranked alongside those of Wellington and Nelson.

But on Saturday mornings, as his car drove through the gates of his home, his spirit blackened. He felt as if he were arriving at the funeral of a man he had murdered. His well-meaning lies to his daughter had destroyed the joy that once sounded through the estate like strings playing in the music room. They had raised barriers between himself and Anne, each sick with guilt for having deprived the other of Jennifer's love.

A servant opened the door and greeted him with a formal acknowledgment as he took his hat and briefcase.

"Mrs. Beecham?" Sir Peter inquired.

"In her room, sir. I'll tell her you've arrived."

"No. No. Quite all right. Don't disturb her." Then, after a moment's pause, "And Jennifer?"

"Out for a walk, I believe."

"Ah, yes. Lovely morning for a walk," Peter said as if the morning mattered. Jennifer walked down to the water even in the rain. When she was home, she was generally in her room, having meals sent up on a tray. "Perhaps a pot of tea," he said, as he started into the library, which had become his own silent prison.

He went to the French doors that opened out onto the terrace. The trees, which only last week had been yellow with new buds, were now green with young leaves. The rolling lawn was coming to life with color, and the slate of the sound was darkening into a deep blue. He touched the door handle, thinking for a moment that he would step outside into the scented spring air. But his hand fell away. The darkness inside the room was more suited to his mood.

Anne entered, carrying the tray with his tea. "Welcome home," she announced with pretended enthusiasm. "I thought I might join you." He took the tray from her and set it down, then embraced and kissed her. He listened as she catalogued the events of the week while she poured and settled into a chair opposite him. Then he interrupted her with the news that had been weighing on him.

"Jennifer has booked passage to England."

Her teacup sagged against her lap. "Dear Lord."

"Second class on *Atlantic*, one of the small Cunarders. Sumner just happened to come across her name on the booking register. He thought it was a mistake and called me for clarification."

"What did you tell him?"

Peter sighed. "Well, oddly enough, they're in the process of transferring the passengers to other ships. *Atlantic* is being held in England for Admiralty alterations. I asked him not to notify Jennifer. Told him that I'd take care of it."

"She was going to leave us without even saying good-bye," Anne guessed. "My God, how she must hate us."

"Nothing of the sort," Sir Peter lied, even though he had thought exactly the same thing. "Just a show of independence. I'm sure she'd still need your help to pack her trunk."

"It's already packed," she answered, her mood growing even more solemn. And then she expressed what was beginning to become her last hope. "Is there any way you might arrange for Commander Day to be transferred back here?"

"Out of the question," he answered abruptly. He jumped up and paced to the French doors. "We can't deliver the man to her doorstep just because it would please Jennifer." He braced his shoulders in a show of determination, but they sagged with his next breath. "Actually," he admitted in a soft voice," I've thought about doing just that. Winston certainly wouldn't deny me the favor. But then, I thought, all this started because I tried to arrange what was best for her. Perhaps we should accept that Jennifer is ready to make her own arrangements."

"You'd let her go?" Anne challenged.

Peter held out his arms, gesturing to the silent household. "Hasn't she already gone? She's certainly not here anymore, is she?"

"At least talk to her," Anne begged.

Peter could see that his wife was near tears. He walked to her and rested a reassuring hand on her shoulder. "Of course I'll talk to her. Who knows? She may even listen."

His opportunity came within the hour when Jennifer stepped through the front door, taking off her sweater as she crossed toward the stairs.

"Jennifer," he called from the doorway of the library. She stopped abruptly, hesitating while she decided whether to acknowledge her father or ignore him. "May I have a word with you."

She walked slowly toward the library, and around him as she entered the room, never even glancing in his direction as he closed the door behind her. Sir Peter walked to his chair before he realized that Jennifer was standing in the middle of the room, like a servant waiting for his instructions. He gestured to a chair.

"Please, sit for a moment. I think this is important."

She moved silently and sat on the edge of the chair opposite him, making it obvious that she didn't plan on staying very long.

"I understand you've decided to go back to England."

Her eyes widened in shock.

"I wasn't prying," Beecham hastened to reassure her. "I just happened to learn, purely by coincidence, that you've booked passage."

"Even Cunard does your bidding," she said coldly.

"Nothing of the sort. It's just that the ship you booked is being pulled out of service. They're moving passengers to other ships. When they saw your name . . . they assumed . . ."

She smiled at the irony. "The one ship I was able to get aboard is being removed from service?"

Peter reddened in embarrassment. "Now really! This certainly isn't my doing. I don't have the power to order ocean liners about."

"No. Only people," Jennifer answered.

For an instant, he thought that he might explode with rage at her effrontery. But as he looked at her, he realized that her wound was even greater than his.

"I suppose I deserve that," he admitted. "I doubt I'll ever forgive myself, much less expect forgiveness from you. But if you're determined to go, at least let me help get you there safely."

"I think you've helped enough." She stood to indicate that she had nothing more to say.

"For God's sake, Jennifer, there's a war on. Ships are being sunk right and left. At least let me get you aboard a safe ship."

She eyed him suspiciously, the settled slowly back down to the edge of the chair.

"All your life, your mother and I arranged things for you. It was the right thing for us to do. And then, suddenly, one day it was the wrong thing for us to do. We made a mistake. We hurt you terribly. But that doesn't mean we can stop loving you."

"You'll arrange my passage?" she asked, not sure that she wasn't being led into some sort of trap.

He nodded. "*Lusitania* sails on May first. It's only one day later than you were scheduled. She makes Liverpool two days earlier than *Atlantic* would have arrived. And she's the safest ship afloat. Let me transfer you to *Lusitania*."

"Thank you," Jennifer said. She stood and started for the door.

"You'll want to let William know that you're coming," he called after her. "If you write him, I'll make sure your letter gets into Monday's diplomatic pouch."

Jennifer turned and looked back at him.

"I will," Sir Peter said. "I swear, I will."

That evening, he and Anne dined alone, sitting at opposite ends of a long table, the sound of the serving dishes filling their empty world. Anne waited patiently for his report on his discussion with Jennifer, while Peter tried and discarded a dozen ways to raise the painful subject. Finally, he settled on the simple truth.

"I'll book Jennifer aboard *Lusitania*. She sails the first of May."

Anne set down her knife and fork. "There's no hope of keeping her with us?"

Peter stood and went to the end of the table where he could sit close to his wife. He took her hand and seemed to study it for a moment. Then he said, "I think letting her go is the only hope we have of keeping her in our lives."

When he returned to the city on Monday, Sir Peter lifted Jennifer's letter from his briefcase and held it in his hand for a long time. What, he wondered, had she told the commander to explain her long silence? What had she said about her father and his ruthless intrusion into their lives? He thought of writing a letter of his own to William Day explaining his actions. Day would certainly understand that he had tried to do what was best for both him and Jennifer. But he realized that it would only be an exercise in self-justification. He had acted shamefully toward a man he thought of as a son. He had abandoned his place in the heart of his daughter. Simple words couldn't restore his honor.

He worried about Day's response to Jennifer's letter. Perhaps he no longer cared for Jennifer the way he had when Peter had seen them together on the terrace. Certainly that was what Beecham had intended when he sent the commander away. What if he wrote back telling her not to come? What if, when she reached Ireland, she found him involved with another woman? Perhaps there was some way he could make sure before his daughter traveled across the ocean only to find her hopes destroyed. He wanted terribly to protect her from pain and disappointment.

But he remembered the pain he had already caused her by trying to protect her from her own life. He slipped the letter into the diplomatic pouch that was being taken down to a departing ship. Then he sent a messenger to Cunard with his request for a first-class suite on *Lusitania*, sailing the first of May.

WASHINGTON

"WILL THIS mean war?"

Robert Lansing put his hand over the telephone. He was still too stunned by the news to think of an appropriate comment. The *New York Times* reporter had just informed him that the British passenger ship *Faloba* had been torpedoed by a German submarine forty miles off the English west coast. American passengers had been killed. Lansing wanted to sound informed, but the State Department had not yet received the information. He had never heard of the Smalls Light, which the reporter had mentioned as the nearest point of land.

"We are still gathering information," he lied. "At this point, it is premature to speculate on the appropriate U.S. response."

He rushed down to the State Department communications center. The single telegraph operator on duty was reading a sports page, his feet resting on an empty desk. His next stop was Secretary Bryan's office, where he nosed around just long enough to be sure that the secretary was away for the day and that no special communications had been received. Then he grabbed his hat and topcoat and rushed off to the British embassy.

Sir Cecil Spring Rice, His Majesty's ambassador, looked exceptionally grave as Lansing was ushered into his office. Sir Cecil, it was rumored, had been born wearing formal attire, and gravity was his natural expression.

"My deepest condolences, Robert," the ambassador said, rising from behind his desk. "All England is saddened to learn that the Germans are now directing their barbarity against your countrymen."

"Shocking news," Lansing agreed, trying to appear as mournful as his host. He turned to Capt. Guy Gaunt, the British naval attaché, who had risen from a chair beside the ambassador's desk. Gaunt was a plant of Naval Intelligence in Sir Cecil's household, ordered to keep the ambassador as uninformed as Lansing kept the American secretary of state. They met frequently, and generally secretly.

"Good to see you, Captain Gaunt," Lansing intoned with a formality feigned for Sir Cecil's benefit.

"A sad day," Gaunt answered, taking up his boss's line of sympathy that America should find itself being drawn into the war.

"Captain Gaunt was just bringing me up to date on this tragic affair," the ambassador said as he pulled up a chair for Lansing. "Perhaps he will start again from the beginning, for your benefit."

Gaunt referred to his notes. *Faloba* had been a small, 5,000-ton passenger ship, unarmed and carrying a standard commercial cargo. She had been torpedoed without warning and then, while dead in the water, shelled unmercifully by the now surfaced U-boat. Half her lifeboats had been destroyed in the shelling, leaving those passengers who were able to make it over the side to fend for themselves in the water. At least one American was confirmed to have died, but there were probably others. Not all the passengers were yet accounted for.

"Cold-blooded murder," Lansing said when Captain Gaunt had finished his report.

"Your government will undoubtedly lodge a formal protest," Sir Cecil speculated.

"More than a protest, I should think." Lansing looked toward the naval attaché. "An unprovoked attack on American citizens constitutes an act of war."

Guy Gaunt nodded wisely.

Extra editions were already on the street as Lansing walked toward the White House. "U-boat Attack Kills Americans" covered the entire front page of an evening tabloid. "Germans attack United States," an enterprising newsboy was shouting.

Lansing was escorted directly into the Oval Office, and within seconds was joined by President Wilson, who was wearing a red satin smoking jacket over his suit trousers.

"Reporters have been calling," the president said as he settled behind his desk. "Everyone seems to know about this except the U.S. government. We've been attacked at sea, but the navy has nothing. Not even a picture of the damned ship. Secretary Bryan can't be reached."

"I have the information," Robert Lansing said confidently, relishing the moment when he was the most informed man in the government. "Personal sources."

Wilson's eyes widened behind his wire eyeglasses.

"I've already been to the British embassy for talks with Sir Cecil and his naval attaché. Their communications, I've found, are generally faster than our own."

"And . . ." Woodrow Wilson was leaning forward in anticipation.

Lansing shook his head slowly. "I'm afraid, Mr. President, that our worst fears have been realized. An unprovoked attack on a passenger ship, known to be carrying U.S. citizens. It could hardly be more blatant."

Wilson's face slumped into his hands. "Dear God," he prayed. When he looked up, there were tears at the corners of his eyes. "Why, Robert? Why would they provoke us? We're the last hope for peace."

"Perhaps, Mr. President, they truly prefer war. God knows you've given them every opportunity for a peaceful settlement. Your offer to mediate. Your open-seas proposal . . ."

"And this is their response," Wilson said.

Lansing nodded. "I'm afraid it is."

The president labored up out of his chair, turned to the window, and looked out over the gardens that were blossoming with spring. "There must be something that we can do. Something short of plunging into this mad war."

"I wish there were," Lansing sympathized. "But they haven't left you much room to maneuver."

"Perhaps a strong protest," Wilson thought aloud.

"We have protested in the strongest terms," Lansing reminded him, "when they stopped one of our ships. But now they have killed our citizens."

"An ultimatum, then." The president was grasping at straws.

"At least that," Lansing advised. "A firm statement that we will consider any further attack on American citizens, or American property, to be an act of war."

Woodrow Wilson shook his head. "That would be as good as a declaration, I think. Unless we embargo our own ships, there's bound to be another incident."

There was a knock on the door, followed by William Jennings Bryan, who was shown in by the president's secretary.

"Mr. President," Bryan began, but he stopped short when he saw Robert Lansing rise from his chair.

"You've heard the news," Wilson began.

"I was just briefing the president," Lansing explained.

Bryan ambled to a chair and sat down heavily. "Yes, I've heard it. And not from those idiot newspaper boys. Where in the name of God do they get their information? 'Americans attacked.' 'High seas slaughter.' A lot of nonsense."

Wilson looked in confusion from one man to the other. "But Robert was just telling me . . ."

"I have it on good authority . . . ," Lansing began. But Bryan cut him off.

"What authority? Your friends at the British embassy? They're probably the ones who are stirring up all the reporters."

"Mr. Secretary!" Lansing's neck stiffened in indignation.

"I've been in touch with our consulate," Bryan continued. "They interviewed the survivors. The passengers blame the ship's captain. They were quite outspoken that he came very near to getting them all killed."

"They were torpedoed without warning," Lansing contradicted.

Bryan pulled two pages of scribbled notes from his jacket pocket and put on his glasses. Then he fumbled with the notes, sorting the pages and turning some of them over until he had them in the right order. "*Faloba* was challenged by a German submarine . . . with the number twenty-eight painted on its side . . . that surfaced next to the ship and put a shot across her bow. The captain tried to run for it, so the submarine fired again, much closer the second time. *Faloba* stopped, and the German came alongside. He announced that he was going to sink the ship and gave the captain fifteen minutes to get everyone into lifeboats. The survivors say that the captain wouldn't swing out the boats. They were all standing on deck, waiting to abandon ship, but the captain did nothing."

Wilson looked at Lansing. "You said they were attacked without warning."

"Exactly as the embassy reported," Lansing defended. "I wonder if the secretary isn't being taken in by German propaganda."

Bryan flourished his notes. "These aren't Germans talking. These are Englishmen who were on the ship. The police kept reporters away from them, but they were afraid to keep officials of our government away. Until British navy officers came and rounded up all the survivors. From then on, His Majesty's navy wouldn't let our representatives near the passengers."

Wilson nodded, then gestured for Bryan to continue.

"After the fifteen minutes were up, the German gave the English captain another ten minutes to put his passengers and crew into the boats. The captain swung out the boats, but he wouldn't let the passengers get aboard.

"Then the U-boat commander extended the deadline for another ten minutes. A half hour had gone by, and the captain still hadn't done anything to save the passengers."

"I can't believe any of this," Lansing interrupted. "There was a British warship on the scene, and its captain confirmed that the attack came without warning."

Bryan tossed frantically through his papers. "That was the problem. The British warship." He found the testimony he was looking for. "While the submarine and *Faloba* were just sitting there, looking at each other, a British warship came into sight. *Faloba*'s captain started his engines and tried to escape toward the warship. That was when the U-boat put a torpedo into her."

"Even though it was obvious that it was an unarmed passenger ship," Lansing pointed out for President Wilson's benefit. "It was a direct attack on innocent passengers."

"Now here's the worst of it," Bryan continued, ignoring Lansing's argument. "The torpedo struck, and the ship began to list. The captain ordered the passengers into the boats and began lowering away. Up to that point, not a single passenger had been hurt. They were in the midst of lowering the boats . . . one of the people our consul spoke with was in a lifeboat, rowing away. Suddenly, there was a terrific explosion aboard *Faloba*. Blew the ship in half. It sank in two pieces."

Bryan dropped his notes into his lap and took off his spectacles. "The ship was apparently carrying explosives." He looked directly at Lansing. "Ammunition and passengers on the same ship."

"Ridiculous," Lansing nearly shouted. "There are any number of factors that could cause a ship to explode." He turned back to Wilson. "Mr. President, the essential fact of this tragic affair is that a German submarine put a torpedo into a passenger ship. And if Secretary Bryan's account proves to be correct, it did so with the passengers in full sight. That's the issue we have to address."

Woodrow Wilson settled back into his chair and folded his hands under his chin. "And yet, Robert, it would appear that the German was very careful to observe the spirit and the letter of the rules of encounter."

"An American was killed," Lansing insisted.

"An American who was traveling on a belligerent's ship through a war zone," Bryan added.

Lansing jumped up from his chair. "Are you suggesting that Americans are no longer free to live and travel as they see fit?"

"Certainly not," Bryan snapped back, his own voice rising in volume. "But if some fool American decides he wants to pick flowers between the German and French lines, he's probably going to get his head shot off. What I'm saying is that Americans who want to travel through battlefields do so at their own risk."

Lansing turned to Wilson. "We have an obligation to assure the right of our citizens to travel on any ship that will sell them passage."

"Bearing in mind," Bryan told the president, "that the presence of a single American on an English ship does not render it immune from German attack."

Wilson's eyes rolled wearily. "Gentlemen, please." Lansing lowered himself back into his chair. Bryan folded his notes and slipped them back into his pocket.

"I'm determined to maintain our strict neutrality," the president said as the starting point for all further discussions.

"Then insist that Germans respect our rights as neutrals," Lansing advised.

"Warn our merchantmen and our people that, when they go into a war zone, they're on their own," William Jennings Bryan countered.

Wilson looked from one statesman to the other. If he followed Lansing's advice, then he would be demanding that the Germans give up their one effective naval weapon, their submarine blockade. They would never even consider it. But if he followed Bryan's counsel, he would enrage the entire American business community, which was getting rich supplying war materials to Britain. "Perhaps," he ventured, "I should reintroduce my open-seas proposal."

Lansing was fuming as he left the White House. A few hours earlier, a reporter had assumed that the United States would be declaring war on Germany. Now, his country wasn't even going to lodge a formal protest. Wilson's open-seas policy didn't have a chance. Essentially, it required that England give up its blockade of Germany in exchange for an end to German submarine warfare. England, he knew, wouldn't hear of it.

When he reached his office, there was a message waiting from Sir Peter Beecham. Beecham would undoubtedly expect that, as a result of the *Faloba* incident, the United States would be coming into the war on the side of England. Lansing couldn't bring himself to call back with the disappointing news.

WILHELMSHAVEN

CAPTAIN BAUER paced the passageway outside of Admiral von Pohl's stateroom aboard *Friederich der Grosse*, the flagship of the Open Seas Fleet, like a schoolboy waiting for his meeting with the principal. More than likely, he was about to be relieved of his command of the German U-boat fleet. Or, if he were left in charge, there would be serious restrictions on his operations. Either way, the undersea war he had been waging with increased success seemed about to end in surrender.

He took another cigarette from the crumpled package that was stuffed into his jacket pocket and lit it from the burning end of the one he was still smoking. He walked to the end of the passageway, then turned and began walking back past the two sailors who stood guard at von Pohl's door. The sentries kept their eyes straight ahead, pretending not to see the flotilla commander in his moment of agony. To acknowledge the fear that was evident in his eyes would have been to confront him with his own human frailty. German sailors were trained to regard their officers as something more than human.

It had been a week since von Pohl had summoned him to the flagship to explain the sinking of *Faloba*.

"A passenger ship?" von Pohl had demanded angrily.

"A passenger ship carrying ammunition," Bauer had countered. "We knew the cargo through our port agents. And we knew where to find her through our Irish agent. She was a legitimate target of war."

"But the passengers . . ."

"That's why U-28 was told to surface and challenge her. We offered the passengers the opportunity to abandon her. Don't you see, Admiral von Pohl? When they carry passengers, they can't carry guns. The passengers would see the guns and talk about them. That's why *Faloba's* captain wouldn't let the passengers leave the ship. He thought they were his protection."

"One of them was an American," von Pohl had reminded him.

"Does an American passenger allow the English to carry munitions through our war zone?"

Admiral von Pohl's shoulders had slumped, his face falling into his hands. He spoke sympathetically. "The emperor has charged me with deliberately violating his order to avoid involving neutrals. When the Americans protest—and they will, my dear Bauer—the emperor wants to offer them the head of a flag officer. We're to apologize abjectly for our sins, and court-martial the man responsible."

Bauer had hardly been able to speak his reply. "Then I'm your man, admiral. They were my orders."

In the days that followed, the fate of Captain Bauer hung like purple bunting over the men of the submarine fleet. They followed the uproar in America through the German newspapers, which reported angry mobs gathered outside the White House, demanding war. The American who had died, an insignificant businessman, had suddenly become a national hero, with news stories of his defiance in the face of his German murderers. He had announced his nationality in a steady voice, a New York tabloid reported, warning the U-boat captain that Americans would search the ends of the Earth to bring him to justice.

Less sensational, but more important, were the reports of deliberations within the U.S. government. A highly placed but anonymous source said that the declaration of war was in the process of being drafted. But an even higher source, also unidentified, claimed that President Wilson was still hoping to keep his country out of the conflict. The submarine crews knew that their commanding officer's future, and perhaps their own, depended on Wilson's response. Each day, as Bauer visited his boats, his officers clasped his hand tighter and held on an instant longer in an expression of personal affection. The boat crews broke the rules of military discipline and greeted his arrival with a loud cheer. They were his men, and they were willing to share his fate.

But at Wilhelmshaven, where he had been summoned this morning, the flag officers turned away from the sight of him. Submarines, they agreed, were an unfit weapon for a great nation, and the men who commanded them were a stain on the purity of the German officer corps. Efficient, effective, to be sure, but hardly gentlemen. The type of men who would respond to a glove across the cheek with a knee to the groin. Sooner or later they were bound to violate the rules of chivalry and bring down the wrath of all civilized nations. It was only a matter of time, they reasoned, until Bauer's conduct would embarrass the kaiser. It was best not to be too close to him when that moment came.

The door of von Pohl's cabin opened, and his aide stepped out into the passageway. The sentries at the door snapped to attention. "Admiral von Pohl will see you now," the aide announced, stepping aside so that Bauer could enter the quarters. Bauer crushed out his cigarette in the butt kit, squared his shoulders, and marched toward his execution.

The man who jumped up from behind his desk seemed anything but an executioner. Admiral von Pohl, glowing in a broad grin, rushed to greet his submarine commander.

"We are vindicated, Bauer. Completely vindicated." He threw his arms around the younger officer and hugged him like a son. Then he stepped back, clasping Bauer's shoulders in his hands. "The Americans are doing nothing. Absolutely nothing. And the emperor is acting as if sinking that damned ship was his idea."

"I don't understand," Bauer managed in complete confusion.

Von Pohl nearly danced back to his desk, where he snatched up a document. "It's not even a protest. President Wilson regards the loss of an American citizen as"—he looked down at the paper and found the words—"as 'the inevitable and unfortunate consequence of blockade warfare.' He has reissued his appeal for freedom of the seas and has offered"—again he consulted the document—"'to personally chair a peace conference which will declare all seas open to the commerce of every nation.'"

Bauer could feel himself beginning to smile. "And the emperor?" he asked.

"In marvelous spirits," von Pohl chuckled. "He has accepted the president's proposals without qualification, leaving the British with the unhappy task of turning their back on their American ally. He knows that England will never agree to lift her blockade. So he becomes a world hero, while King George becomes a warmonger."

"Then there will be no court-martial," Bauer concluded.

"A parade, more likely," said von Pohl. "His Imperial Highness regards the American response as recognition of the legitimacy of our war zone. He feels that President Wilson has recognized our right to sink any ships carrying contraband."

"Passenger ships?" Bauer asked suspiciously.

"If they are armed, or are carrying munitions."

"Without warning?"

Von Pohl's happy expression soured. "My dear Bauer, we must be reasonable. If we know they are unarmed, then surface, and give the passengers a chance to get into the boats. But if they won't stop for our challenge, or if they refuse to put their passengers over the side . . ." He shrugged his shoulders so that Bauer could draw the logical conclusion for himself.

SCHULL

THE BODIES of the four Irish crewmen were carried into the church in plain pine boxes and lined head to foot from the altar rail to the last row of pews. Widows and mothers, their grief hidden in black veils, were led into the front rows; and then the townspeople, with Shiela in their midst, filed in until the tiny church was full. William Day and his English sailors, all in full dress uniform, came in last and stood in the back, realizing that they were not part of the congregation.

Father Brendan Connors had decreed a high mass, and he sang the Latin prayers in a clear tenor. His sermon pulled together the myriad mysteries of Irish theology, proving without argument that their fallen comrades were already in the company of the Blessed Virgin. "But these men are more than saints," he concluded. "They are also heroes in God's army. And their earthly commander is here with us today." He looked to the back of the church. "Commander Day. Will you say a word?"

Even when he reached the pulpit, Day had no idea what he could say to these people. To O'Sullivan's widow, who had cursed him at the dock. Or to Mrs. Delaney, whose two boys had been in the same boat. All he could tell them was what he believed. Without thinking of where it might lead, he began a litany of all the ships that had passed safely down the Irish coast, listing the numbers of their crewmen and the number of passengers they were probably carrying. When he finished, he had counted more than 1,000 people who had sailed under the protection of the Irish boats.

"I have no enemies," he said, "unless they are the kings and princes who declare wars. I believe, as Father Connors does, that we are all brothers. And when we find ourselves caught up in a war, I believe that the best of us do what we can to save one another from the slaughter. These men offered safety to a thousand of their brothers. They are the best of us."

"Not exactly the official Admiralty point of view," Peter Grace whispered out of the corner of his mouth when Day had returned to his place. "I think we've decided that the Germans are the enemy."

"And the Irish?" Day asked in return.

The English sailors formed an honor guard on the steps as the bodies were carried out by men dressed in their best suits, clutching their caps in their hands. They waited at attention until the coffins were secured on a wagon and the procession had disappeared toward the cemetery. They had broken ranks when Emmett Hayes came out of the church and walked up to Day and Shiela.

"Thank you for being here," he said. "We all appreciated your words."

"Not much comfort in words," Day answered.

Hayes shrugged in despair. "I suppose not. But at least they died for something. Most Irishmen aren't given that privilege."

"Will the men go back on patrol?" the commander asked.

"I'm not sure," Hayes said after a moment's thought. "Father Connors will know when it's time to raise the subject. Perhaps in a few weeks."

Peter Grace joined the group, and Day introduced him to Hayes.

"Ah, Mr. Hayes," Grace said after presenting a smart military salute. "I've heard a great deal about you."

"New to the area?" Hayes inquired.

"New to the navy," Grace said. "Fresh out of training school, I'm afraid."

Hayes eyed the new officer cautiously, but the innocent smile stayed fixed on Grace's face.

The English contingent returned to Crookhaven, where Shiela disappeared into the code room while Day began going through the motions of reviewing the previous day's traffic. But after a short while, he jumped up from his desk, left the cottage, and walked to the edge of the cliff beside the antenna tower. He looked out at the empty ocean and realized that his work in Ireland was nearly over.

"Perhaps in a few weeks," Emmett Hayes had said. But Day doubted that the fleet would ever sail again. Even if the men could erase the image of the U-boat, sliding toward them with its guns aflame, the women would never forget the line of coffins down the center of the church. For a year, the widows would be in black, making their way each morning to the saints' altars to light their candles, a constant reminder of the emptiness that awaited wives of heroes.

And there was Lieutenant Grace. He had believed the young officer when he stated confidently that he knew his job. Somewhere in the village, probably among his friends, was an agent working for the Germans. It wouldn't take Peter Grace long to find him. And when he did, then English justice would descend on people who had been its victims for centuries. Once Grace made his arrest, as he had to do, there would be no hope of enlisting Irishmen with the devil's money.

There would be no reason to keep the radio station in operation. Arrest one plotter, and there would soon be another to take his place. They were in a hostile land, with no shortage of enemies. The fact was that Crookhaven was a relic left over from the first low-powered wireless transmitters that had to be set at the ocean's edge if their signals were to reach ships in the middle of the sea. With modern equipment, the Admiralty could just as easily broadcast from Queenstown, or from Milford Haven.

Even his personal attachment to Ireland would soon be broken. Shiela's request for transfer back to England had been genuine. She believed that Peter Grace was her replacement, and that the Admiralty would soon be posting her to a new assignment. Her transfer wouldn't come as quickly as she expected, but in all probability she would be gone before summer.

Day knew that he had done all that he could as area commander for the southwestern coast. He had demonstrated conclusively that a fleet of small coastal boats could keep the submarines out of the sea lanes. Perhaps Admiral Inglefield would organize a new fleet, operating from English ports and manned by English crews. But that wasn't his affair.

"I think I'm finished here," he told Shiela as they drove together back to Schull. "I want a ship that will get me back into the real navy."

"Do you think they'll reassign you?" she asked.

He nodded. "Inglefield likes me. I think he'll pull a few strings if I ask him. The problem will be in telling him that I don't want to join his staff in Queenstown. It will hurt his feelings, but he knows I'd rather be back at sea."

"I'm glad," she said as they turned into her road. "You're better off out of here." As they opened the door to her cottage, she added, "They won't forget the men they buried today. You've overstayed your welcome, if you were ever all that welcome."

They worked in silence as they prepared a simple supper, the question of their future hanging over them. She had requested a transfer to God knows where, willing to leave him behind in order to get out of Ireland. And now he was looking for a ship that would certainly take him away from her. They had come together in a moment of need, when their loneliness had driven them into each other's arms, and acted as if their embrace was never-ending. But now the truth was upon them. Could they simply walk out of each other's lives? Or was there a bond that went beyond their exile in a foreign land that would hold them together despite the separations of the war?

Day mulled the question until they were getting ready for bed. He puffed his pillow and sat up on top of the comforter while she changed into her nightgown. "Can I ask you something?" he tried cautiously.

Shiela glanced at him, looking suddenly defensive.

"You never mentioned your transfer. You didn't even tell me that you had written."

"I had to get away," she answered.

"Away from me?"

"No. Dear God, not from you. Away from this place where neither of us are wanted."

"We could have talked about it," he reminded her. "What you're thinking about . . . what you decide. It's important to me."

Shiela slipped under the comforter and leaned comfortably against his side. "You would have asked me why."

"And you couldn't have told me."

She put her arm around him and held him tightly. "All I could have told you was that I loved you."

"And that's why you wanted to leave me?" Day asked.

"That's why I have to leave you," Shiela answered. She sat up suddenly and touched his face with her fingers. "I know I'm not making any sense. But you have to believe that it's true. Sooner or later, these people will hurt you. I don't want to be here when it happens."

"I don't understand what you mean," Day told her.

"I know," she responded. "And I can't make you understand. I warned you a long time ago that you should leave. And I know you didn't believe me. Everything seemed to be going so well for you. But that's over now." She settled slowly into his arms. "I'm happy that you're finally asking to be transferred."

Day pushed the comforter aside and slipped into the bed beside her. "Maybe we should go together," he whispered. "I think I need to be close to you."

She kissed him gently. "You're close to me now."

"But when you leave?"

"What will happen will happen," Shiela said. "If we're meant to be together, then we'll find each other."

He tried to look into her eyes, but she turned her face away, against the pillow. "Then this is only for now?" Day asked.

Shiela looked up at him, and in the soft light of the lamp he could see that she was crying. "Now is all we have," she told him. She pulled him toward her with all her strength.

SPRING
1915

SCHULL

"CAN I give you a ride, Mr. Corcoran?"

James Corcoran looked through bloodshot eyes and tried to focus on the face that was looking down from the wagon.

"I'm going your way," the voice assured him in a distinctively British accent.

Corcoran swayed unsteadily. He recognized the bright eyes and the generous smile. Someone he had seen before, but who in hell was he?

"It's Lieutenant Grace, Mr. Corcoran. The new officer at the wireless station. I work with Commander Day."

"Oh, yes," Corcoran remembered. "The new lad. With the pretty uniform. God bless you, my boy." His foot missed the step when he tried to climb up to the seat. He toppled forward and crashed against the side of the wagon.

"Let me give you a hand," Grace offered. He reached down and pulled Corcoran up next him, lifting the big shopkeeper effortlessly.

"I'm just up the road a bit," Corcoran said. "It's only a short walk."

"I know where you live," Grace answered. "In fact, I know quite a bit about you, Mr. Corcoran." He clicked his tongue, and the sagging horse began shuffling up the road.

James Corcoran finished every day at the town pub, arriving early, as soon as he had closed up his store, and staying late until the town gathering place was ready for closing. He had buried his wife ten years earlier, and there was never anyone waiting for him at home. Some nights, when the conversation was spirited and the dart board active, he nursed a few pints of bitters through the evening and walked home with a lively stride. But on other nights, when he found himself alone at a corner table, he sipped steadily from a bottle of whiskey, refilling his glass the moment it was empty. Then the road to his small house was much longer, and the hill a great deal steeper. This was one of the nights that he spent by himself.

"And how's business, Mr. Corcoran? Not quite as good as when everyone was getting paid for sailing, I suppose."

"Hard times, my boy," Corcoran slurred. "Hard times."

"And yet everyone seems to be in and out of your store. All the navy people from the radio station. And the townsfolk. Do you know that yours is the only place where Father Connors shops for himself? His housekeeper runs all his other errands."

"They do come by," Corcoran agreed. But he was in no mood for idle chatter. His head was sagging down onto his chest.

"They do, indeed," Grace agreed. "Like the post office. People stop by and leave their letters, and then other people stop by and pick them up."

Corcoran's chin snapped up. "A post office?" he asked. He was seeing a trace of light through the fog.

"For all your old friends in the brotherhood," Grace continued, his head aimed straight ahead, supervising the horse, which knew the road better than he did. "A place where they can exchange ideas. Ideas that they wouldn't want bandied about in the pub."

Corcoran tried to hold his head up and force his brain to think. But he was too far gone in his cups. All he could manage was the fact that he was in danger. But he didn't have the wits left to do anything about it. He recognized the break in the stone wall that marked the path to his house.

"You can drop me here, lad."

"Nonsense, Mr. Corcoran," Peter Grace laughed, pulling the rein to turn the horse onto Corcoran's road. "I'll take you right to your door. That will give you time to tell me about all your neighbors in the Fenian brotherhood. I'd like to get to know them."

The shopkeeper tried to shake his head, but the movement tipped his balance so that he almost fell out of the wagon. Grace's arm shot out and grabbed him by the sleeve.

"What friends?" Corcoran asked as soon as he was steady.

"Oh, let me see. There's Emmett Hayes, the schoolteacher. Father Connors, of course. Joseph Martin. And the mayor. But you don't really tell the mayor everything, do you? After all, he was charged with being a bit loose-lipped when he was living in Kenmare."

"I don't know what you're talking about, son," Corcoran protested. He rolled in his seat and tried to climb down from the wagon. Grace caught the back of his collar and dragged him back.

"But you do, Mr. Corcoran. Why, I'll bet you know things that you don't even know you know. Because you sneak a peek at all those notes they leave in your store, don't you?"

"Let me get down," Corcoran ordered.

"And that's what I'm hoping you'll tell me," Grace continued. "Who's dropping off the notes with the names of the ships. And who picks them up with their groceries."

"I'm not saying a word," Corcoran challenged.

"Just the names," the young man said. "Oh, I don't care about your plans for a rising. Go right ahead and have it whenever you're ready. I don't even want to know who's the general, or where the guns are coming from. Because you see, Mr. Corcoran, all your rebellions are just harmless horseshit. But those notes with the names of the ships, and the times and the locations. Those things are beginning to hurt us. So you'll understand that we have to put a stop to them."

Corcoran's head was clearing rapidly. He saw that they had passed the front door of his cottage and were turning around toward the back of his house.

"Where are you taking me?"

"I thought we'd go around to your well," Grace answered. "It's a nice quiet place to have a chat. We won't be disturbed."

LONDON

REGINALD HALL was splendid in his full dress uniform, his traditional fore and aft hat pinned under his left arm, his gloved right hand resting on the hilt of his sword. He hated diplomatic affairs, preferring the obscurity of his small office in Whitehall and the comfort of a soft woollen sweater. But he never passed up an invitation to the Italian embassy, where the country's military attaché would be present. General D'Sica, who was also a titled prince, was one of his most reliable sources of information.

Not the general himself. Hall had noticed that the more medals a military attaché wore, the less informed he was and the more pathetic was the performance of his country's armies. D'Sica's chest was covered with medallions and starbursts, hanging from a rainbow of colored ribbons.

The information came from D'Sica's secretary, a stunning brunette in her early thirties who, as a native of Trieste, was generally without a country. Everyone in London knew that Maria Agassi was the general's mistress, and nearly everyone but the general knew that she was also a German spy, a fact that made it difficult for Hall to meet her in private. But Hall was the only one among the Allied diplomats and officers who knew that she was actually a double agent, paid from his confidential funds since the beginning of the war. Italian diplomatic affairs were his best opportunities to talk with her.

He bided his time, sipping the champagne and sampling the hors d'oeuvres as he wandered among the guests. You had to give the diplomats and the officers credit, Hall thought. No matter how frightening the carnage that cut across Europe from the Mediterranean to the Atlantic, they still knew how to enjoy a party. Music, wine, and jeweled women, dressed in the latest fashions from Paris under seige. Lead-crystal glasses and fine china service. Apparently not all the money was going into explosives.

He saw General D'Sica and Maria in the process of breaking away from a French officer with a feathered wife and stepped smartly to his opportunity. "General D'Sica. How good to see you." The general smiled broadly while he tried to remember Hall's name.

"Captain Hall," Maria said, coming to D'Sica's rescue while she held out her hand to be kissed.

"A pleasure, indeed, Captain Hall," the general chimed in. "Welcome to our embassy."

"Wonderful affair," Hall answered, glancing around in approval.

D'Sica's head wagged from side to side. "In these times . . . one does the best one can."

They chatted for a few moments with no mention of the war. D'Sica was careful not to allude to the Royal Navy's inability to deal with the U-boats, and Hall, well aware that the Italian allies were in retreat, was equally tactful in never saying the name "Austria."

"Giancarlo," Maria interrupted. "I seem to be getting a headache. There are some pills in the pocket of my cape." He cooed his solicitude, set down his glass, and rushed off to the coat room.

"The Germans are thrilled with the American proposal for freedom of the seas," she said, maintaining her wide-eyed, trivial smile.

"I thought they might be," Hall answered.

Maria sipped her wine. "They've lifted all restrictions from their submarines."

"All?"

"Everything entering the war zone. If it's British, they can fire without warning."

"Passenger ships?" Hall asked.

"Everything," she said.

"You're absolutely certain?"

She shrugged her bare shoulders, which were the color of creamy silk. "Yes, at least until the kaiser has his next change of heart."

"How do you know?" the captain challenged.

"Because I've been told to ask friends at the American embassy whether the United States would consider warning its citizens against sailing on British ships. Von Bernstorff is going to make that suggestion in Washington."

"And?"

"At the American embassy, they don't think such a warning would be appropriate."

Hall wanted to pursue to conversation, but General D'Sica was rushing toward them with a small silver pill case and a tall glass of water.

"General," Hall greeted him, "you're too modest. Miss Agassi was just telling me that you've received a new honor."

The Italian flushed, then lifted a bronze image of Garibaldi from his tunic. "The National Unity Medal," he said. "For diplomatic services." He lifted another glass of wine from a passing silver tray.

"Well deserved, I'm sure," Hall offered.

The captain worked his way to the foyer, found his coat, and left unobserved. He took a cab back to Whitehall, where the light was still burning in the window of the First Lord of the Admiralty.

"You smell of mothballs," Winston Churchill said as soon as he saw Hall's full dress uniform. "On the diplomatic circuit, I see."

"Visiting one of our sources, actually," Reginald Hall answered. "Sometimes a public affair is the best way to conceal a conversation. No one expects anyone to say anything important."

"I trust you didn't stop by for me to admire your attire."

Hall looked down at the fore and aft hat, still tucked under his arm. He tossed it casually onto the cushion of a sofa. "I think the Germans are about ready to go after our passenger ships," he said.

"*Faloba* was an accident," the First Lord of the Admiralty reminded him. They both knew that their official report of a ruthless attack without warning had been purely a propaganda ploy.

"But the Americans took no action. The usual request for explanation, and a simple apology from the Germans. Nothing that would give Admiral von Pohl any reason to think that the Americans would protect their citizens. And we've picked up a few radio signals concerning some of our passenger ships. It would appear that the U-boats have approval to go after them."

"All of them?" Churchill asked, his gaze suddenly sharpening.

"Anything that comes into the war zone," Hall said. "I've heard that from three separate sources. The one tonight works for the Germans. Her information has always been quite accurate."

"Her?"

"A woman with connections in diplomatic circles. The Germans tell her what to listen for."

Churchill slipped off his reading glasses and closed the folder of papers that he had been scanning. "Captain Hall, you know what's at stake here? One insignificant American, lost in a sinking, isn't going to change their national policy. They've already demonstrated that quite clearly in their official reaction to the *Faloba* affair."

"The American public was quite outraged," Hall said.

"The American president wasn't outraged enough," Churchill answered.

Hall nodded. There was no disputing the fact. It was going to take a truly barbarous provocation to tip the United States out of its official neutrality and bring her wholeheartedly into the war. "What we need is a prize valuable enough so that the Germans will try for a ship carrying a good number of very prominent Americans. Something that will make the risk acceptable."

Churchill opened the folder, took out one of the papers, and pushed it across his desk. "Something like this?" he asked.

It was a wire to the Admiralty from Sir Peter Beecham in New York. One of the logistics officers knew of Churchill's distaste for mining and had bumped it up through channels to the First Lord.

HAVE 60 TONS OF PYROXYLIN AVAILABLE FOR SHIPMENT BUT UNABLE TO SECURE WATER-TIGHT CONTAINERS AT ANY PRICE. DUPOINT ADVISES THAT IT IS HIGHLY DANGEROUS TO LOAD PYROXYLIN WITHOUT CONTAINERS. I RECOMMEND THAT SHIPMENT BE DELAYED UNTIL PROPER CONTAINERS CAN BE FOUND.

"The Germans are absolutely determined to keep us from getting the guncotton," Hall said. "Had their agents planning to bomb the train when it reached the New Jersey piers. Probably would have blown out half the windows in Manhattan."

"Then they'd find it an irresistible target no matter what kind of ship it was aboard," Churchill concluded. "Assuming they knew which ship it was and when it was arriving."

Hall flicked the wire against the palm of his hand. "Why don't I respond to this," he offered.

Churchill slipped the reading glasses back onto his cheeks and turned back to the papers he had been reading. "I hoped you might."

CROOKHAVEN

"NEW YORK?"

Commander Day looked again at the address on the plain language copy of the message that Chief Gore had just received by phone line from Queenstown. "We don't handle traffic for New York."

"Never have," Gore told him. "New York traffic generally goes by cable, out of Valencia. Or, if it's radio, it's passed by Lewis, in the Outer Hebrides. They're closer, and they have a bigger transmitter."

"Can we raise New York?"

"Haven't tried," Gore answered. "Maybe, on a clear night, when the conditions are just right."

Day read the message, addressed to WMPB in New York.

EMBARK CARGO OF PRYOXYLIN ON LUSITANIA, DEPARTING NEW YORK, MAY 1. ASSURE MATERIAL IN DRY HOLDS ABOVE WATER LINE. CARGO NOT—REPEAT NOT—TO APPEAR ON EITHER PRIMARY OR SECONDARY CARGO MANIFESTS. GREATEST SECRECY IMPERATIVE.

He knew the WMPB call letters very well from his assignment in New York. They belonged to the War Materials Purchasing Board, headed by Sir Peter Beecham. And he knew the cargo being described. It was the guncotton that he had given Sir Peter as his departing Christmas present.

"There's something wrong with this, chief," he said to Gore. "Call Queenstown and request a confirmation from the sender. I don't believe they want this broadcast from Crookhaven."

It made no sense at all. He had told the Admiralty of his suspicions that the Crookhaven station was being compromised. They had taken him seriously, sending Peter Grace to shut down the leak. Now they were telling Crookhaven to send a message that would link a critical, strategic cargo with a specific ship. If the message were genuine, they would be putting their guncotton—not to mention the passengers of *Lusitania*—at enormous risk.

He folded the message, stuffed it into his pocket, and walked across the grounds to the quarters cottage. Peter Grace, as he suspected, was inside, stirring his breakfast in a skillet on top of the stove.

"Join me for an omelette, commander," Grace said. "They're my specialty."

Day went to the steps in the loft and called up. There was no response.

"We're alone," Grace told him, recognizing the commander's concern. He slid the omelette from the skillet onto the plate with a chef's hand. "Only take me a second to whip up one for you," he offered.

"How's your investigation progressing?" Day asked.

The lieutenant sat down in front of his plate, tucking a napkin into the collar of his shirt. "Still nosing around. A few leads that look promising. But nothing definite."

"Then as far as you know, traffic through Crookhaven is still being compromised?"

"Yes, as far as I know."

Day took out the message and unfolded it. "Then why would they send us this to forward to New York?"

Grace glanced at the message, never interrupting the rhythm of his eating. "Looks routine to me," he concluded.

"Do you know what pyroxylin is?"

Grace shook his head as he swallowed. "Haven't the foggiest."

"It's the chemical name for guncotton. The stuff we use in our mines.

We're out of it, and this is the only supply we'll get for the next six months."

The young officer set down his fork. "A very important cargo, I take it. I suppose that's why they're putting it aboard *Lusitania*. Safest damn ship afloat, from what I hear."

"But why broadcast it over a station that the Germans are probably listening to?" Day asked. "Admiral von Pohl would risk all his agents in New York to get this kind of information."

"Well," Grace thought as he resumed his breakfast, "I suppose you've answered your own question. If the stuff is that important, then I suppose they have to get the message out the fastest way. Speed at the expense of secrecy."

"Except this isn't the fastest way," Day corrected. "Under most conditions, we can't go transatlantic. Chief Gore isn't at all sure he can raise New York until tonight."

Grace was up, walking his empty plate toward the sink. "Does sound silly, I suppose. But then you're taking me out of my element. Radio isn't my specialty. Why not query the Admiralty on it?"

"That's what I've done," Day said. "I just wanted to be sure that this wasn't part of your . . . investigation."

Grace shook his head. "Nothing to do with me. All I'm doing here is poking around. Routine investigation."

Day smiled sarcastically. "Is that how you hurt your hands? Poking around?"

Grace looked down. The knuckles of both hands were swollen, the right hand slightly discolored. "Oh, these. Thought I'd try getting about on a bicycle. Went right over the handlebars. Lucky I didn't break my neck."

When Day got back to the radio cottage, Chief Gore was hanging up the telephone. "No mistake, commander. They want us to call WMPB and keep trying until we raise them."

"Why aren't they using the cable?" Day demanded.

Gore chuckled. "I'm a sailor, commander. And I ended up talkin' to an officer in Naval Intelligence. He wasn't exactly pleased that I was questioning his instructions, much less tellin' him now to route his traffic."

"Naval Intelligence?" Day took another look at the message.

"That's where they routed me," Gore said defensively. "I got my man at Queenstown and gave him the message number. Next thing I knew I was talkin' with an officer in intelligence. 'Follow your orders,' he tells me. 'Code the damn thing and send it.'"

Day couldn't figure it out. It made sense that they would put the pyroxylin aboard *Lusitania*. It was their most valuable cargo and their safest ship. But why the change in the communications routine? And why was Naval Intelligence involved?

"What do you want me to do?" Gore asked, interrupting his deliberations.

"Send it, I suppose," Day said. "Is Shiela here to code it?"

"She should be back any minute," Gore answered. "Some kind of trouble down in Schull that she wanted to look into. Some poor bloke that she knows tied on a snootful and fell into his own well."

NEW YORK

"*LUSITANIA?*"

Sir Peter Beecham could scarcely believe what he was reading. He held the decoded Admiralty message that answered his query concerning the guncotton and read it for the second time. It instructed him to load the lethal cargo, even without protective watertight cases, into the ammunition hold of *Lusitania*. "Is that safe?"

Captain Guy Gaunt, naval attaché to His Majesty's embassy, raised his eyebrows as he read the cable. "Really no way to ship guncotton that's perfectly safe. But I suppose they're right. *Lusitania* is the safest ship we have."

"There could be 1,500 passengers aboard," Beecham protested.

"Which is exactly why the U-boats won't dare go after her," Gaunt countered. "Besides, she'll be heavily escorted before she even reaches Fastnet. And she'll probably be zigzagging all the way up the coast. Safest place in the whole war, if you ask me."

Sir Peter glanced at the requisitions piled high on his desk. Bags of black powder, mortar shells, cases of rifle cartridges, time-delay fuses. There was enough explosive force represented to level one of the continents. Half the material was consigned to ships that carried at least a few passengers. "Damn dirty business," he mumbled half to himself. "On any given day, I could be responsible for the slaughter of hundreds of innocent people."

Gaunt stood and retrieved his cap from the coat rack. "I suppose that's true for any of us. War used to be a soldiers' affair. Now everyone is at risk. It was a lot simpler in the old days."

Well, I'm certainly not going to put Jennifer at risk, Peter decided firmly. Send his daughter off in a cabin that sat on top of a cargo of guncotton? It was out of the question.

He rehearsed his words as he rode in the parlor car out to his Long Island estate. A temporary delay. Just long enough until he could book another ship. Why? Canadian troops! That's it. He could tell her that the cabins were needed for Canadians traveling to join up with British forces. A military necessity that was completely beyond his control.

No, that certainly wouldn't do. Jennifer probably knew people who were booked on *Lusitania*. She'd see through that one in an instant.

Well, the truth then. We're loading a rather dangerous cargo aboard *Lusitania*. If it ever ignited, it would blow the damn ship in half. Certainly Jennifer could see the danger and appreciate his concern. Except she would raise the logical question of why he was allowing any passengers aboard a ship carrying a deadly cargo. How could he explain that he was using civilians to shield contraband? Or why she was an exception?

But it had to be the truth. The first glimpse of civility had returned to his home since he had agreed to let her join William Day. Jennifer was allowing Anne to help her organize her things and to pack her steamer trunks. There were even bursts of laughter as the two women worked together. On the past weekend, Jennifer had joined them for dinner and had begun chatting about the adventure that lay ahead. There was a hint of a smile on her face as she mused over William's surprise when he read her letter and knew that she was coming to join him. Beecham realized that his family had scarcely survived his lies. He couldn't take that risk again.

When the car dropped him at his doorstep, Anne was waiting to greet him. "We have a bit of a surprise for you this evening," she promised. "A fashion show."

"My word!"

"Jennifer's new dresses have arrived. She wants to model them for you."

"For me?" Beecham couldn't conceal his delight.

"It was her idea," Anne said. "She was trying on a simple cocktail dress when she said, 'Won't father love this. I can't wait to show him.' All I did was suggest that you would probably like to see all of them."

He sat in his chair in the library, applauding each of the outfits that Jennifer modeled, offering the comments that he knew would please her. "Very sensible," he said of a plain afternoon ensemble with a full skirt that made walking possible, "yet nicely styled, and the color is perfect for you." And, when she spun around in an evening dress that was well off her shoulders, "My goodness! Would you wear that in public?"

"Really, father," Jennifer laughed. "You're falling hopelessly behind the times. Everyone is showing their shoulders."

Anne watched the exchanges with pure delight as her family came back together before her eyes. She had only just won back her daughter's confidence, and now her husband was being welcomed back into the relationship. Her laughter came spontaneously for the first time in weeks.

"What a wonderful evening," she said to Peter as soon as Jennifer had rushed out of the room in her final outfit.

"Wonderful, indeed," he agreed. But there was a distracted vagueness to his enthusiasm.

"Is something wrong?"

"Oh, no. Certainly not." But then, after a pause, "It's just the danger, I suppose. Traveling through the war zone. There have been several . . . incidents . . ."

"Sinkings?" Anne was suddenly frightened because of her husband's obvious concern.

"I was thinking of suggesting a slight delay." He saw Anne's eyes narrow with concern. "Only a few weeks. Just until the navy gets control of things. Or perhaps a different ship."

"Not *Lusitania*? But you've said she's the safest ship afloat."

"And she is. It's just that now—with all the submarine activity—I thought a slight delay might be a sensible precaution."

She learned toward him anxiously. "Peter, we've only just won her back. Is there something you're not telling me?"

What could he tell her? That he had been using passengers to protect his military cargoes for the past six months? That he was about to use their daughter as a screen for sixty tons of high explosives? That he was weighing the risk of her losing her life against the risk of their losing her affections?

"Please, Peter. If we're going to disappoint her, I have to know why."

"Oh, needless worry, I suppose," he finally decided to answer. "I was talking with Captain Gaunt about *Lusitania* only this morning. He told me it was probably the safest place in the whole war."

Anne's expression relaxed. "Then there's no reason . . ."

"None at all," Beecham said, as he reached out and squeezed her hand in a reassuring gesture. "I suppose, in a war, nothing is perfectly safe. But *Lusitania* . . . she's the fastest ship afloat. And Gaunt was saying that she'll have an escort all the way in. No submarine would even dare to try for her."

EMDEN

"*Lusitania?*"

Captain Bauer looked up from the plotting table at the submarine flotilla headquarters or the north sea. "Where did we get this?" he asked his communications officer, who had just brought him the message.

"Crookhaven," the officer replied.

"Genuine?"

"Most certainly, captain. It was in the proper daily code, signed by Leprechaun. And our operator recognizes his hand. There's no question."

Bauer stepped away from the table and read the message carefully. Just yesterday, he had received a report from his New York harbor watchers, broadcast from the transmitters aboard *Vaterland*. The Admiralty's guncotton, they said, was sitting on a railroad siding in New Jersey. Now, if his Irish agent was correct, the Admiralty was ordering it loaded aboard *Lusitania*.

"The bastards," he hissed. "And they call my submarine crews 'savages'!"

He stood for a moment, tapping the message against the palm of his hand while his communications officer waited by his side. "Contact Admiral von Pohl. Priority traffic. 'Imperative I meet with you, 1800 hours, this evening.' Then get me a car and driver for Wilhelmshaven." He handed the message to the officer, who snapped to attention and saluted. Bauer didn't return the salute. He had already started back to the plotting table.

The table was a twenty-foot-square chart, with the western coastline of Europe projecting from one edge and the Atlantic approaches to the British Islands disappearing off the opposite edge. It included the North Sea, as far east as Jutland, and the North Atlantic, as far west as the Faeroe Islands. Lines of latitude and longitude were drawn in blue. Superimposed was a red grid that marked off the operating sectors for his submarines.

Each of the U-boats at sea was represented by a miniature wooden model, painted white, that was moved around the table to indicate its last reported position and pointed in the direction of its intended course. Incoming ships were represented by other wooden models, of various sizes to indicate the type of ship, and colored according to nationality. They were placed on the table as soon as they entered the war zone and were moved along their intended course at their best projected speed.

Simply by glancing at the table, Bauer had a complete picture of the battlefield in which his boats were operating and all the information he needed to vector a specific boat toward its intended target.

Lusitania, if she followed the normal North Atlantic steamer routes, would enter the western edge of the plotting table at 51°30′ North, 11°30′ West. She would pass about twenty miles off Mizen Head, and then fifteen miles due south of Fastnet Rock. Bound for Liverpool, she would then come to a course of approximately 050 degrees, maintaining a distance of about twenty miles from the shore as she moved up the Irish coast toward Coningbeg Light. At that point, she would turn to course 020 and run up Saint George's Channel.

There were three logical points of interception. The first was out in the Atlantic, before she reached Mizen Head. At that point, she would be unescorted and least alert for submarine attack. But that was also the least-certain point. If she had varied her course anywhere during the crossing, even for a few hours to run around dirty weather, she could easily be ten miles north or south of her preferred course. With *Lusitania's* speed, there was no way a submarine could make up that much distance.

The second point was at Fastnet. Incoming ships used the rock to fix their position. But while the location was certain, so were the dangers. Warships from Queenstown would be waiting there to offer escort. And the Irish fishing boats might well be back on patrol in the area. A boat that stuck up its periscope near Fastnet, when *Lusitania* was arriving, would be placing itself in mortal danger.

The third point was just south of Coningbeg Light. By then, the escorts from Queenstown would have fallen behind, and *Lusitania* would not have yet reached the channel escorts from Milford Haven. It would also be daylight. Masters liked to have full visibility when they made their turn at Coningbeg. The problem here was that Coningbeg was at the extreme of his boats' operating range. Bauer had stopped sending submarines down through the English Channel because of the mines, nets, and constant patrols. Instead, he sent them out around the Orkneys and down the west coast of Ireland. By the time they turned eastward and reached Saint George's Channel, they could remain only two or three days on station. Still, *Lusitania* ran on a precise schedule. A few hours on station was all that one of his boats would need.

If he were going to set a trap for *Lusitania,* Bauer thought, he should try for all three points. One boat, out in the Atlantic, would cover her most likely course of approach. Another boat, off Fastnet, would wait in the hope that she slowed to fix her position before her escorts arrived. The third boat would cruise completely around Ireland and move directly to

Coningbeg. One of them should certainly get a clear shot at The Greyhound.

But should he tie down three submarines just to get a shot at a single difficult target? Even with *Lusitania* in the crosshairs of a periscope, there was no certainty that she could be sunk. Her speed would turn even the slightest miscalculation into a clear miss. One of his boats had held her in its sights off Coningbeg twice during the same day. She had simply turned and shot out of range, leaving the U-boat awash in her wake.

And should he be thinking of attacking *Lusitania* at all? The world's most beloved ship, carrying the cream of the upper class of a half-dozen neutral nations? A passenger ship that the British would certainly claim was unarmed, carrying nothing more warlike than the passengers' luggage as cargo? But he had positive proof that she would be carrying the most important cargo of munitions that had crossed the Atlantic since the beginning of the war. And even the British registries classified her as a cruiser, in deference to the purpose for which she had originally been built.

To Bauer's logical mind, it was the British who were tossing their prize ship, with all its passengers, onto his plotting table. It was their decision that had turned her into an ammunition carrier, and their order that had filled her holds with guncotton. She was a legitimate combatant, and the innocence of her passengers couldn't change that fact. She was a legitimate target, taunting his U-boats with her breathless speed.

But war, he knew, was anything but logical. The monarchs who ruled the warring nations were all cousins, with higher strategies of imperial purpose to be served. Where was the logic of committing the best and brightest of Europe's young men to the trenches while the munitions makers and the money changers were protected in the ballrooms of a floating palace? How could a case of explosives aboard a soot-covered freighter be a legitimate target, while the same case of explosives, under a white-tied dining room, was untouchable? Why was it honorable for the English to starve women and children in Germany with their ironclad blockade but monstrous for the Germans to sink women and children traveling aboard an ammunition ship?

The answers, Bauer knew, would have to come from someone more adept at court politics than he was. He would show von Pohl the message that his Irish spies had stolen, to prove that *Lusitania* was carrying the guncotton. Then he would sketch the outlines of his plotting table and show how his boats could be moved into position for an intercept. The odds of finding her, von Pohl would ask. One in three, he would answer, if he had boats waiting at all three intercept points. And the odds of hitting her? Perhaps one chance in five, he would advise.

His recommendation? He would move the three boats into position despite the long odds. And then he would hope for a stroke of luck. Perhaps a rendezvous message from the Admiralty to *Lusitania* that would give him a more exact intercept point. Or perhaps a weather report that would give The Greyhound a specific course to follow in order to avoid a storm. Anything that would give his boats a more even toss of the dice.

But even as they were talking, von Pohl would know that they weren't discussing the important question. That question was whether or not *Lusitania* was a legitimate target. And to get the answer, von Pohl would probably look all the way up to the kaiser.

CROOKHAVEN

FATHER Connors led the procession through the front door of the church, then stood to one side as the pallbearers struggled to carry James Corcoran down the steps. Across from the priest, William Day stood at attention with a small contingent from the radio station. There was no family to walk behind the wooden coffin, so the mourners were drawn from the town leaders, with Emmett Hayes in the position of honor. Connors dipped a silver wand into a basin of holy water, held by one of his altar boys, and sprinkled the bier as it passed.

"A sad day, commander," he said to Day as soon as the procession had cleared the steps. "Corcoran was a fine man." They watched together as the coffin was pushed up on top of the wagon. "Bitter, I suppose, since he lost his dear wife. But always a kind word for anyone who went into his store. Did you know him?"

Day shook his head. "No. But I see many of the men from the boats here to mourn him. They must have respected him."

Connors pushed the three altar boys into a line and straightened the cross that the boy in the center was carrying. "Will you be walking with us to the cemetery?"

"I have to get back to the radio station," Day explained. "Miss McDevitt will be there for us."

The priest nodded, then prodded the boys forward. He followed the bobbing cross to a position in front of the wagon, then began to lead his parishioners up the hill toward the gravesite.

"I think I'll join the procession," Lieutenant Grace whispered to Day. "Probably a good place to nose around."

"Let them bury their dead," Day said, in a voice that was clearly an order. "You come with me. We have to talk." Grace fell in beside his superior officer and followed him to the car.

"What happened to him?" the commander asked as soon as the car reached the edge of the village.

"Who?" Grace's response was all innocence.

"You know damn well who. The man whose coffin you just saluted."

"I'm told he was drunk," the lieutenant answered.

Day nodded. "That's what the doctor said. But he also told me that he took one hell of a battering in his fall. Broke all the fingers on both hands, and ribs on both sides of his body. How do you suppose that happened? The well's only fifteen feet deep."

Grace sat silently for a moment. Then he answered without taking his eyes from the road ahead. "I suggest you accept the official verdict, commander. Mr. Corcoran fell into his well. That's all there is to it."

"The same night you fell off your bicycle, as I recall. Isn't that how you bruised your hands?"

Grace sighed. "You really shouldn't press this, sir. It's not your affair."

"Everything that happens in this area is my affair," Day shot back. "Now, what happened?"

"He was a Fenian. His store was a drop point. Someone was dropping off your radio traffic, and someone else was picking it up."

"So you killed him?"

"I interrogated him."

"And he died under questioning?"

"Apparently."

Day slammed his foot on the brake, and the car nearly spun as it screeched to a stop. Grace's head snapped forward and cracked against the windscreen.

"Damn you. He was a decent man. And you killed him in cold blood."

Grace pressed his hand against the edge of his forehead. "For Christ's sake, commander, he was the same decent man who called a submarine in to attack your boats. He helped murder four of your crewmen."

Day was stunned into silence. He looked open-mouthed at the junior officer.

Lieutenant Grace pulled a handkerchief from his pocket and dabbed at the trickle of blood that was spreading across his eyebrow. "What the hell do you think spies do? Run around in cloaks and masks? They're all decent, God-fearing men. Until you catch them. Corcoran was a traitor. He killed four of his neighbors. He'd have killed you if he ever had the chance."

Day restarted the car, which had stalled in the sudden stop. He ground it into gear and continued toward the radio station. After a long silence, he asked, "What did he tell you?"

"Nothing much," Grace said. "If he had, he'd still be alive. And I wanted him alive, commander. Once a Fenian tells you something, you own him. They're more afraid of their own than they are of us."

"You don't know who's broadcasting to the Germans?"

"Some ideas. But nothing positive."

"And you don't know who's been stealing our messages?"

"No."

"Then all you know is what I told you. That our traffic is being compromised."

"It takes a bit of time, commander."

Day nodded. "I'm sure it does. But while you're 'interrogating,' Captain Bauer is reading our coded messages. I think the best thing for me to do is to take Crookhaven off the air. Shut it down until we know it's secure."

Grace checked his handkerchief and saw that the bleeding had stopped. He folded it carefully in his lap. "I wouldn't recommend that," he said.

Day looked startled. "I wasn't asking you for a recommendation, lieutenant."

"Then without your permission, sir, I'm going to give you a bit of advice." Grace's tone was polite, but there was an edge of anger beneath the surface. "I don't know a damn thing about ships. That's your specialty, so when I'm aboard I'm going to do things your way. And you don't know a damn thing about intelligence work. That's my specialty. Let me handle it."

"Just keep broadcasting secret messages even though I know the Germans are reading them," Day countered sarcastically.

"Just follow the Admiralty's orders," Peter Grace shot back. "You may not like it, but there are more important issues involved than just a few coded messages."

"Like what?" Day demanded.

"Ask the Admiralty!" Grace nearly shouted. "Press the issue! You think this place is the end of the Earth? You should see some of the stations they have for officers who ask too many damn questions."

Day started to respond but stopped himself immediately. The smug little bastard was right. He had notified the Admiralty of his suspicions, and they had sent Peter Grace as their answer. It was an intelligence matter, and that wasn't his field. For the next few minutes, they said nothing. Then Grace broke the silence.

"I know that you've put in for a transfer."

Day didn't respond.

"I also know," the lieutenant continued, "that you'll be out of here in thirty days. Sixty at the most. Probably to your own command. You have a great record. They still talk about what you did off the Dutch coast. So, just stay out of this. You don't have to get involved. Leave things alone and you'll be out of this damned country before it has a chance to ruin you."

Day weighed the advice. Then he glanced over at Peter Grace. "No more dead men," he offered as his terms of acceptance.

Grace looked away. "I don't enjoy pain and death. I just do my job." Then he turned back to Day with a hint of smile. "So, you see, we're not all that different, are we, commander?"

Chief Gore was waiting at the door when they reached the radio cottage. "Miss McDevitt?" he asked. "We've got some traffic to code."

"She'll be right along," Day answered. "She stopped at the funeral to pay our respects."

He went to his desk and thumbed through the messages. There was nothing that couldn't wait for Shiela's return. Then he opened the pouch of routine naval directions and personal correspondence that was sent out each week from Queenstown and dumped the contents out on his desk. His eyes went to the small, pale yellow envelope that was addressed in a flowing, feminine hand.

My Dearest William,

I have thought of nothing but you since you left, and have written to you constantly. But, as I'm sure you are aware, my parents have had difficulty believing in the inevitability of our meeting and falling in love.

They thought we might not be suited for one another, and in a foolish effort to protect me, have tried to keep us apart. Father never forwarded the letters that I wrote to you.

But, now, all that is in the past. I am free to live, and for me there is no life except my life with you. I am coming across the ocean to be with you because, as my parents now understand, we belong together.

I have passage on Lusitania, sailing from New York on May 1st, and arriving in Liverpool on May 8th. Please write me, care of Cunard in Liverpool, with arrangements for my coming to you. I shall wait in Liverpool until I hear from you, even if it is forever.

I love you,
Jennifer

BERLIN

America's ambassador to Germany, J. W. Girard, and the German foreign minister, Alfred Zimmermann, didn't care much for each other. Zimmermann, despite his diplomatic training, was quick-tempered and abusive, given to issuing orders when he simply meant to offer a suggestion. Girard was emotional and took the rough edge of Zimmermann's personality as an affront to the United States and all its citizens. On more than one occasion, Girard had ignored the time stated in a summons to the German foreign office and had simply dropped by when it suited him. And on each of these occasions, Zimmermann had let him cool his heels in an outer office to remind him that the German imperial government couldn't be kept waiting.

But today's request from Zimmermann had been cordial to a fault. Instead of a diplomatic summons, it had read more like an invitation for cocktails: "Would Mr. Girard be so kind as to stop by at his convenience to discuss a matter of some urgency?" Girard's curiosity had been piqued, and he had rushed straight to the meeting.

"Mr. Ambassador," Zimmermann said, rising from behind his massive desk and crossing the carpeted floor to greet his guest. "How good of you to come."

"Nice to be asked," Girard responded with a nonchalance that he knew would infuriate his host.

Zimmermann watched as Girard dropped into a chair without waiting to be invited to sit. He forced a smile as he circled back behind his desk and untied the ribbon from a legal file.

"I deeply regret any problems that this information may cause your government," he began, "but I believe the issue concerns the safety of U.S. citizens. Specifically, those traveling as passengers on British ships."

"As they have every right to," Girard interrupted.

Zimmermann nodded slightly in recognition of the point, then lifted one of the papers from the folder. "We have positive information that the British are loading contraband aboard their passenger vessels."

"You mean *Faloba*," Girard interrupted again. "I thought we had put that one behind us."

Zimmermann forged ahead. "Specifically, that they are loading high explosives aboard *Lusitania*."

"*Lusitania*? You can't be serious." Girard was stunned at the notion. "We're damned careful about cargoes that get loaded in New York. I mean, you can't just bring a boatload of explosives into Manhattan."

"This message," Zimmermann said, determined to deliver his warning regardless of Girard's impertinence, "was intercepted by the Imperial Navy. I believe it speaks for itself."

Girard took the paper and read it quickly. "Who's WMPB?" he asked, pointing to the address on the message.

"The British War Materials Purchasing Board, in New York," Zimmermann responded, beginning to enjoy the exchange.

Girard tossed the document casually onto the foreign minister's desk. "There has to be some mistake. The English wouldn't simply broadcast something like this in the clear. Anyone in the United States could pick it up."

"It was coded," Zimmermann smiled.

Girard's amazement was obvious. "You've broken a British naval code?"

Zimmermann leaned back in his chair. "I'm not prepared to say how the text came into our possession. But I can assure you that it's genuine. Explosives are being loaded aboard passenger ships in American ports, in total disregard of your laws. But more to the point, these ships then become legitimate targets for attack. My government is deeply concerned about the obvious danger to your citizens who travel as passengers aboard them."

Ambassador Girard wilted under the German foreign minister's smile. He was in checkmate, his government indicted for allowing the British to run roughshod over its laws and risking the lives of its citizens in the process.

"I'm sure there's an explanation," he mumbled.

Zimmermann folded his hands and waited patiently.

"We require a complete cargo manifest of every departing ship," Girard continued.

"Manifests can be falsified," Zimmermann countered. "I'm sure the English have no intention of registering this particular cargo as 'sixty tons of high explosives.'"

"But you'll appreciate," Girard said lamely, "that we can't inspect every package that is loaded in a port as busy as New York."

"Naturally," Zimmermann agreed. "Just as you will appreciate that we must regard English passenger ships as legitimate targets of war. Perhaps your government will want to advise your citizens against traveling aboard them."

Girard reached over and took the message from the desk. He read it again. "May I have a copy of this?" he asked.

Zimmermann stretched out his hand to retrieve the document. "I'm afraid that our possession of this message is considered most secret by our military leaders. I shouldn't have shown it to you. But, in view of our personal friendship, I would have no objection if you shared its general content with your government."

Girard stood awkwardly, fumbling for his hat.

His dispatch was already composed by the time he reached his office:

GERMANY IN POSSESSION OF ADMIRALTY MESSAGE INDICATING CARGO OF HIGH EXPLOSIVES TO BE CARRIED ABOARD LUSITANIA'S MAY 1 SAILING. FOREIGN OFFICE ADVISES GERMANY CONSIDERS LUSITANIA LEGITIMATE WAR TARGET AND SUGGESTS AMERICANS BE PROHIBITED FROM BOOKING PASSAGE. SEARCH OF LUSITANIA CARGO SHOULD CONFIRM OR DENY GERMAN ALLEGATIONS. PLEASE ADVISE WHETHER ANY RESPONSE SHOULD BE DELIVERED TO ZIMMERMANN.

He scribbled the dispatch on a message pad and handed it to his coding officer for immediate transmission. Then he took his hat and his walking stick and stepped out the door into a spring afternoon for his daily stroll down Unter den Linden.

Girard had never adapted to his host country, a fact that helped explain his chilly relations with its foreign minister. In the present conflict, his sympathies were clearly with the Allies. But, still, he was a fair man who valued truth, and he resented being a courier for blatant fabrications, even when they were phrased in the niceties of diplomatic language.

He was perfectly aware, as was Zimmermann, that his country was the arsenal that was keeping the Allies in the war and that, in order to transport the war materials it purchased, England had turned every ship on the Atlantic into an ammunition ship. He knew that the Admiralty instructions to British merchantmen, abandoning the rules of encounter, were genuine, and that an honest copy had been delivered to his government. Yet he had presented to the foreign office a series of American notes and replies that denied all such knowledge and insisted that Germany should be held strictly accountable for compliance with the rules. Great Britain and the United States were involved in a conspiracy of lies, and he was their official spokesman.

But now Zimmermann had thrown the lies back in his face. The German foreign minister had left Washington with one of two choices: Either enforce its own laws that prevented military cargoes from being loaded on neutral vessels and passenger ships or admit its duplicity and warn American citizens that their own government had placed their lives in mortal danger. He never suspected that his government's response would be to concoct an even more deadly lie.

But that was precisely what he learned the next evening when Washington's response was decoded.

THE UNITED STATES GOVERNMENT APPRECIATES THE CONCERN OF THE IMPERIAL GERMAN GOVERNMENT FOR THE SAFETY OF UNITED STATES CITIZENS WHO EXERCISE THEIR RIGHT TO TRAVEL AS PASSENGERS ABOARD BRITISH SHIPS. BUT WE MUST ADVISE THAT THE IMPERIAL GERMAN GOVERNMENT HAS BEEN MISINFORMED AS TO THE LOADING OF CONTRABAND CARGOES IN THE PORT OF NEW YORK. CARGO MANIFESTS OF ALL SHIPS DEPARTING THE PORT OF NEW YORK, AND ALL OTHER UNITED STATES PORTS, ARE CAREFULLY SCRUTINIZED. ONLY SHIPS WHOSE CARGOES ARE IN FULL COMPLIANCE WITH OUR LAWS ARE PERMITTED TO SAIL.

FOR THIS REASON, WE FEEL THAT ANY DOCUMENTS TO THE CONTRARY IN THE POSSESSION OF THE IMPERIAL GERMAN GOVERNMENT ARE QUESTIONABLE AND DO NOT CONSTITUTE A SUFFICIENT REASON FOR DENYING UNITED STATES CITIZENS THEIR INTERNATIONALLY RECOGNIZED RIGHT TO SAIL ABOARD ANY SHIP OF THEIR CHOOSING.

It was signed by Robert Lansing, counselor to the Department of State.

Girard was infuriated by the note he was about to deliver. Cargo manifests are scrutinized, Lansing had written. But that, of course, wasn't the issue. The Germans held an Admiralty message which clearly stated that cargo manifests were to be falsified. It was the cargo that should be carefully scrutinized, and Lansing was offering no indication that the United States would search *Lusitania*'s cargo with extra care.

Then, Lansing used his evasion as a justification for issuing no warning to American passengers. In effect, he was telling the Germans that no matter what cargo *Lusitania* might be carrying, the presence of American passengers rendered her immune from German attack.

He remained standing and silent as he placed his government's answer on Alfred Zimmermann's desk and watched the foreign minister read it several times.

Zimmermann looked up unemotionally. "This is not responsive," he announced.

"My government feels that it is," Girard whispered without a great deal of conviction.

Zimmermann gestured to a chair, and Girard sat slowly. "You know, of course, that we intend to attack *Lusitania*."

Girard nodded, and then he said, "Judging by the content of the note, I think it's apparent that my government will regard such an attack as unwarranted and barbarous."

"*Barbarous?*" Zimmermann hissed the word as if it were a profanity. His voice rose as he asked, "And what would you call the actions of a government that loads women and children on top of a cargo of guncotton? Is that civilized?"

"Officially," Girard said, "there is no guncotton aboard *Lusitania*. As our note states, if there were, the ship would not be permitted to sail."

"Officially? You say, 'officially.'" Zimmermann rose from his chair. "And if it were your wife and children who were boarding the ship, would you tell them that 'officially' they were safe?"

"I'm not here as a husband and father," Girard answered softly. "I'm here as a representative of the United States government."

Zimmermann settled in despair back into his chair. After a long and heavy silence, he asked, "Then you will not warn your countrymen?"

Girard indicated the note that lay on the foreign minister's desk. "I think not."

NEW YORK

Captain Bowler Bill Turner waited eagerly on the wing of *Lusitania*'s bridge as the ship slipped into the New York Narrows. Despite his impatience to see the skyline of Manhattan, he rang his engines back to slow ahead. In the tight confines of the channel that separated Brooklyn from Staten Island, The Greyhound had to move slowly. At full speed, her wake would roll like a tidal wave against the two shorelines, swamping the small boats tied to the docks.

The ship turned slowly, rounding the tip of Brooklyn, and suddenly the city appeared. Turner smiled at the breathtaking view. In all the world's harbors, there was nothing quite like it. At one moment, you were steaming through the world as it had been, with green hills, patched with farms, sloping down to the water. Then, at the next instant, you were racing toward the world as it would be, with its towering monuments to money and commerce rising straight out of the sea. It was as if the ship were carrying him through time.

He moved northward through the inland harbor, his bow pointed directly at the spired tip of Wall Street, his whistle screaming greetings to the ships at anchor. Then he turned a few points to port and entered the Hudson River, which took him up along the west side of Manhattan.

Across the river, her ornate clipper stern poking out past her pier, he could see the German liner *Vaterland*, still held prisoner by the British cruisers that patrolled just outside American waters. *Vaterland* was an elongated copy of his own ship, built with the same arrangement of four turbines driving four propellers. She had been made longer by the addition of two extra frames, and more luxurious by the inclusion of a complete, haute cuisine restaurant, all to win a point in the rivalry between the two countries. But despite the best efforts of her Hamburg builders, she hadn't been made nearly as fast. Turner liked to think that, were he in her place, he would take *Lusitania* out to sea and run circles around the two waiting cruisers.

Not that he was entirely pleased with his new command. He was in his second round-trip crossing since relieving Fairweather Dow, and he, too, was disappointed in the indifferent sea-keeping qualities that had resulted from the alterations of the bow. He now had a new problem. There was a leak in the steam connections to the two astern turbines. He had to back the ship slowly, taking great care not to add astern speed suddenly. Otherwise, he would risk rupturing the crossover lines.

But compared with *Vaterland*, his concerns were insignificant. In a week, with cargo loaded and passengers boarded, he would be heading back into the Atlantic. *Vaterland* and her Ritz Carlton restaurant were going nowhere.

On the stern of the German liner, a group of men watched the tugs nudge The Greyhound into her berth. "There has to be a warning," one of them said, resurrecting the conversation that had been interrupted by the arrival of the very ship they were discussing. "The passengers have to be warned."

The Germans were U.S. citizens, with homes in Manhattan and prosperous businesses that served their new homeland. One was Hermann Prinz, an importer of fine Dresden china. Another was George Viereck, publisher of a German-language newspaper. Until the outbreak of war, they had been members of an ethnic community that lived at peace with the hundreds of other national groups that mingled in the city's multilingual excitement. But with the war, they had become outcasts, victims of propaganda that made them cousins of the Huns who had raped their way through Belgium. They were regularly accosted on the streets by former friends and business associates who demanded to know why they were using French babies for target practice and torpedoing hospital ships.

They met to render whatever trickle of assistance they could to their homeland, trying to counter the flood of support that was flowing to Great Britain. And, they tried to build some bridges over the widening chasm that separated the old country from the new. But now they were facing a crisis. They had been briefed by the German embassy on the fatherland's efforts to warn the United States about the dangers to passengers. They had been told of the government's reaction. Now, they were planning to carry the warning to their American countrymen themselves.

"An advertisement," George Viereck repeated when they had reassembled in *Vaterland*'s first-class smoking room. "We can place a shipping notice in perhaps thirty or forty newspapers. In all the major eastern cities." Prinz was skeptical. Passengers, he had argued, don't read shipping notices. "Merchants read them," he said, "and they already know the dangers. They have insurance."

"But the editors will read them," Viereck insisted. "And then they'll ask questions and write stories. If we place the ad now, the papers will be full of articles about the contraband cargoes. It will become a conversation topic. People will call friends who are planning to sail in order to warn them."

There was silence as the men pondered their alternatives. Finally Prinz asked, "Who will sign the ad? We can't speak for the German government."

"We will," Viereck shot back. "The ad is a warning to our countrymen. We'll sign it as 'the German American Community.'"

Prinz totaled the contributions that each of them was able to make. It wasn't as much as they hoped for; all of them were losing money in their boycotted businesses. Meanwhile, Viereck drafted the ad:

NOTICE

TRAVELLERS INTENDING TO EMBARK ON THE ATLANTIC VOYAGE ARE REMINDED THAT A STATE OF WAR EXISTS BETWEEN GERMANY AND HER ALLIES AND GREAT BRITAIN AND HER ALLIES; THAT THE ZONE OF WAR INCLUDES THE WATERS ADJACENT TO THE BRITISH ISLES; THAT, IN ACCORDANCE WITH FORMAL NOTICE GIVEN BY THE IMPERIAL GERMAN GOVERNMENT, VESSELS FLYING THE FLAG OF GREAT BRITAIN, OR OF ANY OF HER ALLIES, ARE LIABLE TO DESTRUCTION IN THOSE WATERS AND THAT TRAVELLERS SAILING IN THE WAR ZONE ON SHIPS OF GREAT BRITAIN AND HER ALLIES DO SO AT THEIR OWN RISK.

He read the draft to the others, who nodded as they listened. Hermann Prinz raised the only objection, "Perhaps we should clear this with the German embassy. We may be interfering with delicate negotiations. We may be doing more harm than good."

"How can we be doing harm by warning Americans for their own safety?" a stout, formally dressed man who owned a printing company argued.

"Every citizen has a right to place an advertisement," a store owner agreed.

The motion carried. Viereck would make copies of the ad and send it, with payment in advance, to all the newspapers they could afford. But he would clear the ad with the embassy just in case there was some objection to the wording.

Prinz still wasn't sure it was the right thing to do. But when he climbed out onto *Vaterland*'s deck, he saw *Lusitania* across the river, her lines fast and the companionway being lowered into position. He wagged his head from side to side. "I suppose we have to do something. We can't just let them sail out there with the submarines."

From his editorial offices, George Viereck wired the contents of the ad to the German embassy in Washington, along with a list of the publications he hoped to use. It was late at night when a messenger from the wire room brought him the embassy's response. The ad, according to the German government's representatives, was entirely proper. With one exception. "It will appear more official, cause more comment, if it is signed by the Imperial German Embassy." The suggestion was signed by Captain Franz von Papen, naval attaché. Viereck changed the signature and began addressing the envelopes.

In Bayonne, New Jersey, just a few miles south of where *Vaterland* was berthed, a yard engine pushed six boxcars across a pier and onto a car-float. While the float crew was securing the cargo to its tracks, two trucks pulled to the end of the pier and emptied a cargo of their own. A dozen Pinkerton guards, each in civilian clothes and carrying a rifle, climbed down and assembled around their supervisor, Tom Jordan, an experienced strikebreaker from Philadelphia. Jordan spoke in a low, confidential voice.

"Just routine, boys. Six of you on guard at all times while the other six are resting. No one leaves the float for any reason. Any reason at all." He paused and looked each one of them in the eye. They wouldn't give him any problems. No one ever gave Tom Jordan any problems.

"Now, everyone turn your pockets inside out. All of 'em. And hold everything you've got out in your hands." They looked suspiciously from one to another as they did exactly as they had been told. Jordan passed in front of them like an inspecting sergeant, taking their cigarettes and matches. "No one smokes on this watch," he said as he stuffed the material into his own pockets. "You can have this stuff when you get back."

"What the hell are the fire extinguishers for?" one of the men asked. He looked back at the boxcars with the metal seals on their locked doors. Two tanklike extinguishers had been positioned next to each car. "What's in them things?"

"The fire extinguishers are for fighting fires," Jordan said logically. "Just routine. You're not going to need 'em."

"So what do we do if someone tries to torch the stuff?" another guard persisted. "Are we policemen or firemen?"

Jordan laughed. "If that shit starts burning, I wouldn't worry about being a policeman or a fireman if I was you. I'd worry about being a swimmer."

He waited through the nervous laughter. "Tug will pick you up sometime during the night and bring you across to the Cunard pier. They'll take the cargo off sometime tomorrow night. Then you come back here with the float. One day. That's all there is to it."

He looked at the man who had asked about the fire extinguishers. "Any more dumb questions?" There were none. "Okay," Jordan concluded. "I'll see you guys on the other side. And someone better try to stop me from coming aboard."

Captain Bill Turner put one hand up to his bowler hat as he stepped out of the taxi and started toward the Cunard pier. There was no wind, but securing his hat as he left or arrived at his ship was a reflex action. He had watched many a costly bowler sail through the breeze and end up captive to the tide. To his right, the sharp prow of *Lusitania* rose in a graceful curve, reaching six stories above the street. To his left, a car-float loaded with boxcars was being pushed toward the berth by a straining tugboat that seemed near sinking.

Turner strode into the cargo shed between the two berths and headed toward the companionway that reached up to the weatherdeck of *Lusitania*. It had been a delightful evening. Dinner with a daughter who lived in New York, and then a few ales with former shipmates who gathered at a saloon on the Bowery. Good company! Not the collection of starched and feathered monkeys who tried to steal the menus from the captain's table in the first-class dining room. He had no patience for the swells who paraded to his table each evening wearing everything they could pack into a steamer trunk. In fact, he had pursuaded the Line to put an assistant captain aboard, a manicured officer who enjoyed impressing the passengers with sea stories he had read in a book. It gave Turner the freedom he needed to navigate his ship.

"Hey, mack!" Turner turned to one of the crewmen who was leaning over the rotted edge of the railroad car-float, holding the loop of a hawser. "Can you take a line?"

Bowler Bill stepped to the edge of the pier and caught the rope before it could fall back into the water. "Just run it up to the end of the dock and put it over a cleat," the crewman instructed.

The car-float was caught in the tide, moving away from the pier with more force than the tug seemed able to muster. It was obvious to Turner that if he took the line to the end of the pier, it would do nothing to bring the car-float into its berth.

"You don't need a bowline," Turner answered. He walked the loop in the other direction and tossed it on a cleat opposite the stern of the car-float. "Tie it off," he ordered the crewman. And then, "Tell the tug to go ahead slow."

The line tightened and checked the float's forward motion, swinging it snugly against the pier.

"What are you carrying?" Turner asked, looking up at the row of railroad cars.

"Cargo for *Lusitania*," the crewman answered.

"What is it?"

"Dairy products," the crewman said, as he tied off another line. "And I think fur pelts."

Bowler Bill scanned the row of Pinkerton guards and noticed the butts of the rifles sticking out under their topcoats.

"Bullshit," he said to himself.

EMDEN

LIEUTENANT Walter Schwieger boarded the U-20, which was tied to the pier at Germany's North Sea submarine base, and began his inspection. He started at the bow, between the two torpedo tubes that pierced the pressure hull and reached through the plating of the outer hull. He noted that each tube was loaded, and that the two replacement torpedoes, hanging in overhead racks, were tightly secured. He tested the jacks that would lift the spares out of their racks and the chain falls that would be used to lower them into the tubes. Repeatedly, his crew had practiced the back-breaking routine of reloading a fired tube. Their best time, from fire to ready-to-fire, was one minute, twenty-one seconds.

He moved aft, squeezing between the compressor and the tanks of compressed air that would be used to force sea water out of the ballast tanks, adding buoyancy and bringing the boat back to the surface. Then he passed by the pumps that sent water fore and aft to keep the boat level.

In the crew's compartment, he ran his hand over the narrow, miniature bunks that hung from the side of the pressure hull between the cable runs and the water pipes. They were freshly made, the sheets and blankets drawn taut. Once at sea, they would never be made up again. Two crewmen shared each bed, one sleeping fitfully while the other stood watch. And they wouldn't be neat and fresh. Condensation, building up on the inside of the steel tube in which they lived together, would fall on them like a steady rain. Mildew would begin to grow before they turned south around the northern tip of Ireland.

He lifted the deck boards and looked down at the storage batteries, steel containers of lead plates filled to the top with acid. They were his only source of power once the engines were shut down and the boat dived.

He inspected the officers' quarters, framed bunks stacked three high, with a locker at one end and a writing table at the other. There was a curtain hanging from an overhead pipe that could be pulled to provide a few square feet of privacy.

His officers came to attention in the control room, which was the brainstem of the boat. The helm, mounted behind the enclosed gyro compass, to drive the rudder. The wheels that aimed the fore and aft diving planes up and down to control the boat's vertical direction. The levers that opened the outer doors to the ballast tanks so they would fill with sea water, and the air valves used to pump the sea water out. The telegraphs that sent speed orders to the engineers.

Farther aft, Schwieger inspected the magazines for the deck gun, sixty three-inch armor-piercing shells mounted in port and starboard racks, the projectiles pointing at him from both sides of the passageway. Then he stepped through a watertight door into the engine room, walking sideways through the narrow space between the oil-coated diesel engines.

Behind the engines were the clutches, thrown with a long steel lever, that would uncouple the propeller shafts from the diesels. And directly behind the clutches were the enormous electric motors, connected to the shafts by exposed gear trains. On the surface, as the diesels drove the propellers, the gears turned the motors in reverse, making them act like generators. The electricity they produced was used to charge the lead-acid batteries. When the boat dived, the diesels were shut down and disconnected from the propeller shafts. Then power from the batteries spun the motors, and the motors drove the propellers.

Finally, he inspected the after torpedo room, checking to be sure that both tubes were armed. There were no replacement torpedoes for the after tubes. There wasn't any room.

Schwieger returned forward to the control room, where his officers were still waiting. "Let's take her out," he said simply, and he started up the ladder into the conning tower.

The tower was his command post, containing a compass repeater; instruments that reported the trim, speed, and depth of the boat; the maneuvering board for plotting intercepts; the firing calculator for aiming his torpedoes; and the first appearance of the periscope as it rose from a tube that reached to the keel. If the control room was the brainstem, the tower was the cerebrum.

Schwieger climbed one more ladder to the conning tower bridge, an open deck behind a steel windscreen. It was from here that the watch officer maneuvered the boat while it was on the surface, shouting his commands through a voice tube to the control room two levels below.

Schwieger leaned over the windscreen. "Single up," he ordered. His crewmen responded by taking in all but two of the lines that held the boat to the pier. "Slack," he called, and the lines were untied and tended by hand. The boat began to drift away from the dock. "Back one-third," he called into the voice tube. He heard the rattle of the idling engines turn into a throaty growl. "Take in all lines." Seamen on the pier lifted the docking lines from their cleats and tossed them across the widening space of water to the U-20's crewmen. The boat was under way.

"Left ten degrees rudder," Schwieger said into the voice tube. The stern of the backing boat turned out into the channel. He watched until he was certain that his bow would clear the submarine tied ahead. Then he ordered, "All ahead one-third. Right fifteen degrees rudder." The boat shuddered for an instant. Then it moved forward, carving a smooth turn, and headed out toward the North Sea.

U-27 had left just hours before, the first boat in the series of traps that Captain Bauer was setting for *Lusitania*. She was to head north, around the Orkneys, and take a station twenty miles west of Mizen Head. Bauer hoped to give her a more precise position, straddling the steamer lane, based on any further intelligence he could gather on *Lusitania's* course. U-30, already on patrol off the southwestern tip of England, would pause at Fastnet during her return journey. U-20's orders sent it around Ireland, to a position southwest of Coningbeg.

Bauer's instructions to his captains had been incomplete. During the night of May 6, and during the day of May 7, a large British cruiser, operating as a troop carrier and ammunition ship, would be making her way toward Liverpool. The boats were being sent to intercept positions. But they were not yet authorized to attack. Authorization, along with the name and registry number of the ship, would be sent by later broadcast. The hope was that that broadcast would include more useful information of her course, speed, and the presence of escorts, if any. They were to be fully prepared to attack, saving at least two torpedoes regardless of any opportunities that might present themselves as they moved toward their stations. But they were not to attack unless they received the specific order. Their final instructions, Bauer said, had to await decisions of national policy.

It hadn't taken Schwieger a second to fill in the missing details. The ship had to be *Lusitania*. The U-boat commanders were well aware of The Greyhound's sailing schedule, which could be read any day in the newspapers of the world's major cities. She was due to arrive in Liverpool on the morning of May 8. And she was the only ship, listed as a cruiser in official publications, sailing the Atlantic. He could guess at the "reasons of national policy." Along with Canadian troops and stores of ammunition, *Lusitania* also carried legitimate passengers, many of them nationals of neutral countries. Germany risked world outrage should she fire on *Lusitania*.

But Lieutenant Schwieger had no compunctions about the legitimacy of *Lusitania* as a target. She had been built, from the keel up, to serve as a fighting ship, and her potential armament of six six-inch guns was most formidable. Nor did he have any intention of surfacing and putting a gentlemanly shot across her bow. He had done that before, far out in the Atlantic with a freighter called *Hampton*, and it had almost cost him the lives of his crew. Schwieger had a simple resolution to the dilemma posed by the rules of encounter: When in doubt, fire without warning. He had no illusions as to what the reaction of *Lusitania* would be if he surfaced beside her and demanded to inspect her cargo.

"Keep her to our side of the river, Haupert," he said to his executive officer, who had come to relieve him on the bridge. Lieutenant Haupert nodded and did a dance step to move around Schwieger on the tiny deck.

"Speed?" Haupert asked.

"Ahead standard. Take her to full when the river widens. I want to pass through the Frisians in daylight. Call me when you have Borkum in sight."

They were rounding the point of Friesland, with Germany to their right and Holland to their left. It was a two-hour run to the channel through the East Frisian Islands that opened out into the North Sea. British destroyers occasionally dashed right up to the channel entrance in hopes of placing mines that would pen the submarines in. They hadn't been seen in the past few weeks, but Schwieger still planned to slow the boat and post extra lookouts while he passed through.

He dropped down into the tower and checked the course that Haupert had laid out: north, until they were well clear of the Dutch coast, then north northwest to a point midway between the heavily patrolled Orkneys and the Shetlands. It was a day and a half of cruising, which meant that he would pass between the two British strongholds in the middle of the next night.

The Frisians were low and flat, really the high points of the sandy, sloping coastline as northern Europe disappeared into the sea. The channel was shallow, ideal for mining. Schwieger took the conn as they passed through, posting Haupert on the bow. He kept the extra watch on deck until the landfall had disappeared behind him.

Then he tested his radio, sending a plain language message of random words that identified his boat to the radio station at Emden. The response, "Good hunting," meant that his signal had been received loud and clear. When his charts indicated that he had fifty feet of water under his keel, he began the routine diving test.

The ballast tanks were flooded until U-20 reached neutral buoyancy, where the boat would just as soon sink as stay afloat.

"Dive," he ordered from his station atop the tower. He heard the warning alarm sound throughout the hull below. He saw the sudden wave up at the bow, as the planes were turned downward. The boat's forward motion began forcing the bow down, into a dive.

Schwieger dropped through the opening, closing the hatch above his head. He felt a sudden popping in his ears, just as the sound of the diesel engines died. The electric motors were already humming when he reached the control room.

"Level at thirty feet!" The diving officer watched the depth gauge and ordered the bowplanes turned upward in time to level the boat at thirty feet.

"Much too slow cutting off the engines," Schwieger growled to the chief engineer. "You wasted air. We might need that air."

The diesels had to be shut down the second the air vents that fed them were closed. Otherwise, they sucked air from inside the hull. The popping in Schwieger's ears told him that the air pressure had been reduced. Every extra second the diesels ran reduced his ability to stay beneath the surface by ten minutes.

He climbed back up into the tower and ordered the periscope raised. Quickly he scanned the horizons to check that he had clear lenses and full mobility. He felt a drop of water splatter against the peak of his cap, and he looked up just in time to take another drop on his nose.

"Dammit!" he cursed. There was a slow drip of sea water from the packing around the scope. The housing had been crushed in his collision with *Hampton,* and now repaired for the second time while he was in port. But the repairs had obviously been faulty. The seals were not perfectly watertight.

"What's wrong?" Haupert asked, climbing up through the hatch.

Schwieger pointed up to the packing, and Haupert illuminated the wet rubber gasket with his flashlight.

"Just a drip," the executive officer consoled.

"It can only get worse," Schwieger snapped. "Christ, this is the last thing we need." He put his face to the eyepass and swung around the horizon. Another droplet hit his cap. In disgust, he pulled the counter-weight and dropped the periscope back into its tube.

He ordered the boat to the surface and now complained about the time it took to switch back to the diesel engines. He knew he was jumpy. The first hours of a patrol were always the most tense. By the time he ran the British gauntlet between the Orkneys and the Shetlands, very little would bother him.

But still, the periscope was his most important combat weapon. The leak wasn't a good beginning to his hunt for the fastest ship afloat.

LONDON

"They've taken the hook," Reginald Hall said as soon as he had closed the side door into Winston Churchill's office. The First Lord raised his hand to hold off the conversation until he'd finished reading the staff report on the campaign in the Crimea. His admirals and generals simply didn't get the point. They were debating their chances of capturing and holding the Dardenelles. Winston didn't want to hold anything. As soon as the troops from Egypt and Australia were ashore, he wanted them moving northward to threaten the Austrians from the south.

"Problems?" Captain Hall asked in response to Churchill's concerned expression.

"The First Sea Lord," Winston answered, as if Admiral John Fisher were a significant explanation for any difficulty. "He insists that we pull the Mediterranean fleet out of the Dardenelles and go on the defensive. Defend what? The Gallipoli peninsula? What possible strategic importance will it serve?"

Hall had never shared Churchill's enthusiasm for attacking the "soft underbelly of Europe." He was aware that the campaign was burning up scarce resources. "Perhaps the tactical difficulties . . . ," he tried.

Churchill cut him off with a glower. "Tactical difficulties? My dear Hall, tactics are just the details. It's the strategies that have to be served." He closed the report and gave his chief intelligence officer his full attention. "Now, what hook have they taken?"

"The guncotton. I think they're going after *Lusitania.*"

He laid his evidence out before the First Lord. A suggestion to the Americans by the German foreign office that passenger ships were now a legitimate target. A radio intercept indicating that Captain Bauer was vectoring one of his returning boats to a position around Fastnet. Reports of two more boats testing their radios as they departed from Emden. "Three U-boats, taking up stations on the steamer routes, after the Germans have advised the Americans they're going after passenger ships. What else could it be?"

Hall unrolled a chart of the south Ireland coast and indicated how far the two boats leaving Emden could reach in ten days. "By the fifth of May, they can both be south of Ireland. By the sixth, both can be on station off Coningbeg."

"And *Lusitania?*" Churchill asked.

Hall nodded. "On the seventh."

Churchill sat for a moment, digesting the information. Then he selected a cigar and went carefully through the rituals of lighting it. "Can they hit *Lusitania?*" he finally asked.

Hall rolled his eyes. "Dozens of variables," he answered. "If she comes close enough . . . and if they see her soon enough. Let's say that if they can get to within a mile of her course and have something less than a forty-five-degree angle on her bow, they'll have an excellent chance of scoring a hit."

"And their chances of sinking her?"

Hall lifted his palms. "No way of knowing. A single hit might not even slow her down. But, then, *Lusitania* has the same longitudinal coal bunkers as *Aboukir* had. The bunkers would be low by the time she reached Ireland. So, if a torpedo opened one of them up, she'd take on a severe list within a few minutes."

"You're giving me details," Winston chastised.

"Just thinking," Hall apologized. "I think a torpedo hit could cripple *Lusitania*. Perhaps leave her at the mercy of a U-boat's deck gun. But I doubt if she could be sunk."

Churchill puffed patiently. Then he concluded, "So there's no chance of a major disaster here. But we might expect American feelings to be badly bruised."

"Well . . ." Hall was about to qualify his answer.

"Just your opinion, captain," the First Lord growled. "I'm not writing down your name."

"If the Germans hit her," Hall said, "that would be the most likely result."

"Even though she's carrying sixty tons of guncotton?"

"The guncotton," Captain Hall assured, "is three decks above the water line. Thirty feet away from any torpedo hit. Shouldn't even be ruffled."

The First Lord disappeared behind a cloud of cigar smoke. "Well, then, let's hope our friend Bauer decides to have a go at her."

WASHINGTON

William Jennings Bryan arrived at the State Department punctually at 10:00 A.M., strolling past the petitioners in his outer office without seeming to notice them. Normally, he was the most courteous of men, given to profuse greetings and brotherly embraces with perfect strangers. But there were serious matters waiting on his desk that required his undivided attention. He had to get busy if he were to make his normal departure at 3:00 P.M.

An American ship, the tanker *Gunflight*, had become the latest victim of German submarine warfare. According to the Admiralty, she had been attacked without warning by a U-boat off the Scilly Islands as she headed toward France. Three of her crewmen, including her captain, had been killed in the unprovoked attack. British patrol craft were escorting the crippled ship to a safe harbor.

Robert Lansing was already firing off unsolicited legal opinions. "Our failure to defend the rights of Americans, subsequent to the barbarous attack on *Faloba*, has served as an invitation to further attacks on our ships and our citizens," he had written to Bryan, with a blind copy to the president. "Nothing less than a vigorous assertion of those rights will suffice in the present circumstance." His recommendations included a demand for immediate compensation, coupled with a warning that any further attacks on American citizens would be regarded as an act of war.

But Bryan had his own sources. The tanker, he had learned from the ship's panicky radio message to her owners, had been intercepted by the British patrol craft, which thought she might be delivering her cargo to the Germans. She had been attacked, while under British escort, by a submarine that quite naturally assumed she must be a British ship. The lost crewmen, according to another source, had jumped overboard at the sight of the U-boat. And the ship's master had suffered heart seizure under the stress of the moment.

Byran began penning his rebuttal. Americans who travel into a war zone, he insisted again, do so at their own risk. Their stupidity was not protected by American law. He wrote for nearly two hours, interrupting his text with relevant quotations from the Old Testament. "Now, what's next?" he asked his secretary as he handed her the draft for typing.

The woman ran through the situations of the people still waiting in Bryan's outer office. A visa had been denied without reason. Obviously a clerical error, Bryan thought. Then there was a lawsuit moving too slowly through a foreign legal system. Bryan was familiar with the country and knew that its courts counted time by the decade. Another visitor was seeking an immigration waiver for his brother. Probably impossible, since the man had an Oriental name. All fairly routine matters that he was easily able to refer to other departments. But one matter caught his interest. A New York publisher named George Viereck was claiming that the State Department was conspiring to deny his right of freedom of speech. He had been shuttled to a dozen different government offices, first in New York and now in Washington.

Byran welcomed Viereck warmly, draping a friendly arm around his shoulder as he pumped his hand and led him to a chair. He apologized for having kept him waiting, commented on the fine spring weather, and then leaned forward in riveted attention as the man told his story.

"We are American citizens. Of German ancestry, but still loyal Americans. All we are trying to do is warn our American countrymen against sailing as passengers on British ships. So we wrote an advertisement and sent it with payment in full to fifty newspapers. Only one has published it. The others claim to have been advised by the State Department that it is illegal to publish our warning."

Bryan's thick eyebrows arched. He reached across his desk, took the copy of the ad that Viereck offered, and read it carefully. To his mind, the ad made more sense than all of Robert Lansing's convoluted legal arguments.

"Who told you that this was illegal?" he asked.

Viereck mentioned all the offices to which he had been referred. "At first, none of the officials can understand why it should be illegal. Then they call here, to Washington, and when they put down the phone, they agree that the newspapers would risk prosecution by running it."

"Do you know who, here in Washington, they spoke with?"

Viereck tossed through the papers in his briefcase and found a page of handwritten notes. "The counselor to the State Department. A gentleman named Lansing."

Bryan smiled. "May I keep this?" he asked. He was already folding the copy of the ad. "And the names of the people you spoke with. I wonder if you could dictate them to my secretary. I feel certain, very certain, that we should be able to get this matter resolved."

"But there isn't time," Viereck said, suddenly becoming excited. "The ad must appear now. Before *Lusitania* boards American passengers and sails."

"*Lusitania?*" Bryan didn't understand the connection.

Viereck hesitated, weighing his words.

"Why before *Lusitania* sails?" Bryan demanded.

"Because she's a legitimate target of war. She's carrying . . . contraband."

William Jennings Bryan suddenly became the old country lawyer that had launched his public career. He stood menacingly and circled his desk slowly. "Mr. Viereck, you know something about *Lusitania*'s cargo, don't you? Something you're not telling me?"

"It's there in plain sight. For anyone to see."

"What's there in plain sight? You came here, Mr. Viereck, or so you say, out of concern for the lives of your fellow Americans."

Viereck sighed and closed his eyes. He kept them closed as he answered. "Boxcars full of guncotton. On a barge, tied up at the Cunard pier where *Lusitania* is docked. And 600 cases of rifle cartridges in the shed, waiting to be loaded. There are a thousand rounds in each case."

"You know this to be a fact?" Bryan demanded.

"I saw them with my own eyes," Viereck said. "It's all out in the open."

Bryan fixed his withering gaze on the man and watched as Viereck seemed relieved to have unburdened himself of the information. The secretary decided that his visitor was telling the truth. He reached out and placed a comforting hand on Viereck's shoulder, then stepped back behind his desk.

"First, we'll make sure that your advertisement runs," he said as he lifted his telephone. He asked his secretary to connect him with the national press services. "And then, I'd like to discuss this information with a few of my colleagues. One in particular."

His phone rang back, and the secretary of state picked it up. He put his hand over the mouthpiece. "Thank you, Mr. Viereck," he said. "You've done your country a great service."

SCHULL

THEIR separation was approaching. Shiela was expecting her recall back to England at any moment, and Day knew that his transfer was imminent. "Thirty days," Peter Grace had told him. "Sixty at the most."

There was no commitment between them. Shiela still hadn't explained why she had asked for a new assignment without telling him. Nor had she suggested that they might leave together. "If it's meant to be, we'll find each other," she had said, giving him his freedom to find any future he chose.

And yet, he was living a lie. He was taking Shiela into his arms with the words of Jennifer's letter fixed in his mind. It was not that he felt any guilt for his past feelings toward Jennifer, nor that he hoped to take up a relationship that was still clearly impossible. But Jennifer's words had cut through his despair, and the memory of her discovery of life had filled him with hope. If her name, written on a piece of paper, could work changes in his world, then he couldn't deny that she was part of his life. And if she were part of his life, then his fingertips, brushing across Shiela's shoulder, were an obscenity.

He had to tell her. But tell her what? That once, in a different world, he had fallen in love? That wouldn't matter to her. Or that there was a part of him that he had already given away and couldn't share with her? That would matter a great deal. Perhaps just the fact that a young girl he had known in America was sailing into the war zone, and that he was frightened for her. That was true. But only part of the truth. The rest was that if anything should happen to her, he would feel the pain as long as he lived.

William Day wasn't sure what was true. Why had he left Jennifer behind? Certainly not because she didn't matter to him. He still wore her signet ring, although it had been months since he had read the inscription. Or because Sir Peter Beecham thought he was unsuitable? There were those in the Admiralty who thought that someone of his background was unsuitable for an officer's uniform, and that hadn't stopped him for even an instant. Most likely, it had been his blind adherence to the social rules of encounter: They defined which relationships were proper and which were entirely unacceptable. And yet all the canons of behavior were being shattered by the cannons in France, and by the deadly gray wolves that roamed the Atlantic.

"There's something I have to show you," he said suddenly to Shiela when they reached her cottage at the end of the day. He led her to the sofa and took the small envelope from his jacket pocket. Then he went into the bedroom, leaving her alone while she read.

"I had to tell you about this," he said when he returned.

Shiela folded the letter back into the envelope and handed it to him. "What will you tell her?"

"What I told her when I left. That it's just not possible."

"Why isn't it possible?"

Day sank slowly into the chair opposite her. "We're in two different worlds. I knew it. Her father knew it. Jennifer was the only one who didn't understand."

Shiela stood up and started toward the kitchen. "I'll get a dinner started."

But Day caught her hand as she passed. "I thought of not showing you the letter. Of just throwing it away. But that didn't seem honest."

"I don't think we're talking about a letter," Shiela answered. She pulled away from him and went into the kitchen. He followed at her heels.

"At the time, I loved her very much. I didn't want to. I knew it could only disappoint both of us. But I did love her."

"And now?"

"Now, I don't know. I thought it was over."

She answered softly, busying herself with the food. "If it were over, you could have just thrown away the letter. There would have been nothing to tell me. But you had to show it to me. You didn't want to hurt me, but you couldn't hide it from me."

He nodded. "I'm sorry."

"For telling me the truth?"

"Yes."

Shiela looked up at him. She set down the food she was preparing and wiped her hands on her apron. "It's good that I'm going away," she said. "I don't think that I can live with the truth."

She walked past him and into the bedroom, closing the door behind her.

Day waited the rest of the evening without disturbing her privacy. Then he fixed a tray with a cup of tea and a plate of biscuits. She was awake when he brought it to her.

"I think I should leave," he said, when she had finished eating.

"Is that what you want?" Shiela asked.

He couldn't answer her.

"Because I'll be alone soon enough," she continued. "And I'll be alone for a long time."

He put the tray aside and held her in his arms.

MAY 1915

NEW YORK

THIRTY FEET below the river, *Lusitania*'s stokers began pumping life into the great ship. The coal had been drawn out of the bunker doors into huge piles on the boiler room floors. There an army of men, stripped to the waist and coated with a paste of coal dust, shoveled it into the furnaces that fired the ship's nineteen operating boilers. The white flames brought hundreds of tons of fresh water to a boil, creating the nearly invisible steam that rushed toward the turbine throttles.

Sixty feet above, on *Lusitania*'s shelter deck, in a gold-encrusted blue uniform, Staff Captain John Anderson greeted the arriving first-class passengers. Each received a salute and a broad ivory smile intended to pay Cunard's respects to the personal achievements that could afford a first-class fare and to guarantee that social rank would be fully respected, even under the difficulties of an Atlantic crossing. Anderson's task was to assure that the passengers were never aware of the hot hell down in the bowels of the ship that made her great speed possible, and to help people who were used to being in control forget that they were stepping into a world that was dangerously beyond their control.

Sir Peter Beecham climbed out of a car at the end of the pier and flashed Jennifer's ticket to the porters who rushed to take her luggage. Then he held the car door for Anne, who adjusted her dress as she stepped out onto the street, and for Jennifer, who smiled giddily as soon as she caught sight of *Lusitania*'s towering bows. The women walked ahead as Sir Peter completed the arrangements for Jennifer's trunks.

"Sir Peter!" It was a reporter from the *New York Sun*. "Are you planning to sail?"

"My daughter is boarding. A visit home," Beecham explained. "Just seeing her off."

"And you're letting her sail aboard *Lusitania*?"

Beecham's expression reflected his confusion. "Of course . . ." he started to respond.

"Have you seen the German advertisement?" The reporter was already unfolding the paper and pushing it under Sir Peter's nose. "Do you think it's safe?"

He saw the ad, bordered by a ruled line, placed adjacent to *Lusitania*'s sailing notice, and read it slowly.

"Looks like the Germans are going after her," the reporter chattered as Peter read. Beecham folded the paper and handed it back without a comment. He pushed past the reporter and the baggage handlers and headed directly for Charles Sumner's office on the upper level of the pier building.

The area was packed, with passengers pressing against the entrance of Sumner's private office and newspaper reporters spilling out of the door into the corridor. A *Times* reporter recognized him. "Sir Peter! Any comments on the ad placed by the imperial German embassy?" Beecham ignored the comment and elbowed his way through the crowd to where Sumner's secretary was barring the entrance to his office. He glowered at the man, stepped around him, and walked through the door.

Captain Turner was standing next to Sumner's desk. The Cunard official was on the telephone, staring out his window at the riveted side of *Lusitania's* hull, which rose like a wall high above his head. "Of course the manifest is complete," Sumner was screaming into the phone. "*Lusitania* will sail exactly on schedule." He listened impatiently to the comments from the other end of the line. Then he yelled, "She's been cleared for sailing by the collector of customs for the Port of New York. If the State Department wants to inspect her cargo, they can talk to the port officials." He slammed the phone down into its cradle.

"Well?" Captain Turner asked.

"You heard what I just told them," Charles Sumner answered. "We're cleared to sail, and that's exactly what we intend to do."

"And what do I tell the passengers?" Turner persisted. "They're all asking about the advertisement. Some of them have ordered their luggage held on deck."

"Tell them that it's nothing more than German propaganda. *Lusitania* is the safest ship in the world. And when they reach the war zone, they'll be under the protection of the Royal Navy."

"I've already told them that," Turner said. "That wasn't enough. Alfred Vanderbilt is still sitting in the first-class entryway with his steamer trunks stacked beside him."

"Captain Turner!" Sumner's swelling red neck was bulging out over his boiled collar. "*Lusitania* sails exactly at noon. With or without Mr. Vanderbilt. But you might ask him, if he plans to be in Europe this summer, exactly how he intends to get there?"

Bowler Bill lifted his hat, which he had placed on Sumner's desk. "No special sailing orders?" he asked.

"There is nothing special about this crossing," Sumner fired back. "It is routine. Absolutely routine."

"And my orders," Turner persisted.

"The same as your orders for the last crossing," Sumner said. "And Captain Turner. Please leave by the side door. I'd rather if you didn't give any interviews to reporters."

He watched while Turner squared his bowler, and exited quietly through the private door. Then he turned his attention to Peter Beecham, who was standing patiently at the other end of his office. "A madhouse," he complained. "Someone has been sending telegrams to the first-class passengers, warning them that the ship will be sunk. And then, out of nowhere, I'm told that the Department of State is sending a personal envoy of the secretary to inspect *Lusitania*'s cargo."

"Have you notified Lansing?" Beecham asked.

"I have," Sumner answered. "He says we're to get the damn ship out of port. Under no circumstances are we to await any inspection party from the State Department."

Beecham nodded. Whatever problems the American government was having, he could count on Robert Lansing to keep them under control. But at this particular moment, affairs of state weren't his most important concern.

"Is the advertisement authentic?"

Sumner waved his hands helplessly. "The German embassy claims to know nothing about it. Although they agree that the warning is 'timely,' whatever that means. The *Times* says the check for the ad came from a German-language newspaper here in New York. It was signed by the publisher, a man named George Viereck. But he can't be reached. According to his secretary, he's in Washington."

"And the telegrams?"

"All delivered to the same Western Union office. Uptown. They're unsigned."

"So maybe it is just propaganda," Beecham thought aloud. "But why now? Why on this trip?"

Sumner snatched up the cargo manifest from his desk. "How in hell would I know? As you're well aware, Sir Peter, I don't even know what the ship is carrying." He looked down the list of items that were listed as cargo. "Maybe it's this sixty tons of cheese. Do you suppose the Germans are suddenly in need of cheese?"

"Just the usual military shipments," Sir Peter lied. "Nothing particularly special."

"Then I guess there's no particular reason for us to worry," Charles Sumner countered.

Beecham lowered himself slowly into a chair. "Charles, my daughter is sailing on *Lusitania*." He looked up imploringly at the Cunard official.

"And you want to know whether you should take her off," Sumner said. Then he answered, "All I can tell you is what I just told Captain Turner. *Lusitania* is the safest ship afloat. And when she reaches the war zone, she'll be under the protection of His Majesty's navy."

He turned his back on Beecham and walked to the window. He could see the passengers filing up the companionway, into the arms of Captain Anderson and his squadron of smiling stewards. "I suppose you're the only one who can answer that question, Sir Peter. If it's really cheese, then there's no reason why the Germans should single her out. But if it's something else . . ."

Beecham rose slowly. "I'll use your private exit, if you don't mind." He shuffled slowly toward the door.

"Sir Peter," Charles Sumner called after him. Beecham stopped and turned. "If you decide she should leave the ship, would you mind taking her off through the third-class entrance? I think one person seen disembarking could touch off a panic."

Beecham nodded.

As he climbed the companionway, he made up his mind. The "cheese" was the most important military cargo he had ever sent across the ocean. The German warning, appearing just as *Lusitania* was about to sail, was too timely to be a coincidence. Somehow, they knew; probably their harbor watchers who had seen the car-float of boxcars slip across the river. They were going after the guncotton, and they didn't want any American passengers standing in their way.

"Ah, Sir Peter!" It was Captain Anderson, rendering his welcoming salute. "Miss Beecham has already boarded and gone directly to her cabin. Our chief steward will lead you there." He snapped his fingers, and one of his staff jumped forward with a smart salute.

Damn, Beecham thought. "And her trunks?" he asked.

"Sent directly to her stateroom," Anderson was pleased to report. "Just as she asked."

He followed the steward inside, to the elevators that rose from the main deck, up four stories to the boat deck. He rode up one level to the promenade deck, then walked forward to the parlor suites on the starboard side. When he stepped in, Jennifer was already unpacking.

"Look," Anne said, with a sweeping gesture toward the flowers that filled the sitting room. "Compliments of Alfred Booth."

Peter looked at the bouquets that were set on the end tables and the basket of fruit on the service table. Gifts, signed with the name of the Cunard chairman, were standing treatment for passengers who booked the most expensive suites. "Very thoughtful," he agreed.

Jennifer lifted an armful of dresses from her trunk and rushed them toward the oversized closet. "I shall be quite the talk of the captain's table," she teased. "I think I'll choose something more daring each night, as we get closer to England. By the last night, submarines will be the farthest thing from their minds."

Peter waited until his daughter had disappeared into the bedroom.

Then he turned quickly to Anne. "You've seen the German ad in the *Sun?*"

She seemed surprised that he should mention it. "Yes, of course. Captain Anderson told us that it was just German propaganda. No one seems to be taking it seriously. They've all gone to their cabins."

"I'm very concerned," Peter whispered. "Perhaps a different ship. It would only take a few extra days."

"Not *Lusitania?*" Anne questioned. "Is anything safer?"

"Of course not," he snapped. "It's just the damned timing. In another week or so . . . perhaps her next crossing."

Anne's expression sank. And then Jennifer's voice called cheerfully from the bedroom. "Did you hear about the German advertisement, father? Isn't it the most ridiculous thing?"

He looked around the cabin, already littered with Jennifer's personal belongings. He glanced back at Anne, whose expression was pleading with him not to upset her cherished parting moments with her daughter.

"Peter?" It was Anne's whispered voice, begging for his decision.

"Ridiculous, indeed," he called through the doorway into Jennifer's bedroom, forcing a chuckle into his voice. He felt Anne touch his hand, and he took her hand in his. He flashed a reassuring smile, even though his thoughts were locked on the awful cargo that was directly below them.

Jennifer walked with them to the companionway, jostling with the crowds of visitors who were departing the ship. The deck was alive with feigned gaiety, disguising the undercurrent of apprehension. The departing guests were reassuring the passengers that the German warning was absurd, and the passengers were pretending to be completely unconcerned.

Sir Peter watched as his wife and his daughter fell into each other's arms, Anne rocking Jennifer gently as if she were still a child on her knee. Then Jennifer turned to him, hesitated for an instant, and then threw herself against him, her embrace crushing the brim of his hat so that it lifted ridiculously from his forehead.

"I love you, father," she whispered in his ear. "Even when I hated you, I loved you."

He squeezed her until his arms ached.

They stood on the dock, looking up and mouthing words to the tiny figure that waved down at them. Then *Lusitania's* massive whistle shook the sky, and the black wall of steel began easing away from the pilings.

"Slow astern," Captain Turner ordered from his station on the protruding wing of the bridge. Far below him, the engineers tapped the throttle wheels and let steam seep into the astern turbines. They watched apprehensively as the crossover pipes vibrated. Then the two astern turbines began to roll.

Lusitania began to move, imperceptibly at first, but then with gathering momentum, until the steel wall became part of a rapier-shaped hull, and then the hull was miraculously transformed into a ship. She backed straight out into the river, her bow finally clearing the end of the dock.

"Left fifteen degrees rudder," Turner ordered. Five hundred feet behind him, a steam engine drove an enormous steel quadrant through fifteen degrees of its arc. The quadrant forced connecting rods to swing the rudder over. In response, The Greyhound's stern began turning to the north, pointing up the Hudson River.

"Slow ahead," Turner called into the wheelhouse.

"Slow ahead, aye," the first officer chimed. He pushed the handles on the four telegraphs, one for each of the ship's propellers, until the arrows pointed to slow ahead.

In the engine room, throttle valves to the astern turbines were closed. Simultaneously, other valves were spun open, allowing high-pressure steam to roar into the two small turbines that drove the ship's outboard propellers. The steam expanded as it passed through the turbine blades and then was carried to the low-pressure turbines that spun the two inboard propellers.

Turner waited. With its great momentum, *Lusitania* continued to slide backward. But just as she came to a position parallel with the river, she stopped. An instant later, she began to ease forward.

"Right fifteen degrees rudder," Turner ordered. Now the bow began swinging toward the center of the stream. The Greyhound moved past the end of her pier and gathered speed as she steamed by the captive liner *Vaterland*. On the stern of the German ship, a crewman dipped the imperial ensign in salute. Turner ordered his own colors lowered momentarily to return the honors.

She passed the tip of Manhattan, entering the broad harbor between Brooklyn and Jersey City. Next she turned into the narrows, where Captain Turner once again slowed her engines. Then she burst away from the land and entered the Ambrose Channel, which would carry her out to the open sea. All along her rails, the passengers stood in silence, watching the land disappear behind them. The giddy moment of sailing was over. The untameable North Atlantic was ahead.

EMDEN

"DAMN," CURSED Captain Bauer. He crumpled the message from U-27 in his fist and hurled it at the world chart that covered one of the walls in the flotilla headquarters' operation room. It hit just beneath the Shetland Islands, which was the approximate position from which U-27 had radioed that she was turning back to port.

"Bowplanes," he whispered. He turned to his aide, who was standing near his side, trying desperately to make himself invisible. "Klaus, how many boats have had failures to their bowplanes?"

Captain Klaus Schopfner searched through his memory, scanning the hundreds of repairs that were needed each month to keep the boats at sea. "None that I recall, sir."

"Not one," Bauer agreed sarcastically. "Until now. Now, when we need every boat on station, U-27 can't operate her bowplanes."

He shook his head slowly in despair. The boat's captain had no choice. With the bowplanes inoperative, the only way he could dive was by flooding his ballast tanks, and then blowing them when he wanted to surface. Each change of depth would send an explosion of bubbles rushing to the surface, marking his position clearly. He wouldn't stand a chance in combat with even the least capable British warship. The only option available to him was to return on the surface, running far north around the Shetlands to avoid the strongholds of the British fleet.

"God be with them," he said to his aide. He walked slowly to the edge of his plotting table, reached out to the wooden miniature of U-27, and pointed its bow back toward Emden.

The loss of the boat punched a gaping hole in the snare he had stretched across *Lusitania*'s line of approach. It left him without a boat on the western approaches to Mizen Head, drastically reducing his chances of an intercept. That meant that U-30, on her way up from the Scilly Islands to a station near Fastnet, would be the first boat to get close to The Greyhound. But U-30 couldn't stay on station very long. She was already at the limit of her fuel, and he had to leave her a reserve in case she had to maneuver around patrol boats on her way home.

"It won't work," Bauer said.

"Marginal, at best," Captain Schopfner agreed.

The flotilla commander walked around the edge of the table, pausing to examine his prospects from different angles. He lifted the model of U-30 and moved it up to Fastnet. Then he picked up U-20 and juggled it in his fingers. "What do you think, Klaus?"

The captain leaned forward. "Perhaps both boats, here." He tapped the table just below Fastnet. "She'll certainly pass through a bottleneck, minimum five miles off the light, maximum twenty miles. Two boats in a line, five miles between them. The first boat, say, eight miles from the light. That way her probable distance from either boat is three miles. Five miles at the most."

Bauer nodded. "In theory, you're correct. But there could be a British fleet there, waiting to escort her. The boats would have to stay submerged for the entire operation." He set the model of U-30 on the table where Schopfner had indicated. "Besides, this one can't hold station very long. If *Lusitania's* arrival changed by even a few hours, we'd have only one boat left for the trap."

Captain Schopfner shrugged. "I suppose Coningbeg Light would be my next choice. But, of course, U-30 can't wait that far to the east. She'd be too far from home, unless you let her come right up Saint George's Channel and through the Irish Sea, instead of going all the way around Ireland."

Bauer pointed to the narrow North Channel, at the top of the Irish Sea. "Would you send a boat through there?"

"Ordinarily, no. Too dangerous. But this is no ordinary prize."

Bauer knew his aide was right. One submarine for The Greyhound. It was an exchange that even a novice chess player would make immediately. Hold U-30 at Coningbeg, take his best shot at the incoming *Lusitania*, and then take his chances on U-30's making it through the North Channel under the noses of the tight British patrols. That was the military decision. But still, if he could just be sure of *Lusitania's* time of arrival, and the size of the escort being assigned, he might be able to set the trap at Fastnet. Then U-30's chances of returning to Emden would improve dramatically.

"We need more information, Klaus," he decided. "There must be some instructions to *Lusitania* on rendezvous times and locations. Nothing from our Irish friend?"

"He's been quiet," Captain Schopfner said. "Nothing for several days."

"Can we reach him?"

"I think so. He's supposed to be listening for us 2300 to 2315, their time."

Schopfner went to the base communications room and returned with a radio officer at his heels. The man stood at braced attention next to Bauer, his pen poised above a message pad.

"This is for Leprechaun," Bauer began. "You have his call letters and his code. It goes out tonight. Keep sending until you have his acknowledgment." Then he dictated:

Imperative we have all traffic directed to Lusitania. Forward
as soon as copied. We will stay up on your frequency all hours.

Emmett Hayes took a stack of school papers with him into the basement,
lit the oil lamp, and turned its flame low. There were no windows from
the basement that could show a light. And even if a sliver should find its
way through a crack in the floor over his head, there was no one awake
in Schull who could possibly see it. Hayes had survived by being careful.
He had picked the late hours of the evening to guard his frequency
because there was no chance that anyone would come knocking at his
door. And he kept his light low so that no one would ever suspect that he
wasn't long in his bed.

He didn't need much power to listen, just the current from the single
storage battery. He connected the wire, waited for the vacuum tubes to
get warm, and peaked his gauges at his assigned frequency. Then he
spread the pencil-written essays out on the sewing machine's workbench
and screwed the cap from his fountain pen.

He read the first, by an auburn-haired girl who was being raised by
her mother and a maiden aunt. The printing was precise and the
grammar flawless. Even the story, the imagined adventures of a barnyard
animal, was engaging. Hayes searched for some defect that he could
circle with bold strokes. There was nothing, he reasoned, that couldn't be
made better with an added application of hard work. But there wasn't a
single flaw. Reluctantly he wrote "Satisfactory" across the top of the page.

The next paper presented him with a few opportunities, and his pen
sung like a tuning fork as he assigned punctuation and corrected spelling.
But when he was finished, the child's work was only slightly scarred. He
was pleasantly surprised as he reread the story. By God, it was coherent.

In paper after paper, he found improvement. They were beginning to
understand. They had thoughts and ideas that were worth expressing.
And in the expression, the thoughts and ideas became important. When
you came right down to it, that was the difference between masters and
slaves. The masters were certain that their ideas were important. The
slaves were afraid that theirs might be shameful. Maybe, in another
generation or two, assuming he could keep them at their desks, the slaves
would begin to believe in themselves. And then, there wouldn't be an
army or a navy in the world with enough guns to keep them down.

The radio came to life, sounding out a group of letters that he knew
as well as his own name. He could hardly believe it until the irregular
sounds tapped out the letters again. Hayes nearly leaped over the
worktable, scattering the school papers in the process. He threw open the
sewing machine door and began pumping the treadle furiously, trying to
generate enough power to respond. His call letters sounded again, but his

voltage needle was still below minimum. Take it easy, he told himself, slowing his feet into a steady rocking motion. Then the needle reached the green band, and immediately he began keying his call sign, followed by the call sign that the sending station was broadcasting. A moment later, the sender acknowledged his response.

He jumped away from the key, snatched up his fountain pen, and glanced around frantically for a clean piece of paper. The message began coming through as he scooped up the essays from the floor, turned one over, and began writing down the random clusters of letters that were sounding from his radio. As soon as he had them all, he was back at the treadle, generating the power to send exactly the same letter groups in return. The sender would then check his transmission against the coded letters of the original message, correct any errors, and then sign off.

Hayes rushed up the step, banging into the door jamb in the darkness. In his bedroom, he fumbled the key into the lock of the armoire and felt through his shirts. With the laundry cardboard in hand, he rushed through the darkness back to the basement and began breaking the message, letter by letter. When he finished, he had Bauer's request printed out in block letters across the back of a little girl's essay.

SCHULL

Lieutenant Grace recognized the sound of Tom Duffy's truck long before it crested the hill behind him. Even in idle, the engine sounded consumptive. Now, climbing the hill that led south from Schull, toward the tiny town of Colla, it was blasting out a series of random explosions. Grace dropped into the tall grass by the roadside and glanced back. The truck hadn't appeared yet, but the belches of heavy gray smoke had risen into view. He heard the engine falter and gears scream as they ground their way into low. Immediately, there was the sound of a cannon shot, which meant that Duffy had stepped back on the gas.

He had been following Duffy, one of the two names he had been able to beat out of James Corcoran. But he had been following at a distance. Despite his broad smile and explosive laugh, Tom Duffy was a frightening man. He was enormous in stature, barrel-chested, with a great belly that rolled over his belt buckle. His arms were as heavy as thighs, and his hands were massive. Tufts of thick white hair protruded around his ears, framing the freckled dome of his head, and wild, bushy brows hid the tops of his eyes. His nose bore the scars of several shattering breaks and meandered down the middle of his face. There was a perpetual stubble of a beard. The smile was as bright and as satisfying as a lighthouse, casting a beam of good will that made his gargoyle-like features seem almost pleasant. But even Peter Grace made certain to keep his distance. Duffy's strength was legendary.

Supposedly, he had carried the keystone of the church's arched entrance up a ladder on his back and had held onto it when the ladder broke under the weight. He and his truck earned their livelihood by moving things that were too heavy to move, like the boulders that were dumped into the harbor to serve as moorings for the boats, and the flywheel of the steam engine that hauled slabs out of the quarry. But even more legendary was his viciousness. He had earned his way into the Fenian brotherhood as a leg breaker, sent to coax the uncooperative and punish the disloyal. Most Irish loyalists changed their politics the instant his smiling face appeared at their doorsteps. Few persisted in heresy after he had dug his thick fingers into their shoulders and lifted them off the ground to the height of a proper hanging.

Had he killed anyone? Some claimed to have known the informers whom he had snapped like twigs and left by the railroad tracks so that it would appear they had been hit by a train. Others couldn't believe it. "A killer? With that smile? You must be daft." Even the doubters, however, conceded that his arrival had probably caused men with guilty consciences to die of fright.

Corcoran had mentioned Duffy's name as a threat. As his battered body was being tipped into the well, he had gurgled through a bloody mouth, "Tom Duffy will get you for this." Grace had made it a point to find Duffy, and when he did, he returned quickly to the radio station, took a large-caliber pistol from his footlocker, and strapped it to the back of his belt. He wanted to be armed if he and the giant man should ever cross paths, although he doubted that all the bullets in his revolver could make much of an impression on Duffy.

Grace froze in the tall grass as the truck rattled by him. He lifted his head only when the engine sound had faded in the distance. Then he jumped up, brushed the dirt off the workman's coveralls he was wearing, and lifted his bicycle over the stone wall. He pedaled out onto the road and began following at a safe distance. There was little chance of losing Duffy. The puffs of smoke from the truck rose clearly over the tree lines.

Something was up, maybe the break he was waiting for. He had been watching Emmett Hayes, the other name that Corcoran had delivered, and observed several whispered meetings between the teacher and Duffy. It figured. The Fenians were an unlikely combination of intellectuals and dock workers, and the two men represented both wings of the brotherhood. When he'd reached the schoolhouse to take up his daily vigil over

Hayes, he'd found the school closed. "He was called away in a hurry," one of the children had said. "He had to go to Colla." Grace had taken up his post on the Colla road, and only minutes later Duffy had appeared, perhaps racing to a meeting.

The truck turned away from the harbor at the Colla dock and headed inland, toward the poor farms that were squeezed between the rocks of the coastline. When Grace reached the turn, he could see the truck's smoky trail leading up to a nearly toppled barn. He stepped down from his bicycle and pushed it into a hedgerow. Then he left the road and moved on foot toward the barn, using the stone walls that crossed the fields as his cover. He crept up to the back of the barn and looked in through the space between two weathered boards.

There were four of them. Emmett Hayes was facing him, looking down at someone who was apparently sitting in a chair at the center of the group. Tom Duffy's broad back was blocking his view of the person. And another of the townsmen was standing beside Duffy. He could hear Hayes's voice clearly.

"I haven't seen a thing of you since poor Jimmy Corcoran's funeral," Hayes was saying. "I've missed you." Grace couldn't hear the reply, but then the schoolteacher continued, "Ah, that's my point, I haven't had a word from you. I told you that you could leave things with Father Connors's housekeeper."

Again, the reply was muffled.

Hayes's eyes closed, and his chin sank against his chest. Carefully, he removed his wire-frame glasses. "Now, that's not the truth you're telling me. We've been watching you. We've seen you through the window at the radio station, hard at work at your desk. So let's have no more lies between us. What's wrong?"

Tom Duffy turned and walked away from the interrogation, and Peter Grace got his first look at the spy who was compromising the Crookhaven radio traffic.

Shiela was sitting in the chair, wilting under Emmett Hayes's eyes.

"I just can't do it anymore," she answered, her voice suddenly stronger. "When we buried Mr. O'Sullivan . . . the others . . . the information I was bringing you was killing people."

"That wasn't your doing," Hayes reminded her. "Commander Day handed me the patrol schedules himself. We didn't need you for that."

"But the others," she protested. "The bodies from the ships. I was telling you what ships were coming . . ." Her voice trailed to a whisper that Grace couldn't make out.

"English ships," Hayes snapped. "Have you forgotten we're fighting a war? Have you forgotten who the enemy is? The Englishman in your bed may be decent enough. But you're not whoring for the whole damned country, are you?"

Shiela jumped up. "You've no right to talk to me that way. I've worked for the cause. How many messages did I drop off at Corcoran's store? But it's over. I'm being sent back to England, and I'm leaving all this behind me."

"It will be over when we own our own damned country," Hayes said calmly. "Until then, no one leaves us behind. The only way you leave the movement is in your best dress, with your rosary beads wrapped around your fingers. You knew that when you joined us."

Shiela nodded slowly. Then Grace was able to make out, "I didn't know how guilty it feels to be a party to killing people."

Hayes walked away from her, resetting his eyeglasses. "No one knows that at first. We weren't born indifferent to murder. That was something we had to learn from the English."

He stopped and turned abruptly. "But there's something we need right now. Something only you can bring us. Just once more, and then you can take yourself back to England."

She raised her head and looked at him suspiciously. Hayes read her doubts and blessed himself. "My word on it, so help me."

"What do you need?" she whispered.

"*Lusitania*," he answered. "She'll be arriving in three days. I need to know every message that is sent out to *Lusitania*."

"Mother of God," Shiela answered. "You can't be serious."

"Dead serious, lass. Everything that's been sent to her since the last message you gave us. The one about loading the cargo aboard her."

"I don't think there's been anything since," Shiela said.

"There will be. The kind of messages you used to bring us. Who's assigned to escort her. Where they're going to rendezvous. I need it the instant you have it."

"Why? She's a passenger ship."

Emmett Hayes hunched his shoulders. "They don't tell me why. Just what they need. Probably the cargo that the English seemed to think was so special."

Shiela shook her head slowly. "I can't."

Hayes glanced from her toward Tom Duffy, who was leaning idly against the broken frame of the barn door. "There's two places he can take you," he told Shiela. "I was hoping it would be back to your radio station."

Shiela knew the other place. It was a root cellar behind the deserted O'Mara farmhouse. They used it as a holding cell while a proper tribunal was convened. The brotherhood didn't hang women. They turned them over to the other ladies, who stripped them, doused them in tar and chicken feathers, and then paraded them through the villages for the amusement of their neighbors. It was worse than hanging. At least the dead men didn't have to live with the memory of their shame.

She pushed back her growing terror and tried to think carefully.

"Just this once?" she asked. "And then I'm out?"

"Out of the country, yes. We won't try to stop you. And we won't turn you in to your English masters, either. You have my word."

"Anything going out to *Lusitania*. That's all?" she tried to make certain.

"And anything coming in from her."

She stood for a few seconds, looking directly at him and weighing her choices. "All right," she concluded. "And I'm to bring it to the rectory housekeeper."

He nodded. Shiela turned to leave, but Tom Duffy was still stretched across the doorway. She looked back at Hayes.

"Mr. Duffy, would you be so good as to bring Miss McDevitt back to Crookhaven."

Duffy raised his hand and tipped his bushy eyebrow.

"And Shiela, don't try to avoid us. Even if we don't catch up with you, we can make sure that the English do. They're not very kindhearted in dealing with traitors."

THE HEBRIDES

LIEUTENANT Walter Schwieger felt the fresh, warm breeze on his face as soon as he raised his head out of the hatch. He stepped up onto the deck and smiled at the clear, high sky, dotted with fluffy white clouds that gathered over the north coast of Scotland to the east. The ocean was nearly flat, animated only by the long, gentle swells that lifted the boat carefully, then set it back down like a baby being placed in its cradle.

"A good day for sun bathing, Willi," he said to his executive officer, who had the watch.

Lieutenant Haupert nodded. "We don't get many days like this. It might be a good idea to let the crew come topside."

"A very good idea," the commanding officer agreed. "Send them up in shifts. Three or four at a time." Haupert climbed down through the hatch, leaving Schwieger on watch.

They were finally making a good cruising speed, running fast to make up the time they had lost turning the northern tip of Scotland. Twice, on the way north, he had been forced to dive the boat at the sight of an approaching British patrol. On each occasion, he had taken her down sixty feet and shut off his motors, conserving his batteries in case he had been forced to maneuver under water. They had spent half an hour listening for the approaching sound of propellers, and then another half an hour until the sound faded and disappeared. He had been three hours late reaching the Orkneys, and this had cut down the length of darkness available to him for passing through the British stronghold.

They were still in dangerous waters when the sun rose, and once again Schwieger had taken U-20 under in order to avoid being seen. For another five hours he had cruised beneath the surface, scarcely making five knots' headway. He had been tempted to raise the scope to search around him, and then surface if the way was clear. But the leak in the periscope packing worried him. It would probably get worse each time he raised and lowered the scope, so he had decided to make minimum use of it until he had targets in sight.

Now they were in the clear. The British navy was behind him, and looking the other way. He didn't expect to see another warship until he had cleared the Hebrides and reached the sea lanes that converged on the North Channel. By then, it would be night, and the darkness would be his protection as he reached the northwest coast of Ireland.

Three of his crewmen, all engineers, climbed up through the deck hatch behind him and blinked into the sunlight. Theirs was the worst tomb in the pressure hull below. The diesel engines, with their feed lines and exhaust tubes, filled the hull's eleven-foot diameter, leaving a ten-inch-wide aisle as a work space. The temperature alongside the engines' exposed cylinders was well over one hundred degrees. The engine noise was deafening, and the air was foul with the stench of oil. The men stretched out on the deck and uncoiled like snakes, peeling open the work shirts that were nearly glued to their bodies. "Like a cruise ship, captain," one of the engineers called up to the tower.

Schwieger laughed. "Like first class on *Vaterland*," he shouted back, sending the men into howls of laughter.

He raised his binoculars and searched the sea ahead. Nothing but a horizon that rose and fell gently with the long, smooth swells. Then he swung the glasses gently over the port bow and began tracing the distant land line of the Hebrides. He was stunned when the framed focus of the binoculars stopped abruptly on the bow of a British destroyer, throwing up an even white wake as it charged toward him.

"Clear the deck," he screamed over his shoulder, but he kept the glasses locked on the destroyer. It was about two miles away, just emerging from the dark line of land that had masked its approach. From the angle on its bow, he could tell that it was on an intercept course. The height of its bow wake showed that it was making flank speed. Clearly, it had seen him and was rushing in for the attack. He waited until the engineers had disappeared, locking the hatch above their heads. Then he dropped down into the conning tower and yelled his command to dive.

Haupert charged up from the control room. "What's wrong?"

"An English destroyer," Schwieger said, spinning the locking wheel on the hatch.

"Has she seen us?"

"She's seen us, dammit!"

The diesels were already stopped, and after the clatter of the clutches, he heard the electric motors start up. "Level at fifty feet."

"Fifty feet, aye," came the response from below.

He heard the ocean close over his head, and then came the deathly silence that confirmed they were beneath the surface, where the destroyer couldn't see which way he turned. "Right standard rudder." He turned away from the last course line the destroyer had observed, swinging to the west and then to the north. By the time the destroyer reached the intercept point, he would be a mile away.

The decision he faced now was when to shut down his electric motors. The longer he kept them running, the more distance he could open between him and his potential attacker. But the British destroyers were now being equipped with hydrophones that let them listen to noises under the water. If the English commander guessed the direction of his turn, he might get close enough so that the sound of U-20's propellers would give its position away. He could raise his periscope and see which way the destroyer was headed. But on the flat seas, in clear daylight, there was every chance that the scope would be spotted. Best not to take any chances, Schwieger thought. He had the whole ocean to hide in. Just sit still and let the Englishman try to find him.

"Shut down the motors, Haupert," he said. "We'll wait him out."

The whine of the motors died. The order for silence was passed from man to man. U-20's crewmen settled into the tight living spaces available to them, looked up at the beads of condensation already beginning to form on the steel hullplates, and waited.

At first, there was nothing but the silence. The destroyer's commander had to guess which one of the infinite number of possible courses the submarine had taken from the point where it submerged. By all odds, he was headed off in the wrong direction.

But then they heard the first faint rumbling of distant propellers. The Englishman had picked the right number on the roulette wheel. He was heading in their direction.

Still, there was no reason for panic. What did it matter if he passed right above their heads? As long as they remained silent, he would never know that they were sitting twenty feet under his keel. Schwieger was the only one with any cause of apprehension. As he sat quietly, his boat at dead still, he was falling still further behind schedule. And his problems were mounting. Lose another few hours, and tomorrow's sunrise would catch him in the well-traveled approaches to the North Channel. He would probably have to dive again, giving up still more time in his race to be on station when *Lusitania* arrived from her Atlantic crossing.

The propeller noises grew louder. The Englishman's luck knew no limits. The destroyer was heading directly toward him.

"We should pop up the minute he passes," Haupert whispered, "and put a torpedo right up his ass."

Tempting, Schwieger conceded with a nod. Except if they missed. Then they would give up their hiding place and be forced into a duel in which the destroyer would have the advantages of speed and maneuverability. Surprise was the submarine's best weapon, and he didn't want to sacrifice it for the sake of a single try with a torpedo. Besides, his real target was still three days away. He couldn't afford to waste torpedoes in a duel he had no reason to fight.

The distant rumble of the destroyer's propellers was turning into a distinctive throbbing. She was getting closer, still on a course that aimed directly toward them. He could imagine the growing fears of his crewmen, their eyes turning upward toward their attacker. They would prefer any action to just sitting and waiting. But sitting and waiting was exactly what Schwieger intended to do.

The destroyer passed above them, less than a hundred yards to the south. "Good guess," Schwieger congratulated in a whisper. But he could imagine the confusion of his adversary. The English captain had to be looking about helplessly, wondering if he had made the right decision. He was so close. And yet, for all he knew, his target might be miles away.

The propeller noise began to fade. "Think he'll turn back?" Haupert asked.

Schwieger shrugged. "Probably not. My guess is he's headed up to the Orkneys." He smiled. "Good riddance to him."

The noise had become faint. "Let's just make sure," Schwieger decided. He ordered the electric motors to "slow ahead," getting up just enough headway to use his bowplanes. "Level at fifteen feet," he called. He gestured to Haupert to raise the periscope slowly. Immediately, a fast trickle of sea water started down from the packing.

Schwieger lifted the instrument slowly until it barely broke the surface. At the boat's slow speed, the periscope would show no wake. Then he turned it to the north and began searching down toward the west. When he saw the destroyer, it was in the middle of a sharp turn, swinging back in his direction.

"Damn," he cursed, starting the scope back down into its housing. "The son of a bitch is coming back."

"Take it down to fifty feet," he yelled into the control room. Then he waited as the boat slowly descended.

"Steady at fifty feet," the diving officer called back up into the tower.

"Stop motors," Schwieger called in response. When the electric motors were silent, he could hear the distant rumble of the destroyer's propellers growing louder as it headed back toward its prey. U-20's crew settled again into an anxious silence.

Minutes passed, and then they turned into an hour. And then the hours began to add. Overhead, there was the ever-present sound of the destroyer, criss-crossing back and forth. Within the submarine, there was the mounting apprehension as the walls continued to sweat and the air grew stale. The boat was dark, with every spare light turned off to conserve the dwindling electric power. Diesel oil fumes pressed down from above, and there was a faint odor of sulfur from the battery banks under the deck plates.

Some of the men were coiled into the narrow, damp bunks. Others were squeezed into corners, resting their heads against the bends in piping or against the cold, flat surfaces of silent machines. Still others were slouched at their watch stations, their faces resting on the control panels they were assigned to guard. They stirred only enough to raise their heads when the propeller noise grew deafening as the destroyer pounded overhead.

Wait, Schwieger kept saying to himself. She won't keep searching forever. But he knew that the English destroyer could stay on station far longer than he could hold out under water. Up there, the supply of fresh air was endless. The bunkers were full of coal to power the engines. The galleys were alive, preparing hot food. An hour, a day, counted for nothing. But his clock was registering the seconds and the minutes. Each tick brought closer the moment when he might have to stir his crew to battle stations so that they could fight for their lives. Each minute narrowed his chances of reaching the point near Coningbeg Light where he would wait for orders to intercept *Lusitania*.

THE ATLANTIC

"I THINK, perhaps, the pheasant," Alfred Vanderbilt told the starched waiter who hovered near his elbow. "Miss Beecham will have the fillet of sole." He tipped his head toward Jennifer. "Amandine?" he asked.

"Please," she answered.

"Yes," he said to the waiter. "The fillet of sole amandine."

He turned his attention back to Staff Captain John Anderson, who was holding court at the head of the table. Anderson was explaining the importance of fixing the ship's position immediately, when they raised their first sight of land.

"The warm spring air, blowing over the cold sea water, naturally raises a blanket of fog, which can obscure the horizon for two or three days at a time. And that, of course, makes it impossible for us to get a precise celestial fix of our position." He looked at the blank faces that surrounded him. "The stars," he said. "We fix our position by measuring the angle of elevation to certain stars. If we can't see the horizon, we can't measure the elevation."

"But surely you know where we are going," a plump woman, encased in lace, asked. She seemed suddenly concerned that *Lusitania* might be lost.

"Of course," Anderson hastened to reassure her. "But there are many forces at work during an Atlantic crossing. Ocean currents. The winds. They all tend to move us off our course. Perhaps by several miles. At sea, that's of no concern. There's more than enough ocean for us to sail on." He chuckled and took in the knowing smiles of the gentlemen at his table. "But when navigating near land, even a few thousand yards can be critical. So, when we near land, we stand off at a safe distance until we are absolutely certain of our exact position."

"I would certainly hope so," the woman said. "But how?"

Anderson looked perplexed. "How?"

"How can you be absolutely certain of your exact position?"

"Ah," Anderson said. He began arranging the salt and pepper shakers as props for an explanation of a two-point fix.

"Does this interest you?" Alfred Vanderbilt whispered to Jennifer Beecham. He rolled his eyes in an expression of boredom.

"Oh, certainly," Jennifer lied. "It's fascinating."

Vanderbilt squinted skeptically, bringing a smile to Jennifer's face.

"I don't care how he gets us there," she admitted. "I just can't wait to be back in England."

"You seem . . . distracted," he said. "I hope you're not worrying about the German warnings."

Jennifer was surprised. She had put the rumors of a German attack out of her mind the moment she had heard them. "Not at all," she answered. "It's just that I'm expecting to be met. It all seemed quite simple. But now . . . perhaps the arrangements . . ."

Vanderbilt understood immediately. Sir Peter Beecham's daughter would never have to worry about travel arrangements, or even social arrangements. This was something that even her father couldn't arrange.

"A young man?" he asked.

Her skin flushed red. "A naval officer," she answered. "I have no idea where he might be stationed."

They were interrupted as the waiter leaned between them and placed their hot plates carefully on the table. Then Vanderbilt leaned close to Jennifer and said, "I wouldn't give it a moment's thought. If I were your naval officer, I think I would take my ship right up onto the beach in order to be waiting for you."

She smiled at his kindness. But it didn't really help. It had all seemed so simple when she had written William Day about her arrival in Liverpool. Now, with each mile closer toward her destiny that *Lusitania* carried her, her doubts grew stronger. With each passing hour, her simple plan to rejoin the man she loved seemed more ridiculous.

They hadn't exchanged a word since he had left her home and headed off toward a new assignment. Even then, he had held out no promise of a future. "There are things we can't change," he had told her. And when she had insisted that their love could change everything, he had simply answered, "Not everything."

He was fighting a war. His ship, his men, would be his all-consuming concerns. Was there any room left to shelter a memory of a love that he had left far behind?

Had he even received her letter? Postmen didn't simply carry their letter bags to the front lines of a world war. Perhaps, even if he cared, he had no idea that she was on her way to him.

And there was the most frightening of all possibilities. What if he had fallen in love with someone else? A woman more beautiful. More daring. Stronger than she was. A woman free from the titles and trappings that he had seen coming between them.

How foolish she had been to assume that all he cared about was hearing from her. How ridiculous to expect that he would be waiting when *Lusitania* reached her destination. There were moments when she wanted to climb up to the bridge and beg the captain to turn the giant ship around.

Anderson droned on, explaining every aspect of the crossing until the fruit compote, served in crystal dishes set into a bed of crushed ice, had been finished. Then he explained the pressing demands of duty and rose to indicate to the first-class dining room that dinner was over. For the men, it was a signal to adjourn to the richly paneled smoking room with its wood-burning fireplace. There, they would second one another's criticisms of the management of the war while hinting at the enormous personal profits that the slaughter was yielding. The ladies gathered farther forward, in the library and writing room. On the first night out, Jennifer had accepted an invitation to join them. But she had no interest in wailing over the wartime inconveniences of maintaining a proper social schedule. Nor could she share her anxieties. None of the ladies would have understood why a gentleman of breeding would leave his beloved just because of a war.

She rode with her dinner companions on the elevator to the boat deck, two levels above the dining room. But as the women headed forward and the men moved aft, she stepped out into the open night and found a space between two of the lifeboats where she could see the Atlantic sliding past.

Jennifer wondered what was waiting for her. Perhaps William himself, looking up from the pier and then waving wildly when he caught sight of her looking down from the railing. That was the image that she took with her to bed each night and that she held in her arms as she fell asleep.

But it vanished each morning with the light of day. It was absurd to think that he could simply leave his post just to come and meet her. Most likely there would be a letter with specific instructions as to places and the names of people who would make her welcome until he could return. It could easily be weeks before she would see him. But at least she would be there, where he lived, waiting for the moment his ship turned into the harbor.

Her thoughts turned darker in the afternoon. A letter, courteous to a fault, filled with concern for her feelings. But somewhere toward the bottom of the first page, the tone would change abruptly to one of frank honesty. It would restate all the things he had said at their parting, pointing out concisely why their lives could never fit together. And then it would urge her to return home, bringing his deepest respects to her parents. The letter would leave the most intimate questions unanswered. She would never know whether it stated his true feelings or whether hidden behind its concern was the fact that he no longer loved her. Perhaps that he had realized that he never loved her. But it would announce an end to her dreams from which there could be no appeal.

Her worst fears came in the evening, as she prepared for dinner and realized that she was dressing for no one. What, she wondered, if he had found someone else? What if there were no letter at all?

She saw herself, at the end of a deserted dock, sitting on her steamer trunks as the last carriages carried the last passengers away. The Cunard people would be most gracious, finding her suitable accommodations and taking great care that her things were delivered promptly. And they would show great patience each day when she stopped by to ask for a letter, looking sadly after her as she left empty-handed.

Oh God, William, she thought. Tell me something. Even if you are sending me away, tell me so that I'll know. But don't leave me to wonder. Don't leave me hoping for things that will never be.

"You'll catch a death of cold." Jennifer was startled by Alfred Vanderbilt's voice as he stepped up beside her. He already had his topcoat off and was placing it over her shoulders. "You shouldn't be outdoors on the Atlantic until at least the middle of July."

"It doesn't feel cold," she answered.

He smiled. "No, I suppose it doesn't. Not at your age. But it's the wind. It cuts right through you. Let me walk you inside."

Jennifer took his arm and started across the deck.

"Still worried about your young man, I imagine."

She smiled in embarrassment. "The one you're so certain will be waiting, Mr. Vanderbilt."

"And you're not? Why?"

"We quarreled," she admitted.

"Then he'll certainly be waiting. To apologize for whatever foolish thing he said."

"What he said was that he wasn't from a very important family."

"And that concerns you?"

Jennifer laughed. "No. But it concerns him."

"Ah? The arrogance of the working man. A terrible burden to carry through life."

She shook her head. "It's just that, after the war, he thinks we'll all have to go back to where we belong."

Vanderbilt stopped as they reached the door. "I don't think so," he told her. "I think this damned war may finally teach us that we all belong together. I think that the old ways are finished, and good riddance to them."

She looked pleasantly surprised.

"The war throws us all together. It shows us that we need each other. It breaks all the rules, and once they're broken I think we'll all be amazed at how well we can live without them." He opened the door and then reached out to retrieve his topcoat from Jennifer's shoulders. "You said he was a naval officer."

"Yes," she nodded.

"Then I'm sure he's learned to break a few rules already. Take my word for it. He'll be waiting."

Vanderbilt stayed out on deck as Jennifer stepped through the door. "Aren't you coming in?" she asked.

He swung the coat around his own shoulders. "No. I like to walk out here in the fresh air. I really can't stand all that damned cigar smoke."

LONDON

Reginald Hall sat alone in his conference room, staring up at a map of the war zone and sipping slowly from a glass of deep red port. It was nearly midnight, and the windows throughout Whitehall were darkened. The only light in his office slipped beneath the closed door of the communication room, where the night watch officer slept at his desk.

He had taken off his jacket and tossed it carelessly on a chair. His necktie was pulled down, and his shirt collar, released from its button, was sticking out under the sides of his jaw. This was how he did his best work, alone and unhurried. This was when his mind could roam freely, unencumbered by the constant stream of new information that filled his days, undistracted by the whine of the radios and the clatter of the coding machines.

It was all quite simple, really. Like a chess game. You watched the enemy move and tried to deduce his plan. Then you made your move to frustrate his attack and, one hoped, to launch your own strike at the same time. He and Flotilla Commander Bauer were at the opposite ends of Europe. But they might as well have been sitting across a table from each other, their heads nearly touching as they bent over the chessmen. He had made his move, pushing *Lusitania* out into the center of the board. Bauer had studied it and then countered by moving his submarines toward the sacrificial queen. Now he was studying Bauer's response. Not so much for what he saw, but for what it told him about his opponent's thinking. Had Bauer missed the trap? Was he reaching thoughtlessly towards the obvious capture? Or was this a feint? Did the German submarines have some other prize in mind?

What were his options? He had every reason to take *Lusitania*. His information about her cargo had come from a coded message, so he would feel sure that the English were trying to keep the cargo secret. No reason for him to be suspicious. But he was making no effort to hide the presence of his U-boats. The two that had left Emden had announced their departure by testing their radios as soon as they reached the North Sea. One had broadcast a long, coded message when it rounded the Orkneys. And the boats already on station certainly weren't lying low. Four ships had been sunk off Land's End in the past two days. Perhaps the German admiral figured that all the British escorts would be circling around *Lusitania*. He might be making us think he's going after the cargo of guncotton so that he can have a field day sinking everything else while we're focused on the one target he isn't going after. Not a bad plan, Hall thought—feinting toward your opponent's queen and then taking the bishops that he had forgotten to protect.

Hall might counter by moving the escorts away from *Lusitania*. But Bauer was no fool. If *Lusitania* were suddenly left open, he would certainly wonder why. Without doubt, he would pause to study the board before he rushed to the attack.

He took the port with him as he stood and circled the conference table toward the map. There were three—possibly four—German boats within striking distance of *Lusitania*'s course line. They knew about the cargo, and every source available to him confirmed that they were interested. Perhaps the normalcy of their operations was Bauer's cover, his attempt to convince the English that no particular trap was being set.

So, what move should he make? Probably to respond with a normalcy of his own. Show Bauer that the Admiralty was concerned about *Lusitania*'s safety. He would expect that, since the British were obviously aware of his warning in the American newspapers. But at the same time, Hall's move should advance his own strategy. He had to make *Lusitania* appear to be an impossibly well-protected target. And yet, with the same move, he had to make certain that Bauer would go for her. The question was how.

It was ironic that it all came down to this. All the ships and all the guns, and yet the war didn't hinge on tonnage and firepower. It came down to 2 men, 400 miles apart, trying to determine what the other was thinking. Trying to guess what the other would believe and what he would distrust.

What would be normal? To station escorts to meet *Lusitania* and guide her up the Irish coast. Bauer would notice that and appreciate how important the cargo was to England. But would he attack in the face of an escort of warships? Probably not, unless he could find a gap in the coverage. And how could Hall indicate a safe place for Bauer to set his trap? Make it too obvious, and his German opponent might see the subterfuge. Make it too obscure, and he might miss it.

How did the British typically escort ships into Liverpool? The Queenstown fleet met them somewhere near Fastnet and escorted them up the coast. At Coningbeg, they turned them over to the ships from Milford Haven, which then took them up Saint George's Channel. The break in the coverage, if there was any, had to occur around Coningbeg. It was precisely at that break that a U-boat had gotten close to *Lusitania*, forcing her into a wide course alteration and into zigzag maneuvers. Bauer had to know that.

But he also had to know that the British had fixed the situation. Now the rendezvous with the Milford Haven fleet was generally set south of Coningbeg instead of farther up the channel. If Hall were going to reopen the gap, he needed a damned convincing reason. Like the one that was on the map right in front of him.

The sinkings off Land's End. There were four red pins in his map, clustered around the Scilly Islands, marking the four ships that had gone down under U-boat attacks in the past two days. Pushed in among them were four blue pins, indicating submarine attacks and sightings. Bauer was raising hell off the southwest tip of England.

Maybe, Hall thought, this is Bauer's feint. He was littering the seas directly south of Milford Haven. The logical English response, the one Bauer might be hoping for, was to pull the Milford Haven fleet out of Saint George's Channel and send it rushing to the south. And that would create an opening for the U-boats.

Hall tossed down the rest of the port. "All right, Herr Bauer," he whispered to the map. "I think I know what you're up to. Now let's just hope that you don't know what I'm up to."

CROOKHAVEN

"THERE'S CODED traffic," Chief Gore told Shiela when she stepped out of Day's car in front of the radio station.

She felt the fear tighten in her throat, but then forced a smile so that neither the chief nor Day would notice her reaction.

"Not a lot, I hope," she said.

"Just two," Gore told her. "Short ones. Won't take you long."

She walked to the coffee pot that had already filled the room with its heavy aroma. "Who are they for?"

"Two ships," he answered. "Don't remember their names."

She breathed easily. The chief would certainly remember the name *Lusitania*. She'd been given another reprieve from the terrible choice that was rushing toward her.

Since Tom Duffy had dropped her at the station the previous morning, she had thought of nothing but the next message that would go out to *Lusitania*. The Germans knew The Greyhound's call letters as well as she did. They would spot the message and then ask Emmett Hayes for its contents. She would have to deliver it to him before the German request came in on his radio.

But Shiela knew that she couldn't. She had reached the decision to break from the Fenians when she had finally admitted to herself that William Day was the center of her life. That was when she had requested her transfer, hoping that the Admiralty would end her deceit by taking her out of Ireland. It would mean leaving William. But away from Ireland, there was at least a glimmer of hope for her future. If she stayed by his side, the lie she was living would inevitably destroy them both.

The fact that it was *Lusitania* reinforced her decision. Left with no alternative, she might well have pointed her finger at one more insignificant ship, a cargo-laden steamer whose crew might be given the chance to take to their boats. But Emmett had been interested only in *Lusitania*. She knew about her special cargo. She'd coded and delivered the message that had ordered the cargo to be loaded aboard her. But this ship was alive with passengers, many of whom had little stake in the war, and probably none an interest in Emmett's damnable Irish cause. She couldn't betray them to the madness that was gripping the world.

And then William had shown her the letter. The thought of another woman's coming to him had crashed the fragile hopes she had been protecting. Yet, the fact he had told her meant that he shared at least some of the feelings she had for him. It was obvious that Jennifer was very important to him. And while she wished she had never learned about her, or even heard her name, Shiela knew that placing Jennifer in danger would be a total betrayal of the decency she was trying to reclaim. There was no possibility that she would ever give Emmett Hayes any information concerning the arrival of *Lusitania*.

So she prayed that there would be no more coded traffic for *Lusitania*. That somehow, she wouldn't be caught in the trap that she herself had set when she first returned to Ireland and agreed to work with the Fenians. The trap she had armed when she fell in love with William Day. But with each passing moment, her chances of escape grew slimmer. The Greyhound was only a day away, racing toward a rendezvous off the Irish coast. There would surely be messages to arrange her escort, to time her handoff to the Milford Haven fleet when she made her turn at Coningbeg, and confirm her passage over the bar at the entrance to Liverpool.

She had worked out and discarded her possible plans. Her first thought had been to make a run for it: Code the message whenever it came in, deliver it to the chief, then pack a few essentials and catch the next train for Cork. But she knew she was being watched. Emmett even knew when she was at her desk in the coding office. Would he simply let her climb aboard the daily train that ran from Schull to Skibbereen? And if he did, where would she go? To the naval station at Queenstown to confess that she had been supplying information to the Germans? Back to England, where the Admiralty would certainly be able to find her, once Hayes had informed them of the reason for her absence from her post? Or perhaps to the north, in hopes of vanishing into one of the small Irish villages? What hope was that? In Ireland, every stranger was an event. It would take just a few hours before the townspeople knew where she had come from. Just a few days before the movement's messengers had told Emmett where she could be found.

She had thought of changing the message. She could change the bearings and the distances that located *Lusitania*'s rendezvous, and even the time of her arrival. Then she could deliver the altered text to the rectory housekeeper, exactly as she had been ordered. Would Hayes ever know that she had lied? When the Germans missed their intercept, they would undoubtedly question the information they had been sent. But even *Lusitania* was insignificant in the vastness of the sea. Perhaps Emmett would think that The Greyhound had simply slipped through the Germans' fingers.

Shiela had even decided, at least for a moment, to confess everything to William Day. That she had been working for the Fenians, knowing that they were helping the enemy. That she had stopped and had tried to break free from the conspirators. That they had refused and were holding her hostage for one last message. The message that would finger *Lusitania*. She knew he would find a way to warn the ship. She could even hope that he would protect her from her own countrymen and stand beside her when she confronted the Admiralty with her confession. But she was terrified of the moment when she would say the words of her confession and see the stunned impact in his eyes. Would they soften with understanding? Or would they fill with hatred and disgust at the thought that she had used him?

"Just two ships," the chief had said. "Don't remember their names." His words had bought her another hour. Perhaps another day. But *Lusitania* was on an inbound course. There would have to be a message.

Day had taken his coffee and stepped outside, walking to the edge of the land near the steel lattice of the radio tower. His eyes searched the horizon where The Greyhound would soon appear, but his mind was locked on the letter that he had dropped into the mail pouch for Liverpool.

He had written twenty pages, tearing them to shreds as he read them.

The truth seemed too abrupt, but each time he tried to soften it, it became less true. His meaning was simple. She had to go back to America. But the explanation baffled him.

Because he couldn't take care of her. He was a soldier at war, with no way of knowing where he would be needed. She might arrive only to see his ship sail. She might wait, only to have him gone for years. That was true enough. But, of course, it was entirely beside the point. A million women were waiting without knowing. That was why she had come across the Atlantic. There was also a hidden promise. It implied that the war was the only thing that stood between them. But someday the war would be over, and no matter how he worded his thoughts, they seemed to say that someday Jennifer and he would be together. That wasn't true. He couldn't let her leave, thinking that their time would come. That would be the cruelest lie of all. He had torn the letter up, squeezing the pages into a tight ball.

Because there was someone else. True, again. And those words were unambiguous. They ended all hope, all thought of a future. But the someone else was leaving. There was something standing between them that he couldn't understand. Some dark secret that Shiela couldn't explain. "If it's to be, we'll find each other," she had told him. Yet, despite the words, he knew she was telling him that it could never be. Shiela wasn't the reason he was telling Jennifer to go home. And he couldn't use her shabbily. He had crossed out the words with a furious hand and then tore the page into tiny pieces.

Because he didn't love her. Certainly words that would leave her with no reason to stay. But the lie was so transparent to him that he knew she would see through it. He could have ended it all in her garden on Long Island if he could only have told her that he didn't love her. He couldn't tell her that now, either.

How could he make her understand the simple truth? That there were barriers separating people, dividing them into different worlds. That she couldn't long live in his, nor could he in hers. That there were rules that regulated their lives, and that there was great peril to anyone who broke the rules. He tried to put it into words, but his explanations fell far short of his meaning. He had torn up page after page.

He had finally realized that a letter couldn't tell her what he knew and what he felt. He would have to see her again and try to make her understand. He would have to take her to the ship, put her aboard, and watch her sail back to where she could live the life that was hers, but not his.

His letter had been short. His delight that she was visiting in England. His excuses that he couldn't be there to meet her. His advice that she go immediately to stay with family friends. His promise that as soon as he was able, he would come to England to see her. It said nothing that would answer her question. That was an answer that he had to deliver to her face. The truth didn't fit into a letter. But she would hear it in his voice and see it in his eyes.

He walked back to the radio cottage. Shiela was locked in the code room, translating the two outgoing messages into the day's cipher. Chief Gore was busying himself, filing old traffic and filling out the message logs. A seaman was in the process of spooning coffee for a fresh pot. The duty radioman was slouched by the telegraph key, his feet crossed on the edge of his desk. It was the chief who picked up the Queenstown telephone when it buzzed.

"One for *Lusitania*," he said absently when he set down the telephone. He was still writing, filling in the header of the message form. Day walked around him and read over his shoulder.

RENDEZVOUS ELEMENTS CRUISER SQUADRON E, 7 MAY, 0600 HOURS, 260 FASTNET, 40 MILES, THEN ELEMENTS DESTROYER SQUADRON A, 1800 HOURS, 120 CONINGBEG, 7 MILES.

"My God," Day whispered.

Gore looked up. "Something wrong, commander?"

Day reread the message. Squadron E was the patrol ships out of Queenstown that met incoming vessels at Fastnet and escorted them up the coast. It was normal to send arriving ships the time and coordinates for the rendezvous. But the details of the second rendezvous, with the Squadron A ships from Milford Haven, were never broadcast. That information was signaled over to the ship by the Squadron E vessels.

"Who originated this?"

"Admiral Coke," the chief said, checking the call letters that signed the message. "From Queenstown."

"Get me a confirmation," Day ordered.

"From Admiral Coke?"

"From whoever actually drafted this."

The chief sighed and lifted the telephone.

"Where's Lieutenant Grace?" he asked while Gore was waiting to be connected.

"In his quarters, I think."

Day took the message pad and pulled out the carbon copy.

Grace was at his wash stand, hunched over a shaving basin so that he could see himself in the small mirror that leaned against the wall. His chin was hidden in a thick lather.

"Good morning, commander," he said to the image that suddenly appeared behind him.

"Do you know anything about this?" Day responded, thrusting the message into his line of sight.

Grace read, the razor still poised against his throat. "Who's MFA?" he asked, looking at the call letters in the message head.

"*Lusitania.*"

He shrugged, then carefully touched the blade to his skin. "Seems routine. Don't you set up the meetings for all the incoming ships?"

"Not like this," the commander answered. "Look at it."

Peter Grace set his razor down carefully and took the message in his hand. "The Queenstown lads meet her at Fastnet, and then they turn her over to the Milford Haven fleet at Coningbeg." He gave the paper back to Day. "Makes sense to me."

"That's the problem," Day countered. "It will make sense to the Germans, too. With these two points, I can plot her course all the way up the coast. Christ, I can even figure her exact speed. We never send anything this specific."

Grace went back to his shaving. "I have no idea," he concluded. "Escorting ships is really not my cup of tea."

"No, but security is. Do you have things under control here? Or is there still a chance that the Germans are reading our traffic?"

"If you mean do I have our spy in leg irons, the answer is no. I'm afraid he's still out there. Of course, James Corcoran's terrible accident has probably shaken him up a bit. More than likely he's lying low. I'd guess you're secure until he thinks we've given up on him. And by then, I should have the son of a bitch."

"But you don't know who it is?"

"I have a few ideas."

"Lieutenant, this message will be coded and on the air in less than an hour. Can I be sure that the Germans won't read it?"

"Sure?" Grace lifted the razor from his cheek long enough to chuckle. "Commander, in my line of work we're never sure of anything. I'm not even sure that you're not working for Admiral von Pohl. But I doubt it. And I doubt that you have to worry about your message."

"There are 2,000 civilians aboard that ship. Women and children," Day reminded him.

Grace began toweling off the lather. "The Admiralty knows that. And they know what I've been doing."

There was a moment of temptation when Day wanted to pick up the razor and use it on Grace's smug face. He turned on his heels and stormed out of the cottage, back toward the radio building.

"Who sent it?" he demanded of Chief Gore as he burst through the door.

"Dammit, commander, I got routed to intelligence again. Got my ass reamed quite properly. 'Send it,' he tells me. 'And be quick about it.'"

"Where is it?" Day asked.

The chief nodded toward the locked door. "Miss McDevitt is translating it right now."

He started toward the door of the coding room, then stopped himself. Shiela was just doing her job. It was pointless to interrupt her. And the chief was just doing his job. He still had time to think. The decision of whether to send the message was still his to make.

Day refilled his coffee cup and walked outside. Why was Naval Intelligence involving itself in routine traffic? First, concerning the loading of a cargo in New York. And now the day-to-day escorting of incoming ships. None of this was their affair. And why had Queenstown suddenly changed the information it was sending to the ships? There was no reason to broadcast the coordinates of the second rendezvous. That could be passed on, with far greater security, by the escorts from Squadron E.

The only answer he could think of was that the message was a plant, requested by Lieutenant Grace, to help him track down the spies who had been compromising Crookhaven traffic. But Grace claimed to know nothing about it. Was he lying? Why would he withhold information from his commanding officer? Did he suspect that his agent might be someone within the station? Someone whom Day might accidentally tip off? Chief Gore? Shiela? One of the radiomen? Ridiculous! They were all people with long service to the Admiralty.

But if the message were genuine, wouldn't it increase the danger to *Lusitania?* Unless they were certain that Crookhaven was now completely secure. But if they were, then why was Peter Grace still here? Why had he said that he couldn't be sure of anything?

There were no answers that made sense. Except the one answer that had been drilled home during his first week in officer training. You don't question orders. You carry them out immediately, to the best of your ability.

"Message is ready." It was Chief Gore calling from the open doorway. Shiela was standing beside him, running a final check on the seemingly meaningless page of characters she had delivered.

"Send it, chief," Day said. All he could do was carry out his orders.

LONDON

STAFF ADMIRAL Oliver stood next to the wall chart, a rubber-tipped pointer held under his right arm like a field officer's baton. He stared blankly at Admiral John Fisher, who had just asked an embarrassing question.

"Why in God's name is the Milford Haven fleet rushing down to Land's End?" Fisher repeated. "What are they supposed to do down there?"

Oliver stammered as he aimed his pointer toward the area off the southwestern tip of England. "Well, sir, the submarine activity here. Six ships sunk in two days. Our thinking—"

"Whose thinking?" Fisher demanded. He glanced around the room at the other officers of his staff. To his mind, none of them had ever had a useful thought in his life. Then his squinting eyes found Winston Churchill, and Captain Reginald Hall, who was sitting at Churchill's elbow. "Only thing they can do down there is get themselves sunk."

"Sir John," the First Lord of the Admiralty answered, "we can't just sit back while German U-boats run unchallenged ten miles off our coast. We have to do something."

Fisher shook his head. Gestures, he thought. More pap for the newspapers. Winston simply wanted to tell his fancy friends that he had the German submarines under attack. The man was bright enough to know that the ancient destroyers operating out of Milford Haven couldn't find a submarine in a wash basin. Even as escorts, their best hope was that the torpedo would accidentally hit them before it got through to the ships they were escorting. He turned his attention back to Admiral Oliver, who was delivering the daily status briefing.

"We have six ships coming up to Coningbeg tomorrow," Oliver said. He pointed to the blue disks that were fixed to the map, each with an arrow that indicated its heading. Then he slipped his glasses down on his nose so that he could read the names of the ships.

"Escorts?" Fisher asked.

"Squadron E will meet these four, coming in from the North Atlantic, and take them to Coningbeg. From there"—he hesitated in embarrassment—"with the Milford Haven fleet operating in the south, I'm afraid they'll be on their own."

"And the other two?" Fisher demanded.

Oliver squinted at the disks. "That would be *Candidate* and *Centurion*. They will be unescorted."

Admiral Fisher studied the map. There were two red squares, near

Land's End, indicating the U-boats that Squadron A was going after. Another square indicated a U-boat off the southwestern coast of Ireland, about to turn around Fastnet and head in along the southern coast. He looked back at Winston Churchill.

"With all these submarines, maybe we should send *Candidate* and *Centurion* around Ireland. Have them come in through the North Channel."

"Except," Churchill answered, "this submarine might decide to stay outside Fastnet. Then we would be sending the ships directly to it. There are dangers either way."

The First Sea Lord nodded. Churchill was right.

"Now, the day after tomorrow, we have *Lusitania*, due off Fastnet at dawn," Oliver continued. "Squadron E will provide the escort as far as Coningbeg. From there"—his voice trailed off—"once again, with the Milford Haven ships out of position, there would be no further escort."

Fisher frowned as he studied the chart. "I'm not sure I like this," he concluded. "That German ad in the American papers. Seems to me they're too interested in *Lusitania*. Has she been warned about all this submarine activity?"

"We've put out a general warning," Hall said. "I'm sure *Lusitania* has it."

"She'll be escorted part of the way," Winston Churchill added. "And if there seem to be unusual dangers, we can pull her into Queenstown until the danger passes. Anger a few passengers, I suppose. But I think we can protect her."

"I'm sure," Fisher agreed. "Escorts really don't do much for *Lusitania*, anyway. She has to slow down so that they can keep up. If you ask me, the damned escorts are in more danger than she is."

Reginald Hall smiled. "An excellent point, admiral. We don't want to slow her down. The U-boats can't hit what they can't catch."

Fisher rose, signaling the end of the briefing. His staff jumped up in unison. "Well, I suppose that tidies up everything," he announced. Then he turned back to Churchill. "You'll be on call during the weekend?"

"No," Winston said. "Captain Hall will be here, but I'm afraid there are pressing duties in France."

Fisher was surprised. He glanced back at the chart and took in the markers for the German submarines and the large disk that indicated *Lusitania*. "Is that wise?" he wondered.

"Can't be helped," Churchill said. "General French is a bit out of sorts over the supplies going to the Crimea. There's a meeting in Paris. He asked me to attend."

The First Sea Lord left, his staff following like a flock of ducklings.

Churchill and Hall stayed behind, along with Admiral Oliver, who was picking up his briefing papers.

"I suppose the First Sea Lord is right," Churchill pondered aloud. "Who would Squadron E send as an escort? Probably *Juno.*"

Admiral Oliver looked up and blinked in his direction. "I imagine so," he agreed.

Churchill shook his head. "Smoky old bucket," he said. "All she'll do is give away *Lusitania's* position, and slow her down in the process."

Hall nodded in agreement. "She's certainly no match for a submarine."

"Then perhaps we should cancel the rendezvous," Admiral Oliver suggested. "I mean, if she adds nothing to *Lusitania's* safety . . ."

"An excellent observation," Winston Churchill said. He looked toward Captain Hall.

"I would certainly agree with Admiral Oliver," Hall responded.

Churchill looked back to Oliver. "Then you'll see to it, Admiral."

Oliver was pleased to have made a contribution. "I'll draft a message to all parties right away."

"I don't think I'd broadcast it," Hall offered. "I think, if you would just contact Admiral Coke and advise him to recall the escorts."

"Of course," Oliver agreed. He gathered his papers and left the briefing room.

Churchill struck a match and gave his full attention to sealing a cigar. He fit it carefully into the center of his mouth, then struck another match to light it. "Any thoughts?" he asked Hall when he was satisfied with the dense smoke.

"I still think they'll go after her," Hall said.

"They'll know where to find her?"

The intelligence officer nodded. "If they're still reading Crookhaven, they will."

"Where?" the First Lord asked.

Hall went to the map and tapped his finger at a point south of Coningbeg Light. "Right here. Their submarines will report the Milford Haven fleet rushing to the south. They'll know that Coningbeg is unprotected. My guess is that they'll have two boats waiting, flanking the entrance."

Churchill grunted. "That would be Saturday evening."

"Just before sunset," Hall agreed. "If she keeps to her schedule. And Bowler Bill Turner is very meticulous about schedules."

"Should raise one hell of a row," Churchill said as he reached for his hat. "American citizens violated by an unprovoked submarine attack. You'll want to have reporters waiting when *Lusitania* limps into port."

"If the Germans manage to hit her," Hall cautioned.

Churchill paused in the doorway. "Just the fact that they attack will help. It will get Woodrow Wilson leaning in our direction. And maybe we'll get lucky. The Germans might just manage to kill an American or two. Then Mr. Wilson will fall right into our lap."

THE IRISH COAST

"Fastnet," Walter Schwieger told Willi Haupert. He glanced down at his watch. "And right on schedule."

"I didn't think we'd make it," Haupert answered. "What did we have to make up? Ten hours?"

They had been lucky. The seas had stayed flat, and there had been a blanket of fog for cover. They had been able to stay on the surface, running at flank speed, covering the 500 miles from the Hebrides in 35 hours. That left them a day and a half to reach their station at Coningbeg, only 170 miles away. It would be an easy passage.

"Maybe we'll get in some hunting while we're waiting," Schwieger mused.

His executive officer laughed. "The crew would enjoy that. They owe somebody for making them spend all that time hiding."

Haupert was right, Schwieger knew. It had been a difficult voyage for the crew. They had sat for hours beneath the surface, being hunted by the ships above, without even attempting a counterattack. Then, in their race southward, they had heard a ship sounding its horn in the fog. "Close enough to touch," they had complained to one another. But their captain hadn't tried to follow the wailing whistle. He hadn't made any effort to stay close, waiting for a clearing. Instead, he had passed it by. They were hunters, they all agreed with pride. Yet on this patrol they had done no hunting. Instead, they had either hidden or run.

But Schwieger's orders had been specific. He was to get to the south Irish coast, making certain to arrive before the sixth of May. Once on station, he could hunt to his heart's content. But his primary target was the "large troop transport." He had to be ready for the order to attack her.

When Fastnet was off his port quarter, he ordered the turn to east northeast. Now he was moving parallel to the coast, making his best speed, hidden by the dark of the night.

They caught a brief glimpse of sunrise just as they were passing ten miles off the Old Head of Kinsale. But the coastline quickly disappeared in the whisper of fog that rose from the water, and within minutes they were moving in fog so dense that Schwieger couldn't see his own bow. There was suddenly the danger of running into one of the small bum boats that traded up and down the coast, or into the nets dragged behind a fisherman. He changed his course to east, widening the distance to land as he continued to race ahead.

Haupert came back up on deck, balancing a steaming mug of coffee fresh from the mess. "Breakfast is ready," he told his captain. "I'll take over if you like."

"Porridge?" Schwieger asked suspiciously.

Haupert nodded. "From here on. The eggs were finished yesterday."

Schwieger made a face. "I think I'll stay up," he said. He took the coffee and lifted it to his lips without ever taking his eyes from the wall of fog directly ahead.

As he sipped, the sky began to lighten. U-20's bow appeared, tossing up an even wake as it sliced through the flat seas. A patch of blue appeared overhead, and then U-20 broke out into daylight. Almost at the same instant, the gray hull of a ship materialized out of a wall of fog only 500 yards off his starboard beam.

Schwieger was about to scream the order to dive. But atop the hull, two cargo masts appeared, and then the small superstructure of a freighter. "Battle stations," he yelled. "Slow to all ahead one-third." At his flank speed, he would have run away from the ship. Then "right standard rudder," swinging his bow toward the first target of his voyage. The deck hatches sprung open and his gun crew leaped out on the deck. Just forward of the conning tower, his boarding party came up, dragging the collapsible boat behind them. The freighter suddenly turned to its right. Before his gun crew was in position, it disappeared back into the fog.

Now, Schwieger had to guess, just as the destroyer that had closed on him off the Hebrides had had to guess. Would the freighter continue turning back to the west? Or would her captain order his rudder amidships as soon as he found the protection of the fog? "Steady as she goes," Schwieger decided. He was guessing the captain would stop his turn, and he was aiming his boat to follow her into the mist.

If he was right, then he was running right behind her, closing under his momentum. As his boat lost speed, he would settle in no more than 200 yards off her stern. If he was wrong, then he was moving south while the freighter was moving west. He would probably never see her again.

"What do you think, Willi?"

Haupert pointed straight ahead. "She'll run south until she thinks it's safe. Then she'll turn back to her course."

Schwieger nodded. He leaned over the conning tower rail, searching the few hundred feet of water he could see for some sign of the freighter's wake. "Put a lookout right on the bow," he told his executive officer. He wanted every inch of visibility he could buy. "Switch to the motors." The noisy diesels immediately went silent, letting him hear the movement of the air and the sea around him.

He was risking losing his target. With the electric motors, his best speed was only seven knots, less than what the freighter was making. But, blinded in the fog, he had only his ears as a detection device. He strained over the sound of the water splashing over his bow.

For a while, there was nothing. But then, scarcely noticeable, was the distant throbbing of a reciprocating engine. He turned his head from side to side, trying to locate the sound.

"Port bow," Haupert whispered.

"I think so," Schwieger agreed.

He felt the boat rock slightly. A wave had rolled gently against his starboard bow. He followed the angular line of the wave and watched it narrow as it disappeared ahead of him. It was the ship's wake.

"She's turning," he told his executive. Then, in a stage whisper into the voice tube, "Left standard rudder." He was turning back to his target's original course.

He couldn't hear the engine any more. He was still behind the freighter, but she was moving away from him. "Switch to the engines," he told Haupert, who bent into the hatch and repeated the order. The diesels chugged for an instant, then roared to life. "All ahead two-thirds."

They picked up speed, chasing the ghost they could no longer hear. But then the wake was visible again, a rolling wave that moved across his bow from starboard to port. He had turned a tighter circle than his prey, and now he was coming up along her port side. An instant later, the sky lightened. They broke out of the fog and saw the side of the freighter no more than fifty yards off their starboard bow.

Another instant decision. If he fired a torpedo, it wouldn't have enough time to arm itself before striking the target. But if he slowed to open space, he would be giving the ship time to turn back into the fog bank. He screamed down to his gun crew, "Put a shot ahead of her." The crew was already swinging the gun out over the starboard side. They fired almost immediately, sending a tower of water crashing over the freighter's bow.

An officer rushed out onto the wing of the ship's bridge and began waving both arms toward Schwieger. Seconds later, steam blasted from her escape pipes. The throbbing of her engines slowed to a stop. The ship and the submarine came to rest in bright daylight, less than one hundred yards apart. U-20's deck gun was trained directly at the officers on the bridge.

Haupert loaded his boarding party into the boat and rowed across to the freighter. In the dead-calm seas, it was a quick crossing. He climbed to the bridge, saluted the captain, and demanded the ship's papers. When the captain claimed to have sailed without the final manifest, Haupert ordered the hatches broken open and sent his boarding party to search.

Schwieger grew nervous as an hour passed. He was dead in the water, in a sunny clearing, less than twenty miles from the Irish coast. The ship, named *Candidate*, had had ample time to radio to British patrols while they were maneuvering in the fog. For all he knew, a British cruiser might be bearing down on him, and his boarding party still hadn't returned. He could sense the tension growing in his gun crew, who still held the deck gun focused on *Candidate*'s bridge.

Suddenly Haupert appeared on the wing and held a three-inch cannon round high above his head. He had found contraband in the ship's holds, and he was ordering her crew to take to their boats. As Haupert rowed back to U-20, Schwieger watched *Candidate*'s crew lowering their lifeboats. When Haupert was aboard, the loaded lifeboats of the freighter were already a hundred yards clear of their ship, pulling strongly toward the north.

"Cannon shells. Cartridges," Haupert explained as he climbed to the top of the tower. "Half her cargo is ammunition."

"Then she goes to the bottom," Schwieger smiled, still scanning the horizon for an approaching man-of-war. He started the diesels and swung a quarter mile turn to the north of the ghost ship.

"She was armed," Haupert added. "A three-incher and two machine guns behind sandbags on her fantail."

"Christ," the submarine's captain cursed. When they broke out of the fog, they had been right under *Candidate*'s transom. If the three-inch cannon had been manned, U-20 would have been blown in half.

"Son of a bitch," Schwieger said as he lined up his bow with the abandoned ship's smokestack. He gave the order to fire. In the flat seas, the torpedo's wake drew a straight line between the two vessels, and then *Candidate*'s hull exploded at the water line.

Instantly she took on a list, while clouds of soot shot up from her funnel. U-20's crew watched, expecting her to continue her roll until her decks were awash, and then begin sinking by the bow. But *Candidate* steadied with a twenty-degree list and showed no signs of sinking.

Schwieger waited another five minutes, looking about constantly for the warships that might be drawing near. There was nothing in sight, except the drifting, wounded ship, and the lifeboat, now half a mile off and still pulling furiously toward the shore.

"All ahead slow," he ordered, moving toward *Candidate* and getting up enough headway to bring his deck gun to bear. "Tell the gun crew to fire when ready."

The deck gun cracked, blasting a hole high up in the superstructure. The next shot punched a hole in *Candidate*'s flank, a foot above the water line. They kept firing as U-20 drew closer, blasting hole after hole in the hull. Fifteen shots later, an explosion blasted up through the inside of the ship, and she began to roll abruptly. In two minutes, her stern was high in the air and she was plunging toward the bottom.

"Let's get the hell out of here," Schwieger said, taking the submarine at full speed toward the fog bank that still lingered to the south. The last thing he saw was *Candidate*'s stern, armed with a cannon and machine guns, disappear into the sea.

As soon as he was concealed in the mist, he turned back to the east. His chances of finding another ship in the fog were slim at best. His best course was to get to Coningbeg and wait for the radio message that would aim him directly toward *Lusitania*.

THREE HUNDRED miles to the west of Fastnet, crewmen began unlashing the whitewashed canvas covers that were stretched across the tops of *Lusitania*'s lifeboats. The wooden blocks, hanging from the davits, were connected, and the boats were lifted out of their chocks and swung out over the rails.

"Just routine," Staff Captain Anderson told the curious couples strolling along the boat deck in their topcoats. "Just keeping everything in tiptop working order."

He threw a smart salute to Alfred Vanderbilt, who had Jennifer Beecham on his arm. Vanderbilt stepped to the rail and looked down nearly fifty feet to the ocean rushing past below. He glanced back up at the boat, swinging from its rope falls. "I hope you don't expect me to ride down in that thing, Captain Anderson."

Anderson laughed. "Hardly, Mr. Vanderbilt. The elevators will be at your service. We simply have to assure that the boats can be swung free. Admiralty orders."

Other strollers imitated Vanderbilt and stole a glance down the dizzying height of the ship. The men forced smiles at the absurdity of the exercise. But the women were plainly frightened. When the boats were swung out, there was a three-foot gap between the railing and the gunwales of the boats, far too great a distance to cross in a long skirt. And even if they should get aboard a boat, the thought of being lowered on rope falls fifty feet into a churning sea was terrifying.

"I'd stay with the ship," a broad matron decided. "I could never get across."

"Ah," Anderson smiled, understanding her concern. "But you

wouldn't have to. We load the boat before we swing it out. Quite safe, you see."

He sped through an explanation of the procedure. The boat would be filled, maneuvered between the davits and out over the side, and then gently lowered with the block at tackle. While it was on its way down, the crewmen would raise the canvas sides on the collapsible boats that were fixed to the deck directly under the lifeboats. The collapsibles would be filled, and then connected to the rope falls that would be recovered from the already launched lifeboat. Then the collapsible would be lowered. "Really very simple," Anderson concluded.

"And how long does all this take?" Alfred Vanderbilt asked.

"Just a few minutes."

Vanderbilt arched his eyebrow skeptically.

"Fifteen minutes at most," Anderson assured.

When the women returned to their staterooms, they found the cabin stewards closing their portholes. "We don't want to show any lights," the stewards explained. "Just a precaution. I hope you aren't inconvenienced." When the men reached the smoking room, they were greeted by waiters who conveyed the captain's request that they not bring their cigars out on deck at night. "The light, you understand, sir. When it's dark, the light of a cigar can be seen from a considerable distance."

By tea time, the signs of approaching danger had dampened the anticipation of the last night's festivities. Everyone seemed suddenly to remember the German ad that warned against booking passage on an English ship. "The maid left our life jackets on the beds . . . right next to the pillows," a silver-haired woman complained.

"Very uncomfortable, with the portholes locked," a friend in a huge hat agreed.

"Are there submarines out there or not?" a portly gentleman demanded of a wheezing companion. "One minute, they say there is absolutely no danger. The next, they're worried about the light from a damned cigar. Just what in hell is going on?"

"Well, I suppose the German warning couldn't be any plainer," the companion remembered. "It was printed right next to the *Lusitania* sailing notice!"

A delegation from the smoking room demanded an audience with Captain Turner and assembled in the captain's day room, just beneath the bridge. Turner donned his officer's cap for the occasion.

"Of course there's danger," he snapped, interrupting the gentlemen's litany of concerns. "There's always danger when you cross the Atlantic."

"We're referring specifically to submarines," a frock-coated delegate said, gathering nods of approval from the other self-appointed representatives of the passengers.

Turner sighed. "There are no submarines this far out in the Atlantic. And it will be dark when we make our approach to Ireland. Not much chance of a submarine seeing us in the dark."

"What about the morning?" a voice challenged.

"When you wake up in the morning," Turner answered wearily, "there will be a British cruiser and a couple of destroyers standing alongside. I don't think you'll find any submarines hanging around."

"Then there's nothing to worry about?"

"There's always something to worry about. But you're on the safest ship afloat. And you'll soon be in the hands of the Royal Navy. Frankly, gentlemen, I'd be more worried that you might get a bad bottle of claret at dinner."

There was uneasy laughter as the delegates filed out of the day room and headed back to the smoker.

But Turner *was* worried. He had been unable to get a morning fix of his position because of the fog, or to determine his latitude from the noontime elevation of the sun. There were still patches of fog rising from the water all around him, and if he couldn't get the evening stars, then he would be approaching his rendezvous after thirty-six hours of dead reckoning. He could easily be several miles off course, and that could be more than enough to cause him to steam right past the waiting escorts.

Without the escorts, he would have to get a certain fix of his position before moving up the coast, particularly if the fog persisted. So he would have to move in close to land, where his ability to maneuver was restricted. Either that or turn back out to sea, which would mean missing his rendezvous at Coningbeg Light and perhaps even missing the tide over the Liverpool bar.

When he reached the bridge, he sauntered out onto the port wing. Sunlight streamed in columns through the low overcast. Even if he could see the horizon, it didn't look as if he would be able to find the evening stars. Chances were that he wouldn't be able to establish his position until morning. And by then, he would be off the south coast of Ireland where, according to the Admiralty, "submarines were very active." Active, he thought. The military certainly had a nice way with words.

It was mid-afternoon when U-20 broke out of the fog. Schwieger was still running on the surface, making his best speed toward Coningbeg. In fact, he was almost an hour ahead of the schedule he had charted after he had left *Candidate* sinking in his wake. He bent over the voice tube. "Slow to all ahead standard," he called.

"All ahead standard," a metallic voice repeated from the control room below. The furious roar of the diesels seemed to relax, and the wild spray from the bow grew calmer.

Schwieger had heard nothing from Emden. Bauer had promised to confirm his order to attack the large troop transport that everyone understood would be *Lusitania*. He had told his submarine captains that, when the order came, it would include the precise position of the intercept. But, so far, the flotilla commander had said nothing. Schwieger had questioned his radioman. "Anything from the flag? Any traffic addressed to other boats?" He had gone over the radio log, confirming the silence that the radioman reported. He had even ordered the antennas checked to make sure that his equipment was still in working order.

"Maybe while we were down," Haupert had suggested. If Emden had broadcast during the long hours that U-20 had spent lying beneath the surface, they would have missed the message. But if an operational order had been directed to them, they would have acknowledged by simply keying their call letters, a message too brief for the British to home in on. Without the acknowledgment, Bauer would continue to rebroadcast his instructions.

Perhaps the operational message had been sent to one of the other boats. Perhaps *Lusitania* was already under attack, somewhere west of Fastnet. Bauer couldn't hold up the war just because one of his boats failed to respond.

Schwieger couldn't send a message asking for instructions. The U-boats went into radio silence as soon as they entered British coastal waters. All he could do was wait until he was on station, and then send his call sign. That would tell Bauer that he was still alive, in position, and waiting for instructions.

He was weighing his choices when his binoculars found a trace of smoke on the southern horizon. He squinted and made out the outlines of a ship, still too indistinct to determine whether it was a man-of-war or a freighter. But after a few minutes, he was able to determine that it was on a constant bearing and closing the distance. Whatever it was, it was heading for Coningbeg Light, just as he was.

Haupert came to the deck and leaned over the railing beside him, fixing his binoculars on the same target. "Freighter," Haupert decided at exactly the moment when Schwieger could see the cargo hoists forward of the superstructure. "Do we have time for a bit more hunting?"

"Plenty of time," Schwieger said with a smile. He turned to the voice tube. "Come to course one two five," he ordered, calculating the approximate point of intercept.

"Gun crew up?" Haupert asked.

"Not yet," Schwieger said. "This one may have cannons and machine guns, too."

They watched the target as it drew closer, now at a faster rate since Schwieger had ordered the course change. There was no doubt about it. The long superstructure and the after cargo hoist came into view. It wasn't a naval ship.

"Christ," Haupert suddenly whispered. "It's the same ship. It's the one we just sank." He was staring in disbelief through his glasses.

The captain laughed. "You're crazy, Willi. No one will ever see that ship again." He braced his elbows to steady the binoculars. The same bow lines. The same Mediterranean deck. Even the paint scheme seemed identical. "My God, you're right."

"It can't be," Haupert said, still staring at what seemed to be a ghost.

Schwieger called down the voice tube to the control room. "Rolph," he said to the quartermaster. "Break out the shipping manual. See if *Candidate* has a sister ship."

They were now less than three miles apart, the freighter clearly visible because of her height above the water. U-20, her decks nearly awash, was still too small to be spotted. The voice tube whistled. "*Centurion*," the quartermaster called up from below. "Same design, but launched six months later. They both belong to the Harrison line."

Haupert shook his head. "Crazy," he said.

"Same ship," Schwieger thought aloud. "Probably the same armament. Get me a course and speed, Haupert. We're going to take this one from under water."

Haupert plotted a new intercept point based on the five-knot speed that U-20 could make running beneath the surface. "One zero zero," he concluded.

Schwieger nodded and ordered the new course. "Let's take her down," he told his executive officer.

They blew the ballast tanks for just a few seconds, until they could feel the boat begin to settle. Then they dropped down through the hatch, ordered the diesels shut down and the electric motors started, and finally the bowplanes turned to the diving position. Slowly, U-20 cut into the ocean's surface and slid gradually down into the sea.

The torpedomen had already reloaded the spare torpedo into the tube they had used on *Candidate*. Both bow tubes were armed, with one spare still waiting in the overhead rack. Both stern tubes were live. Haupert checked the clock. "Fifteen minutes," he suggested. Schwieger had been running his own mental calculations. Fifteen minutes was just about right. By then, they should have *Centurion* about 2,000 yards off the starboard bow. Plenty of room to calculate a shot into her beam.

The crew was relaxed, joking with one another as they waited for the attack to begin. This was the safest kind of combat that they could ever expect to see. An attack from the hidden safety of the depths, against a target that had no means of counterattack. Most likely, they would hit her with the first shot. They wouldn't surface until she was dead in the water, her crew away in the lifeboats, so that there was no one left aboard to fire back. It should be as easy as target practice. If they missed her, there would certainly be a gloomy moment of disappointment. But disappointment was much easier to take than the return fire they risked whenever they attacked on the surface.

Schwieger grew impatient after just ten minutes. "Let's have a look," he said to Haupert. The executive officer brought the periscope up from its tube, and Schwieger bent down to the lens. At that instant, a stream of water fell down on top of him, soaking through his sweater and shirt.

"Christ," he cursed. He jumped back and looked up at the periscope packing. A steady jet of water was blasting from the packing against the overhead. From there, it was tumbling down on top of him.

"Give me your jacket," he told Haupert, and waited impatiently while his executive fumbled out of his windbreaker. Schwieger threw the jacket over his head like a tent and bent back down to the eyepiece. He tried to ignore the flow that was pounding down on top of him as he carefully lifted the scope into the sunlight.

Centurion was visible immediately, steaming across his bow on a straight, unsuspecting heading. He called out the calculations to Haupert, who repeated them as he cranked the range, speed, and relative heading into the firing calculator. The precise gears within the calculator were driven by U-20's speed and heading. Given the speed and heading of the target ship, they instantly calculated the exact moment at which the torpedo should be fired. "Twenty-three seconds," Haupert reported, as soon as the machine had reached its conclusion.

"Mark," Schwieger ordered.

Haupert hit the firing button. They waited as the calculator's gears spun off the seconds. A red light flashed, announcing the moment of firing. But neither officer needed the light. They heard the blast of air that pushed the torpedo out of the tube, and they felt the bow jerk upward as soon as it was relieved of the weight of the torpedo. Schwieger had already pushed the periscope back down into its tube. He stepped away from it and slipped Haupert's jacket from his head.

"How long?"

"Twenty-eight seconds," the executive officer answered, giving the time it would take the weapon to reach its target if all the inputs had been correct. It didn't really matter whether the lookouts on *Centurion* saw the trace of air bubbles that the torpedo left in its wake. At this close distance, they would hardly have time to throw the rudder over. Before the ship responded, the torpedo would be into their engine room.

They weren't alarmed when the clock ticked past the twenty-eighth second. It would take time for the shock wave from the explosion to reach them. It moved past the thirty-five-second mark, and then they felt the boat shudder. They heard the soft thump, followed immediately by an angry growl. An instant later, a cheer rang out through the pressure hull. Schwieger ordered U-20 to a course parallel to the one that *Centurion* had been steaming. Then he draped Haupert's windbreaker over his head and pointed toward the periscope.

Centurion had been hit directly beneath its funnel, and the heat of the explosion had set fire to the coal dust in its nearly empty bunkers. Dense smoke rolled from the hole in her side, mixing with the white steam that was venting through her stack. She seemed terribly wounded. But the crew, moving about her deck, was making no effort to lower her boats. Instead, the men were forming a bucket brigade, attempting to douse the red flame that was licking at her afterdeck cargo. The ship was still moving forward and, at least for the moment, was riding on an even keel.

"Damn," Schwieger reported to Haupert, who was looking on anxiously. "Direct hit, but she's shrugging it off." He lowered the scope and stepped out from the stream of water that was tumbling from the packing.

"Should we finish her with the deck gun?" Haupert asked.

Schwieger shook his head. "Not while she can still shoot back." He thought for a moment and then decided, "We'll give her a few minutes and see what happens."

They could still hear the ship's propeller throbbing as they continued on a parallel course. The beat of the engine was slower, but steady. She was still making a decent speed, probably a knot or two more than the submarine could make while running submerged. Walter Schwieger tapped his foot impatiently. Then he ordered the periscope up for another look. More water cascaded in on top of him. He looked up at the packing. "We'll sink before she does," he said to Haupert.

Through the scope, he could see that the coal dust fires had burned themselves out. A gray haze surrounded the jagged hole in her side, and dark smoke poured from a small deck fire. But the ship was still riding even in the water, and with enough speed to pull away from U-20. He was now off *Centurion*'s stern quarter, well within the arc that would be covered by a deck gun. If she were carrying the same armament as her sister ship, it would be suicide to come to the surface.

"Left standard rudder," the captain announced, starting the boat into a sweeping turn away from the target. "We'll try another one," he told the executive officer. "This time from the stern tubes." Schwieger could reload the tube he had just fired at *Centurion*, leaving himself with both bow tubes loaded. If he fired again from the bow, he would have only one forward torpedo left, and he wanted both bow tubes armed if he were ordered to go after *Lusitania*. One torpedo into *Lusitania* would be meaningless. His periscope gave ample evidence as to how insignificant a single hit could be. He stopped his turn when he was headed directly away from the wounded freighter. Then he gave Haupert a new set of range, speed, and bearing to feed into the fire control calculator.

He watched the second torpedo through the scope, following the trail of air bubbles as it sped toward the ship. For a moment, he thought he was going to miss. The trail seemed to be drifting toward the stern of the target. But then there was a flash of light a few yards forward of *Centurion*'s propeller wash. The stern seemed to jump out of the water for an instant, then tossed a large, white wave as it dropped back down into the sea. Her speed died immediately, and as she slowed, she began to settle, her bow lifting up out of the water.

Despite the flood splashing down around him, Schwieger kept his face pinned against the periscope. He watched as a lifeboat lowered down the side and saw the men jumping over the railings. The angle of her deck grew more severe as the bow raised and the stern pushed under the surface. Men scampered down the slope of the deck until they reached the rising sea, then simply stepped over the side.

"Take a look," he offered to Haupert, holding out the windbreaker so that his executive could use it as an umbrella. Haupert saw the bow pointing toward the sky while the twitching forms of men fell from the decks. As he watched, an internal explosion shook the hull until the forward cargo mast fractured and collapsed. He was stunned by the image of hellish destruction.

"I'm glad she's not *Lusitania*," he said as he stepped away from the periscope.

Schwieger sent the scope back down into the pressure hull. "Nothing we have could do that to *Lusitania*," he assured his aide.

JENNIFER Beecham fastened the garter clasp to the top of her silk stocking, stood up straight before the mirror, and smoothed the ruffles of her bloomers. She ignored the dressing gown that she had laid out on the bed and walked in her stocking feet into the sitting room, wearing nothing but her corset. The dressing maid was waiting, carefully arranging the white dinner gown that she had just finished touching up with a hot iron.

"A beautiful dress, Miss Beecham," the maid said, trying not to notice Jennifer's immodest attire.

"It's my favorite," Jennifer answered, holding out her arms so that the woman could fit them into the sleeves. "I saved it for the last night."

"Most ladies do," the maid chattered. "Save their best for the last night. I don't know why."

"To leave a memorable impression," Jennifer answered quickly.

"Seems it would be more important to make an impression when you're meeting people, rather than when you're leaving them," the woman answered.

"Oh, no. If you wear your best on the first night, then everyone will be disappointed by the last night." But then she stopped. That wasn't really true. Sometimes the first impression was terribly important. She turned to a mirror as the woman began fastening the score of buttons that ran up the back. The dress flowed with her slim figure, and the color deepened her skin and set off the brilliant dark lights in her hair. "I wish I could wear this when we arrived in Liverpool," she admitted.

"I hardly think so, miss," the maid answered. She had reached the last button, which was well below Jennifer's shoulder blades so that much of her back was daringly exposed. "Not unless . . ." She smiled, and then when Jennifer answered with a smile, she broke out in a giggle. "A man couldn't be held responsible if you looked like this."

"Is it that obvious?" Jennifer asked.

"I think it would be, Miss Beecham."

Jennifer sighed. "But just a plain walking dress?"

"I wouldn't worry a bit," the woman answered. "Not if I looked like you."

Jennifer laughed at the compliment. But the laughter did nothing to calm the fear that was growing inside her. It was evening. And that was the time of day when she began to fear that William had found someone else, and there would be no letter waiting for her.

SCHULL

Day saw the hostility on the housekeeper's face as soon as she opened the door.

"Father Connors?" he asked.

"Father's not home," she answered, almost before he finished saying the priest's name. She started to push the door closed.

"Do you know where he is? It's important."

"He can't be disturbed."

Day held one hand against the door. "He'll want to see me," He insisted. "Where can I find him?"

The small woman hesitated, studying Day's British uniform as she tried to make up her mind. "He's in the garden, reading his prayers." He bolted down the few steps and started around the corner of the building. "He can't be disturbed while he's reading his prayers," the housekeeper screamed after him.

Father Connors was pacing on a stone path in his flowered garden, mouthing the words of the breviary that he held in both hands. He looked up, nodded toward Day, but continued reading until he finished the verse. Then he pulled the red ribbon through the pages and closed the book.

"Good evening, commander."

Day opened the gate. "I'm sorry to interrupt you, Father. You know I wouldn't if it weren't important." The priest settled onto a stone bench, leaving a place for the naval officer to sit beside him. "I need the fleet," Day said as he walked toward the bench. "I need the boats, out on their stations, by dawn tomorrow."

Connors eyes widened. "Tomorrow?" His fingers came up to his lips. "Mother Mary!" He shook his head slowly. "That's a difficult thing you're asking. I suppose, if we had a few days . . ."

"We don't have a few days. There are submarines out there. I was just at the radio station, and we picked up calls from two ships that were sunk in the last five hours. There were two sunk yesterday. And there's a ship coming in tomorrow. A passenger ship. I think it may be in danger."

"Passengers?" The priest was startled. They had never been concerned with passenger ships before.

"I should tell you it's an English vessel."

"That won't make it any easier for the lads to decide."

"Not all the passengers are English, Father. And the babies don't know what country they're from."

Connors nodded. He climbed to his feet and began walking the path. Day fell in next to him.

"Have you spoken with Emmett Hayes?" the priest asked.

"I can't find him. School is closed. I thought you might know where he is."

"No," Connors said. "I haven't seen him either. But it would be good if we could find him. The people respect Emmett."

"They respect you, too, Father. If you could talk to them . . ."

"Oh, I'll talk to them," he agreed. "But you have to understand, commander, that Irishmen aren't always that fond of their priests. We talk about patience. We tell people to bless the crosses they have to carry and to look forward to a world that's to come. Sometimes a man wants to get the damned cross off his back and do something about the world he has now. When that happens, then the priests begin to sound like the traitors."

"But they listened to you before," Day reminded him.

"That they did," Connors agreed. "But I was telling them that it was all right to help themselves to English money. God knows they deserved it, and most of them would be going out to sea anyway. But then their neighbors began washing up on the beach. They saw the danger. And now I'd be telling them that they should risk their lives for the English. That gets pretty close to sounding like treason."

"But if you reminded them that there are women and children on the ship?"

"Ah, yes. Women and children." He nodded his sympathy. But then he stopped pacing and turned to face the British naval officer squarely. "Shiela tells me that she once took you to visit the children's cemetery. She said it brought tears to your eyes. There are children's graves all over this country, William. But we can't cry over them. There are just too many."

Day's shoulders sagged. He understood the priest's meaning.

"You're a fine man, Commander Day. I remember your words at the funeral. 'The best of us try to stop the slaughter.' That's what you're doing now, and that's why I'll try to help you."

Day nodded in appreciation. "What do you think my chances are?" he asked.

Connors put his arm around the younger man's shoulders. "I'll do what I can. I'll get word out to you at the radio station."

It was growing dark when Day left the garden and ran back to his car. He started the noisy engine, turned on the arc lamps, and headed back toward the Mizen Head road. As he passed the path to Shiela's cottage, he was surprised to see a dull lamp glowing in the window. He braked, backed up to the path entrance, and turned through the gate. Shiela was startled when he opened the front door. She stood as still as a statue in the middle of her parlor, unable even to mouth a greeting.

"I thought you were still at the station," Day said.

"I got a ride from the postman," Shiela answered, as if that explained what she was doing at home.

He looked into the bedroom. Her carpet suitcase was open on the bed with two stacks of her clothes resting beside it. Shiela followed his eyes, then looked back at him. "I'm leaving," she said, confessing what she knew he understood.

Day looked bewildered. He knew that no orders had come in for her. "You can't," he said. "Not yet."

She broke from his gaze and rushed into the bedroom, where she began pushing the clothes into the suitcase.

"You can't," he repeated, following her as far as the doorway.

"I have to." She didn't look up from her work. "I can't stay here any longer."

"Why? Another few days. A week or so. Your orders will come through."

"I don't have another few days," Shiela answered.

He watched her for a moment as she tried to close the suitcase over the thick stack of clothes. Then he bolted into the room and pulled her hands away from the valise.

"What are you talking about? Why don't you have another few days? What's wrong?"

She tore away from his grasp and backed away from him into a shadowy corner. "Leave me alone," she shouted. She kept retreating until she was pressed into the corner. Then her hands came up to her face, and the fight drained out of her body. She slid down the wall until she was sitting with her knees drawn up in front of her. From the darkness, Day heard her gasping sobs.

"Shiela, tell me! What's happened? Let me help you." He dropped down in front of her, reached out, and tried to lift her face from her knees. She shook her head and slapped his hands away.

"Leave me alone," she begged breathlessly. "Just let me go. Please."

Day stood slowly. He backed away as far as the bed, never taking his eyes off the raglike figure hunched in the corner of the room. "Is it me?" he asked carefully. "Did I do this?"

Through the wracking sobs, she said, "It's you. It's them." Her face lifted slowly, and Day could see her eyes glistening in the dim lamplight. "It's me. I did it to myself."

He watched as Shiela struggled to her feet. She stayed back in the shadows, leaning against the wall. "Please let me help you," Day whispered.

"You can't help me," she answered, but she was speaking more to herself than to him.

"Why?"

"Because I'm a lie," her voice came back. He could hardly hear her when she said, "I'm Grace's spy."

For a second, he didn't understand. Then, in the next instant, it was all perfectly clear. Every word he had spoken to her, every thought he had shared in the night, had all been heard in a German officers' mess. She had used him. His need for her had made it easy.

His eyes fired and his fists clenched. He took one murderous step toward her. But then he stopped. Shiela was standing helplessly, not even bothering to raise her hands to defend herself. It was as if she were already dead with shame, and nothing he could do could hurt her any more. His rage subsided as quickly as it had flashed. Shiela, Day saw, was one of the victims. He was the traitor. He was the one who had doomed the ships and delivered innocent men to the slaughter. He backed away and sank slowly to the edge of the bed, his eyes falling away from her. "Everything?" he asked. "Did you tell them everything?"

"Oh, God, no!" Shiela rushed to him, dropping on her knees so that she could see his face. "Not what you said to me. Not what I knew you were thinking. Just the radio messages. I couldn't have told them anything about you. I love you," she said. "That's why I can't let you help me."

"And I . . ." he started.

She pressed a finger to his lips. "Don't. You've never lied to me. Don't lie now. You love her, and you always will. It would be worse if I believed you loved me."

He reached up and took her hand. "I won't leave you like this. We'll go to them together. To Queenstown. We'll make them understand."

Day stood up suddenly, thinking he had found the answer. "You'll be all right. You're going to them with the truth. It's not as if they had to catch you."

"It's not the English I'm running from," Shiela said. "It's the Irish. They want something from me, and I'm not giving it to them. They'll find out. They may know already. They'll be coming for me."

"Who?" he demanded.

She spun away from him, shaking her head. "I've betrayed enough people already. Don't ask me who. Just help me get away."

"Get away to where?"

She screamed. "I don't know to where. I just can't let them find me. You don't know what they do to their traitors."

Day turned away in confusion and paced back out into the parlor. "What is it that they want?" he asked her.

"*Lusitania*," Shiela told him.

Instantly he remembered the message. The coordinates that gave away *Lusitania*'s position mile by mile along the coast. He had handed the information to Shiela.

"But I didn't give it to them," she continued. "I couldn't. They'll find out, and then they'll come looking for me."

"Who?"

She studied him for an instant, then turned away, back to the unfinished packing on her bed. He rushed into the bedroom, his anger flashing. "Who are they? You've got to tell me. There are thousands of innocent people on that ship."

She turned at him in her own anger. "They're safe. I didn't give them up. That's why I have to get out of here. The Germans will know about the message. They'll demand a translation. And then my people will know I've lied to them."

Day tried to think, but it was all happening too fast. The Germans wanted *Lusitania*. The Fenians were supposed to get them the information they needed. Shiela had withheld it. But that wouldn't stop the Germans. They had other sources of information. The ship was in mortal danger. *Lusitania* had to be warned.

"You've got to come with me," he decided. "We have to get this to Peter Grace. He's with Naval Intelligence. He'll be able to help."

"Peter Grace knows," Shiela said. "He knows about all of us. He's been watching me. Watching the others."

"He doesn't know. Not everything," Day told her.

"He does," she fired back. "It was Peter Grace who killed James Corcoran. And Corcoran was one of us."

Day was stunned. "He can't know," he insisted. "He was the one who told me to send the message. He knew I would give it to you. If he knew about you—"

His words stopped. The station was compromised. Peter Grace knew it, and, if Shiela was right, he knew that Shiela was the agent. Yet he had given her the information that would sink *Lusitania*. Which meant . . .

"They want her sunk," he whispered.

She looked at him and read the horror in his eyes. "The English?"

"The English want the Germans to sink *Lusitania*," he told himself. "Oh, sweet Jesus. It's the Americans they want killed."

"What are you saying?" Shiela asked, trying to break through his deadening shock.

He focused on her. "They're using you to talk to the Germans. You and your poor patriots. You're all being used."

He grabbed her arm and pulled her into the parlor, where he pushed her down into the sofa. Then he leaned over her, his face nearly touching hers. "You've got to tell me everything. Everything you know. Who gets your messages? And how do they get to Germany?"

Shiela tried to look away, but Day's huge hand locked onto her face and held it toward him. "Dammit, listen to me. When the Germans sink *Lusitania*, they sink themselves. And your Irish friends go down with them. You're not protecting them. You're destroying them. You're not a traitor. You've been used. Not just you. All of us. We've been used to set up a shipload of Americans. We have to stop it."

Now the shock was in Shiela's eyes. She understood. He released his hold from her cheeks.

"Who talks with the Germans?"

"Emmett Hayes," Shiela said.

"Come on," he ordered, already dragging her toward the door.

"They'll kill you," she warned him.

"If they don't, then Peter Grace will. But they're not going to kill the people on *Lusitania*. We're not going to let that happen."

She pulled free from his grasp, but ran with him toward the car.

THE IRISH COAST

U-20 RAN slowly, cruising in a five-mile square box, hiding under the cover of darkness. Schwieger had moved twenty miles south of the lightship, far off the shipping lanes that converged at the entrance of Saint George's Channel. Without doubt, potential targets were slipping by to the north. But he had more pressing matters to deal with.

The periscope had to be repacked. In the few times he had used it for his attack on *Centurion*, nearly a hundred gallons of water had poured into the boat. It had spilled over the lip of the hatch in the conning tower and down into the control room. Haupert had shut the hatch, but that made communications with the men below difficult. If he was going to stalk *Lusitania*, he might well need to use the scope over and over again. And he would need to have an instant response to each of his commands.

His engineers had fashioned a new gasket from the rubber pads that had supported his spare torpedoes. To install it, they had had to remove the top of the periscope housing on the top of the conning tower, and then mount a jack that could force the packing into position. That meant he had to stay on the surface for two, perhaps three hours. He didn't want any ships stumbling on him while his men were working and he was unable to dive.

And then there was the radio. To mount the jack, the men would have to disconnect the boat's low-frequency antenna. He would be without communications until the repair was completed. Schwieger had sent his call letters the minute he was on station. Seconds later, the call letters had been returned, acknowledging that Emden knew where he was. But there had been no follow-up message. No order to strike at the large troop carrier, and no vector to lead him into her path. He had waited as long as he could before starting the repair. But the work had to be finished before daylight, even if it meant that he couldn't receive the most important message that Captain Bauer had ever sent him.

"They'll keep resending," Haupert encouraged him when he finally gave the order to disconnect the antenna. It was true. Emden wouldn't consider the message delivered until they received on acknowledgment. But Schwieger could envision the confusion at flotilla headquarters. When U-20 didn't respond, they would figure that the boat had been forced to submerge. Perhaps it was lying helplessly at the bottom while British destroyers circled overhead. Or, worse, perhaps it had been sunk. At some point, Bauer would have to discount U-20 as part of his trap. He would begin flashing orders to the other boats, repositioning them as best he could. By the time the antenna was reconnected and Schwieger could announce his presence, the entire attack could have taken another turn.

"Let's get moving," he snapped impatiently at the engineers who had brought their heavy tools to the top of the tower. "I want this finished in one hour."

Their glances told him he was demanding the impossible. But the men set to work, locking a huge wrench on the first of the bolts that circled the periscope housing, cracking it free.

BOWLER BILL Turner stood at the window of the wheelhouse, in one hand a cheese sandwich that oozed mustard onto his shirt cuff, in the other a mug of tea. Four decks below, in the two-tiered first-class dining room, the menu included Peking duck and Dover sole, with a choice of 200 wines to wash either down. But Turner rarely visited the dining room, and he had never tasted the duck. To his mind, meals were an inconvenience that should be dealt with as quickly as possible. A captain shouldn't be looking down at a menu. He should be looking out at the sea.

They hadn't been able to get an evening fix. Even with the fog lifted, the horizon had remained an indistinct blur, and the haze overhead had obscured the first stars. Now he was in the clear, with a hundred stars overhead to choose from. But without a horizon they were useless, except for the pale glow they threw across the wave tops that made him a more visible target for submarines.

He walked to his speed indicator. Twenty-one knots. The best speed he could make with the number four boiler room shut down to save coal. If he had his way, he would be firing the cold boilers right now, giving him an extra six knots of speed in reserve. Twenty-one knots was fast enough to pull away from any submarine the Germans could build. But if a U-boat were in the right position, with a decent angle on his bow, the twenty-one knots were only marginal. They certainly weren't enough to outrun a torpedo. "Fastest ship afloat," the passengers told one another whenever the subject of the German warning was raised. And neither

Captain Anderson nor any of the officers who mingled with the passengers would say anything to change their minds. But they all knew, as did Bill Turner, that with one boiler room shut down, *Lusitania* was just another passenger ship. The accountants at Cunard had taken away her best weapon.

Turner ran the possible arrival plans through his mind. If he made his rendezvous with Squadron E, then things would be relatively simple. The cruiser would take position dead ahead, and one destroyer would cover each beam. He would slow to about seventeen knots, the best speed the cruiser could maintain, and then move up the coast under their protection, holding a distance of about twenty miles from the shore. They would deliver him to Squadron A at Coningbeg Light, which would put two destroyers off the port and starboard bows, and two more on his quarters. They would ease back up to about twenty knots and then charge up Saint George's Channel.

But he had doubts about the rendezvous. Without a good fix, an open-sea rendezvous was chancy. Worse, the weather conditions promised more fog in the morning, as soon as the sun began to heat the air. In fog, a rendezvous was nearly impossible.

If he couldn't find Squadron A, then he would have to turn north in hope of sighting land. He could get a certain fix from any of the prominent bluffs that dotted the south Irish coast and then head toward Coningbeg on his own. He felt safer with escorts. But without them, he could at least run at his best speed, which gave him an added measure of safety. Though not the full measure that *Lusitania's* designers had intended.

"Home tomorrow," the first mate said as he stepped up beside the captain.

Turner grunted. "I certainly hope so."

SCHULL

DAY PARKED the car at the edge of town, and then he and Shiela turned off the main street, toward Emmett Hayes's house. They walked around the pools of light from the flickering lamps in the houses and found a darkened corner diagonally across from Hayes's front door. Then they waited.

During the short drive into Schull, Shiela had spilled out her involvement with the Fenians. In the first days of the war, the Irish patriots had gone over to the Germans, hoping that the defeat of England would bring freedom to their country. German submarines had smuggled them guns, and German officers had promised a strike from the sea to aid their Irish rebellion. But the most important weapon they had been given was a radio. With the radio, the Irish could organize coastwatchers, keeping track of the English ships that patrolled the Atlantic approaches and delivering this information instantly to the Germans. And with the information, the U-boats could operate safely off the coast of Ireland.

Shiela's arrival had been a godsend. An Irish woman working inside the English radio station! Now they could know the movements of the ships days in advance. Instead of just safety, they could give their German liberators targets. All they had to do was get the woman working for the movement. And that wasn't very difficult at all. She had relatives in the coastal villages with memories of fathers and uncles who had died fighting the English. They could be used to encourage her participation and to serve as hostages to her loyalty. She had parents who had been uprooted from their home by English landlords and forced into exile on the docks of Liverpool just to feed their family.

Shiela had resisted Emmett Hayes's first overtures. The Germans, she had told him, weren't liberators, and she had suggested he read the reports of their liberation in Belgium. She had even threatened to expose him to her British superiors if he ever approached her again. She was sympathetic to the centuries of Irish poverty and slavery and wished the Irish patriots well. But she was English now, and treason was a worse fate than slavery.

But then Emmett had made it impossible for her to be English. He had taken her to the children's cemetery and led her through the crumbling tombstones. He had described the little girls who had died lying on the ground with their mouths full of grass and the boys who had collapsed gnawing at the moss on the side of a rock. She had looked about sadly, but then the sadness was pushed aside by screaming rage. She had never hated anything as much as she hated the people who could do such a thing to children. And right there, standing on top of the babies' bodies, she had joined the movement.

Then fresh bodies had floated ashore. At first the bodies of English sailors, burned and bloated by horrors worse than hunger. Then Irish bodies. Those of her townsmen who were trying to protect the ships. She understood very clearly that past murders couldn't be undone by new murders, and she had decided to break away.

As he listened, Day had understood. He knew why Shiela had warned him that Ireland would destroy him. It was destroying her. And he knew why she could say she loved him and yet insist that they had to part. How could she love a man and still betray him? He knew why she had taken him to the children's cemetery. Once he saw it, he would be able to understand the crimes that she knew she would someday have to confess.

But there was still time. If she could help save *Lusitania*, she could undo the treachery in her past. A life saved was the only payment for a life wasted. It was Shiela who was at risk. She was as much in jeopardy as any of the passengers who were steaming toward the killing grounds off the coast of her murderous country.

They save Hayes as he passed under the light of a window. They waited as he vanished in the darkness, only to reappear on his front steps. Day bolted immediately, darting across the street to reach Emmett just as he turned the lock in his door. He grabbed the schoolteacher by his coat collar and threw him into his own parlor. Shiela followed him and closed the door behind them.

"Stay down," Day ordered. He pulled the shades in the window, then touched a match to the wick of the lamp. As the light spread, it found Hayes sitting on the carpet, with Shiela and Day standing above him.

Hayes's shock gave way to indignation. He looked from face to face as he scampered to his feet. "What in hell do you think you're doing?" he demanded of the naval officer. And then to Shiela, "Have you lost your senses?"

Day took him by the shoulders and placed him firmly in a soft chair. Then he set a straightback chair directly in front of the teacher and sat down. Shiela remained standing near the window.

"I know who you are and what you've been doing," Day said calmly. Emmett's eyes widened. He shifted his focus over Day's shoulder and looked at Shiela. She responded with a small nod that said, Yes, he knows; I told him.

He looked back at Day. "I don't know what you're talking about. What have I been doing?"

"Sending shipping information to Germany. You're a German agent."

Hayes started to get up. "That's ridiculous—"

Day reached out and, with the flat of his hand, sent him flying back into the chair. "There isn't time to argue. Right now I don't give a damn what you've been doing. I need your help."

Hayes's expression narrowed. "What help?"

"I need to talk to the Germans. Whoever your contact is, I need to get him on your radio. Right now."

Emmett blinked in bewilderment. He studied Day's face and realized that the man was serious. Then he turned to Shiela. "For the love of God, what's he talking about?"

"We've been used, Emmett," she answered. "The English have made fools of us."

"How do we raise Germany?" Day asked.

It's a trick, Hayes thought. He can't prove anything. He's trying to get me to give myself away. "Commander, I don't know what she's been telling you. But it's crazy. I teach school. What in the name of Christ would I know about raising Germany?"

"Listen carefully, Emmett," Day began, "because we don't have time to discuss this. Right now, there's a flotilla of submarines waiting for *Lusitania*. And she's steaming right into their trap. The Germans asked you for information about *Lusitania* because they know she's carrying a valuable cargo. And the English provided the information because they want to help the Germans sink that cargo."

Hayes threw his hands into the air. "This is a fairy story." Once again he started out of the chair. But he froze as William Day's jaw tightened in anger.

Day waited until he settled back and then continued with his explanation. "The reason the English want the Germans to attack *Lusitania* is that she's carrying nearly a thousand American passengers. The English want the Germans to attack the Americans. Can you understand that?"

Hayes's pretended confusion disappeared as the pieces began coming together in his mind.

"England wants America to join the war," Day went on. "And America won't have much of a choice once a U-boat torpedoes a shipload of Americans. Don't you see? The English know all about your little nest of spies. They're using it to bring America into the war."

He turned to Shiela for confirmation. She answered his expression. "They gave us some genuine targets, Emmett, just to string us along. *Lusitania* is the target they've been waiting to give us."

Then he snapped back to Day. "How do you know? How do you know it's a setup?"

"Because there's an English intelligence officer at Crookhaven. He knows that Miss McDevitt has been giving you messages. Yet he gave her this message to code, knowing that she would bring it straight to you and that you would send it to Germany." He lifted a copy of the *Lusitania* rendezvous message from his pocket and handed it to Hayes. Hayes took the message, his eyes remaining locked on Day. Then he fumbled for his glasses and started to read.

"Do you know anything about points on a chart?" Day asked him.

Hayes shook his head, indicating that he didn't, as he studied the text.

"Each of those numbers is a range and bearing from a point on the chart. If I know the exact time that a ship is to be at one point, and then the exact time it is to be at another point—"

"Then you know exactly where it will be at any given time," Hayes said, completing the thought. He looked up at Day and saw the naval officer nod. His hand, holding the message, dropped despairingly over the side of the chair. "Sweet Mother Mary," he whispered.

"That's why we have to raise Germany," Day concluded. "We have to convince them that they're the ones walking into a trap. We don't have much time." He pointed to the message. "If you believe that, *Lusitania* arrives off Fastnet in about five hours."

Emmett lifted the message and read it again. He handed it back to Day as he took off his glasses. "There's just one thing wrong with all this, commander. You're English. If this is a trap for the Germans, then it's your trap. Unless that's a German uniform you're wearing."

"It's English," Day said. "But we all have to draw the line somewhere, Emmett. I draw it short of women and children."

"It's your countrymen who are setting them up," Hayes said.

"It's your liberators who are going to fire the torpedo," Day answered.

Emmett Hayes smiled. "God should have stopped on the fifth day," he said. "The sixth day's work has never measured up to his expectations." He turned to Shiela. "There's paper and pencils on the kitchen table. Write down what you want to send to the Germans."

They huddled together in the kitchen as Day wrote.

Cargo not repeat not aboard Lusitania. England wants Germany to kill American passengers. High-placed Americans ready to declare war. Sources are within Royal Navy. Most reliable.

Hayes looked up at William Day. "A bit melodramatic, I'd say—'High-placed Americans ready to declare war.'"

"I had dinner with one of them," Day answered. "He's been ready for a long time."

They rushed upstairs, and Day watched as Emmett pulled his code books out of the shirt cardboard. He looked over the schoolteacher's shoulder as Emmett began translating the message.

Hayes covered the code book with his hand. "Commander, I'm helping you save *Lusitania*. I have no intention of helping you defeat Germany."

"Fair enough," Day smiled. He turned his back and walked across the room.

Hayes worked for nearly half an hour, retranslating each coded phrase back into plain text to make sure of its accuracy. Then he insisted on locking the code books back in the armoire before starting down to his radio. They rushed down the stairs and were halfway across the parlor when they stopped short.

Peter Grace was lounging casually in the kitchen doorway. A large-caliber revolver was dangling from his fingers.

"Well, now, this is a surprise," Grace said. "You two, I expected." He gestured with the barrel of the gun toward Shiela and Emmett. "But you, commander? I had no idea you'd gone over to the Irish." He nodded toward Shiela. "Although I suppose I understand why."

"Peter, we're setting up *Lusitania* for sinking," Day tried.

Grace shook his head. "That's not our affair, commander. Higher-ups, you know." He reached out for the papers that Emmett Hayes was holding. "May I?" Reluctantly, Hayes handed him the message. Grace let the page of code drop to the floor and read the plain language version.

"Talking directly to the enemy? That's not very bright, Commander Day. You should have taken my advice. You could have had your own ship." He stuffed the message into his pocket. "No, this one will never do. I think we should send the original version. You have a copy, don't you, commander?"

"No," William Day lied.

Grace raised the revolver and pointed the muzzle into Shiela's face. "You have a copy, don't you, commander," he repeated. Day remembered James Corcoran's broken body. He had no doubt that Grace could pull the trigger without a second's thought. He reached into his pocket and held out the message.

"Give it to our unassuming German agent," Grace said, holding the pistol at Shiela's eyes with a steady hand.

Emmett took the message.

"Good," Grace smiled. "I think we'll send that one instead. Now, Emmett, why don't you run back upstairs and put that one into code. I'll give you exactly twenty minutes. You'll know when your time is up because you'll hear a bullet going through Miss McDevitt's head. So try not to dally."

Hayes looked at Day, who nodded. He started for the stairs.

"And, Emmett," Peter Grace called after him, "bring the code books back down with you. I'll want to check a word or two just to be sure you haven't made any mistakes."

Hayes disappeared at the top of the stairs.

"We're going to be waiting for a while," Grace said to Shiela and Day. "Why don't you two sit right over there. With your hands in your laps. And try not to move too suddenly. We wouldn't want poor Mr. Hayes to think that his time was up."

Hayes unlocked the armoire and carried the code books to his desk. But before he began working, he lifted the lamp from his desk and placed it carefully in his window, making sure that it was far to the left. Then he raised the shade.

EMDEN

Captain Bauer was up from the dayroom bed at flotilla headquarters the instant he heard the light tapping at his door. He brushed his hair down with the palm of his hand as he reached for the uniform jacket he had left draped over the back of his chair. He stepped into his shoes and walked out into the operations center.

"Message from Leprechaun," his communications officer told him. Bauer snatched the paper from the clipboard and rushed to a light.

It was the information he had been waiting for, the coordinates of *Lusitania*'s two rendezvous with her escorts, one off Fastnet, the other near Coningbeg Light. He took the message to his plotting table and tossed it to the night operations officer. "Plot these, Klaus," he ordered.

The officer leaned over the table and marked small circles at each of the coordinates. Then he took a cloth tape measure, stretched it between the two circles, and laid out *Lusitania*'s course into Liverpool. He stepped back from the table when he had finished.

Bauer looked down at the Irish coast. He moved the models of the Squadron E ships out of Queenstown and aimed them toward the Fastnet rendezvous. He twisted the model of *Lusitania* until it was headed for the same point. Then he took the U-30 marker and moved it from Land's End toward Fastnet, duplicating the course that the boat's commander, Lieutenant Rosenberg, would take as he headed for home from the Scilly Islands.

"How long will it take Rosenberg to reach here?" He touched the table at a point to the west of the Fastnet rendezvous, where *Lusitania* would still be traveling without her escorts.

The operations officer did a quick calculation, then shook his head. "Too long," he answered. He measured the course lines of U-30 and *Lusitania* and ran another calculation. Then he drew another circle, this one on *Lusitania*'s course line, but due south of Cape Clear. "This is the best intercept that U-30 can make. Half an hour after *Lusitania* meets her escorts."

"Just so!" Bauer said, satisfied that he knew the situation at the western end of his table. Then he stepped toward Coningbeg. The small U-20 marker was alone, surrounded by open water. The replicas of the Squadron A destroyers were far to the south, where they had gone to chase after Rosenberg. "Then this is where we will have to attack."

He turned to his communications officer and began dictating messages. One was for Lieutenant Rosenberg on U-30. It gave him the intercept point that the operations officer had plotted and authorized the attack. But it cautioned that *Lusitania* could be heavily escorted. He was not to risk his boat if enemy warships were close at hand. The other went to Lieutenant Schwieger on U-20, giving him an intercept point southeast of Coningbeg Light. It advised that when *Lusitania* reached that point, she should be steaming unescorted.

Bauer reread the messages. He looked up at Klaus Schopfner and the other staff officers who surrounded the table. "Anything else?" he asked. There were no comments. Each of the boats had been given the best opportunity for attack that was available.

"Send them," he told the communications officer.

SCHULL

PETER GRACE smiled. "Nicely done, Emmett. You should have taken a position with naval communications. At least you would have been on the right side."

They were in the cellar, Hayes seated at the sewing machine, where he had just received the acknowledgment of the message he had sent to Germany. Day and Shiela were standing against the back wall. Grace had checked the coded message that Hayes had brought down from the bedroom, assuring that random words matched the code tables. Then he had marched the three down the stairs to the basement, positioned Day and Shiela at a safe distance, and watched Hayes as he set up the radio and brought it up to power. He had bent over Emmett, watching each letter and listening to be certain that it was keyed accurately. Then he had waited until the German operator's call letters sounded from the speaker.

"We won't be needing the radio any longer," Grace told Hayes. "Just pull it free and set it down on the floor."

Hayes did as he was told, pulling the antenna wire and the power cord from the sheet-metal box and placing it carefully on the hard dirt floor.

"Now smash it," Grace ordered.

Hayes looked horrified at the suggestion.

"Smash it!"

Emmett kicked at the instrument. At first it withstood the force of his shoe, but as he continued kicking, the hollow back panel collapsed, and the glass vacuum tubes burst. He stood panting over the bent metal and glass shards.

"Come to think of it, we won't be needing you any longer, either, Emmett," Grace said.

Hayes had barely understood the meaning of the words when he felt a hot flash burn into the center of his back. He tried to scream, but there was no air in his chest. As he fell forward, over the ruins of his radio, Day and Shiela saw the handle of a knife sticking out of his coat. Blood was already bubbling up around it.

Shiela screamed, but her voice cracked before any sound could escape. Day started forward toward the dying man but stopped as Grace cocked the hammer of his pistol. He looked from Hayes to the young lieutenant and saw the satisfaction in his face. Another assignment completed with the usual efficiency. Peter Grace wouldn't think twice about firing. He backed up to the wall next to Shiela.

"We'll be leaving together," Grace announced. "I'm going to back up the stairs, and you two are going to follow me."

Day stepped carefully toward him.

"Miss McDevitt first, if you don't mind," Grace said. "I'd like to keep her between us, commander." He backed toward the stairs, and then onto the first step. Shiela fell into line in front of him, and Day followed behind Shiela. "When we get to the parlor, you two will go ahead of me. We're going to walk to your car, and then we'll drive back to the radio station. The code room should hold you nicely until the military police come for you."

He was halfway up the stairs, with Shiela and Day following on the lower steps.

"Not much I'll be able to do for you," he said to Shiela. "Fenian. German agent. I think your goose is cooked." He backed up another few steps. "But in your case, commander, I think we may be able to buy a bit of leniency. Taken in by all this Irish nonsense. The wiles of a seductive woman. Not really a traitor. Of course, I wouldn't count on getting your own ship . . ."

He was still taunting when a massive fist fired across the doorway. Grace's head flew sideways, and then his body followed as he staggered and then fell across the parlor floor. Tom Duffy's giant form moved in front of Shiela, across the doorway, in pursuit.

Grace skidded on his back, the carpet crumpling up under him. He raised his head, and his clouded vision caught the enormous shape lumbering across the room toward him. He lifted the gun, levering it from his elbow, which was pinned to the floor, and fired wildly. He got off three shots before Duffy's hands reached down and closed around his neck. Then he felt himself being lifted into the air.

He pressed the muzzle of the pistol into Duffy's massive gut and tried to pull the trigger. But suddenly his arm was wrenched away. Day had lunged and grabbed his hand, twisting it around behind him. Grace's shoulder tore out of its socket. The revolver dropped to the crumpled carpet.

Day dove for it and caught the gun in both hands. In the same motion, he rolled onto his back, aiming the muzzle up toward Peter Grace. He was about to fire when he saw that Grace's toes were already a foot off the floor and rising higher into the air. Duffy held him by the neck and was hanging him in the noose of his fingers.

"Let him down," Day screamed. But Tom Duffy wasn't taking any orders. He had come in response to Emmett Hayes's signal, only to find his leader murdered. Now the murderer had to be executed.

He held Peter Grace's quivering body high above his head, watching his eyes bulge and his face contort. Then, with a quick shake of his arms, he snapped the head like a whip. The sound of the English officer's neck breaking was almost as loud as a pistol shot. Duffy turned and walked to the top of the cellar stairs, carrying the limp, swinging body by its shattered neck. He tossed it through the doorway and watched it bounce down the steps. He took a deep, discouraged breath. Then he started down the stairs to retrieve his fallen field commander. The cellar was good enough for the English bastard. But it was no fit place for Emmett Hayes.

Day sat up and saw Shiela. She was on her knees, bending over the discarded warning message that Hayes had been going to send to Germany.

"Are you all right?" Day asked as he scampered toward her.

"I can send this from the radio station," Shiela answered. "The call letters are here. And Emmett's identification letters. We can still warn them."

"Can you drive my car?" He reached down and helped her to her feet.

"I think so," Shiela said. Then she added, "Mr. Duffy can drive me."

"Then go!" Day said. "Tell Chief Gore I'll have him shot if he doesn't get that message out. I'll get down to the dock. Father Connors is trying to get the fleet together." He saw that Shiela was not yet steady on her feet. "Are you all right?"

She nodded at him. "I'll be fine. Get to the dock. I'll take care of the message."

Day rushed out through the front door. When he was gone, Shiela reached around to her back and touched the point of pain that had nearly made her faint. When she brought her hand back, it was stained with blood.

THE IRISH COAST

Schwieger looked at the message that the radioman had brought to the top of the conning tower. He smiled and passed the clipboard to Haupert. "She's ours," he said.

Haupert read the orders from Captain Bauer. "Unless Rosenberg gets to her first."

"Not likely," Schwieger told his executive. "With the escorts, he'll never get close enough. And what could he have left? One torpedo? It would be too risky. Rosenberg has courage. But he's no fool."

"He's been ordered to an intercept point," Haupert reminded his superior.

"In case *Lusitania* has no escort. On the chance that she steams right under his nose. Believe me, Willi. We're the ones who are going to get her . . . if this damned periscope is working."

He glanced to the east, where the morning horizon was brightening. "Let's take it down and try her out!"

His engineers had finished their work less than an hour earlier. The fabricated gasket had been packed into the housing and sealed against the periscope casing. The deck plate had been refitted while the jack was being disassembled and the low-frequency antenna restrung. Moments later, Haupert had come to the bridge to announce that a long coded message was coming in. And now they had the message. Everything was falling into place. Haupert closed the hatch over their heads, and Schwieger shouted the order to dive. U-20 switched to its electric motors and slipped slowly under the surface.

Schwieger stood inside the tower and listened to the sea close over his head. He looked up at the packing. It stayed dry. He glanced at the depth gauge and followed the boat's gradual descent, letting the pressure build on the new gasket. At forty feet he ordered the bowplanes turned up and then brought U-20 to an even keel. Even at this depth, as far down as he would probably have to go, no water was leaking into the boat. So far, so good. The real test would come when he tried to raise the periscope.

"Up to fifteen feet," he called down into the control room. Again, he watched the depth gauge and brought the boat to level when it was at periscope depth. "Let's try it," he told Haupert, and the executive officer reached for the counterweight cable. Nothing happened.

"It's jammed," Haupert said in horror.

"It was working," Schwieger answered in disbelief. They had run the periscope up and down right after the engineers had forced the new packing into position. He tugged on the counterweight cable himself. The periscope didn't budge in its housing.

"The deck plate must have squeezed it too tight," Haupert guessed.

"Shit! Of all the damn luck!" Schwieger ripped off his cap and fired it at the deck. But in an instant, he was back in control of himself. The first thing he had to do was get back to the surface. The sun was rising, and once he was in daylight it was a gamble to come up without checking with the periscope. He might come up under the guns of a cruiser.

"Surface," he screamed into the control room. Then he scampered up the ladder, ready to turn the hatch as soon as he heard the tower break the surface.

There was light in the sky. He spun quickly, checking the sea around him, and found that he was still alone. "Repair crew topside," he shouted down to Haupert. Then he began to calculate.

How long would it take? They had to open the deck plate, cut away some of the packing, and then replace the plate. An hour, at most. And then he would test the scope with the deck plate in place, this time while they were still on the surface. So he would be up for how long? Not much more than an hour. The problem was that the sun was rising. In a few minutes, he would be in open daylight and, while the repair was in progress, unable to dive. He had to move farther away from the shipping lanes so that he wouldn't be sighted. The last thing he needed now was to have an English destroyer looking for him.

"All ahead standard," he called into the voice tube. he listened as his order was repeated from below. "Come to course two zero zero."

"Two zero zero, aye!"

He would run to the southwest, into the space between the coastal shipping lanes and the southern lanes coming up from Land's End. Then, with everything in order, he would turn around and head back toward Coningbeg Light. He had plenty of time to get back on station. And his batteries would be fully charged when he got there.

Two machinists squeezed through the hatch and dragged their tools up behind them. Schwieger stepped to the edge of the deck to give them room and reached out for the radio mast to steady himself. He nearly toppled over the edge. The radio mast was gone.

He wheeled around and looked toward the stern. The stub of the low-frequency antenna was flapping from the insulator near the end of the deck. "Christ!" he cursed. The mast had obviously not been fully secured. It had torn away in the dive and trailed the antenna out behind the boat. When the antenna reached its full length, it had snapped like a piece of bakery string.

U-20 had no communications with Germany.

*   *   *

CAPTAIN Turner paced out onto the starboard wing. There was light in the eastern sky, but he knew that he wouldn't see the sun breaking the horizon. He could smell the fog in the air. It was beginning to build even before the early heat of day.

"You won't be able to see your own nose," he told the watch officer when he returned to the wheelhouse. He walked past the helm and leaned over the chart table.

By dead reckoning, he was only half an hour from his rendezvous. But he had little faith in his course line. The warships could be fifteen miles to the north, or just as easily fifteen miles to the south. There was no way to be certain.

Maybe he'd get lucky. Maybe the fog would hold off just long enough for him to see the horizon while the morning stars were still visible overhead. Then he'd get his fix and head straight for the rendezvous. But Turner had spent more than thirty years on the Atlantic. When you could smell fog this early in the morning, there wasn't much point in taking the sextant out of its case. Most likely, he would be in thick soup until early afternoon.

He wouldn't waste a lot of time looking for the warships. They'd be just as blind as he. They could steam within a mile of one another without ever making contact. Oh, he'd sound *Lusitania*'s deafening horn as he got nearer to where he thought Squadron E might be waiting. And he'd listen for a return signal. But more than likely, there would be none. Then he would continue eastward, on his own, keeping well clear of land. And around noon, when the fog would lift, he'd duck in toward the beach to fix his position.

"Should we begin sounding the foghorn?" the watch officer asked over his shoulder.

"Why not?" Bowler Bill answered. "It's time the passengers were getting up, anyway."

CROOKHAVEN

THE GUARD at the radio station gate waved into the headlights of Day's car, and Tom Duffy stepped on the brake. Shiela pushed herself painfully up in the seat and leaned out through the open side window.

"Ah, Miss McDevitt," the guard said.

"Let us through," she managed. "We have to get to the station."

"You can't drive up there," he answered. "It's just a path."

"Please," Shiela begged.

"I'm sorry, Miss McDevitt, but you know the standing orders."

Duffy's fist flashed past Shiela's face and struck the young sailor on the point of his chin. He shot backward, through the door of the guard shack, and slammed against the far wall. Then he deflated into a heap on the floor. Duffy had already pulled the transmission back into gear. He hit the gas, the fragile gate shattered, and the car bolted toward the radio station.

Chief Gore jumped up as the door blasted open. Shiela came in with a giant man squeezing through the door next to her so that he could keep his massive arm around her waist.

"Miss McDevitt," he said. But his eyes locked on the man's round, red face. He thought of the pistol resting in his desk drawer.

"I've got a message to send," Shiela said. She pulled away from Duffy and came toward Gore, unfolding a paper as she walked. "It's priority. I've already coded it."

Gore looked from Duffy to Shiela and finally to the paper that she was holding out. He took it and turned away toward his desk as he read it.

"Whose call sign is this?" he asked.

"It's German. A radio station somewhere in Germany," Shiela said.

Gore looked up in confusion. He brushed his fingers across the message. "This isn't one of our codes."

"It's a German code. Please, chief. Just send it. Commander Day wants it on the air immediately."

Gore reached behind him and began easing the desk drawer open. "Where is Commander Day?" he demanded.

"In Schull. At the dock." Shiela's voice was fading. "He's sending the boats out to escort *Lusitania*. Please. Send the message. That's what it's about. Saving *Lusitania*."

Gore's hand found the pistol. He eased it slowly out of the drawer and then snapped it in the direction of Tom Duffy. "All right. Both of you back up," he ordered. Neither of them moved, so Chief Gore began backing toward his radio transmitters. "I don't know what this is all about. But I'm not sending any messages to the Germans. Not until Commander Day gets here."

"There isn't time," Shiela begged. "The Germans are trying to sink *Lusitania*. That message will stop them." Instead of backing away, Shiela began walking toward the Chief. But her step faltered. She staggered sideways, then fell against the chief's desk. She had to grab the edge of the desk to keep from falling to the floor.

Gore's eyes widened. He saw the dark, wet stain that was soaking down the side of Shiela's dress. "Mother of God!" he dropped the pistol next to the sending key and rushed to help her. But Duffy was already there. He lifted Shiela in his arms as if she were a doll.

"What happened to her?" the chief asked.

"Your lieutenant shot her," Duffy said. Then he screamed at Gore, "Send the damn message. She's been bleedin' to death just to get it here."

Gore saw the blood drip down onto the floor. "She needs a doctor," he said to Duffy.

"I'll get her to a doctor," Duffy yelled. "You send her message."

Gore nodded. He turned and rushed to his radio while Duffy ran out the door with Shiela in his arms.

The chief's hand trembled as he dialed in the frequency. He peaked his power gauge, and then he tapped in the strange call letters. He was astounded when a response came back immediately, loud and clear.

Carefully, he began sending the coded letters, working his way through the message line by line. Uncharacteristically for his experienced hand, he stumbled on a letter group and had to send the repeat signal and then correct his error. He was soaked in sweat when he finished the message.

He signed off the coded characters that spelled *Leprechaun*. Then he lifted his hand from the key and waited for the acknowledgment. There was a long silence. Then the speaker hissed, and Emmett Hayes's call letters sounded. It was the first time Chief Gore had received a coded acknowledgment from a German operator. He had no idea who he was, or where he was. But when he turned, he saw the bloodstain thickening down the side of his desk. He knew he had done the right thing.

EMDEN

"IT WASN'T sent by our agent," the communications officer was telling Captain Bauer. "It didn't come from Leprechaun."

"But it's his code," the flotilla commander argued. "And those are his call letters. It looks like everything else we've gotten from him."

"But it didn't sound the same. It wasn't his hand, sir. We know the way Leprechaun keys his letters, just the way you know someone's voice. This wasn't his voice. And it was a different radio. Much more powerful. Leprechaun has a portable field model. It's low powered with a good deal of background noise. This was a loud, clear signal."

Bauer was angry. It was a vital message, and he had only an hour to act on it. Maybe less. By now, *Lusitania* should be past Fastnet, headed up the coast. U-30 should be racing to intercept her. They might be only thirty miles apart. But his communications officer was telling him that the message might not be genuine.

"Try again for a confirmation," Bauer ordered.

"But, sir . . ."

"Try again," the submarine commander snapped.

The officer saluted and raced off to the communications center.

They had tried for a confirmation. As soon as they had translated the code and realized it was a complete reversal of Leprechaun's earlier message, they had become suspicious of the strange hand and the different radio transmitter. They had sent out Leprechaun's call letters and waited for a response. Nothing had happened.

Bauer looked at his operations officer. "What do you think, Klaus?"

"I think it's a trick," Schopfner answered without hesitation. "It says that the guncotton isn't aboard *Lusitania*. But our agents in New York saw it put aboard."

"Not quite," Bauer contradicted. "They saw railroad cars barged across the river to *Lusitania*'s dock. They can't be sure of what was in those cars. And they don't know for a fact that they were ever loaded aboard."

"But why would the British . . ."

"To make us do exactly what we're doing," Bauer said. "To make us attack American passengers." He looked at his copy of the message and read aloud. "High-placed Americans ready to declare war."

"The Americans did nothing over *Faloba*," the operations officer reminded his commander.

Bauer nodded. "But that was one man. This is hundreds of women and children. Worth the risk to get the guncotton. But without the guncotton?"

Had he been outmaneuvered? Captain Bauer wondered. First the English break the rules of encounter, arming their merchant ships and ordering them to ram submarines that challenge them. Then he responds by ordering his boats to fire without warning. And then the British send him the one ship that he can't fire on. Only they fill it with a cargo that he can't resist. Was he playing into their hands? Their queen exposed on the chessboard! And now a message warning him not to rush in and take it. Was there a trap lurking somewhere else on the board? Perhaps on the far edge, all the way across the Atlantic?

"I would act on the first message," Schopfner said decisively. "It came from Leprechaun. From his radio. It delivered the coordinates you asked for. Up to that point, everything makes sense."

"And simply ignore this warning?" Bauer asked, brandishing the copy of the message.

"But it came from a high-powered transmitter, captain. Where would Leprechaun get a high-powered transmitter? The only ones in Ireland belong to the English. It has to be an English trick."

The communications officer rushed into the room, shaking his head as he reached Captain Bauer. "No response whatever, sir. We keep sending Leprechaun's call letters. He doesn't answer."

"So it can't have come from him," the operations officer added.

Bauer held up his hand to silence them. He walked away to a corner of the room where he stood alone. Then he turned abruptly. "It can't be the English. Don't you see, if they sent this message to trick us, they would be standing by to confirm it."

The two officers looked at each other in confusion.

"To send this," Bauer said, "the English would have had to capture Leprechaun. Or found some way to turn him. How else would they have his call sign? And his code?"

The operations officer nodded to concede the point.

"So they get to this man," Bauer continued, "and decide to send us a hoax. They use his call sign. They use his code. So tell me. Why don't they answer to confirm their message?"

"Perhaps," the communications officer pondered, "they're not listening."

Bauer frowned. "Who's more likely to be away from his radio? A single agent? Or a British communications station?"

He dashed to his communications officer, snatched the message pad, and began writing. "Something happened in Ireland," he told his officers as he wrote. "Between the first and second messages, something changed. I don't know what, but I think this warning is genuine."

He tore off a message addressed to U-20 and U-30:

DO NOT REPEAT NOT ATTACK LARGE TROOP CARRIER. BRITISH TRAP. STAND CLEAR.

"Get that off immediately."

He paced back and forth under the questioning eyes of his operations officer, rerunning the decision he had just made. The "high-placed Americans" rang true. There were people, high up in the American government, who had suppressed the warning advertisement. They obviously didn't want to discourage Americans from booking passage on *Lusitania*. And then the convenience of the British using a compromised radio station to order the guncotton loaded aboard. Did they know that he was reading the radio station's traffic? Did they know that he would get the message that gave the rendezvous points that *Lusitania* would reach, and the precise course she would have to follow? They were either very stupid, or very cunning. And if they were cunning, then he had been played for a fool.

His communications officer rushed back into the room. "We can't raise either boat," he announced. There was an edge of panic in his voice.

"They must be submerged," Schopfner said.

Bauer went to the plotting table. U-30 was near shore and close to the warships that were serving as escorts. More than likely she was submerged. But U-30 was a long shot at best. The boat that had the best chance of attacking *Lusitania* was U-20. And she was still hours away, in an area that the Milford Haven squadron had vacated. She should be on the surface. She should be answering.

"Keep sending," he told the communications officer. "No other traffic is to interfere. Just keep trying to raise them. U-20 has to acknowledge that message."

THE IRISH COAST

Lusitania's great horn bleated out into the dense fog. She was moving slowly, making barely fifteen knots, feeling her way across what Captain Turner hoped was the rendezvous point. But there was no answering call from the ships of Squadron E.

"Could be anywhere," Turner told his watch officer. He checked the ship's chronometer. It was nearly eight o'clock. He had already lingered too long in hope of a long shot. Without a fix, he could be as much as fifteen miles away from the cruiser *Juno* and her destroyers. They would never hear him.

"Full ahead," he decided, watching as his deck officer ran to the engine room telegraphs and signaled for the new speed. "Steer course zero six zero."

"Zero six zero, aye," the helmsman chimed.

No matter what errors he had made in the past two days of dead reckoning, Turner knew that he was at least twenty miles off Fastnet. The course he had ordered would bring him no closer to the Irish coast, keeping him well clear of land and outside the traffic of small boats that ran up and down the shore. His plan was simple. Later on in the morning—certainly before noon—the fog would burn away. When he could see land, he would turn in closer to the coast, sight one of the many readily identifiable landmarks, and get a positive fix on his position. In the meantime, he would be moving in the right direction, closing on his second rendezvous near Coningbeg Light.

He would have preferred to have the escorts. And maybe they would have the sense to realize that he had missed the rendezvous and would start back up along the coast in the direction they knew *Lusitania* would have to take. There was a chance, Turner thought, that they would see one another when the fog lifted.

But *Juno* had already broken out of the fog. She was thirty miles to the east, steaming toward Queenstown. Admiral Oliver's order, recalling *Lusitania*'s escorts, had been received two hours earlier, while *Lusitania* was still well out at sea. *Juno* had no intention of meeting up with The Greyhound. She was heading back into port for an easy weekend that would be spent tied up to the pier.

ABOARD U-30, Lieutenant Rosenberg saw *Juno* through his periscope. Something was terribly wrong. According to the coordinates he had received from Bauer, she should still be well to the west at her rendezvous with *Lusitania*. Or, if she had made the rendezvous earlier than expected, then *Lusitania* should be steaming in her company. *Juno* was also in much closer to the beach. The course line he had laid out for *Lusitania* between the two rendezvous points had her nearly fifteen miles off the coast. Rosenberg had taken a position along that line, but *Juno* was at least five miles inside him. Perhaps there had been some new information from Emden. Information he couldn't know because his radio was useless when he was running under the surface.

"Down scope," he snapped to his executive officer. Then he stood back, leaning against the bulkhead of the tower, and tried to think. *Lusitania* was coming in. There was no doubt about that. Probably right behind *Juno*, and along the same course line that the decrepit cruiser was traveling. His best chance was to move in toward the beach as quickly as possible. Ideally, he would run on the surface in order to make his best speed. But he couldn't risk being sighted by the cruiser. His next choice would be to keep his periscope up, so that he would see *Lusitania* the instant she appeared. But even that was too risky. The damned Irish fleet had reappeared. The sea was dotted with small workboats and fishing boats. They would certainly see a periscope cutting through the flat sea.

"All ahead full," he ordered. "Take her down to thirty feet."

He had just one chance. Get to *Juno*'s course line, and then take one quick look through the periscope. If *Lusitania* was there, he would take her. If not, he would drop the periscope and get out of the area before the Irish boats spotted him and called in the British fleet. His batteries were low, so he couldn't do a great deal of maneuvering under water. And he had just two torpedoes left, hardly enough to do battle with a squadron of British destroyers. He'd take one look. If *Lusitania* wasn't there, then he would head for Fastnet and begin his long journey home.

WALTER Schwieger screamed in frustration. It was another freighter, steaming leisurely, no more than three miles off his port quarter, the second one that had come into sight in the past hour. But he couldn't dive to avoid being spotted. His machinists were just now tightening the bolts on the deck plate that protected his periscope.

"Christ," he cursed to Haupert. "The son of a bitch is probably on his radio right now. The whole damned English navy will know we're out here."

Haupert winced. There was nothing he could say to his captain. They were having impossible luck. Everything was going wrong. Schwieger had made a good decision in running out of the shipping lanes while he made the repairs. There was no way he could have guessed that he was moving right into the path of two meandering tramp steamers. His plan to fix the periscope and then return to Coningbeg should have worked. Now, there was no way he could head back to his intercept point. The whole Milford Haven squadron would probably be there waiting for him.

"If we only had a radio," Schwieger lamented.

Haupert understood. Now that the British knew where he was, Schwieger was willing to break radio silence to let Bauer know his new position. Perhaps Emden could give them a new vector toward their incoming target.

"Finished," the machinist announced proudly, standing up over his work.

Haupert knew that Schwieger wanted to throttle the man. But the captain simply nodded. "Let's hope it works this time," he said to the machinist.

They waited on the deck while the men dragged their tools down through the hatch. "We can't head back to Coningbeg, Willi," Schwieger said, thinking aloud more than asking Haupert for his opinion. "And we sure as hell can't stay here."

"You did everything you could, captain," Haupert consoled. "Things just went wrong. Perhaps it was just never meant to be."

"Perhaps," Schwieger admitted. He looked at the sea around them, clear and bright, marked by small patches of hazy fog. In another hour, visibility would be unlimited. It was a perfect day for making an intercept. "But we might not be finished yet. She's still coming toward us. Somewhere, in the next few hours, our paths could cross."

He couldn't go back to the east. But he could head to the northwest, away from the Milford Haven ships and toward *Lusitania*. He could run northwest until he reached *Lusitania*'s course line. Then he could turn southwest and travel along that line in the opposite direction. There was a chance that by midday, his target would appear on the horizon directly on his bow.

"Bring her to three zero zero," he told Haupert. "Flank speed. We'll give it one more try."

"Should we dive and test the periscope?" the executive officer asked.

Schwieger shook his head. "We'll find out soon enough. If it works, we'll use it. If not, we're heading toward home anyway." He dropped down through the hatch to get himself a cup of coffee.

LONDON

It was all coming apart, Reginald Hall admitted to himself. All the pieces so carefully assembled, like the springs and gears of a fine watch. He had wound the spring to set it in motion, but the watch wasn't ticking. The pieces weren't working together.

He held copies of the sighting reports. Two freighters had spotted one of Bauer's submarines thirty miles southwest of Coningbeg Light, well off the route that *Lusitania* would be taking into Saint George's Channel. What in God's name was she doing so far out of position? And there had been the panicky phone call from Admiral Coke in Queenstown. The Irish fishing boats, operating out near Fastnet, had spotted a periscope only ten miles from shore. That was well inside *Lusitania*'s course, and with the boats all around her, Bauer's second submarine probably couldn't do anything even if she sighted The Greyhound. Why in hell were the damned Irish out there anyway? He had counted on Lieutenant Grace's keeping that situation under control. But Grace was obviously having difficulties. He hadn't even reported in.

Worse, the sighting reports had brought the Milford Haven fleet back up from Land's End. That was exactly what they should do when they learned that there was a submarine operating near the Irish coast. And he certainly couldn't order them to stay away. What possible reason could he ever offer to Admiral Fisher for telling English warships to ignore a submarine? Especially one that might be in a position to threaten *Lusitania*.

Now Admiral Coke had figured out that *Lusitania* was in great danger. He had wired Admiral Fisher that there were submarines operating all along the Irish coast and requested permission to divert The Greyhound into the safety of Queenstown harbor. It was a prudent request. *Lusitania* could wait in Queenstown until the submarine threat subsided and then chart a new course for Liverpool. Or, she could even disembark her passengers and cargo at the British naval base. Fisher would undoubtedly agree and order *Lusitania* to turn inland, out of harm's way.

So, the chess game he had been playing with Flotilla Commander Bauer was over. A stalemate, Hall supposed. He had failed Winston Churchill's hope of drawing the United States into the war. Bauer had failed to stop the cargo of guncotton from reaching England. It was time to pick up the pieces and reset the board.

There would be other matches, he consoled himself. *Lusitania* would make many more crossings from America. And there were other ships. Ships that would carry American passengers, and that he could load with other irresistible cargoes. But this one had been so perfect. His strategy had been nothing short of genius. He hated to see it end without a victory.

EMDEN

STILL NO response. It had been more than an hour since Flotilla Commander Bauer had fired off the message to his two boats canceling the attack on *Lusitania*. Neither of them had responded.

What a damn fool I've been, he thought mournfully. I should have seen the trap. I should have known.

He had spent the past hour alone in his day room examining the clues that now seemed so obvious. The message to New York ordering the guncotton to be placed aboard the great ship. The Admiralty had never talked to New York through the Crookhaven radio station. And Crookhaven had never handled any traffic concerning cargoes. He should have been suspicious of that message the moment it was received from his agent in Ireland. It should have told him that the English knew about the leak in Crookhaven and were sending the message directly to him. He should have recognized the bait they were pushing under his nose.

Then there was the warning to the American passengers. Common sense said that the U.S. government should have taken steps to protect its own citizens. Yet the American State Department had done just the opposite. It had suppressed the warning. Certainly that should have gotten his attention. The Americans must have known about the guncotton. It had been financed by one of their own banks and manufactured in one of their own factories. Why would they load their own citizens on the same ship with such a deadly cargo? Unless they knew there was no cargo. Or unless someone in the American government had a more important agenda than simply protecting innocent lives. He couldn't blame himself for not knowing all the answers. But at least it should have raised his suspicions.

And then the rendezvous message. He had been so delighted to get it from Leprechaun that he hadn't really studied it. If he had, he would have realized that it was much more detailed than the other rendezvous messages that Crookhaven had been broadcasting to incoming ships for the past six months. It made it easy for him to plot *Lusitania*'s course and pick his intercept points. Too easy! Why hadn't he asked himself, "Why?"

He remembered how brilliant he had felt when the English took the bait he had offered. When he had sent U-30 to raise hell off the Scilly Islands, the English had pulled their whole fleet away from Coningbeg. Now he realized that they had recognized his feeble attempt to fool them. They must have been toasting one another with their best port when they pretended to have been taken in by his plan.

But there was still time. There were still perhaps a few hours left to call off his attack. All he needed was a response from U-20 that she had received and understood his message.

He jumped up from his chair and charged out into his operations center. Klaus Schopfner saw him coming and simply shook his head in response to the question he knew Captain Bauer would ask. There was still no acknowledgment. His message had not yet gotten through to Lieutenant Walter Schwieger.

THE IRISH COAST

SUDDENLY, William Day was caught up in the hunt. The image of the brutality in Emmett Hayes's cellar, which had paralyzed him since he had rushed from the house, had quickly faded. The sight of the periscope that had sneaked up through the surface, only a hundred yards from Sheehy's boat, had snapped him back to life.

"There," he had screamed, pointing to the glass lens that sparkled brilliantly as it turned into the sun. "Come about."

Sheehy had swung his tiller and fired up the engine to a deafening roar. The boat had bolted forward, closing quickly on the searching pole and its white wake.

Day had pulled the cap of a flare, launching a stream of bright white smoke. Immediately, the closest boats had turned toward him, converging on the periscope.

They had closed to fifty yards when the scope slipped downward and disappeared below the surface. The U-boat's captain had seen them coming and was diving to safety. Day could see the huge dark shape falling away below him when his boat sped over the point where the periscope had disappeared. He pointed in the direction that the submarine was headed. Sheehy followed his hand signal and turned the boat, keeping it directly over the fleeing submarine.

He had the advantage. Even Sheehy's ancient long boat, with its two-cylinder engine, was faster than a U-boat running under water. And the other Irish boats were drawing near, forming a tight circle that blocked the submarine's escape in any direction. The German couldn't surface. His crew would come under small arms fire the second they opened the hatches. All he could do was dive to the bottom and go into hiding.

Day looked up to the west, where a low wall of fog still obscured the horizon. *Lusitania* would be coming out of that fog at any moment. But where? He wanted to maneuver his fleet between the submarine and her target so that she wouldn't be able to raise her scope and begin taking bearings. At the same time, he had to be careful not to let the German open up distance between his fleet and the beach. If the U-boat got far enough away from them, it could surface safely. And once her crew got out to their deck gun, they would have the Irish boats cut off from their port. The Germans could finish them at their leisure.

He decided to move his formation to the south, toward the fog bank, putting them between the submarine and the direction in which *Lusitania* would most likely appear, while still leaving the boats an escape toward land.

"Spread out," he screamed over the water. The dark form below him was no longer visible. The U-boat had gone down deep and could now turn in any direction. His best hope of keeping her down was to broaden his coverage.

Where would she go? If she had come for *Lusitania*, then her first thought wouldn't be to punish his boats. She would probably try to break out into the open sea, where she had the most room to maneuver into an intercept position. Day pointed his arm toward the south, and Sheehy turned the boat to the seaward end of the formation. "Okay, you bastard," he whispered. "Come on up and take a look. I'm waiting for you."

"COME TO one five zero," Rosenberg called down into his control room. "Level at forty feet." He knew he was too far down to be seen from the surface. Now he was trying to escape from under the damned Irish boats, out into open water, which was the only way he had a chance of raising his scope for a shot at *Lusitania*.

"Fifteen minutes," he told his executive officer. "Then we'll go up for another look." The Irish, he reasoned, would keep circling around the spot where he had dived. In fifteen minutes, he could open a mile or more away from them. And if he were lucky, *Lusitania* would be out of the fog and into open water, close enough for his two final torpedoes.

"THERE SHE is," Sheehy shouted, his finger jabbing to the south-west. Day turned and saw the ship, her shape still indistinct in the distant haze. But there was no doubt it was *Lusitania*, riding high above the water, with four funnels towering above her decks.

Day remembered where the submarine had vanished. He took a quick bearing on *Lusitania*'s bow and calculated that she would pass well out to sea of them. To have a chance for attack, the submarine would have to run to the south.

"Slow her down a bit, Mr. Sheehy," Day advised. "We don't want to get too far ahead of our friend down there." The Irishman tapped his throttle back, and his old boat slowed to a leisurely speed that probably matched the speed that the U-boat was making.

"SOMEDAY, I'm going to come back here and shoot these damned boats into driftwood," Rosenberg told his executive officer.

"We could take them all right now," the executive answered.

Rosenberg sneered. "Not now. We have a bigger fish to fry."

He glanced at the clock. Ten minutes had passed. If he had guessed right, the Irish boats were all far behind him. But if *Lusitania* were there when he raised his scope, he didn't want any interference while he lined up his shot. Best to wait a bit longer. Just another few minutes.

*   *   *

DAY COULD see the giant ship clearly now. She was crossing due south of him, more than a mile away. And yet, her size made her seem much closer. He could make out the graceful curve of the white wave that rose behind her bow. He thought of Jennifer, probably standing on one of her open decks, looking in at the coast of Ireland. For an instant, he even remembered the words of the letter that would be waiting for her. But as soon as his attention wandered from the killer that was lurking somewhere under his keel, Shiela's frightened eyes reappeared. And he felt a pain of guilt, as if even the thought of Jennifer was somehow betraying her.

"LET'S TAKE a look," Rosenberg decided. "Take her up to fifteen feet." The bowplanes tipped upward, and U-30 began rising up from the depths.

He was on his knees, waiting for the periscope to come up from its trunk. As soon as the eyepiece appeared, he pressed his face against it. He saw the daylight the instant the scope broke the surface. Immediately, he swung it to the south and gasped as the lens filled with the image of *Lusitania*.

"Jesus!" We've got her," he said. He began twisting the rangefinder to start calculating his firing commands, when a small boat cut across his field of vision. It was one of the Irish boats that had moved out ahead of him and were waiting for him to show his periscope.

"Damn!" Rosenberg screamed. He pulled the counterweight, dropping the scope down into the hull. "Dive," he yelled into the control room. "Dive!" Almost immediately, he felt the deck begin to tip as his boat started back down into his hiding place near the bottom.

"That devil. That son of a bitch devil. He read my mind. He was waiting for me."

He turned to his executive officer, who was standing helplessly to one side. "We had her. We had *Lusitania* right in our sights." He pounded his fist against the bulkhead. "To lose her! To a damned rowboat!"

And he knew he had lost her. He would have to maneuver again, far below the surface, until he got free from the fishing boats. By the time he was in the clear, and able to come up for another look, all he would see was her stern as she raced away from him.

"We should make them pay," the executive officer threatened.

Rosenberg waved his hand. The target was lost. He had nothing to gain by taking out his anger on a few wooden boats. "To hell with it," he decided. "Let's go home."

*   *   *

ONCE AGAIN, Day watched the dark shape of the submarine dive into hiding. But this time he knew it was over. *Lusitania* was crossing safely behind him. She would be long gone by the time the submarine came up for another look.

"She's safe, Mr. Sheehy," he announced with a smile. "Let's gather up our boats and take them home."

Sheehy laughed. "A good day's work, commander. A good day's work!"

CAPTAIN Turner squinted at the message that his wireless operation had rushed to the bridge. He held it out at arm's length, and still the words wouldn't come into focus. He needed his reading glasses, but they were on the desk in his cabin. He thought it unseemly for a ship's master to admit his failing eyesight by wearing spectacles in front of his crew.

"Read the damn thing," he snapped at the wireless operator.

SUBMARINE ACTIVITY SOUTH OF CONINGBEG LIGHT. DIVERT TO QUEENS-TOWN TO AWAIT FURTHER INSTRUCTIONS. PILOT WILL BOARD AT HARBOR ENTRANCE, 120 CROSSHAVEN 1 MILE.

"Queenstown," Bowler Bill mumbled. "Well, I won't be stopping to pick up any damn pilot. I've been taking ships into Queenstown since Admiral Coke was a seasick cadet."

He bounded out onto the port wing and raised his binoculars over the port bow. The coastline was still hazy, but he had no trouble finding the Old Head of Kinsale. It stood like a mountain on the end of a finger of land, reaching half a mile out into the sea. He could run in toward the beach and put the lighthouse atop the Old Head off his port beam, at perhaps fifteen miles. That would give him the precise fix he needed before he approached the shore. From there he could plot a direct line to Queenstown, less than an hour's steaming ahead.

"Left fifteen degrees rudder," he screamed back into the wheelhouse. "Come to course zero four five."

That would aim him directly at the Old Head, only an hour ahead of him. With a bit of luck, *Lusitania* would be tied up in Queenstown in less than three hours.

"KEEP A sharp eye," Lieutenant Schwieger screamed down to the lookout on his foredeck. They had raised land directly off the starboard bow. If his plotting was correct, it would most likely be Ballycotton, just ten miles to the east of the entrance to Cork Harbor and Queenstown. He was entering the home waters of the British fleet that guarded the Irish coast, a very dangerous place for a German submarine to be running on the surface. He had to be sure that he would see a British ship before it had a chance to see him. He guessed that he was about fifteen miles off shore, crossing the course line that connected *Lusitania's* two rendezvous points. If he were going to find her at all, it would have to be on that line.

"Come left to course two four zero," he called into the voice tube.

"Two four zero, aye."

Slowly, his bow began to swing away from the shore.

Haupert stuck his head up through the hatch. "Are we there?" he asked.

"On her course line, and turning toward her," Schwieger answered. "If we're going to find her, it will be someplace between here and the Old Head of Kinsale."

Haupert climbed up and stood beside him. "Unless Rosenberg has gotten her already."

"Not a chance," Schwieger answered. And then he said thoughtfully, "Not much of a chance for us, either." He had already made up his mind. He had been without communications from his commanding officer for over five hours and had no way of knowing what further information had been sent. He didn't know whether he had a working periscope. He did know that he had been sighted and that, in all probability, the British Queenstown fleet was out looking for him. He had no intention of lingering around Queenstown on the long chance that *Lusitania* would steam right down his torpedo tubes. All he could do was follow his new course another hour or so toward the west. Probably no farther than the Old Head. If he had made no contact by then, he would assume that *Lusitania* had already passed him, either inland, while he was still far out at sea, or outside of him right now, as he was closing on the coast. At that point, he would turn back out to sea and plot a course for home. He still had three torpedoes left. And he would probably come across other ships as he worked his way up the western Irish coast. It wouldn't have been a wasted voyage.

"Ship ahead!" Schwieger's attention snapped out over the starboard bow where his lookout was pointing. A smear of smoke was rising above the land line. He raised his glasses and picked out the hazy outline of a ship nearing the entrance to Queenstown.

"Is it her?" Haupert asked, leaning on the railing beside him.

"I can't tell," Schwieger said. "If it is, she seems to be heading into Queenstown. But maybe she's just running right up on the beach." He guessed at the bearing to his target. "Come right to two eight zero," he ordered. His bow swung back toward the patch of smoke.

For the next ten minutes they crouched against the rail, staring at the form of the ship, ignoring the fact that they were rushing into dangerous enemy waters. "How many stacks do you see?" Schwieger asked.

"I think two," Haupert said. "And I think it's too small to be *Lusitania*."

"Too slow," Schwieger added. "She can't be making more than twelve knots."

"Jesus, it's a cruiser," Haupert nearly shouted. "I think it's *Juno*."

Schwieger squinted into his glasses. "Damn! You're right. But isn't she supposed to be escorting *Lusitania*? What's she doing heading home alone?"

Haupert chuckled. "Maybe we should follow her in. Wouldn't it be something to sink the English flagship right in the middle of an English navy base?"

Schwieger wasn't amused. "This is crazy, Willi. The escort is running for home. Where in hell is the ship she's supposed to be escorting?" He turned his glasses to the west. The sky was clear. There was still no trace of the ship they were after. And then he thought, *Lusitania* isn't coming. We were sighted. They knew that there was a submarine ahead. *Lusitania* has turned back out to sea, to wait until the ships from Queenstown have cleared her path ahead of her. Maybe *Juno* wasn't going back to port. Maybe she was joining up with the rest of Squadron E to begin the search. And he was racing right up to the entrance of the naval base, making himself very easy to find.

"Let's get out of here," he said to Haupert. He leaned to the voice tube. "Come left to course two one five." Then he turned to his executive officer. "Not this time, Willi. If we're going to get *Lusitania*, it will have to be another day."

They kept a cautious eye on *Juno* as they pulled away from her, watching as the English cruiser turned into Cork harbor. Even after she disappeared, they kept their glasses fixed on the harbor entrance, nearly certain that they would soon see the Squadron E ships coming out in pursuit. But there was nothing. The English seemed to have forgotten about them.

"Old Head of Kinsale," Haupert said casually. He pointed to a shape of land just coming into sight off the starboard beam. Schwieger raised his glasses and nodded in agreement. The shape of the landfall was unmistakable, a mountaintop thrust out into the sea. He swung his glasses slowly toward the bow to make sure that his course was clear. And then he saw the haze of smoke on the horizon. There were ships ahead of them, racing across his bow toward the Old Head.

"There they are! Squadron E!" he told Haupert. Then he asked, "What do you make out? Two ships? Or is it three?"

"Looks like two. Two big ships. Probably both cruisers."

Schwieger steadied his binoculars. "In a tight formation," he said. "Or . . . my God, Haupert. It's one ship with four stacks. It's *Lusitania!*"

"Headed into Kinsale?" Haupert asked.

"Not if we can get there first," Schwieger said. He called into the voice tube, "Right standard rudder. All ahead full."

The diesels growled, and the bow began swinging toward the landmark. He watched until he was headed to the harbor entrance, just to the east of the rock. "Steady as she goes," he ordered.

"Steady on new course three one zero," the helmsman told him.

The boat quickly added speed, its bow beginning to throw up a white spray.

"Do we have a chance of catching her?" the executive officer wondered aloud, his glasses still fixed on the hazy target.

Schwieger could see that his relative bearing to *Lusitania* was slowly changing. The damned Greyhound was too fast. She was closing on his estimated intercept point much more quickly than he was. In open sea, he would have turned farther ahead of her, moving his intercept point farther to the east. But that was pointless. If she were headed into Kinsale, he couldn't cut her off farther to the east. He had to beat her to the Old Head.

"We can try," he answered. "Maybe something will happen. We're overdue for a bit of luck."

JENNIFER Beecham stood on the portside boat deck, a scarf wrapped over her head against the twenty-knot wind that *Lusitania's* speed was generating. The shoreline was rapidly coming into focus. She could see the pale gray of the rocks and the patches of deep green where farm fields bent over the edges of the cliffs. Dead ahead was the jagged edge of a mountain, and if she squinted, she could make out a lighthouse on its crown.

"Beautiful, isn't it?" Alfred Vanderbilt said as he stepped up behind her.

"What is it?"

"Ireland. The Old Head of Kinsale. There's a harbor behind it that used to be a refuge for Spanish pirates. A lot of battles were fought here."

"But it looks so peaceful. Like paradise!"

"Hardly that," Vanderbilt laughed. "I was just taking a stroll. Would you care to join me?"

Jennifer took his arm, and they started toward the fantail along the first-class promenade.

"I have the lighthouse," the watch officer called to Captain Turner, "bearing zero one zero."

Turner checked his chart. "Very well," he answered. He drew a bearing line and marked the time. He would hold this course for another ten minutes and then shoot another bearing. Then all he had to do was advance the first line by ten minutes along his course line, and he would have a running fix. At that point, he figured, he would be about sixteen miles from the Old Head. Then he would turn to the east and run a straight line into Queenstown.

He stepped to the wheelhouse windows. The sea seemed to be empty. The escorts that he had been sure he would eventually meet up with were nowhere in sight. He hadn't even seen a small boat since he had raced past the group that was scattered near Fastnet.

"It's quiet," he commented to the watch officer, who was returning from the wing.

"We seem to have it all to ourselves," the watch officer answered.

"It's LUSITANIA, all right," Haupert said. "Four stacks. Two masts. Look at the height of her!"

"She's getting away from us," Schwieger snapped back. He thought of the course change he had made, away from the coast to avoid *Juno*. That had been his mistake. If he had held course, he would be three miles closer to the beach. *Lusitania* would be headed right across his bow.

Haupert looked up from his binoculars. "Can we keep running like this? On the surface? She'll be able to see us in a few minutes."

He was right, of course. Even though they were low to the water, they weren't invisible. And the bow was tossing up explosions of foam whenever it caught the top of a swell. But he had no chance if he took the boat under. *Lusitania* would simply run away from him. He had to stay up, hoping that her lookouts were concentrating on the shoreline. Then, when he got into range, he would fire his bow torpedoes perhaps with a five-degree difference in their heading. The odds of one of them finding its mark were slim. But it was better than doing nothing.

"BEARING ZERO zero zero," the watch officer called out.

"Very well," Turner answered as he plotted the second leg of his fix. The two lines on his chart intersected at a point sixteen miles south of the lighthouse. He had his position.

"Right fifteen degrees rudder," he ordered the helmsman. He was swinging toward Queenstown, only an hour ahead.

Jennifer and Vanderbilt had turned across the fantail and were starting up the starboard side of the promenade. Suddenly, the deck tipped beneath them and began to move out from under their feet. Jennifer lost her balance, and Vanderbilt caught her in both arms. He looked up to the starboard wing of the bridge, 300 feet ahead. "Captain Turner must think he's in a yacht race. That was a very sharp turn." He held onto Jennifer until the deck leveled itself. "I hope there will be no more of those," he said. Jennifer laughed, and they resumed their walk toward the bow of the ship.

"SHE'S TURNING," Schwieger shouted. "She's turning toward us." He studied the swing of the towering bow and the blasts of white spray it threw as she cut through the sea. She hadn't taken off any speed, but she was turning to the east. Apparently she was headed farther up the coast.

"Queenstown," he nearly laughed. "She's going into Queenstown. We've got her, Willi. We've got her." He ordered a small course correction. Then he scampered down the right hatch behind his executive officer. "Dive! Dive!" he screamed as he pulled the hatch closed.

He leveled off at twenty feet. Then he took a deep breath. "Bring the periscope up," he ordered. Haupert reached for the cable, hesitated for just an instant, and then tugged it down. The periscope began to rise through the repaired packing. He looked at Schwieger, and the two officers smiled at each other. "Our luck is changing, Willi."

He dove to the eyepiece, ignoring the slight drip of water that was falling from overhead. As soon as he saw daylight, he saw *Lusitania*. He was on her starboard bow, and she was racing toward him.

"Set the torpedoes for eight feet," he said. That would put them a full deck below *Lusitania*'s waterline. If she held course, there was little chance of his missing. She would pass less than 700 yards across his bow.

"We'll fire one at a time," he told Haupert. "See what the first one does, and then decide where to put the second one."

He knew a torpedo hit couldn't finish her off. His first torpedo hits hadn't been enough for either *Candidate* or *Centurion*. But if the first one slowed her down, then maybe he could put the second one into her propellers and rudder. If he could stop her, then his deck gun might be able to riddle her hull. It would be just a question of time. It would probably take half an hour for *Lusitania* to put her passengers into the lifeboats. And he was only an hour away from the British warships at Queenstown. Not much of a margin. But for *Lusitania*, he would play it as closely as he could.

Haupert cranked his firing orders into the calculator. "Twenty seconds," he announced. Schwieger lowered the periscope and began counting down the moments.

JENNIFER AND Alfred Vanderbilt had passed beneath the soaring second stack and were walking up the starboard side toward the ladder that led up to the bridge. They were suddenly hot, warmed by the bright sun that was high in the southern sky. Jennifer had brushed the scarf back from her hair, and Vanderbilt had slipped out of his topcoat and folded it over his arm.

"You have no idea where you will be going?" he asked, and once again Jennifer told him that William Day was probably at sea. "I'm sure there's a home port that he sails from. Probably up in Scotland, from what I've read. Although it could be right here in Ireland. I won't know until we reach Liverpool." She tried to sound very sure of at least that simple detail, but even as she said the words she was wondering if she would ever know. The fear had been growing that there would be no message waiting for her.

"I certainly admire your courage," he said, shaking his head in amazement. "Traveling halfway around the world without being sure of where you're going. But, then, none of us is ever sure. Each journey begins with an act of faith." He smiled at her. "I suppose falling in love is the greatest act of faith of all. Once you love someone, I wouldn't imagine anything is really frightening."

They were startled by a sharp crash from somewhere up ahead. Before they could turn toward the sound, the deck lurched beneath them. Vanderbilt heard Jennifer scream and felt her arm slip from his grasp. He watched helplessly as she toppled away from him and fell against the bulkhead. An instant later he lost his footing, staggering across the sloping deck until he landed beside her. He reached to catch her, but a torrent of water began pouring down on top of them. The sea had exploded into the air, and the giant waterspout was washing down the side of the ship.

Suddenly the deck was pitching in the opposite direction, and they were both sliding across the wet wood toward the rail. Vanderbilt grabbed the back of her jacket and reached out frantically for the base of the davit that held the first lifeboat. He caught it with one arm, but Jennifer broke free and crashed against the collapsible lifeboat that was fastened to the deck. Then Vanderbilt lost his grip and rolled on top of her.

"What's happened? What's wrong?" Jennifer cried.

He braced himself against the collapsible lifeboat and struggled to his feet, lifting her up with him. "An explosion, I think. But we're all right.

It's perfectly all right." He put his arm around her and tried to lead her up the angle of the deck. The ship had first lurched to port, but now it had rolled much too far to starboard. It had taken on an almost instant list.

"Are we going to sink?"

Vanderbilt could see that she was close to hysteria. "Of course not. We're perfectly safe. They'll be able to right her. It will only take a few moments."

He clutched at the handrail that was fastened to the boatdeck bulkhead and began leading her toward one of the doors. "Everything will be all right," he kept repeating. But he was battling his own fears. *Lusitania* had already taken on a ten-degree list and still seemed to be falling toward starboard. Whatever it was—a mine, or possibly a torpedo—it had obviously opened the starboard side to the sea.

"Up periscope," Walter Schwieger ordered, the instant that the concussion from the explosion rattled against the sides of the boat. He was down on his face, fixed to the eyepiece as it came up through the deck. He saw *Lusitania* as soon as the scope broke through the surface.

"A hit!" he told Haupert, who was already dancing with joy. "Just forward of the number one funnel. Maybe in the first boiler room. There's a hole in her side. I can see flames inside. My God, she's already listing to starboard. Ten, maybe fifteen degrees to starboard. She looks as if she might roll. One torpedo! And she's already leaning way over."

Below the water line, the torpedo had blown its way into the front end of the nearly empty coal bunker that ran along the side of the ship. Sea water rushed in, instantly drowning the buoyancy along *Lusitania's* starboard side. But the heat of the explosion had ignited the coal dust fumes that filled the bunker. As the gas was compressed by the rising sea water, it burst into flames. The fire roared through the bunker, jetting out its front end like the flame of an acetylene torch. The flame climbed past the torpedo hole and licked against the giant cases of guncotton that were stacked in the cargo hold two decks above.

Vanderbilt had reached the door and was trying to push Jennifer inside. But he couldn't get any footing against the slope of the water-slick deck. He was suddenly aware of a distant rumbling, a sound like a freight train running through the hull of the ship far below. It quickly grew louder, as if the train were thundering toward him. Then there was a flash of light, blue white, like lightning on a dark summer's night. The deck lurched violently beneath him, tossing him off his feet. He caught the edge of the door and held on for dear life. Jennifer spun through the doorway and was tossed into the passageway on the inside.

Sweet Jesus!" Schwieger said in horror. He watched as an enormous explosion tore through *Lusitania*'s bow. A white flash lifted her foredeck right off the hull, and the graceful schooner mast shot into the air and disappeared over the far side. He wrapped his arms around the periscope. "Brace yourself, Willi," he screamed.

The shock wave slammed against U-20 like an enormous fist, stopping her dead in the water and driving her bow to port. Haupert spun against the bulkhead and grabbed a cable rack to keep from falling. There were screams from the control room below, immediately canceled by the deafening thump of a great bass drum.

"What the hell happened?" Haupert demanded.

Schwieger turned slowly from the periscope, wide-eyed with fright. "The whole front of the ship," he said. "It just . . . blew off."

Captain Turner had heard his starboard lookout scream, "Torpedo! Torpedo wake!" He had barely looked up from the course he was drawing into Queenstown when he felt the ship shake. First he was slammed against the chart table. A moment later, he had to hold onto the table to keep from tumbling across the wheelhouse, which was quickly rolling into a starboard list.

He knew immediately what had to be done. The starboard bunker was flooding, and the ship was in mortal danger unless he could stop its roll. "Call the engine room," he bellowed to his watch officer. "Order them to flood the port coal bunker."

The watch officer blinked at the order.

"Now!" Turner screamed.

He rushed to the damage control status board, an outline of the ship dotted with small red lamps, that was mounted against the center of the wheelhouse's forward bulkhead. Two of the lamps, positioned just beneath the outline of the bridge, were blinking furiously. He had a fire in the transverse coal bunker, just forward of the number one boiler room. But he knew there was no longer a coal bunker. It had been ripped out to make more room for cargo. The fire was in the Admiralty's secret cargo stores. He threw the toggle switch that would close the enormous watertight doors, separating the bow from the boiler rooms. Then he turned on the first extinguishers that would begin pumping smothering steam into the forward cargo spaces.

Turned started out to the starboard wing. He had to grab onto the engine order telegraphs and move carefully from one handhold to another. The ship was already over by about fifteen degrees, and he knew from the builder's specifications that if it rolled past twenty-five degrees it could never right itself.

"Call out the list. Every degree," he ordered the quartermaster. "Tell wireless to send out a plain language signal. All stations. 'S.O.S. *Lusitania*. Come quickly. Listing severely.'"

He was nearly to the bridge wing hatchway when his whole world exploded.

The jolt knocked him down as if he had been hit with an ax. A deafening blast set his head ringing. He felt ice-cold hail pouring down on top of him, and it was a moment before he realized that it was the shattered glass from the wheelhouse windows. Lying on his back, he could see the damage control status board. A dozen lights were blinking crazily. The forward boiler room bulkhead had been incinerated, and firy gases were rushing through the hull. The whole front of the ship had been opened to the sea.

Turner climbed to his feet and felt the quartermaster trying to help him. "Sound abandon ship," he said, then worked his way as quickly as he could out onto the starboard wing.

The ship was still rolling, and he doubted that anything could check its list. But there was a more immediate danger. *Lusitania* had no bow, no foredeck. Yet she was still racing ahead, the full force of the sea pounding into her forward boiler room. Turner knew that the next bulkhead, separating the number one and the number two boiler rooms, could never withstand the pressure. When it gave way, his ship would sink instantly.

He needed to keep her afloat long enough to launch her lifeboats. But he couldn't put the boats into the water with *Lusitania* moving. If anyone were to be saved, he had to stop the ship.

Turner staggered back into the wheelhouse, took the handles of the telegraphs, and threw them to full astern. He would back the propellers with all the power that was left to him. It was his only hope of stopping The Greyhound before her own speed destroyed her.

Seven levels below, and nearly 500 feet astern, a dazed engineer saw the command on his telegraph. He threw his own handles to full astern, telling the bridge that he had received the order. Then he began spinning the valves that turned the steam from the high-pressure turbines toward the backing turbines. Above his head, the crossover steam lines began to vibrate like guitar strings. As he looked up, the piping parted, and jets of scalding steam fired down on top of him.

*   *   *

"HER ENGINES are exploding," Schwieger announced, his face still pressed in morbid fascination against the periscope. He was watching the angry clouds of steam that were suddenly blasting from *Lusitania*'s funnels. "Jesus, Willi, the whole ship is coming apart. She's diving. Like a submarine! What's left of her bow is already under water. But she's still moving forward. And still rolling to starboard. She's twisting herself into the ocean. Like a screw!"

VANDERBILT knew even before he had recovered his footing from the staggering explosion that *Lusitania* was doomed. The list was too severe, and already the bow was beginning to dive. He stumbled into the passageway and found Jennifer crumpled on the carpeted floor. He reached under her arms and locked his fingers across her back. She opened her eyes as he was lifting her to her feet.

"Come with me," he told her, the gentleness gone from his voice. "We have to get you to your lifeboat."

She hesitated, trying to pull free from his hold.

"Dammit, come with me." It was a stern order, and she obeyed immediately. "You have to get to your boat. This damn thing is sinking!"

"It can't," Jennifer protested feebly.

"It can, and it is," he said, pulling her after him through the door and back out onto the boat deck.

The ship's officers and groups of seamen were already rushing toward the boats. Then, overhead, there was the repeated blasting of the ship's whistle. "They're putting the boats over," Vanderbilt told her.

The first starboard lifeboat was directly ahead of them, and Vanderbilt led Jennifer toward it. Crewmen were taking up on the rope falls, lifting the boat from its steadying chocks. But the instant it was free, it swung away from them, out over the side. *Lusitania* was now listing twenty degrees to starboard. As the boats were lifted free, they hung straight down from the davits, their gunwales almost ten feet from the side of the ship. They were much too far away for the passengers to reach them.

The crewmen tried to haul the boats in close, using the stubbing chains that were supposed to check their swing. But each of the boats weighed several tons. With the list of the ship, no number of men could pull them back alongside.

"Stay here," Vanderbilt ordered Jennifer. He pushed through the crowd of passengers that was rapidly assembling next to the first boat and scampered up the sloping deck. He picked up one of the deck lounges and carried it back to the boat.

The officer saw what Vanderbilt was up to and reached out to help him. They turned the lounge chair over and stretched it like a gangplank from the ship's rail to the gunwale of the boat. A crewman began handing life jackets to the women in the first row of passengers.

Vanderbilt helped Jennifer get her arms through the holes in the jacket. He tied the belt across her chest, then tied the collar strap under her chin. "Get aboard," he told her.

She stepped to the rail, then looked down through the open wooden slats of the deck lounge. She couldn't see the side of the ship, which was already curving in under the deck. All she could see was the angry wash of white water that raced past almost fifty feet below. She jumped back into Vanderbilt's arms. "I can't," she screamed.

Vanderbilt leaned his face close to her ear. "Get out on that chair and get into the boat," he ordered menacingly. "Don't look down! Just look ahead of you."

"I can't," she cried, trying to pull away from him.

He took her chin in his hands and turned it toward him so that he was talking directly into her face. "If you go, the other women will follow. If you don't they'll all drown. Now get into that boat!"

The ship lurched another degree to starboard. The boat jumped inches farther away, and the crude gangplank shook for an instant.

"Go!" Vanderbilt told her. "Go before it's too late."

Jennifer stepped up to the rail. A seaman helped her find a step on top of the collapsible boat and took her arm to steady her. She reached out and grabbed the edges of the lounge chair. Then she pulled her dress up above her knees and knelt on the back of the chair.

Don't look down, Jennifer reminded herself. Then slowly but steadily, she began to crawl out into the gaping space between the ship and the lifeboat. Once she started, she never hesitated. In a few seconds, she was able to catch the gunwale of the lifeboat. Then she scampered forward and threw herself aboard.

A seaman stretched another lounge chair over the abyss, and within seconds other women were following Jennifer's lead. Some refused, determined to take their chances with the sinking ship. But within two minutes, the boat was filled with women, and with a half-dozen children whom they had brought across with them.

One of the crewmen scampered across the bridge and went to the stern of the boat to tend the falls. Another crossed and went to the bow.

"Lower away," the officer ordered. Crewmen freed the lines from the cleats, and the number one lifeboat began to sink toward the rushing sea below.

Vanderbilt touched a finger to his forehead in a salute toward

Jennifer. "He'll be waiting," he called to her. Then he turned away from the boat and sauntered back up the deck. Vanderbilt had no intention of trying to save himself. This, he thought, was as good a place to die as any. But he might still have a few minutes left. And there was another task he wanted to tend to.

Turner climbed to the signal bridge on top of the wheelhouse. He had backed his engines and could do nothing more to slow the ship. He had turned her toward the Old Head of Kinsale, hoping that every second she kept moving would carry them that much closer to shore. But he knew she couldn't go far. The shattered remnants of his foredeck had disappeared beneath the sea. The wave, created by the ship's momentum, was already crashing against the face of the superstructure, only two levels below. He guessed she might have a minute left, two at the most.

He turned aft to look after his passengers and screamed in rage at the slaughter he saw. Unlike the boats on the starboard side, the portside boats had swung inward as soon as they were raised from their chocks, crushing the crewmen who were tending their falls. Then they had dropped onto the deck and slid forward, cutting like a scythe through the passengers awaiting their escape. One of the boats had been levered out over the railing, only to be torn to pieces by the spike-like rivet heads that grew out of the ship's steel-plated side.

The passengers who saw that there was no escape from the port rail had rushed across the ship to the starboard side, pushing into those who were waiting to cross out onto the deck chairs and into the dangling starboard boats. In the confusion, two of the chairs had been jostled off the rail and fallen into the sea, carrying passengers with them. *Lusitania* was down to her last moments, yet only one of her lifeboats had been lowered away.

The number one boat had almost reached the water. It was dangling in open space, now almost twenty-five feet from the side of the ship and fifty feet below the davits from which it hung. After the swaying journey down, with the boat lurching unsteadily each time the falls were payed out, the sea seemed like a safe haven. The terrified passengers felt themselves breathing again.

And then the bow dropped. High above, on the boat deck, the two seamen who were tending the rope falls had misunderstood the officer's command. He had ordered the stern of the lifeboat to be lowered first, hoping to drop the boat into the rushing sea with the bow falls still taut. Instead, the bow hit the water while the stern was still suspended on the ropes. It swung wildly with the flow of the sea until the boat broached.

Jennifer felt herself being tossed through the air, with screaming bodies flying all around her. She slammed into the water and was buried in darkness as the huge lifeboat came down on top of her.

Lusitania's stern was climbing high out of the sea, her four propellers twisting slowly in the air. She was now leaning more than thirty degrees to her starboard side, her bridge buried in a torrent of white water. The Greyhound screamed in her death agony, a metallic roar as her machinery tore free from its mountings and slid forward, crashing through all her internal bulkheads. High above the dying ship, the weight of her towering funnels began to strain on the cables that supported them. There were loud whip snaps as the cables parted. The second stack broke free and fell over the side, landing like a giant tree across the flotsam of struggling survivors.

There were only seconds left, so Alfred Vanderbilt had to work quickly. He had taken the baskets as they were brought up from the ship's nursery and tied a life jacket around each one. He tucked the blankets tightly around the tiny mattresses so that each of the babies were held securely, as if by a safety belt. Now he was carrying the baskets out onto the deck, where they could float free as the ship sank.

A steward took him by the arm and tried to force him into a life jacket. "There's no time," he screamed. "You have to get over the side."

Vanderbilt tore free from the man and raced back into the writing room, where more babies were waiting. The steward threw the life jacket down on the deck and followed him inside to help him with the baskets.

"SHE'S STOPPED," Schwieger said. His voice had become a monotone, as if he were commenting on the play of a lawn bowling match. "Her stern is high in the air, swinging back and forth as if she were standing on her bow. Now, she's settling, rolling over on her starboard side as she slips under." Haupert endured a long, tense silence. Then Schwieger continued, "There she goes. She's slipped under rapidly. She's gone."

He remained crouched against the periscope for another minute, watching a sea that was clotted with bodies, some thrashing about wildly, others staring open-mouthed at the afternoon sun. He panned from side to side, finding nothing but clumps of deck debris and an ocean of human devastation. There wasn't a single lifeboat floating anywhere.

"Down scope," he whispered.

He stood silently, then dropped slowly down the ladder into the control room.

"Take her down to thirty feet," he whispered to his silent crewmen. "Set course for Fastnet. All ahead two-thirds. We'll stay under until sunset."

He stepped forward through the men, unable to look any of them in the eye. When he reached his cabin, he pulled the curtain closed behind him.

SCHULL

Day saw his car waiting before Sheehy's boat reached the dock. He jumped over with the first line and then ran to Tom Duffy.

"The message is sent," Duffy told him. "Your man at Crookhaven took it. But Miss McDevitt . . ."

Day looked into the car and saw that the passenger seat was empty. "What about Miss McDevitt?"

"She was hurt. Hit in the shooting at Emmett's place. I took her to Dr. Tierney. She's there now, and in a bad way, I think."

Then Day saw the awful stain on Tom Duffy's sleeves and the smear across the belly of his shirt. "Take me there. Please!" He ran around the car and started to climb into the passenger seat. But he stopped when he saw the blood clotted into the folds of the cushion and felt a sudden sickness rising in his gut. He knew that Shiela was finished, and he could only pray that he got to her in time.

"She asked me to take her to the radio station," Duffy explained, as he drove. "But then she sort of fell as we were gettin' into the car. I saw the blood and I wanted to take her straight to the doc's place, but she wouldn't hear of it. She said they'd never be sendin' the message if a stranger brought it to them. She had to take it to them herself."

He sped around a curve without slowing down, rocking the car onto two wheels. Neither of them noticed the danger. "Such a little thing, she is," Duffy thought out loud. "And so much blood."

He skidded the car to a stop in front of a row house with a fresh coat of whitewash. The lamps in the windows were still bright, left burning from their all-night vigil. Dr. Tierney had thrown his trousers and a collarless white shirt over his nightshirt. The tail of the nightshirt hung out over his beltline. He smiled, but there was no joy in his eyes.

"I'm sorry, commander," he said. He turned to lead Day into one of the bedrooms. "It was such a terrible wound. I couldn't close it. All I could do was take away the pain."

When the door opened, Father Connors turned away from the bedside. "I gave her the last rites," the priest told Day as he lifted the purple stole over his head and folded it carefully into his jacket pocket. Then he explained, "A final forgiveness," and stepped out of the room.

Shiela's white face was staring at the ceiling. She tipped her head as she heard him enter, and her eyes flashed with fear. "Don't let them take me," she begged in the little voice that was left to her. "Please, don't let them take me."

He rushed to her side and reached for her hand. It was icy cold. "Who, Shiela? Who's going to take you? There's no one here but me."

"You won't let them take me," she repeated, trying to raise her head from the pillow. Day knew who "they" were. The English. The Irish. Everyone in her life. In Shiela's mind, they all hated her. She thought she had betrayed them all.

He fell to his knees beside her bed. "You saved them," he told her. "The message got through. You saved them."

Her eyes brightened. "Oh, thank God." He felt her squeeze his hand. "Then there'll be no more children for the cemetery," she whispered.

"No," Day told her. "No more children. You saved them all."

There was a moment of peace in her smile. And then her breathing stopped.

Tierney came quietly beside Day and put his hand on his shoulder. With the other hand, he lifted the sheet over Shiela's face. "It was a terrible wound," he repeated. "I don't know how she ever made it all the way out of Crookhaven."

"She had children to save," Day told him.

Father Connors was waiting in the parlor. "I'm sure she's already in heaven," the priest consoled.

If heaven was a land of peace, Day thought, then Shiela was surely there. The razor-edged loyalties that were cutting her to pieces no longer mattered. In death, she had found a place she could call home.

"Will you tell them?" Day asked.

"The townspeople?" Connors said.

Day nodded.

"Is that a good idea, commander? I mean for your sake. Do you want the word getting out that she died carrying a message to the Germans?"

"I want her neighbors to know that she died trying to save people. No matter whose side they think she was on, I want them to know what she was trying to do."

The priest sighed. "I'll tell them at the graveside."

"Where?" Day asked.

"At our cemetery. There's a place we use for strangers. A lovely place." He put a fatherly hand on the commander's shoulder. "Or maybe you'd like to tell them yourself. You know her better than we did."

"I won't be here," Day answered.

Father Connors looked stunned.

"I'm a traitor, Father. It *was* a message to the Germans. The British sent a man to stop me. They'll be sending another."

"Surely they'll understand," the priest protested. "It was innocent lives you were thinking about."

"War isn't about life, Father Connors. It's about death. My job is destroying the enemy. Talking with the enemy is treason."

"But where will you go?"

Day shrugged. "Someplace where Shiela would have gone. I'm a man without a country."

The undertaker stepped up close to Connors. "Where should I take her, Father?" he asked.

Connors looked puzzled. "There'll be nobody to sit with her. I suppose you should bring her to the church."

The two of them started into the bedroom.

"Father Connors," Day called after them. The priest stopped in the doorway.

"Could you bury her in the children's cemetery?"

"The deserted place, where the little orphans are?"

"Yes."

He came back into the parlor. "I don't know. No one's been buried there since . . . I don't know how long."

"I think Shiela would like to be there," Day said. "It was important to her."

"But it's so far from . . ." He was about to say that it was far from her home. But he realized that she had no home. "Yes, I suppose we could do that. If you think that's where she would like to be."

Day walked out to his car, started the engine, and drove the short distance to Shiela's cottage. He found the suitcase that she was going to carry into exile still on the bed where she had left it. It was open, with her few things flowing out. He packed them carefully, and set the suitcase next to the closet. Then he began throwing his own things into a bag.

There was a pounding on the front door. He jumped away from the window, pressing himself into a corner of the bedroom.

"Commander Day! Commander Day!" It was Chief Gore who was calling as he continued rattling the door.

He edged to the window and glanced from behind the curtain. The chief was alone. He bolted to the door and snapped it open.

"It's *Lusitania*," Gore screamed into his face. "She's been sunk. We got the S.O.S. at the station. Then *Juno* went out and radioed that she was gone."

"Where?" Day demanded. "Where did she sink?"

"Off the Old Head of Kinsale. There are no lifeboats. Everyone's in the water."

KINSALE

SMALL BOATS from all along the coast converged on the Old Head of Kinsale. The first arrived at twilight and began sorting through the floating debris in search for survivors. They could be selective. Even in the fading light, they could see an arm waving from atop of a piece of decking, or the splash of a swimmer whose stroke was failing. They could rush through the wreckage of the dead and save the living.

It was after dark when the boats from Schull reached the scene, and they could see nothing beyond the small circle of light that fell from their lamps. They had to rush to every shape that appeared on the surface, reaching out for corpses as well as for survivors. They stacked bodies on their decks like cord wood, leaving space for the living they hoped they might find.

Day was on the bow of Sheehy's boat. They motored into a drift of debris, the random artifacts of a world that had disappeared. There were upholstered chairs that had broken free from the library, and dining room tables, one still covered with a linen cloth. There was a broad-brimmed lady's hat, with a bow at its crown and a pale satin ribbon trailing behind. Wine bottles bobbed like buoys, and deck chairs, still folded to a comfortable angle, lay inches beneath the surface. Life jackets were everywhere, floating empty with their belts and ties open. A raft drifted by, a pair of men's shoes set neatly at its center.

He asked Sheehy to shut down the engine while he listened to the stillness. "Hello!" he called, and then waved the lamp in the air. But the only response was the gentle slapping of the sea against the boat.

The tide was coming in, so he pointed Sheehy farther out to sea. If this were the front edge of the debris, then there would certainly be more behind it. The motor coughed and they chugged past a piano bench that had a window curtain tangled on one of its legs. Day held the lamp higher and was startled by the graceful curve of a lifeboat's hull that drifted directly ahead. Sheehy yelled as he saw it, sure that they had found survivors, and tried to pull his boat alongside it. But the hull flipped over in his wash. It was only a small piece of a boat, strakes that had been torn away from the hull but had held together in their original shape.

They saw a man's body, face down and spread-eagled, the tails of the jacket pointing in opposite directions. They dragged it up over the side and laid it gently in the bilge. There were arms protruding from a floating life jacket. Beneath the jacket they found a young boy dressed in knickers.

He had slipped through the oversized life preserver and drowned with his hands tied over his head. As they reached the dark water, they saw a colorless face staring back up at them. It was a matronly woman with a jeweled necklace resting on her shoulders. The top of her body was formally attired, but someone had torn her skirt off at the waist to make it possible for her to swim.

"They're all dead!" one of the men said, looking around at the desolate waters.

"The earlier boats must have gotten the survivors," Sheehy answered.

"Let's keep searching," Day said. "There might still be someone out here."

He was thinking of Jennifer, as he had every moment since Chief Gore had pounded on the door of the cottage. He had sailed from Schull with the thought of her trembling in a lifeboat perhaps battered and bloodied by her terrible ordeal. He had to get to her. But now he was afraid of finding her. He fought against the image in his mind of her still face staring up at him from the water. As they came alongside each drifting corpse, he felt a shameful joy that it wasn't a young woman, that the hair wasn't long and dark, that the sea had claimed someone else.

They stopped the engine again, and Day was about to call out. But the instant the engine stilled, he heard a gasping voice from the darkness of his starboard bow.

"Don't!" he cautioned, as Sheehy was about to restart the engine. Day carefully lifted an oar and dipped it over the side. He used it as a paddle, moving the boat silently toward the failing voice.

It was a cork raft with two men clinging to its edge. The forms of two women were sprawled across the net of roping that served as its deck. One of the men saw them, let go of the raft and started to swim to the boat. Before he had made two strokes he disappeared.

Day threw the oar back into the boat and plunged over the side. His momentum carried him down into the blackness, where he collided with the sinking man. He clutched under his arms and kicked back up to the surface. Sheehy and his crew reached out over the gunwale and hauled the man out of the water.

He swam to the raft, grabbed the rope at its edge, and then stretched up for Sheehy's hand. Together, they hauled the raft alongside. One of the women on its rope deck was alive, weak with shock but still breathing. The other was dead. The man whose voice they had heard was hauled aboard last. He began to cry hysterically as soon as he found himself safely in the boat. The two men, he told them, had made it to the drifting raft and then hauled the women out of the sea. One, he thought, was already dead when they brought her aboard. They didn't know one another. He didn't remember seeing any of them aboard *Lusitania*.

They continued on further, stopping again and again to call and listen. They heard another cry and hauled aboard a young girl in a sailor dress who seemed none the worse for her hours in the water. She had been with her mother until they were separated by a mob rushing to *Lusitania's* fantail. The rising sea had simply floated the girl off the deck.

Another woman, dressed only in her underwear, was clinging to a half-submerged deck chair. They thought she was dead until one of Sheehy's crew reached down and grabbed her hair. She screamed, slapping his hand away, but then cried when she saw the faces of her rescuers.

All through the night, they cruised back and forth. They stopped bringing bodies aboard in order to leave room for any survivors they might find. At first light, they turned and headed for the dark shape of the Old Head. They carried five living passengers from *Lusitania* and a cargo of six dead bodies.

The sun was up when they turned into Kinsale harbor, where a decrepit flotilla of small boats jammed the piers. The docks were a confusion of seamen, some with old blankets wrapped around wet clothes that were sticking to their bodies. There were faces animated with tales of rescues made off the keels of capsized boats, from floating deck planking, and from the sea itself. There were expressionless faces, stunned by a hundred images of death that had come suddenly, catching its victims in random moments of life. A British naval officer rushed to the dock as Sheehy tied up his boat. He gathered the survivors and hurried them up to the shore without even sparing a glance for the dead.

Day worked his way up the pier, questioning the seamen who were able to talk.

"Were there many survivors?"

There were. Most of them had been brought in early and taken into family homes. The British were rounding up all they could find and bringing them to a church and a schoolhouse.

"Was there a list? Was anyone keeping a record of their names?"

He must be crazy. Boats had put in all around the harbor, some farther west at Courtmacsherry Bay and Clonakilty Bay. It would take days to get a full accounting.

"And the dead?"

There was morgue in a warehouse by the harbor head. One of the seamen pointed out the building. In Courtmacsherry, the dead had been laid out in a field right next to the mud flats where the bodies had been left by the tide.

Day started at the church. A British sailor in white leggings guarded the door with a rifle carried at the port. No one was being admitted, and

Day was referred to the officer in charge, a lieutenant who had been rushed over from Queenstown.

"Name?" the lieutenant demanded.

"Her name is Beecham. Jennifer Beecham."

"No," the officer corrected. "Your name. I need the name of anyone who inquires."

Were they already hunting for him? he wondered. The Royal Navy had a disaster on its hands. He was a witness who knew that England had played a role in the atrocity.

"Day. Mr. William Day."

"Nationality?" the officer demanded as he wrote.

"English," he said. "I'm a personal friend of Sir Peter Beecham's. It's his daughter I'm looking for."

"Oh, excuse me, Mr. Day." The officer was suddenly solicitous. "There are reporters, you know. Many of them from foreign papers. We don't want them talking to the passengers." He was already flipping through a handwritten list of names. "I'm sorry. Jennifer Beecham doesn't seem to be here. I don't think she's at the school, either." He looked up from his list, his expression turning solemn. "Have you tried the warehouse?"

The navy, Day understood, had already begun its coverup. They were frantic to find the passengers before they could speak with the press. They didn't want any witnesses to the absence of escorts. And they wouldn't want witnesses to the messages they had been sending through the compromised radio station at Crookhaven. He guessed that there were navy people looking for him.

He used another name when he reached the warehouse but repeated his connection with Sir Peter Beecham. A naval officer led him inside, where a medical officer insisted on tying a surgical mask across his face. Then he was escorted up and down the aisles that were formed by the rows of bodies laid out on the floor.

He walked quickly, embarrassed to stare at people who had been reduced to carnival displays. There had been no time to compose the bodies. Mouths were gaping open, and limbs were scattered at awkward angles. Hair was tossed wildly, and clothes were colorless, matted across the forms that they covered.

He slowed only when there was a young woman's form, and he glanced at the face for just the instant it took to be sure it wasn't Jennifer's. Then he stopped dead.

There was a slim woman in what seemed to be an ivory-colored gown, a tone that Jennifer favored. Long, slim legs protruded from beneath the hem of the dress. The hands seemed familiar. The wide collar of the bodice showed a graceful shoulder and a long neck. Still secure around the neck was a string of pearls. He raised his glance. Long dark hair was matted over the face.

"You recognize her?" the doctor asked.

Day couldn't speak, but his stare said that he did.

The doctor stepped carefully between the bodies, bent over the young woman, and gently parted the hair.

Day's breath escaped. It wasn't Jennifer who was staring wildly up at the ceiling.

"You've been to the church?" the doctor asked as soon as they finished their search. Day nodded, pushing the mask down from his face.

"There's still hope," the doctor said. "Hundreds are unaccounted for. Many of them are being cared for in homes all along the coast. It may be days before we have them all."

"Thank you," Day answered. There was certainly reason to hope. But he knew that many of those not accounted for would float in with the next tide. And many more would forever be locked in the steel coffin that rested at the bottom, fifteen miles from the beach.

He wandered through Kinsale, asking anyone who seemed to be involved with the rescue. An old fisherman directed him to a house on the hill where a woman fitting Day's description had been brought. He raced to the house, where an Irish family was caring for three of the survivors. Jennifer was not one of them.

In the afternoon, he begged a ride on a small farm wagon around the Old Head, to Courtmacsherry Bay. The town, he found, was nearly under military siege. Navy units were guarding the bodies that were being carried in from the mudflats. The survivors had been herded together like prisoners and were being taken in a commandeered bus to Kinsale.

"Damned English are acting as if this were a battlefield," an American reporter complained to him, taking him for one of the Irish fishermen. "They won't let us near the survivors."

It was evening when he returned to Kinsale. Here, too, he found martial law. The navy had set up tables in front of the church. They were answering all inquiries with a printed list that alphabetized the names of the survivors. Day approached the table cautiously, making sure that none of the officers standing by looked familiar. He scanned the list. Jennifer wasn't named as one of the living.

"William! William!"

He turned to his name and saw Father Connors coming down the church steps, the dark stole of the death rites flapping from his neck. Connors wrapped a strong arm around his shoulders and led him forcefully away from the tables.

"They're looking for you," the priest whispered as he guided him across the street. "There are naval officers in Schull, asking for you."

"I was expecting them," Day said, showing little concern.

Connors was plainly frightened. "They took over the radio station. Your chief told me that they've taken all the files. There are two armed guards standing in front of Emmett's house. They found him this morning. Him and your young officer friend. The bastards even came into the church to make certain of poor Shiela."

"Bastards," Day agreed.

"You can't go back, William. You've got to get out of here."

"I'm looking for someone, Father," he answered angrily. "I have to find her."

Connors shook his head furiously. "Don't be daft, man. You don't have time. We'll find her for you. We've got to get you off the streets."

He had ushered William Day across the square in front of the church and into one of the narrow streets that climbed the hill. "I have friends here in Kinsale. They'll take you in. And they can find anyone you're looking for."

He pushed on the picket gate of a small whitewashed house, glancing back over his shoulder as he prodded Day up the path. "Believe me, lad. We'll find your friend. You just stay inside. Do you hear me?"

Day stopped at the doorstep. "Your friends could get in a lot of trouble, Father. I'm a fugitive."

"My friends have been in a lot of trouble for 300 years, William." He tapped on the door. "Now get yourself inside. I'll be coming back for you."

EMDEN

She was down! Bauer's little boats had done what the kaiser's Imperial Navy had dared not even attempt. They had picked the prize out of Britain's seafaring empire and sunk her in her home waters.

The staff officers at the flotilla headquarters were ecstatic. They had watched their commander focus on *Lusitania* from the moment he had learned of her valuable cargo. They had seen him feint part of the British fleet out of position, sending them off to Land's End. Then they helped him set his trap against impossible odds. Now they rejoiced in his success.

Emden's radios had picked up *Lusitania's* S.O.S. She had been hit within a few hours of the time they had predicted—incredibly precisely, considering that she was on the end of a transatlantic voyage. She was listing, which meant that Schwieger had put several torpedoes below her water line. Would he be able to surface and shoot her to pieces with his deck gun? Then they had heard *Juno*'s report. *Lusitania* was gone, a spreading wake of wreckage marking the spot. With no report from U-20, all they could do was speculate as to how it must have happened.

"It had to be the guncotton," Klaus Schopfner assured Captain Bauer. He was well aware of his commander's last-second effort to call off the attack. The hoax message from Ireland had made him doubt his own decisions. But now Bauer was vindicated. U-20 didn't have the firepower to sink *Lusitania*, unless she was incredibly lucky. Or unless The Greyhound was carrying a cargo that needed little incentive to explode.

Then came a congratulatory message from Admiral von Pohl. It praised Bauer's genius and told him that the German submarine was now the most important warship in the world. "Never again," von Pohl exalted, "will England dare to hide her war cargoes behind women and children. Never again will civilians dare to put their faith in the Royal Navy."

But then the British accounts came in over the radios. Torpedo after torpedo pumped into the crippled ship while women and children struggled for their lives. Lifeboats machine gunned. Rescue ships driven off by murdering Huns.

Bauer sank into melancholy silence as the British reports continued. Some survivors had seen two submarines, both cruising through a sea of drowning women, refusing to offer a hand of rescue.

"Transparent lies," Bauer's officers assured him. "No one can believe such nonsense." Of course they were lies. Bauer knew there could have been only one submarine at the scene.

"Where's Schwieger?" he demanded. "We need to know the details. We have to report what actually happened." But his radio stayed silent. Schwieger had nothing to say about the greatest triumph of his life.

They opened a bottle of brandy to toast their brave crewmen, and the flotilla commander had no trouble raising his glass. He loved the men who took his frail boats out to battle, and he was in awe of their cheerful courage. But then someone proposed a toast to the great German victory in the shallow waters off the Irish coast. Bauer set down his brandy and retired morosely to his quarters. "Inform me the instant we hear from U-20," he said as he left the celebration behind.

His operations officer waited a polite interval, then knocked on the captain's door. He carried Bauer's half-filled glass with him as he entered.

"She was carrying guncotton, captain," he said again. "An armed cruiser carrying contraband. You can't let yourself listen to the English lies."

Bauer took the drink and sipped it. "I'm thinking about the Americans who are listening," he said. "They don't know anything about guncotton. But they know about women and children."

He stared for a moment at the brandy, then handed his glass back to his staff officer. "I'm afraid it may be an English victory that we're drinking to."

LONDON

CAPTAIN Reginald Hall was exhausted. He sat at a desk illuminated by a single lamp, pressing his fingertips into his burning eyes. Was there anything he had forgotten? Was there anything more that he could do? Go over it again, he told himself. Make sure. Even the most insignificant mistake could be disastrous. He opened the folder on his desk and turned again through the orders he had issued and the messages he had sent.

The passengers. Admiral Coke was rounding up the survivors and taking their official depositions. The testimonies would be rushed to the Admiralty, sorted, and edited. Then a few carefully selected "eyewitness" accounts would be given to the press as full documentation of the German atrocity. A few passengers might decide to speak for themselves. Someone might tell a reporter that he had not seen the submarines cruising through the wreckage with their machine guns blazing. Or someone might remember that none of Lusitania's boats had ever been launched. But these petty inconsistencies would be lost in the blare of lurid publicity that the Admiralty was already orchestrating. The world would believe the first account, and he had that account well under control.

The official inquiry. There would have to be a legal proceeding to firmly establish the cause and the guilt for the disaster. He couldn't stop the donkey coroner of Kinsale from holding the hearing he was proposing to establish the cause of death of the bodies that populated his city. But he could control the testimony that the man would hear. And that little sideshow would be lost in the public trial he was planning for London. A trial that would exonerate the Admiralty of all responsibility, admit certain inadequacies of the ship's master, but convict the German submarine captain of mass murder. Hall had already sent his recommendations for the men who should serve as the judge and jury. The Admiralty was already busy writing the verdict.

The guncotton. He had cabled Sir Peter Beecham in New York and asked for the list of items in Lusitania's cargo manifest. There were cheese, firs, and several hundred barrels of iced oysters. New York port officials had signed a manifest that made no mention of guncotton. Beecham had done a thoroughly professional job!

The Americans. He had been certain to deliver minute-by-minute accounts of the atrocity to the American ambassador, all through a dinner party he was hosting at the embassy. His radiomen had intercepted the report that the ambassador rushed to Washington, and his cryptographers had broken its code. "An unnecessary and unprovoked attack on a civilian passenger ship," the ambassador had written, "followed by a wanton disregard for human life."

Perfect, Hall told himself. The ambassador had even shared the report with his guests, the representatives of half a dozen other governments. That was an unexpected bonus. The guests had promptly sent similar reports to their own capitals.

The Crookhaven radio station. Hall had ordered his men to confiscate the message files. The official radio logs that would be presented as evidence at the inquiry would contain no reference to the course instructions he had sent to *Lusitania*. There would be no mention of a rendezvous at Coningbeg with a fleet that he had already ordered to Land's End.

The radio crew at Crookhaven wouldn't be a problem. The chief was a career man who would know that his choice was between a pension and a naval prison. The coding clerk was dead.

Events, Hall concluded, were pretty much under control. But there were still a few open items. Admiral Coke had sent a message recalling *Lusitania*'s escorts, and there was no way he could change the admiral's message log. People were bound to ask why, with submarines active in the area, the ships intended to protect *Lusitania* were tied to their piers in Queenstown? But perhaps Coke would have enough sense to edit his own logs. Or perhaps they could fall back on Admiral Fisher's view that the ancient escorts were more a danger to themselves than a source of survival for *Lusitania*.

Hall's biggest problem was the area commander for the southwestern coast of Ireland, Commander William Day. He knew about the course message to *Lusitania*. Hall's own agent had reported that the commander had even argued against sending it. And then he had authorized a message in a German code to a radio station in Germany. What, Hall wondered, had he told the Germans? What would he tell a court of inquiry?

Commander Day would be easy to discredit. An officer of the Royal Navy sending coded information to Germany. He could easily be made to appear an enemy agent, perhaps even connected with the sinister German scheme to sink The Greyhound. But first, Hall had to find him.

The man had disappeared, and, so far, the Naval Intelligence officers who had been sent to get him had come up empty-handed.

But where could he go? An Englishman couldn't simply disappear in Ireland. Sooner or later he would have to come back to England. And Hall would be waiting for him.

He closed the file and switched off his desk lamp. He had done all that he could. Now it was up to the Americans.

WASHINGTON

PRESIDENT Woodrow Wilson wore his bathrobe into the Oval Office where the secretary of state and his counselor were waiting. He had been relaxing in his bed, reading the afternoon papers, when news of the attack on *Lusitania* had reached Washington. Now he was about to hear the grim details.

"Mr. President," Lansing said, rising as Wilson entered. William Jennings Bryan tried to clear his lap of papers so that he, too, could stand, but Wilson was already seated before he could get up.

"Americans have been killed?" the president asked, referring to the note that had been brought upstairs to his bedroom.

"That seems to be the case," Bryan reported. He had the cable from the ambassador to the Court of Saint James, and he held his glasses up to his face as he searched for the relevant information. "There are over a thousand passengers dead or unaccounted for. It appears that at least a hundred of them are U.S. citizens."

"Dear God. How could so many . . . weren't there lifeboats . . ." Wilson was stunned by the count.

"Apparently she sank very quickly," Bryan said.

"There seems to have been several submarines," Lansing explained. "If they were all firing torpedoes . . ."

"We really don't have the facts," Bryan interrupted. "Our ambassador is simply relaying what he was told by the British. He hasn't had time to verify any of this. And the newspapers are complaining about an Admiralty blackout. I don't think we'll have all details for several days."

"But I'll have to say something," Wilson reminded them. "The American press will be calling for a statement." He looked from one adviser to the other, searching for a suggestion.

"Perhaps you should simply lament the loss of life and tell them we are trying to ascertain the facts," Bryan offered. "That would certainly sound prudent . . . responsible."

The president nodded as he considered the idea. Then he looked toward Lansing. "Do you agree, Robert?"

"With all respect to Secretary Bryan," Lansing began, "I think something much stronger is required. The Germans have knowingly attacked American citizens. They have killed a hundred of our countrymen. To my mind, that constitutes an act of war."

Bryan's round face swelled with outrage. "Rubbish," he snapped. "The Germans have sunk an English ship. They're already at war with England!"

"An English ship known to be carrying Americans," Lansing snapped back. He turned to Wilson. "Americans whose lives they were responsible for protecting."

"An English ship known to be carrying ammunition," the secretary of state countered. "We can hardly hold the Germans responsible for Americans who choose to book passage on ammunition ships."

"Ammunition?" Wilson's eyes widened beyond the wire frames of his glasses. "*Lusitania* was carrying ammunition?"

"Ridiculous," Lansing said. "I can assure you, Mr. President, that there is no ammunition listed in *Lusitania*'s cargo manifest. But even if there were, it would be totally beside the point . . ." He stopped when he saw the president raise a hand in the plea for silence.

"If there were ammunition aboard *Lusitania*, we certainly should have known about it," Wilson mused. "And if we knew about it, then we certainly should have prohibited Americans from boarding her. Either way, we stand indicted." He glanced at his two advisers and saw that neither understood the point he was trying to make. "If we didn't know about the ammunition, then we're terribly stupid. And if we did, then we're totally insensitive to the safety of our own people. Either way, this administration is indicted." Lansing, he saw, was beginning to understand. A tight smile was appearing under his meticulous moustache. "So," Wilson concluded, "our position has to be that there was no ammunition aboard *Lusitania*. Isn't that so?"

"I agree completely," Lansing said.

Bryan was already shaking his head in protest. "But still, the Americans were sailing into a war zone aboard a belligerent ship. It isn't as if the Germans had shot them down in the streets of Berlin."

It was the same debate they had had after an American had been killed aboard *Faloba*. Only this time the stakes were much higher. Wilson could hide behind legal niceties when one obscure citizen had been victimized. Now he would have to explain why a hundred dead Americans weren't a sufficient provocation for him to take action.

He stood and paced behind his desk, his chin high, his hands folded behind his back. "As I see it, we have only two choices. Either deny the German right to attack ships carrying Americans and call them severely to task, or grant their right and prohibit Americans from sailing on English ships."

"We can't force the Germans to assure that there are no Americans aboard before attacking an enemy ship," Bryan said.

"We can't prohibit Americans from their constitutional rights," Lansing countered.

But Wilson wasn't weighing legalities. He was guessing at public reaction. He wouldn't be pleading his case before German voters. When he stood for reelection, it would be Americans who would be casting the ballots.

He turned to his advisers. "I think we have to condemn this barbarous assault on U.S. citizens," he decided. "I think we have to hold Germany strictly accountable."

William Jennings Bryan folded the papers in his lap, then slowly removed his glasses. "If that is your decision, Mr. President, then I must respectfully ask you to accept my resignation. I simply can't support such a one-sided policy."

Robert Lansing tried to look humble. He was the obvious choice to be the new secretary of state. His political star was rising.

PARIS

WINSTON Churchill folded the cable he had just been given and turned to General French. "I'm afraid, general, that I have to get back to London immediately." He stood and stuffed the message into his jacket pocket. "*Lusitania* has been sunk."

"*Lusitania?*" General French went white with shock. "How? Where?"

"Off the Irish coast," Churchill said, retrieving the brandy from the table beside his chair and downing the few drops left in the glass. "I don't have the details. Just that it was submarines, and that there is a considerable loss of life."

"My God," the general said, rising to console his friend. "The audacity. The damned audacity." He placed a hand on Churchill's shoulder. "I'm just thankful that you were here. Not back at the Admiralty, at the helm. There will be hell to pay for this."

Churchill shrugged. "I can't say that it much matters where I happen to be. The fact is that she was sunk during my watch. So I bear full responsibility. An old navy tradition."

"You're not going to resign?"

"I suppose I'll have to." Then the First Lord of the Admiralty gave a puckish smile. "But don't worry, general. It's not nearly as permanent as falling on one's sword."

Churchill went to his bedroom to pack his things while General French summoned a staff car to take his guest back to the channel. The general was waiting in the foyer of the mansion when Churchill came down the curved stairs, ahead of the corporal who was carrying his luggage.

"You should reconsider, Winston. The king will need your services now more than ever."

"I have considered," he answered, holding out an arm so that a private could help him on with his topcoat. "I've been considering for a long time."

General French was plainly puzzled. "But . . . this just happened. How could you have known?"

"It was inevitable," Churchill said. "If not *Lusitania*, then some other ship. Once the Germans departed from the rules of encounter, it was only a matter of time before they'd involve themselves in an atrocity. Only a matter of time before the First Lord of the Admiralty would have to shoulder the blame. But there's a bright side, general. The stalemate in the trenches? I think you'll soon have Americans to tip the balance in your favor. I think that at this very moment, for the first time, you can count on winning the war."

"Americans?" French questioned.

Winston Churchill found a cigar in his jacket pocket and placed it unlit in the corner of his mouth. "*Lusitania*," he reminded his host. "She's a favorite with American society. It wouldn't surprise me if some of Woodrow Wilson's closest friends were aboard."

He winked at General French, whose expression showed that he was beginning to understand.

"So try not to take this too hard," Churchill recommended. "I'll be back!"

NEW YORK

SIR PETER Beecham had rushed back to his post as soon as he received the first fragmented reports of the sinking. The news hadn't been all that distressing. According to the reporters who called his Long Island home, *Lusitania* had been hit but was still afloat. One reporter thought she had been beached along the Irish coast. The other had it on good authority that she was already safe in Queenstown. They knew his daughter was among the passengers and wondered what he had heard from her.

"Everything is perfectly all right," he had assured Anne, who had begun to cry as soon as he told her. "They say *Lusitania* may have put into Queenstown."

"But the passengers?" Anne had begged. "Jennifer?"

Peter had called Cunard with Anne standing by his side and been put through to Charles Sumner, who had just rushed back from his own weekend. "She put out an S.O.S. and reported a list," Sumner told him. "That's all I know. I haven't heard anything about her being in Queenstown, although that would be the most likely place for her to put in."

"Sumner feels she's probably in Queenstown," he'd told his wife, putting the best possible inference on the meager information he had received. Then he'd promised her he would call as soon as he heard anything, kissed her goodbye, and headed back to his office in New York.

The first hint of a disaster was waiting for him. His clerk handed him two cables, one from the Admiralty reporting that *Lusitania* had gone down. The other was from Naval Intelligence, demanding to know the complete content of *Lusitania*'s official cargo manifest. He had told his clerk to respond with the cargo list. His own difficult efforts had gone into a message that he penciled directly to the First Lord of the Admiralty and had sent out over his priority channel.

MY DAUGHTER, JENNIFER BEECHAM, ABOARD LUSITANIA. PLEASE ADVISE ME OF HER WHEREABOUTS AS SOON AS POSSIBLE. PLEASE.

He waited throughout the night, long after he had sent most of his staff home, counting the hours until it would be dawn on the south Irish coast. Surely, by then, the passengers would be landed and his daughter would be found. Someone would get back to him.

Charles Sumner called. Cunard had forbidden him to make any statement, but he thought Beecham should know that the ship had sunk quickly. "I'm sorry to be telling you this," Sumner said, "but apparently there were heavy losses. Cunard says they could run into the hundreds."

"Are there any names?" Beecham begged.

"No. None at all. But I'll be staying here, Sir Peter. As soon as something comes in, I'll let you know."

The *New York Times* reached him. They were retracting their earlier story that the ship was safe. They now had a man in Queenstown, and he was reporting a horrendous loss of life. Had he been in contact with anyone in England? Had heard anything from his daughter?"

"No," he whispered. "Nothing. Nothing at all."

If the papers had it, then Anne could learn the horrible details at any moment. He had to prepare her. He lifted his telephone and listened patiently while one operator handed him off to another, until his butler came on the line.

"Is she awake?" Peter whispered, as if his voice might disturb her.

"She is, sir," the man answered. And after a brief pause, "Sir Peter, the *Times* called. They told her Miss Jennifer's ship was sunk."

"Damn!" he cursed. He should be there with her. But he couldn't leave the radio that might bring him word that Jennifer was safe.

The phone was quiet for several moments, and then he heard Anne's anxious voice. "Have you heard from her, Peter?"

"Not yet, my dear, but it's much too soon. I've wired London, and . . ."

"The *Times* said there were few survivors," Anne interrupted frantically.

"Nonsense," he said angrily. "The damned newspapers never know what they're talking about. Sumner tells me that there were some losses but that . . ."

"Sumner told you she was in Queenstown," she cut in. He could hear an edge of hysteria in her voice.

"Anne, listen to me. *Lusitania* is a huge ship. They would have had plenty of time to put the boats over the side. And Jennifer would be in one of the first boats over. First-class women are always the first to be put into the boats."

"Are you certain, Peter?" his wife begged.

"Of course I'm certain. I'll probably be hearing from her at any moment."

He suggested that she try and get some sleep, promised that he would call the instant he heard, and sent her a kiss. He hung up the phone, hating himself for the lies he was telling her. *Lusitania* was a huge ship. And they should have plenty of time to put boats over the side. Except for the guncotton. If it had exploded, then there wouldn't have been any time at all. He would never be able to tell Anne the truth about the guncotton.

Midnight passed. It was already daylight in Ireland. And there was still no response to his cable to Churchill. He phoned Cunard, and Sumner answered the telephone quickly. "No. I'm sorry, Sir Peter. There's been nothing more. The Admiralty has taken over all the radio and telegraph stations. Even Alfred Booth has no idea of what's going on."

Peter went down the hall to his radio room. The operator was sitting at his station, drinking coffee to keep himself alert.

"My message to the First Lord," Peter said.

"Nothing yet," the man answered sympathetically. "There's been nothing at all on the London channels."

"Send it again," Beecham said. "And this time please copy it to Admiral Fisher."

The radioman set his coffee aside and reached for the message.

Beechman was sitting drowsily at his desk when his telephone rang. He snatched it up and heard Anne's voice. Only then did he realize that it was morning.

"Peter, I'm frantic," Anne began. "You must be able to find out something."

"I know, my dear. I'm concerned myself. But the communications facilities in Ireland are quite primitive. And the Admiralty seems to have them tied up with emergency traffic. It may be a while before we hear from her."

"There are no reports?" she said incredulously. "Peter, are you telling me everything?"

"Of course I am. I'm quite sure she's safe. Probably furious that she can't get a message to us."

He finished the conversation, then walked down the hall toward the radio room. It was noontime in Ireland, almost a full day after *Lusitania* had been hit. Someone had to know who had survived.

Beecham heard the dots and dashes of an incoming message as soon as he opened the door. He rushed over to the radio operator and read the words as the man was writing them down on his message pad. "Several submarines." "Torpedo after torpedo fired into the sinking hull." "Lifeboats machine gunned." The words sickened him like fists punching into his gut. His head flooded with horrible images of Jennifer's last moments. He began to feel the terror she must have felt when a submarine slid up next to her lifeboat and the leering gunners took their aim.

"Jesus," he cried out in his agony. He staggered out of the room and, steadying himself against the corridor wall, managed to get back to his desk. He lifted the telephone and dialed the Cunard number.

"Have you seen it?" he begged Charles Sumner. "Is it true?"

"It just came in," Sumner said in a barely audible voice. "I can't believe it. They must have known her course. They must have had all their submarines waiting for her. Why, Peter? What in God's name was she carrying?"

He hung up the phone and tried not to think of *Lusitania*'s cargo. He fought back the images of Jennifer's last moments. But there was one image that he could not stifle. That was their moment of parting on the deck of *Lusitania*, when his daughter had told him that she loved him.

It was the most painful image of all.

KINSALE

DAY JUMPED up from the parlor chair as soon as he heard the squeak of the front gate and rushed to the top of the basement stairs. He closed the door behind him and then pressed against it, waiting for the knock on the front door. The soft tap told him that the caller was a friend.

"Father Connors sent me," a man's voice whispered.

Day heard the door close quietly, and then the landlady stepped toward the cellar steps and called his name. He came cautiously out of hiding and found a tall young man, scarcely through his teens, standing in the center of the room.

"Tom Downey." They shook hands. "Father Connors has a boat waiting for you in Courtmacsherry. He said he has an errand to run and that he'll be meetin' you there."

"Courtmacsherry?"

"We can't go from Kinsale. The Brits are all over the docks. They're finished with Courtmacsherry."

He touched his forehead in a salute to the landlady. "We won't be forgettin' your kindness, Missus McGrath." Then he held the front door open for William Day.

Downey led the way up the narrow street to a flat horse-drawn wagon. Day stopped short when he saw the six newly made wooden coffins that were stacked on the back.

"These damn things are gettin' to be a boomin' business," Downey said. They lifted one of the coffins aside, and then Downey pulled the lid off one in the bottom row. He looked at the narrow space inside, then took in Day's size. "I suppose it wouldn't make a damn bit of difference to you if you was dead," he said.

"It'll do nicely," Day answered. He climbed up onto the wagon and then squeezed himself into the coffin, his knees bent and his shoulders hunched. "This may just kill me," he joked grimly.

"You should be able to push up the lid a bit to change the air," the young man guessed as he fitted the top of the coffin over Day's face. Then he replaced the box that had been on top.

Day felt the wagon jerk beneath him, and then they began moving in time with the slow, steady metronomic pace of the horse's hoofbeats. Downey tugged the reins, aiming the horse toward the main square at the foot of the hill. He tipped his cap to the armed British sentries who waved him onto the main east–west road.

Crushed into the dark tomb, Day had no image of the new world he was moving toward. He could think only of death. Of Sheila, her wounded, shrouded body waiting alone in the church for burial alongside other nameless, wasted children. Of Jennifer, the horror frozen on her blinded eyes as she was lifted out of the sea. He tried to think of them as martyrs to some cause, to find a purpose more important than the first glimpse of the new day's sunrise that had been taken from them. But there was none. They weren't martyrs, only victims. Victims of the holy causes of great men determined to reshape the world in their own likenesses. In their global strategies, *Lusitania* was just a small, expendable piece. The people who would die aboard her, or die trying to save her, had no significance at all. No more than the soldiers poured into the trenches, whose names weren't as important as the names of the battles that tortured them and killed them. Was Irish freedom more important than an Irish girl's life? Or the honor of an English king more valuable than the next breath of one of his subjects? Perhaps. But from the darkness of his coffin, Day couldn't see anything more important than life. Even the uncertain life that was awaiting him.

They had been traveling for hours when he heard hushed voices, then felt the wagon stop. There was a shuffling of the boards over his face, and then a crack of pale morning light.

"Good as new," Tom Downey said as he lifted the lid away from the coffin. His strong arms helped pull Day free then steadied him while he tried to find his balance. He was standing on a rotted pier, next to a small decrepit schooner with tattered canvas resting on her booms. The crewmen were leaning along her gunwales, dark figures who stared at him curiously.

"She's Portuguese," Downey explained. "You're her new deckhand."

The schooner's captain swung himself over the rail and onto the dock. "This him?"

Downey nodded.

The captain took Day's measure. "Then get him aboard. I'm missing the tide."

"Where's Father Connors?" Day asked Downey. "He was going to find someone for me. One of the passengers. He was going to bring me information about her."

Downey looked around, then lifted his hands helplessly. "He'd be the one to try. But there's so many of them."

Day turned toward the schooner and saw the captain was climbing aboard ahead of him. He took a step, then stopped and walked back to Downey. "I can't." The young man looked shocked. "I can't," Day repeated. "Not without knowing. Not without ever knowing."

"It may be that no one will ever know," Downey reminded him. He gestured out toward the ocean. "There's some that won't be givin' their names to anyone."

Day heard the captain bark an order in a strange tongue. The crewmen began taking in the schooner's lines.

"They're looking for you, commander," Downey said. "There's no goin' back. You'd best be gettin' aboard."

Day hesitated. The mooring lines were slipping across the pier toward the boat.

The grind of an automobile engine broke the morning stillness. They turned together and saw a black car bounce around the curve of the harbor and head toward the pier. "It's him." Downey said, slapping Day on the back. "Wait here." He ran up the pier. Day waited for only a second, and then ran after Downey. He saw Jennifer as soon as she stepped down from the car.

She rushed toward him, bursting into tears before he could get his arms around her. She said his name over and over again as he rocked her in his strong embrace. "You're safe. Thank God, you're safe," Day kept repeating. He looked over her shoulder at Father Connors, who was beaming like an angel.

"In the hospital," Connors explained. "Right there where you'd expect her to be. Asking everyone did they know Commander William Day. And still the Brits couldn't find her."

He stepped back and held her at arm's length. She looked ridiculous in an oversized dress that Connors had obviously borrowed and in the work shoes that were much too big for her feet. "You're beautiful," he told her, and then he took her back into his arms.

"The tide," the captain shouted from the fantail of the schooner. He waved his arms in frustration. "The tide!"

"He has to get aboard," Downey told the priest.

"I need a minute," Day begged. "Just a minute."

Connors nodded. "A minute, then," he answered. He looked at Downey. "Run down and tell that savage I'll excommunicate him if he sails without Commander Day."

"A minute?" Jennifer was suddenly frightened. She looked at the boat and at Day, and then she made the connection. "Where are you going? Why?"

He turned her away from Father Connors, pulled her close to him and walked her slowly down the pier.

"I have to go away," he began.

"Where?" She tried to pull away, but he held her tight to his side.

"I don't know. Wherever they take me. But I can't stay here, and I can't go back to England."

"Why? What's wrong?" She broke his grasp and turned to confront him.

"Because I know things. Things that England has to keep secret. I betrayed them, Jennifer. They're hunting for me."

"Betrayed them? What are you taking about? What things?"

He took her shoulders. "I can't explain. There isn't time. And it would be dangerous for you to know. Just believe that there's no other way. I have to go into hiding."

She pushed him away and looked at him with sudden determination. "Then I'm going with you."

"You can't. There's no future for me. But at least I know that you're safe. I couldn't have gone away without knowing that you were safe."

"I came to be with you," Jennifer insisted. "I'm going to stay with you."

"No," he said, with a hard edge to the word. "No. You're going back to your home. To your parents. That's where your life is."

"But my life is with you." She threw her arms around his neck. "I won't let you go."

"Commander." Father Connors was standing beside them. "He has to cast off. He can't miss the tide." Day saw that the sails were already hoisted, luffing in a breeze that came over the schooner's bow. He reached behind his neck and broke Jennifer's grip. Then he placed her hands in Father Connors'.

"Go home, Jennifer," William told her. "You have a life to live."

He looked at the priest.

"I'll take care of her," Connors promised.

Day turned away and jumped aboard the boat.

The captain took in the last line, and the crew hauled the sails across the breeze. The schooner began sliding forward, her side scraping against the pilings.

"I love him," Jennifer whispered helplessly.

"And he loves you," Connors said. "That's why he's doing what's best for you."

She looked at the priest, her eyes suddenly flashing in anger. She broke away from him and rushed down the pier, stumbling on the hem of the borrowed dress. When she caught up with the boat, she saw Day, standing at the gunwale, slowly drifting away from her as the schooner moved off the pilings.

"William," she screamed. "Do you love me?"

He looked blankly toward her.

"Do you love me?" she demanded again, still running to keep up with the boat.

He knew he should lie to her. Only by denying what was true would he be able to send her away. But it was as impossible now as it had been when he'd left her once before.

"I love you," he called back, his face dark with despair.

Jennifer ran to the edge and leaped out over the water, just reaching the edge of the boat.

Day's face exploded in laughter as he caught her hand and pulled her aboard.

The schooner heeled as her tired canvas locked onto the breeze. She gathered speed and headed out into the ocean, passing due south of the Old Head of Kinsale.

July 21, 1915

Dearest Mother and Father,

I am so sorry for not having written to you immediately to tell you that I am well, and blissfully happy. But that was not possible. As father may explain, there were circumstances involved in the sinking of Lusitania which must forever remain secret. William knows the details of England's involvement and has been made a fugitive from his own country.

Because I love him, I am going with him into exile. I won't tell you where, nor shall I be able to write you. Knowing where he can be found would pose great difficulties for you, and great dangers for him. But please believe that at every moment I will love you both, and regret the sorrow that I have caused you.

I don't know what our future will hold. I can only hope that some day our world will find the peace that I have found, and that William and I will be able to come home to you again.

> *With all my love,*
> *Jennifer Day*

AUTHOR'S NOTE

TIME OFTEN blurs the distinction between fact and fiction, and that is certainly true of *Lusitania*. For the facts, I have counted heavily on Colin Simpson's beautifully written history *Lusitania*, published by Little, Brown in 1972. As Simpson documents:

LUSITANIA had been substantially altered, turning its forward spaces into cargo holds, and explosives were a frequent cargo. On its final crossing, it was carrying not only sixty tons of guncotton but also substantial stores of artillery shells and rifle cartridges.

British representatives purchased war materials from American manufacturers and were aided in shipping these materials by U.S. officials. German protests were suppressed at the highest levels of the government, including the counselor to the secretary of state, Robert Lansing.

The Admiralty was copying German radio traffic and had reason to know that submarines were being sent to the Irish coast to intercept *Lusitania*. The master of the ship was never informed, and the escorts scheduled to meet the ship were recalled as it approached Fastnet Light. Immediately following an Admiralty meeting, at which the dangers to *Lusitania* were discussed, Winston Churchill departed England for France.

Rescue ships, racing toward the passengers who had abandoned the stricken *Lusitania*, were recalled when they were in sight of the sinking ship.

The Admiralty carefully censored all information that was presented to the board of inquiry, including radio messages sent from Queenstown and from the radio station in western Ireland.

THOSE ARE facts. Other characters and events of the story are fictional. There was no Jennifer Beecham traveling aboard *Lusitania*. The Royal Navy had no officer named William Day. And still others fall into that uncertain gulf between truth and fiction. For example, I doubt that any Admiralty radio station ever made a last-second effort to warn the Germans. And yet one message from a British radio station in Ireland, sent only a few hours before *Lusitania* was attacked, was erased from the message log. Its content and its destination have never been revealed.